PUFFIN BOOKS

2001   1912   1957   1941   2066

THE INFINITY CAGE

Praise for *TimeRiders*:

'A thriller full of spectacular effects' – *Guardian*

'Insanely exciting, nail-biting stuff' – *Independent on Sunday*

'This is a novel that is as addictive as any computer game'
– *Waterstone's Books Quarterly*

'Promises to be a big hit' – *Irish News*

'A thrilling adventure that hurtles across time and place at
breakneck speed' – *Lovereading4kids.co.uk*

'Plenty of fast-paced action . . . this is a real page-turner'
– *WriteAway.org.uk*

'A great read that will appeal to both boys and girls . . .
you'll find this book addictive!' – *Redhouse.co.uk*

'Contender for best science-fiction book of the year . . .
an absolute winner' – *Flipside*

Winner of the Older Readers category,
Red House Children's Book Award 2011

ALEX SCARROW used to be a graphic artist, then he decided to be a computer-games designer. Finally, he grew up and became an author. He has written a number of successful thrillers and several screenplays, but it's YA fiction that has allowed him to really have fun with the ideas and concepts he was playing around with when designing games.

He currently lives in Norwich with his family.

Sign up to become a TimeRider at:
www.time-riders.co.uk

TIME RIDERS

2001   1912   1957   1941   2066

THE INFINITY CAGE

ALEX SCARROW

PUFFIN

PUFFIN BOOKS

Published by the Penguin Group
Penguin Books Ltd, 80 Strand, London WC2R ORL, England
Penguin Group (USA) Inc., 375 Hudson Street, New York, New York 10014, USA
Penguin Group (Canada), 90 Eglinton Avenue East, Suite 700, Toronto, Ontario, Canada M4P 2Y3
(a division of Pearson Penguin Canada Inc.)
Penguin Ireland, 25 St Stephen's Green, Dublin 2, Ireland (a division of Penguin Books Ltd)
Penguin Group (Australia), 707 Collins Street, Melbourne, Victoria 3008, Australia
(a division of Pearson Australia Group Pty Ltd)
Penguin Books India Pvt Ltd, 11 Community Centre, Panchsheel Park, New Delhi – 110 017, India
Penguin Group (NZ), 67 Apollo Drive, Rosedale, Auckland 0632, New Zealand
(a division of Pearson New Zealand Ltd)
Penguin Books (South Africa) (Pty) Ltd, Block D, Rosebank Office Park,
181 Jan Smuts Avenue, Parktown North, Gauteng 2193, South Africa

Penguin Books Ltd, Registered Offices: 80 Strand, London WC2R ORL, England

puffinbooks.com

First published 2014
005

Text copyright © Alex Scarrow, 2014
All rights reserved

The moral right of the author has been asserted

Set in Bembo Book MT Std 11/14.5 pt
Typeset by Palimpsest Book Production Limited, Falkirk, Stirlingshire
Made and printed in England by Clays Ltd, St Ives plc

British Library Cataloguing in Publication Data
A CIP catalogue record for this book is available from the British Library

ISBN: 978-0-141-33720-3

www.greenpenguin.co.uk

MIX
Paper from
responsible sources
FSC   FSC™ C018179
www.fsc.org

Penguin Books is committed to a sustainable
future for our business, our readers and our planet.
This book is made from Forest Stewardship
Council™ certified paper.

*I dedicate this last book to three teenagers I've grown
to love as my own children. They live on in my head
(yapping away even when I'm trying to get some sleep).*

To Maddy, Liam and Sal

PROLOGUE
2044, Chicago

Waldstein stared out through the wire mesh of the displacement cage. In the dimly lit space of the abandoned warehouse, he could see the first two rows of the plastic bucket chairs he'd set out and, sitting on them, the tech journalists he'd personally invited to attend tonight's demonstration.

Wide-eyed and utterly bewildered by his presentation thus far. All of them.

They think I'm insane. Worse than that, he suspected they thought he'd invited them here this evening to witness some crazy old loon fry himself in his own electric cage. There seemed to be a lot of loons these days, like the woman who'd invited several digi-networks to film her setting herself on fire for world peace.

As the power generator beside his cage began to hum with the build-up of stored energy, getting ready to discharge itself and electrify the entire mesh, his eyes met one of them, a female journalist. She was shaking her head frantically, mouthing . . .

'Don't do this . . . please . . . for God's sake, don't do this.'

He smiled at her. 'I'm going to be fine,' he called out, but his words were lost beneath the increasing hum and the growing murmur of concern and disquiet among the small audience.

I'm going home. I'm going to see them again.

The countdown on his watch reached zero, and the building hum from the generator suddenly became a crackling discharge. Sparks showered around the cage, cascading down on to him from the mesh roof above, stinging his cheeks, his hands, his neck.

I'm going home.

Home.

Home, to that morning: 18 February 2028. To that precious breakfast-time; a low winter sun streaming into their small kitchen through a fogged window, piercing its way through a half-drawn venetian blind, dancing dust motes trapped in shafts of light and a small table for three striped by ladder lines of light and shadow. A twist of steam from a teapot spout, curling lazily in the sun. A haze of tangy toast smoke hanging like swamp mist above them. Gabriel's contented chuckling as he sucked on a plastic spoon. In the background, a digi-news station waffling about a troubled world. A world so far away from this – their cosy little family bubble.

He remembered that last time together. Eleanor had pushed the kitchen stool back and got up, finishing the dregs of her tea. Lifted their son from his booster chair and wiped away the smear of food from his cheeks.

'I'm running so late, Ro',' she'd said. 'I've really got to scoot.'

And that was it, pretty much: their final precious moment. The last time he'd see his son alive and the last few words he was ever going to exchange with his wife.

And, Christ, what had he said? Something loving? Something profound? Something poetic? Gentle? Intimate? No.

'Don't forget, we're completely out of soyo-milk.' Had he even bothered to look up from the physics paper he was reading? No. He didn't think so.

She'd leaned over and planted a kiss on his rumpled forehead.

'You need a cut, by the way. Your hair's looking wild and woolly again.'

She'd turned with Gabriel on her hip, who was burbling his version of *Goodbye, Daddy, I'm off to playschool*. She'd stood in the doorway, turned and smiled at him. 'Don't stay in all day, Ro'. It's lovely out there. Get some daylight. Feel a bit of sun on your face, OK?'

Then she was gone.

Now Waldstein felt the hairs all over his arms lifting. His same wild hair, even wilder now, lifted by the currents of static electricity. Through the showering sparks he caught one last glimpse of the female journalist, out of her chair now and hurrying forward, begging him to stop this stunt before he killed himself. She was almost right up to the cage . . .

Then it all vanished. No warning. Just. Gone. Replaced by a bland whiteness and silence. He sensed weightlessness and wondered whether he was floating or falling.

Is this it? A transition through dimensions? Or did I just kill myself?

The white seemed endless, utterly featureless. For the briefest moment Waldstein allowed himself to hope that, perhaps, he'd been so very wrong. That a lifetime of scoffing disbelief in something so naive and wistful as the notion of an afterlife . . . a heaven . . . had just been the blinkered myopia of a scientist. That Eleanor would emerge out of this mist, whole, intact, no longer torn in half by the accident, her cheeks spattered with the ink spots of her own dried blood. And Gabriel, once again balanced on her hip, burbling his own language.

If not that, then he wasn't dead. This wasn't Heaven. He'd been successful and managed to punch a hole through the Cartesian axes and was now floating in some 'other', in

3

dimensional transit. Any second now he was going to appear back in their old apartment in Brooklyn.

Eleanor would be there, still sat finishing her toast and yet to stand up and tell him she was running late. And this time he'd put down that damned science paper, look into her eyes and tell her that he loved her. And, yes, he was going to be strong . . . he absolutely *must* resist the temptation to change things, to suggest she should *not* go to work this morning (so the automated freighter pod that was due to plough into the side of her e-Car and cut her clean in half would pass on its way without incident).

Right then he decided he'd be quite happy with either: this being Heaven, or having that second chance to tell her he loved her.

The mist stirred, like breath on a spider's web. He sensed shifting densities, could now perceive a depth to it. Through veils of white, as frail and immaterial as the finest linen, he thought he could make out *something* just a little more substantial drawing closer to him.

'Hello?' His voice sounded suppressed. Blanketed. Smothered. As if the sound had carried no more than a few inches from his mouth, then evaporated. 'Who is that?'

'*Roald* . . .' A thin voice. A whisper. Certainly not Ellie's.

The *something* drawing closer to him seemed to lack a clear outline. One moment possibly a human figure, the next elongated like an eel. Then an ethereal wisp of smoke disintegrating and re-forming again.

'*Roald . . . We know who you are . . .*'

'Who is that?!' Waldstein heard the shrill pitch of terror in his own muffled voice. Almost feminine in tone. He wanted to sound more commanding. '*Who are you?*'

Just then he felt something firm beneath his feet. Solid

4

ground. Gravity seemed to have returned to this white no-place. Then the mist itself suddenly vanished.

He found himself standing in a small kitchenette bathed with morning sunlight, which streamed in through a venetian blind.

'*I did it. I'm home,*' he whispered. '*I'm finally home.*'

Eleanor looked up at him and smiled as she stirred the last of their son's breakfast in a plastic bowl. Here they both were. Ellie for real, not a software simulation. But flesh-and-blood real. And his beautiful son. The sunlight made the fine blond baby-hair fuzz on the top of his head glow. The warmth of the sun coming in, the cosy fug of the kitchen, the smell of lightly burnt toast and milk-soaked rusks; it was all too much for him. Too much.

He buried his face in his hands and began to cry.

'Roald . . . we need to talk.' A soft voice, almost that of a woman's. But not Ellie's.

He looked up.

'Roald Waldstein . . . we need to talk.' The voice seemed to have come from his baby son. Gabriel had twisted in his booster seat towards him and was staring at him intently, small pudgy hands palm-flat on the table in front of him.

'This is a pocket of reality that we have temporarily borrowed so that we can talk to you.'

Waldstein looked at the moving lips of his son. The words, impossibly coming out of his mouth, were slurred and delivered in a clumsy, laboured way, limited by the small unpractised muscles.

He shook his head. Struggling to rationalize this. Not Heaven. Certainly he wasn't back home. Was this a dream, then? A hallucination? Was he now lying on a hospital gurney being worked on by a crash team trying to revive him?

'This is only a temporary reality, Roald. An isolated pocket of higher-dimension space–time. We duplicated the destination that you intended to arrive at.'

He couldn't take his eyes off Gabriel's lips. 'Who . . . who . . .?'

'Who are we?' Gabriel smiled. 'Those that care.'

Waldstein looked around the small kitchen. So real. There, stuck to the fridge door, were the plastic farmyard-animal magnets Gabriel liked to play with. On the counter, Ellie's touch-screen recipe tablet, beside it the old-fashioned moleskin notebook in which she hand-wrote her shopping lists.

'Those that care?' That meant absolutely nothing to him. 'Who are you?'

'You can call us . . . the Caretakers.'

'I . . . I . . . are you –'

'Roald, this is our chance to warn you.'

'Warn me? About what?'

'About time travel. You are the first human to turn this dangerous theory into a *very* dangerous reality.' Gabriel's eyes narrowed. 'You're not the only species to have stumbled upon this technology . . . there have been others before. When we detect the unique signature of this technology, we come.'

'You . . . you're talking about . . . *tachyon particles*?'

Gabriel nodded. 'They're the telltale first sign. What we look out for. And we come, always, with the same message, with the very same warning.'

The shockingly adult expression on his son's infant face melted away. It was Gabriel once more, his hands patting the table impatiently, fumbling at the plastic bowl.

Eleanor spoke to him now. 'Time travel is an open door to dimensions beyond your comprehension. To a destructive energy that can destroy everything. Not just this world but this universe. It is corrosive; the more often it happens, Roald, the more vulnerable we *all* are.'

Eleanor stopped stirring Gabriel's mushed-rusk breakfast. She looked up at him with her intense grey eyes. Just then she looked every bit as beautiful as that very first time their eyes had met across the noisy chaos of a street-food fair. Beautiful. But now, with some other intelligence behind them, *terrifying*.

'We present an ultimatum. The strictest possible ultimatum. This technology cannot be used. We cannot allow it to develop any further, to spread . . .' She smiled sadly at him. 'We know why you worked so hard on your device. To see your loved ones again. Perhaps to alter events so that they would live. But, Roald, history has a way it is supposed to go. There are no choices in this matter.'

'All I want . . . ever wanted . . . was to be with you . . . with *her*, again.'

'I know.' She shook her head slowly. 'That can't be. I'm sorry. Our ultimatum is strict. It has to be.' She got up and came round the table towards him. 'It has to stop. Or we will have no choice in the matter.' She took one of his hands and held it gently, stroking his knuckles with her thumb. 'We don't do this lightly, Roald. We're not monsters.'

'Do . . . do what?'

He noted tears in her eyes. 'Extermination, Ro'. The complete annihilation of your species, your entire world. Everything. We'll leave behind no trace that this world ever existed. There'll be nothing but dust.'

He felt his scalp suddenly prickle with dawning realization. This one flight of fancy, this one fool's errand into the past . . .?

God help me. God help me. What have I gone and done?

'But, Roald, it's not too late. That can be avoided. It *can*.' She squeezed his hand. 'There is a chance that we won't be forced to do this. We've seen a way through. And, believe me, we don't want to wipe out life if we can avoid it. Life is so very precious.' She stared at him intently. 'Roald . . . you can help us save humanity.'

CHAPTER 1

1890, Albert Docks, Liverpool

So now look at me. I find myself writing all my thoughts down like Sal once used to do. In the very same notebook, as it happens. Every now and then I flip back through the dog-eared pages and find solid blocks of her tidy, tiny writing and read some of it and remember the moments she was writing about; as clear as yesterday, they seem to me.

Why the hell do I keep doing that? Reading her old entries? Every time I do, it makes me feel so low. Then, of course, if Maddy or Rashim look over at me and ask what's up . . . I do that thing I always do: grin like a fool and throw it away as nothing, or I just say I read or thought of something funny.

Truth is I'm the one who's having to keep us all going. Maddy is damaged goods. And Rashim? Well, I suppose, to be fair, he does his share of hand-holding. But this trip was my idea. This extended sightseeing jolly to experience some of the British Empire, Africa, the Far East; eighteen months of remarkable sights and sounds and smells. We've seen so much, so many amazing things and not once needed to step into that awful chaotic white mist to do it.

Liam's eyes drifted from the smudged words he'd just written to the fountain pen in his hand. Not for the first time, he wondered if they would ever need to, or should, do that again. There was enough in this world that was racing towards the twentieth century. So much to explore. And this trip had been a useful distraction for them all. Particularly for Maddy. It had taken her mind off dwelling morosely on the loss of Sal. On losing Adam. More than that, it had been a much-needed distraction from endlessly pondering the purpose of that artefact they'd discovered in the Nicaraguan jungle. They'd glimpsed a scheme they couldn't possibly begin to understand: some impossibly large design by beings who could just as easily be angels or aliens as people from the far future. Perhaps even God Himself.

It was enough to drive a mind to the very edge of insanity.

Liam looked up from the diary. Their ship was waiting for its turn to berth somewhere along the Albert Docks in Liverpool. Thick funnels were tossing snow-white plumes of steam up into a promising blue sky, and the wharves were alive with cranes and teams of stevedores noisily barking orders at each other. On the deck beside him the railing was lined with their fellow passengers, excited at the sight of the busy port before them.

Why can't we just be like them?

But he, Maddy and Rashim weren't like them. They were separated from normal people – and always would be – by the simple fact that they knew what others didn't. A curse, or a gift, they knew that time was a stream that could be swum up or down. They knew reality was as malleable as clay, as impermanent and insubstantial as a wisp of smoke . . . Nothing, *nothing*, was forever . . . or even safe.

I suppose the question is this: what's best? To be ignorant – or to know?

CHAPTER 2
1890, London

Rashim turned the brass key in the padlock. Its unlocking *clack* reverberated around the dark interior beneath Holborn Viaduct. He unlooped the padlock from the latch and briefly inspected it by the light of his oil lamp. He turned and showed the others some scuff marks on the locking bar.

'Looks like Delbert has had a go at fiddling with this while we have been away.'

'That doesn't surprise me,' said Maddy.

She stared into the darkness beyond the partially opened small oak door. Eighteen months of daylight and sunshine they'd experienced. Eighteen months and travelled so far. Seen blue skies rimmed with snow-capped mountain peaks, the stepped terraces of paddy-fields, the lush sloping carpet of tea plantations. Endless days savouring the warmth of the sun on her face and listening to and smelling the world about her. The aroma of spices and ripe meat of a hundred different marketplaces. The clamour and chorus of teamed manual labour; the crank and grind of coal-powered machinery; the hoot of steamships coming in and setting sail; the energetic symphony of a bustling, busy colonial empire feeding voraciously hungry mouths thousands of miles away.

Liam had been right. She'd soon realized that on their travels. It was the tonic she'd desperately needed: to witness this vibrant world, alive and industrious, mobilizing itself for the looming twentieth century. For once to just be a tourist, someone passing through without a care. Miss Madelaine Carter – an apparently well-to-do young American woman – with her curious coterie of travelling companions.

And now, after visiting a part of the Raj that would one day become Mumbai, after taking a train journey across the Kashmiri mountains and a paddle steamer down the River Nile, they had finally returned home to London.

'Back to living like a bunch of weird mole people again.' She sighed solemnly.

'Aye, well . . . it's not like we have to hide away in here all the time.'

'And maybe it's time you got a haircut, Liam?'

He shook his head stubbornly. His dark hair had grown down to his shoulders and was now tied back into a ponytail that swung and batted his ears. 'I'm getting rather used to it.'

'You look like a hipster.' She folded her arms. 'That's not a good thing, by the way.'

'And what about the beard?' he asked, stroking his chin. Eighteen months of not shaving and he'd just about managed to grow a half-convincing goatee.

'With that grey bit at the side of your head, and that face fungus . . . it really ages you. Do you actually want to look old?'

He looked at Rashim. 'Does it?'

Rashim frowned, hesitating with his hand on their small arched doorway. 'I would say it is a *distinguished* look, Liam. But then it looks good on me too. I suppose I'm biased.'

He pushed the door inwards. It creaked loudly and echoed into the dark space beyond. He ducked through, and Maddy followed him in, with Liam right behind her. The two support units squeezed through after them, Bob laden down with travel valises and Becks pushing a heavy leather trunk on castor wheels.

Maddy stepped cautiously across the stone floor towards the computers, wary not to trip over the cables she knew were snaking from one side to the other. She noticed the dungeon was *completely* dark.

'It's all off in here. Everything's been turned off!'

Rashim held out his oil lamp in front of him. He weaved between the armchairs and leaned over the table to try the lamp. He flicked the switch on and off a couple of times. 'That circuit breaker I installed must have tripped while we were away.'

'Is that good news or bad news?' asked Liam.

'Good news,' replied Rashim. 'If there'd been a power surge, then without the breaker there would have been damage to the circuit boards in the computers and the displacement machine.' He headed over towards the rear wall of their archway, where a nest of thick insulated cables spilled out from a jagged hole. He squatted down and examined a fuse board. 'Yes. That is exactly what happened.'

He flipped a breaker switch and the electric bulb imprisoned in its wire cage above the table glowed softly amber, while standby lights beneath the row of computer monitors blinked a muted neon blue.

'I'll start up the computers,' said Maddy. She hefted her heavy skirts up, knelt down and crawled under the table, flicking on each computer one after the other. The faint, deep hum of the Holborn Viaduct generator, coming through several brick walls, was now accompanied by the soft chorus of a dozen hard drives clicking and heat fans whirring.

'SpongeBubba's . . . uh . . .' Liam nudged the lab robot several times. Normally a light knock was enough to trigger the robot's inertia sensors. 'I think he's dead, Rashim, or broken or something.'

Rashim came over and gave SpongeBubba's squat frame a

gentle kick. 'Hmmm . . . he is just completely powered down. I suspect the circuit breaker must have flipped several weeks ago. His internal standby battery can last up to two hundred hours if he turns off all but his essential functions.' He rapped his knuckles on the unit's yellow casing.

'Awww.' Liam patted the top of the unit. 'Poor little fella.'

'He will be all right. He just needs to charge for a few hours.' Rashim checked round the back of the robot. 'Ahh, do you see? He is plugged in. He must have been in the process of recharging himself when the breaker tripped. Give him twelve hours to get his AI and language rebooted and his motorized circuits charged up and, once again, he will be annoying all of us as usual.'

Across on the far side of their brick dungeon, the monitors flickered to life one after the other, each now displaying diagnostic boxes running software-module checks as computer-Bob's AI awoke from his enforced slumber.

'Would you like me to put the kettle on and make some coffee, Maddy?' asked Becks.

Maddy turned round and cocked a brow at her. 'Tell me, why is it that out of the pair of you it's the *female* meatbot that thinks to ask that?'

Both support units looked at each other for a moment.

'Would you prefer me to make this hot beverage instead, Maddy?' asked Bob.

Twenty minutes later, Maddy, Rashim and Liam were sitting round the table, reminiscing about all the things they'd seen over the previous year and a half. In particular, Rashim had been astounded by the sight of tens of thousands of springboks moving together like a school of fish across an African savannah, cunningly herded by a pride of lions towards a bottleneck.

'Attention,' said Bob. He nodded at one of the computer monitors. On the screen, a dialogue box had been silently flashing. The cursor was blinking red. 'Attention: computer-Bob has an important message.'

All of them turned to look at the monitors. Text was now flashing on every screen. Computer-Bob's equivalent of shouting for attention. Maddy jumped up and hurried over. She quickly squinted at the text before her breath caught in her throat.

'What is it, Mads?' asked Liam. 'Mads?'

She let it out with a slow whooshing noise. 'What the . . .?!'

Liam was up out of his chair now. 'Mads? What is it?'

She turned to look at him, then at Rashim. 'OhMyGod, it's . . . it's a message.' Her mouth hung open. 'A message for us!'

'A message? From who?'

They both joined her at the computer bench and stared at the array of monitors. On each screen was the same dialogue box, text laid out in bold and red.

> **Broad-sweep tachyon signal. Decoded signal reads: 'All past sins forgiven. Come and seek me out. Your work is done.'**

CHAPTER 3

1890, London

> My calculations indicate the message comes from the first three months of the year 2070.

'Can you identify the location it came from?'

> Negative. It is a broad-sweep signal, which makes it impossible to calculate a precise origin point.

'It's a message from Waldstein . . .' Maddy looked at Liam and Rashim. 'Right? I mean, that much is obvious!'

Liam sucked air between his teeth like a dodgy building contractor considering bumping up a quote. 'I dunno . . .'

'I dunno? Great,' she said, sighing. 'What's *that* supposed to mean?'

'It means, I dunno . . . maybe it's a trick, Mads?'

'A trick?'

'A trap,' he clarified. 'If that is Waldstein, then maybe he's trying to lure us into an ambush? But, hold on . . . maybe it's not even him. It could be someone else trying to flush us out into the open?'

Rashim nodded. 'Liam is right. If it is not Waldstein, then it might be a third party that is aware of your agency. If it really is Waldstein . . . then it is clear he has only a vague idea of where we are.'

'The broad-beam signal?'

He nodded. 'If he knew exactly where we were, well . . . he would be here talking to us face to face. I suspect he knows he cannot find you, certainly not if you continue to choose not to correct any further time waves.' Rashim stared at Maddy pointedly. 'And that was the message you quite clearly communicated to him, wasn't it?'

The impulsive ultimatum Maddy had communicated forward to Waldstein so many, many months ago . . . that unflinching demand that Waldstein had better start explaining what the hell 'Pandora' meant, otherwise they were not going to correct any more time contaminations – the message that had caused them to run for their lives. How often had she quietly regretted shooting her mouth off like that?

Rashim shot a quick glance at Becks. 'Since no other clones have followed us here to Victorian London, it is fair to assume he has no idea where we are. At the very least, this message indicates we are actually perfectly safe here. That he can't find us.'

Maddy nodded thoughtfully. 'So . . . he's got no alternative but to appeal to us to make ourselves known. To step out into the open. To come to him.' She pressed her lips together and frowned. 'It could be a trap . . . or maybe . . .'

'What?'

Maddy considered that for a moment. If it wasn't a trap, what was it? She settled back in the wooden chair in front of the computer table, fingers absently stroking the soft flesh beneath the corner of her jaw.

Bob came over with a tray of steaming mugs. He set down one of the mugs heavily on the table in front of her. 'Coffee,' he grunted.

'Rashim's right. We haven't been visited by mad killer meatbots,' said Liam, 'so Waldstein doesn't know we're sitting pretty.' He shrugged nonchalantly. 'We did it, Maddy . . . we escaped him. We're out of sight.'

'But now comes this message,' said Rashim. 'If this is him, is his only option to try to lure us out?'

'And kill us,' added Liam.

Maddy shook her head slowly. 'Or maybe he wants to explain himself.' She turned to Liam. 'This feels . . . I don't know, it feels kind of *genuine*. Maybe he's ready to talk with us? Make peace with us?'

'What?!' Liam looked at the monitor in front of them. 'That's —' he raised his finger and counted up the words on the screen — 'that's thirteen words, Maddy. You get *that* — you get "genuine" — from just thirteen flippin' words?'

'Yes, I do.' She turned in her seat and stared at the monitor in front of her. 'You know what I think? I think all we're ever going to have is a bunch of theories, suspicions . . . speculations. We're never going to find out anything sitting here. We're never going to know why we were given the job of steering history towards disaster. We're never going to find out what that large transmitter in the jungle was all about — right there in the middle of that ancient Mayan temple . . . unless we go find Waldstein and talk to him face to face.'

'You've got to be flippin' joking, Mads!'

'No. I'm quite serious.'

'He already tried to kill us once! You want to give him another go?'

'Look . . . all right. I've been thinking about that. My message was . . . OK, it was an ultimatum. It was a challenge. All right, it was pretty —'

'Stupid?'

'*Combative* . . . I think what I did was make us sound like we were turning on him. So maybe he had no choice? Maybe he just panicked?'

'I wouldn't trust that insane old bugger . . .' Liam shook his head. 'You want answers? Well, Jay-zus, we *all* of us want answers, Mads, but this is stupid. You go to him . . . even if he doesn't have us all killed as soon as we arrive . . . tell me, are you actually going to be able to trust a single thing he says?'

She looked down at her lap and sighed. 'Liam, I suppose I'm tired of guessing. I'm tired of half knowing things, speculating on Waldstein's motives. I'm tired of worrying that someone's out there looking for us, that there might be another batch of support units roaming around. And you know what? What if we really ARE meant to be doing something important, and instead we're just sitting here and it's not being done? We literally have No Idea what the hell we're supposed to be doing any more.' She sighed again. 'I'm tired of that too.'

'And I want to know these things, just as much as you: why we're here, why we were made, why we have to see to it that mankind ends up wiping itself out!' He laughed drily. 'I know you think I make a joke out of everything . . . but I want to know what that thing was that we found out there. I want to know what it does, why the hell it's doing what it does . . . and who put it there!'

'Right . . . so, we can ask Waldstein about those transmitter things as well as everything else that –'

'Jay-zus! What makes you think he even knows those transmitter things exist?!'

They sat in silence for a while, giving that idea a moment to sink in.

'Seriously, Maddy . . . if we're getting ourselves involved again . . . if we're going to go down that road and get some answers, then the only things we can trust for sure are what we find out for ourselves.'

'So? What are you suggesting?'

'Well, for starters . . . we don't serve ourselves up to Mr Waldstein like lambs to the slaughter.' He shrugged. 'Perhaps we go find that other transmitter. Maybe we'll come across one of the people who set those things up?'

'And of course they'll open right up to us, Liam, and explain everything, right? Just lay it all out there for us?'

'At least *they've* not tried to kill us.'

'Yet.'

He looked at Rashim. 'What do *you* think?'

'I think we may, if we are lucky, find another "transmitter". So, all we will have found then is another large stone column covered with symbols that we cannot begin to decode. And that is all we discovered in Central America: a device that is channelling tachyons to the far side of the world. We do not know who set it up or why it is doing this. All we discovered is there is some *other scheme at work* . . . that is all.' He shrugged. 'And we lost two friends in the process.'

Liam looked at him, wide-eyed. 'What are you saying? We just ignore that thing sitting there in that city in the jungle, doing God knows what?!'

'Oh, I want to know what its purpose is . . . but I suspect that Maddy may be right. Perhaps our best chance at getting answers is agreeing to meet with the one person we can guarantee knows more about things than we do. Waldstein.'

Maddy nodded. 'He *must* know about them. I can't imagine for one moment that he doesn't.'

'I think it's dangerous,' said Liam. 'I think it's bloody stupid! We should go and find out what we can in Jerusalem first.'

20

'Liam?' Maddy sat back. 'Come on – let's not fall out over this. We need to stay together.'

'I'm not falling out with you, Mads . . . but –' he made a face – 'this has got to be the stupidest idea you've had yet. You're suggesting we walk right up to Mr Waldstein's front door with our hands in the air and hope he'll say, "*Come on in, chaps. I'll put the kettle on and tell you e-e-e-verything!*"'

He looked at Rashim. 'Rashim? Come on, fella . . . back me up here!'

'I believe we have two options, Liam. We walk away from everything we do not know and live out our lives in – some might say – blissful ignorance. Or we go in search of the answers.' He looked at the message sitting on the screen. 'I believe our best hope of getting those answers – a risk though that might be – lies in meeting with Waldstein.'

'This is crazy! Maddy? You're gambling, so you are! Gambling that what he –'

'God, Liam . . . *everything* we've done so far has been a gamble!' She laughed. 'Jesus, we've been rolling the dice blindly ever since . . . ever since I found that Pandora note!'

He shook his head. 'I can't agree with you, Maddy. Not this time. We had to run for our lives because Waldstein decided we were a problem. You remember that? You remember those things coming after us, again and again? You remember them gunning down Foster?'

She did. She'd seen it with her own eyes. Those killing machines calmly raising their guns and brutally slaying him in that shopping mall.

'Do you honestly think he's gone from *I want them dead* to *Come on over and have some tea; we're all friends now*? Huh?'

'Maybe something's happened. Maybe something's changed?'

'Like what?'

'I don't know.'

Liam shrugged. 'That's why it's a crazy decision. You don't know.'

'I'll go on my own, then.'

'Are you *that keen* to die, Maddy?'

She pulled in a long, slow breath. 'I'm tired of second-guessing. I'm tired of not being able to settle my mind. I'm frikkin' exhausted with stressing over whether at any second another squad of killer meatbots are gonna appear right here and kill us in our sleep.' She nodded at the message on the monitor. 'There's the invitation. Right there. We get a chance, hopefully, to meet with him face to face. We can tell him about those tachyon transmitters. We can ask why the hell we're having to steer mankind towards doom. I mean . . . there's got to be a reason why we have to do that.'

'Maybe he *is* crazy. Maybe he's just like that insane guy who helped Hitler win the war . . . that Kramer fella.'

'And maybe not. What if there's something worse than Pandora . . . that virus? Huh? What if avoiding the end takes us someplace far worse? What if we should be doing our jobs instead of sitting round here drinking . . . coffee!'

'And what if you end up walking into an ambush?'

She sucked in a breath. 'Then it's my mistake . . . and it's just me paying for it.'

Liam sighed. 'Well, if you'll not listen to me . . . Rashim? Please . . . talk some sense into her.'

'I want answers from him too,' Rashim replied. He looked at Maddy. 'I will go along with you,' he said. 'I believe this is our best chance. Perhaps our only chance to get all of the answers.'

'And a chance for him to wipe us all out in one go.' Liam shook his head. 'This is insane.'

'It's what I need, Liam. I can't go on bumbling along . . . I need answers,' said Maddy.

'You're goin' to go and find him whatever I say, aren't you? This isn't a vote, is it?'

She nodded. 'I'm sorry, Liam . . . I have to know. But obviously . . . I'm not asking you to come too.'

'There's no way I'm going to convince you not to go, is there?'

'No.'

He sat down in a chair and narrowed his eyes.

'What are you thinking?'

'I'm thinking we have two courses of action. Two plans . . . you and Rashim go into the future so you can get yourselves ambushed by Waldstein . . .'

She smiled at that. 'And the other one, smart-ass?'

'I go into the past to take a look at that other transmitter.'

'Two missions?'

'Aye. We do both. I'll take one of the support units, you take the other. We both find out what we can and hopefully . . . we all make it back here and get to compare notes.'

Maddy looked at Rashim. He shrugged. 'It does make some sense. Exploring two avenues. More to the point . . . if Waldstein's intention is to wipe us out, it would be better that one of us is still at large. There may be some leverage gained by that.'

'I guess.' She sighed. 'I just hate the idea of us being separated.'

'It's not like we haven't been separated into teams before, Mads.'

'I know, but . . . I'll be worried about you.'

'I'll have a support unit along with me.' He smiled. 'Been there, done that.'

'But what if I'm wrong? What if it is a trap and Waldstein wipes us out?'

'Then you'll feel like a right idiot.'

She laughed sadly. 'No . . . I mean, what about you? You'll be left alone.'

He shrugged. 'I'll find something to do with my time.'

CHAPTER 4
1890, London

'So? Where do we go to find him?' Maddy was looking at Rashim expectantly. 'You're the one who was living in Waldstein's time. I was hoping you'd have some thoughts on that.'

They were sitting in Bentham's Pie Shop. Liam's choice. Eighteen months of dodgy mutton curries and oven-baked flat breads had taken its toll on him and now all he wanted was stodgy, steaming British comfort food: viscous beef-and-gravy fillings topped with thick flaking pastry lids.

'Yes, I'm from his time,' replied Rashim, 'but that does not mean I was intimately acquainted with the man.'

'You know about him.'

'Of course I do. Any scientist or theoretical physicist from the forties onwards knows all about Waldstein. Just as any scientist in the twentieth century would know about Einstein.'

'Stein!' Liam blurted out. The others turned to look at him. 'Just thinking,' he said. 'Why is it every brainbox science fella has a name ending with "*stein*"? Einstein, Waldstein, Frankenstein.'

Rashim rolled his eyes. 'Newton, Tesla, Hawking, Higgs, Koothrappali, Chan, Lee . . . shall I go on? Yes? Maynard, Watt, Kaspersky, Vasquez –'

'OK,' cut in Maddy, 'I think he gets the point.' She dipped

a hunk of bread into the beef stew in front of her. 'Rashim, we need to know when and where we'll have our best chance at getting to him.'

'The obvious and best-documented moment where Waldstein could be met would be the Chicago demonstration in 2044,' said Rashim. 'I mean, that is very well covered. There is footage of the event that we can look at. But —'

'But we'd be talking to a younger Waldstein who'd have no idea who the hell we are because he wouldn't have set up the TimeRiders agency by then.'

'Precisely. Not for at least another fifteen years or so.'

'Right, so that's clearly no good. He said in the message that "your work is done". Which I presume refers to the virus. Either it's happened or is about to happen. So I guess it's safe to presume Bob's calculation was correct; that message came from the first two or three months of 2070?'

'Hmm. After his spot at the last international TED Talks in Montreal in 2050, Waldstein became a complete recluse. His business had a number of locations. I think he had —'

'Information: Roald Waldstein's commercial empire, W.G. Systems, has the following publicly listed premises,' said Becks. 'A New York-based patent and legal office, a Californian software-development campus, a carbon-fibre fabrication plant in Tokyo, an Oregon-based genetic research division, a Denver-based energy-research campus and a Wyoming-based research and development facility.'

Rashim nodded. 'He also had a number of private retreats. I do recall reading that he owned one of the artificial islands-on-stilts off the coast of Dubai.'

'So he could be hanging around at any one of those places at any time?' Maddy puffed her cheeks. 'Great.'

'I remember while I was working on phase one of Project

Exodus, in 2068, there was a digi-docu on one of the news-streams about Roald Waldstein. That was the summer before the Japanese/North Korean cold war turned into a hot war. And then –' Rashim rolled his hands, one over the other – 'you, of course, know how it all goes from there.'

Maddy and Liam nodded.

'Anyway, the two most likely locations that the message was transmitted from in early 2070,' said Rashim, 'would be the W.G. Systems' HQ in New York or their research campus near Denver, Colorado. Waldstein's base of operations for his agency would require privacy, energy, security. The corporation's head office and research campus were both known to be hard places to gain access to.'

'We may need to try both those locations. How far apart are they?'

'Quite far.'

'So, I guess we'll portal to one, then the other.'

'That might be unwise, Maddy.'

'Why?'

'Think about it . . . this is 2070. There are many monitoring agencies in this time scanning for tachyon particles. When we open a portal, we run the risk of being picked up on someone's particle-scanning array. We may be attracting attention.'

'Seriously?'

Rashim nodded. 'Trust me, in 2070 *every* world power is busy scanning for tachyon emissions.' He shrugged. 'Just as every world power is busy, secretly, racing to build their own time machines. Portalling in once, we will attract someone's attention. If we're portalling around all over the place, we will get zeroed in on.'

'Well, OK . . . if we open one, say, in New York, and Waldstein's not there, I guess we can catch a plane or something to Denver?'

Rashim shook his head. 'It is not quite that simple. America is not like it was in *your* time.'

Maddy raised an eyebrow, querying him. 'There *are* planes, right?'

'My time is in chaos. Things were beginning to break down. Law and order, government control. There were . . . *will be*, I should say . . . food shortages, power-outs. It is a very difficult time. A dangerous time. America is fragmented badly.'

'Fragmented?' Liam looked up from his pie. 'What do you mean?'

'In 2070, it is called the Federated States. It is a much smaller nation that extends from the west coast to the Midwest. All of the eastern states have been abandoned.'

'Abandoned?'

'It is a wilderness. Ungovernable. Largely unpoliced, chaotic. A no-man's-land of refugee camps.'

'Why?' asked Maddy.

'There is the rising Atlantic, the rising Gulf of Mexico; the eastern coast and many of the southern states are partially flooded. The Capitol was relocated from Washington to Denver in 2063.'

'Why didn't he just send a location data stamp with the message?' asked Liam. 'If he really wanted to meet, surely he'd do that?'

'Well, obviously he didn't want to broadcast who the message was from,' replied Maddy. 'That was a broad-bandwidth message computer-Bob picked up. He's just being super-cautious. Rashim, come on . . . where do you suggest we go first?'

'New York, perhaps? There was the W.G.S. Tower, overlooking Times Square. Even when the levees eventually failed and Manhattan became waterlogged, a section of the business district remained open, operating several floors above street level. I know Waldstein spent some of his time living at the top of the W.G.S. Tower.'

'Why there? Why not one of any of the other more secure places where W.G. Systems had facilities?'

'I don't know. I do remember, in that digi-docu programme, one of the last interviews he gave was from there. From the rooftop of his tower. He said something about loving the view from up there. The sunrises and sunsets across the sea. "Watching the green lady slowly wading into the deep."'

'You mean the Statue of Liberty?' said Liam.

'Yes,' replied Rashim. 'He said watching the sea level rise made it look like she was a bather slowly wading out into deeper waters.'

'So . . . we aim for the beginning of 2070. New York, then. If he's not there, we've got enough time to make our way across to Denver before that Kosong-ni virus outbreak begins.'

'That's your plan, Mads?' said Liam. 'That's it? A leisurely stroll across America in the hope of bumping into Mr W.'

'It's the best plan I've got. So what's yours? Huh?'

He shrugged. 'First-century Jerusalem, round about the time of you-know-who. I'll go back there and see what I can see. Might even get his autograph if I can.'

She shook her head. 'Sheesh, so just about as concise a plan as mine, then?'

He shrugged. 'Details to be ironed out. The difference is nobody's scanning for tachyons back then. Nobody's out to kill me back then and nobody's got guns back then . . . and, of course, I'll have Bob.'

'Uhh . . . actually, I was thinking we'd have Bob along with us.'

'All right, so then we'll toss a coin to see who's having him.'

Maddy buried her face in her hands. 'Jesus . . . Liam, are we really going to do this? Fling ourselves out there in different directions with just a frikkin' hope and a prayer? Are we being stupid? Reckless?'

'Haven't we always been?' He laughed. 'As far as I can see, we've never had much of a plan. We've just dealt with whatever came our way.'

'Great . . . and look where that's got us.'

'Alive, Mads . . . we're alive.' He leaned forward on to the table and nudged one of her shoulders with his. 'We should be dead. In fact, we were never meant to be alive in the first place. So . . . everything we have now, every moment, every memory, and all that we know . . . it's all a bonus.' He grinned. 'And, I promise you, we'll be back in that dungeon in a few days' time . . . and we'll have all those answers between us.'

She looked at him. 'Liam, what is it with you? Nothing ever worries you, does it?'

'Ahh, I do my fair share of worrying . . . to be sure.'

'But you always bounce back up with that dumb-ass grin on your face. Shiny, like a new penny.'

'Speaking of pennies . . .' He pulled a coin from his waistcoat pocket. 'For Bob this is, OK? Heads or tails?'

CHAPTER 5

2070, New York

Maddy decided to open a portal somewhere familiar. Somewhere they'd know and at least be able to get their bearings. A quick pinhole viewing confirmed what they'd expected to see: Brooklyn's streets lost beneath a permanent, stagnant carpet of water. Rooftops and windowsills growing green and wild with tall weeds and saplings.

The first two to go through, Rashim and Becks, burdened with backpacks crammed with tins of food, readied themselves on the sawdust plinths. Maddy counted them down and, with a hum building up to a crescendo, then a puff of evacuated air, they were gone. Just Maddy, Liam and Bob left.

She looked around their dungeon as the displacement machine recharged itself for the next release of energy. This place had begun to feel just as much a home to them as their archway beneath the Williamsburg Bridge once had. The modest touches of comfort had begun to clutter and cover the dungeon like barnacles on a ship's hull: the hammocks strung up behind the curtains, the commode in the corner hidden by a sky-blue satin drape on a loop of rope, the threadbare armchairs round their communal table, messy with mismatched crockery, their kitchenette with its modern, out-of-place electric kettle, toaster and a single-hob stove, and a rack of shelves where plain vanilla cartons of milled oats jostled for space with the last boxes of

Rice Krispies. Beside the armchairs and table, a small coal burner with a smoke hood and a chimney flue improvised to direct the smoke out of the archway through a hole in the wall on to Farringdon Street. Damp clothes hung on wooden laundry frames round it. Normally it glowed a welcoming, flickering amber. Now it was all cold grey ashes. In one corner were several tall oak wardrobes in which the accumulated clothing from several trips into the past hung tidily from coat hangers.

She looked around and felt sad. Yes, it was just beginning to feel vaguely homely. Well, it *had* been . . . then events had once again spun out of her control: the trip to the jungle . . . the tachyon beam there, Sal's and Adam's deaths . . .

Liam and Rashim had made a supreme effort to yank her out of the spiral of depression that she'd begun to orbit. They'd nagged and cajoled until she'd wearily given in and let them drag her away to explore the furthest reaches of the British Empire. An extended holiday travelling on steamships and trains to the Far East, India, Africa and back again. Bless them for trying so hard . . . all of that had helped. Had lifted her spirits. She suspected Liam was not only trying to keep her mind off grieving but also trying to show her that an exciting world lay out there beyond the soot-filled skies of London. That there was a life to be lived beyond the burden of what they knew about the future. If the end of mankind was just shy of two hundred years away from now, all three of them could still live out their natural lives, even find partners and, perhaps, if their engineered bodies allowed it, maybe even have children. And their children would have time to have children and grandchildren. Five, perhaps six, generations could live out their lives before the end of humanity finally arrived. That was a future worth living for, wasn't it?

But, since they'd returned from their travels, this place hadn't once felt like a home. With Sal gone, it seemed different. It was no longer some thrilling twilight Batcave from which the six of them could plan their next exciting adventure. Instead it felt like a truly melancholic place; like a party where too few guests arrive, shuffle their feet and mutter niceties before excusing themselves early. Maddy noted Sal's few possessions lying around: her diary (that Liam seemed to have taken over), a loose folder of pencil sketches she'd made of them — some of them pretty good — and there was her hoody, still hanging over the side of her hammock, and a pair of her trainers tucked side by side beneath it.

She sensed the loss of Sal like she now felt the creeping damp in here. It no longer seemed like their home, more like a dark and dank prison cell. A place to escape from.

SpongeBubba sat inert in the corner beside the computer bench like a broken toy. Rashim had flipped his power over-ride switch so that he was properly off and not just in a dormant low-charge state that he could emerge from at will. There was no knowing for sure when they were all going to be returning.

'Why the hell does this feel like a goodbye, Liam?'

'No reason why it should. You're seeking answers, I'm seeking answers. We'll be back here comparing notes before you can say "Tawamattawockymickytata".'

She smiled. 'Oh yeah, that "Bend in the River" place in the jungle? I see you've been practising.'

'Aye. Stupid name for a village, anyway.'

She stepped towards the desk and threw an arm round him, hugging him tightly. 'Just you be very careful back there.'

'Are you kidding? I've got Bob. He's a one-man Roman legion. It's you that needs to be careful, Mads. The future? Well, you know what I think about heading there.'

'I can't ignore the invitation. That's the first and only time

33

Waldstein has ever attempted direct contact with us. I have to go . . . I need this. You know that.'

He looked at her for a moment, then nodded. 'Aye. But it's stupid.'

'It's necessary.' She stepped back and smiled. 'A few days or weeks from now, we'll all be back here. We'll know everything there is to know.' She shrugged. 'And maybe then we can make an informed decision for once . . . instead of winging it.'

'Decision? About what?'

'Whether we go on. Go our separate ways. Whatever . . . At least we'll be free to go about our lives without having to look over our shoulders all the time.'

'Go separate ways?' Liam looked down at his hands. 'Is that what this is?'

'What?'

'This . . . going to speak to Waldstein –' he stroked the bristles on his chin – 'is this you looking for a way to leave? Is this you asking his permission to cut free . . .? To go your own way and know he won't be hunting you down?'

'I'm after some answers, Liam. That's all.'

'Aye, and when you've got them?'

'I don't know. Who knows what the hell we're going to find out? What that might change about us?'

'I'm after answers too, Maddy. We're here for a purpose.'

She glanced at Bob. 'A mission?'

'Aye. A mission. Maybe it's Waldstein's mission. Maybe we now have to work against him. I think we need to know that. And I think that giant tachyon transmitter is the bigger question, to be sure. Not the old man.' He puffed air and shook his head incredulously. 'I can't believe that you're not as curious about them as I am.'

'Oh, I am . . . but . . .' What she didn't want to admit to him was that that giant transmitter in the jungle terrified her. It radiated more than energy. It radiated menace. 'Waldstein's the one person we know who's going to have answers, Liam. You want my opinion?'

'You're going to give it to me anyway.'

'You're going on a wild-goose chase.'

'Aye, well . . . we'll see.'

They stared at each other, sharing an awkward silence. Maddy cracked first. 'So, have you decided your call-back window?'

'Aye. I'll give me and Bob a week back in Jerusalem to see what's what.'

'A week?'

'I wouldn't mind seeing what it's like in Bible times. Anyway . . . we'll be back here long before you, I'm sure.'

Liam was probably right. They were going to have to find out where the reclusive billionaire, Waldstein, was hiding away. The only return window she'd scheduled was an hour after the outward one. In the same spot. Just in case they needed to beat a hasty retreat. But, in truth, she had no idea how long or difficult or dangerous their jaunt into the future was going to be. Maybe *her* mission was going to be the wild-goose chase.

They were probably pushing their luck. Two missions at the same time? No one back in the dungeon keeping an eye on things, waiting for a sign, a time wave, on the lookout for a *get-me-back-home-now* message?

She glanced at the monitors on the computer bench. A row of twelve quietly humming personal computers wired together, working in parallel to host an artificial intelligence that she'd come to view as a trustworthy colleague, if not a friend.

Computer-Bob. If Liam ran into trouble, there might be some way he could leave a message through time for the AI to pick up. Maddy on the other hand . . . she was relying on finding

35

Waldstein, who obviously had a displacement machine of his own. There was, however, the distinct possibility that both teams could end up being marooned. Which was why she'd given computer-Bob some instructions to carry out in the event that he found himself all alone here in London.

One of the screens displayed a dialogue box with text written in a font large enough so that she could see it from the square plinth of sawdust she was standing beside.

> **Charge complete. Are you ready to go, Maddy?**

She stepped up on to the plinth. 'And don't forget – if you do bump into *you-know-who*, get him to say something really useful.'

'Like what?'

'Like . . . *Blessed are women, for they make far smarter decisions than dudes.*'

He laughed. 'Right.'

'And it's totally OK to be gay, straight, black, brown . . . and listen to banjo music.'

'I'll try to remember.'

'And . . . I want an autograph.' She grinned. 'Can you imagine what I'd get for that on Craigslist?'

'I'll do my best, Mads.' He reached out and grabbed her arm. 'Stay safe . . . and come home, all right?'

She nodded. 'I better go . . . Rashim will be wondering what's happened to me.' She nodded towards the webcam on the bench. The nearest equivalent to direct eye contact. 'Computer-Bob?'

> **Yes, Maddy?**

'In the event of . . . of the worst-case scenario – the one we talked about earlier – you know what you have to do?' That was something she'd discussed with Liam and Rashim – the possibility that some self-destruct process needed to be agreed. If they all went missing, this place couldn't be left intact.

> Yes, Maddy. I will ensure the displacement machine is rendered inoperable, then complete a hard-drive wipe across the computer network.

They'd agreed that if Liam's return window didn't bring them back, and if she wasn't able to request a return portal from the future, computer-Bob was to allow six real-time months to pass here before destroying the machine and erasing himself.

'And . . . meantime, if anyone unauthorized enters this archway without us . . . then you do the same. Wipe everything. Do you understand?'

> Yes. I understand. We have already discussed these protocols.

She rolled her eyes. 'Yes . . . yes, of course we have.' She looked at Liam. 'I'm just –'

'I know. Clucking like a mother hen.'

'Being thorough . . . I was going to say.'

> Do not worry, Maddy. I will make sure this technology does not fall into the wrong hands.

'Good. Right. Then . . . I guess I'm ready to go. You better give Liam the countdown.'

A digital display appeared on one of the screens. One minute to go. She watched the seconds tick down.

She listened to internal circuit switches clicking, the building hum of energy peaking held at bay and ready to be released. A sudden and melancholic notion occurred to her.

This could be the very last time I see this place.

A stupid thought really. After all, every time they'd opened a window to the past, it could quite easily have been her last jump. There was no knowing what fate existed round the very next corner. All the same . . . it did somehow feel a little bit like a goodbye.

'Liam?'

'Aye?'

She couldn't think of anything meaningful to say. Nothing that could sum up the confusing swirl of thoughts and emotions inside her. 'Just be careful, OK?'

'Always am, Mads. Always am.' He looked at the countdown display. 'Ten seconds. Hands by your side and stand still like a good girl.'

'Liam, you know I love you, right?' she blurted as the noise of the displacement machine began to fill their dungeon. She wanted to quickly add something about not in 'that way' . . . but as a dear friend, as a brother, as a comrade in arms. But, as always seemed to be the case, her farewell words were being cruelly drowned out and she'd have to bellow them to him. But she saw she didn't need to. He nodded back at her and mouthed, '*I know. Me too.*'

The countdown on the screen showed five seconds. Time for one last reassuring smile. He replied with a wink . . . and a wave.

Then she was gone and Liam watched the displacement field collapse to a pinprick of light, then vanish.

CHAPTER 6
1890, London

The dungeon was quiet once more, with nothing but the distant muted chug of the Holborn Viaduct generator, the whir of computer fans and the clatter-click of hard drives to keep them company. He turned to Bob. 'So, it's just the two of us once again, big fella.'

'Yes, Liam. Just the two of us.'

'I suppose we'd better start identifying *exactly* where we're deploying. Biblical Jerusalem, I suppose, is a bit on the finger-in-the-air side.'

'Recommendation: we identify a specific time first.'

'Aye. I recall you and Becks had a jolly good go at calculating the start and end times of the beam when we were back in the jungle?'

'Correct. I have the data stored.' He reeled off the statistics and figures on his hard drive, then broke the numbers down into the conclusions they'd come to eighteen months ago. The beam in the jungle had appeared to be deliberately directed through the very centre of the earth and out of the other side. Emerging, of all places, in the middle of the city of Jerusalem. More specifically, somewhere beneath the big temple in the city. The decay rate of the tachyons suggested the beam either started, or ended, at the very beginning of the first century.

The time of Christ. Liam wondered whether that was significant or not.

'You know the ideal time we need to aim for, Bob?' Liam said. 'Just before that thing is switched on. Like the day before or something. Perhaps we'll even catch whoever these people are with their launching-ceremony party hats on, cracking open a bottle of champagne, passing around a bowl of peanuts . . . or something.'

'You need me to calculate to a particular day?' Bob looked at him. 'I am unable to guarantee that kind of precision, Liam. I can attempt a best-guess calculation, but we may arrive days, weeks or even months before or even *after* the origin time of the beam. This will be an imprecise calculation.'

'Well, let's get as close to the beginning as we can. Even if we miss it being turned on, surely one of *them* will be hanging around to make sure that beam thing is working properly, right?'

'That is a reasonable assumption.'

'All right, then . . . you better start working on your numbers.'

Bob nodded. 'I will commence calculating.' He closed his eyes.

And, while he was doing that, Liam decided he was going to head on down to the market at the bottom of Farringdon Street and get in whatever useful things he could find for their trip to biblical times. As he headed out through their low door, he decided to pay a visit to the library too, to see if he could find anything about the temple itself; a history of the building perhaps, with information about the sacred ground beneath it.

'This is not a suitable place,' said Bob.

Liam nodded. The density graph was spiking every few seconds. He looked at the grainy, pixelated image they'd just snapped from the past. It wasn't showing them very much: a section of sun-bleached stone wall and a long hard-edged shadow cast diagonally across it. As far as Liam could make out, the shadow could have been cast by a person, a camel, a palm tree . . . a large dancing banana . . . for all they knew. And there was something blurred on the left of the low-resolution image, perhaps someone's robe or cape swishing past. Whatever it was, this narrow backstreet in the upper city was just as busy as the last half a dozen locations they'd density-tested.

They'd also been experimenting with different times of day. This current time-stamp was at dawn. Their version of seven in the morning. They'd tried midnight, three in the morning, midday – Liam had bet midday would have been quiet. Surely, with the sun at its highest and hottest, things would slow down a little? But no. It seemed Jerusalem was a city that never settled down.

'Seriously? Don't these Judaeans ever sleep?'

'We may have picked a busy period in their year, Liam.' Bob turned towards the webcam. 'Computer-Bob, reference the historical database.'

> I am already checking, Bob . . . one moment . . . one moment.

Liam grinned. 'What's it like talking to a copy of yourself?'

Bob frowned. 'Which version is the *copy*, Liam . . . and which is the original?' He frowned. 'My AI is inherited from the first organic unit. The one that was incapacitated by Kramer and his men. As was computer-Bob's. As such, we can both be considered "descendants" of the original AI. However, I have acquired additional first-generation memories, which computer-Bob has inherited and –'

'All right, all right. Clearly a sore point. Sorry I asked.' He patted the support unit like a scolded pet. 'I was just attempting a bit of light-hearted banter there. My mistake, Mr Sulky Pants.'

Bob cocked his head and smiled – unpleasantly. All tombstone teeth and pink gums. 'As Maddy would say . . . *goofing around*?'

'Yeah . . . something like that.'

The dialogue box on the monitor in front of them flickered to life.

> **Information: the time-stamp you have chosen coincides with a Judaean religious holiday called 'Passover'. The religious holiday lasts for a week. In first-century Judaea, the city of Jerusalem is a major attraction for the local population to celebrate Passover. Expect this location to be busy.**

'Great.' Liam sighed. 'So maybe we're going to have to head further out.'

> **That is recommended.**

'All right, then, I suppose we'll have to take it outside the city. Computer-Bob, can you find us some quiet place not too far away? I don't want the same back-breaking hike we had getting to Rome.'

> **Affirmative. Checking . . .**

'By the way . . .' Liam turned to Bob. 'I picked up some things while you were sleeping.'

'I was *not* sleeping. I was calculating our time-stamp.'

'Aye, yeah . . . sure. I bet you calculated that in about three seconds and used the rest of this afternoon to get in an old-man nap.'

Bob's thick Neanderthal brows knitted together.

'Just messin' again.' He slapped Bob's shoulder. 'Now, I got us some clothes that should just about pass as suitable for this time. I should be OK. But, as usual, you're going to stick out like a brontosaurus.' He looked at Bob. The support unit's coarse, springy, wiry hair had grown long enough during their time abroad that it was now hanging in thick corkscrews to his shoulders. His normally smooth, square jaw had sprouted a thick thatch of dark bristles. Maddy had been nagging the pair of them to get down to the barber's at the end of the street and tidy themselves up. Rashim, on the other hand, kept his beard meticulously trimmed and his long hair tidy, thus escaping her disapproving scowl. Luckily they hadn't listened to her. Liam looked at Bob; the scruffy, unkempt look would probably help them. He could imagine Bob passing as some simple-minded gentle giant. Perhaps an ex-Gallic slave.

'And . . . I picked up an old goatskin bag, a satchel-type thing, I've packed a couple of those torches. Oh, and I bought a second-hand copy of the King James Bible for reference and this . . . I nicked from the library.'

Liam produced a burgundy-coloured, leatherbound hardcover book. *A Remarkable Exploration Beneath the City of Heaven*, by Sir Richard F. Barton. 'I flicked through some of this. Some gentleman explorer messing about in the sewers and Roman-era aqueducts. It might be useful.'

'Liam, the Bible is not a reliable source for historical data.'

He shrugged. 'You never know. There might be something we can use.'

'Suggestion: you should download the appropriate language into one of the babel-buds.'

'Done that . . . while you were napping.' He smiled. 'First-century Hebrew, Greek and Aramaic. You'll need to download those into your hairy nut too.'

'I will do that now.'

An hour later, computer-Bob finally came up with a suitable location for them. The slopes of a hill overlooking the city to the east. They examined the pinhole image and saw dry clay-orange ground and the twisted thick trunks of stunted olive trees. In the distance . . . the cluttered, labyrinthine mess of a city crammed within the confines of a salmon-pink stone wall. All flat roofs and terraces, narrow streets and crowded marketplaces that shimmered with colour.

'To be clear . . . that is Jerusalem, right?'

> **Of course.**

'Good, then that looks to me like a short downhill stroll. Good job.'

They ran a density scan and got nothing on the display but a gentle undulation that could have been the swaying of dry grass nearby or a passing bird.

'I think we've got ourselves a winner,' said Liam. 'But let's just be cautious. Let's go in after dark.'

> **Good idea, Liam. I will advance the time-stamp by six hours.**

'All right, computer-Bob, looks like we're good to go. Can you start charging her up once more, please?'

> **Of course, Liam.**

Liam settled on the edge of the desk. As soon as the displacement machine was charged, they were ready to go. He found himself staring affectionately at the row of monitors sitting on the bench and at the webcam.

Maddy's final instructions to computer-Bob had been quite right. A perfectly sensible precaution. If for some reason his expedition to biblical times went wrong, as well as Maddy's trip to meet Waldstein, then this dark refuge tucked away at the back of the brick labyrinth was destined to remain deserted for years, decades even. But one day, for certain, somebody would force that padlock and enter. What they'd find would be covered in dust. None of it would be functional, of course, but *when* it was discovered would determine how much of a stir it would cause. He imagined someone discovering these inert pieces of technology during, say, the Second World War

44

would attract the attention of the highest levels of British government. However, someone coming across the same things forty or fifty years later might think they were looking at the abandoned props for some low-budget science-fiction movie, or think it some abandoned backstreet computer workshop.

If both their missions went wrong, computer-Bob was going to have to destroy the displacement machine, completely erase the hard drives and erase himself – an act of digital suicide.

Sorry, ol' fella.

He heard the displacement machine starting to hum as it began to accumulate a reservoir of stored energy. The first three charge-indication lights were already flickering amber.

> **Caution: preparing to open Maddy's one-hour window . . . in ten . . . nine . . .**

Liam turned to look at the space in the centre of the dungeon where the sphere routinely opened. A part of him was hoping that a few moments from now they'd emerge from the hovering portal. Already confounded by some problem or obstruction or threat, and deciding instead to come along with him and Bob for an adventure in the past.

Space–time suddenly warped into a sphere and a gentle gust of displaced air disturbed the drapes round the hammocks, sending several pieces of paper skittering across the computer table. And there the portal hovered and flexed two feet above the ground. He could see a rippling oil-painting depiction of the future – the sky tones of sickly sepia, the ground a drab, lifeless grey. He couldn't make out any details clearly, but from what he could see the future was not a particularly colourful or inviting-looking place.

More to the point, he saw no dark silhouettes preparing to

45

come through. His heart sank a little as he realized they'd already set off on their quest. They were gone.

Just us, then.

The sphere hovered for another few moments, then collapsed with a soft pop.

'OK, that's it . . . now it's our turn, Bob.'

In silence, they stripped out of their Victorian clothes, Liam carefully folding his smart trousers, morning shirt and waistcoat and placing them on his hammock. Then he pulled over his head and narrow shoulders an extra-large cotton nightshirt that hung down to just above his knees. It looked close enough to the pale-cotton jellaba that he'd researched most Judaeans wore in this time. A pair of leather slippers were as close a match as he could find to sandals.

He looked at Bob. The same-sized nightshirt that hung loosely on Liam was tight round his chest and bulging biceps. The hem hung only as far as his pelvis. Luckily he was wearing a pair of leather breeches. Hardly authentic clothing for the time, but nothing that would catch a person's attention any more than the sheer ox-like size of him.

Liam reached for the goatskin bag he'd bought from the market. In there were a few essentials he was going to have to keep from prying eyes, the torches in particular.

'You all ready to go, Bob?'

'Yes, Liam.'

He turned towards the screen beside him. 'Computer-Bob?'

> Yes, Liam?

'Just thought I'd better say, you know . . . just in case . . . it's been an honour and a privilege working with you.'

> Thank you, Liam. It has been an honour working with you also.

The cursor blinked silently for a few seconds before finally jittering across the screen.

> Your last statement suggests you anticipate not coming back?

He was going to say no. That it was nothing. No big deal. Just something nice to say to fill the time. But that would be disingenuous. Computer-Bob wasn't just a bunch of looping code. He was a friend. A friend who deserved the truth.

'I certainly intend to return. But I won't lie . . . this time it feels like we're pushing our luck.'

> Maddy's strategy is a calculated risk. I am sure she will return safely.

'Really? How can you even begin to predict that?'

He had no idea what they were going to learn from Waldstein, if anything at all. That is, if he didn't have them wiped out by another group of meatbots ready and waiting to jump them as soon as they came knocking. And, if he *did* lay out some profound revelation before them, what was that going to do to Maddy's already-troubled mind? Make everything all right once again? Was the truth from him – whatever it was – going to set her free . . . or send her over the edge?

> Just a 'hunch'.

'A hunch?!' Liam laughed. 'Jay-zus, don't tell me even you can think like a mushy-headed human now?'

The cursor blinked for a moment.

> Negative. I have no soft-logic circuits. That was just appropriately deployed humour. Designed to make you feel better.

'Right. Darned hilarious.'

> The humour was amusing?

'Hmm . . . I suspect you've been whispering too much at

47

night with Becks. Someday I'll have to teach you and her what actually constitutes *funny*. It's all about –'

> **Timing.**

'Oh, ha ha . . .' He slapped his hand gently against one of the monitors. 'Everyone's a comedian here.'

> **:)**

Five amber-coloured charge lights were on the board now.

> **Liam, I now have enough power to activate your portal. You and Bob should take your positions, then I will initialize the one-minute countdown.**

'Thank you.' He gestured at Bob to take his place on one of the plinths, then stood beside him on the other one. 'So, here we go again, big man.'

'Here we go again, Liam,' Bob rumbled. He turned to look at him. 'For your information, I believe your objective is the correct one to prioritize. We will soon understand the purpose of those tachyon transmitters. That is important.'

'And what about Waldstein?'

Bob frowned. 'I predict he may have some critical information. But not all of it.'

> **Ten seconds, Liam. Remain perfectly still.**

He squinted at the monitor on the bench and watched the last few seconds count down. Listened to the hum of energy reach a buzzing crescendo echoing around the dungeon, and felt the air around him become charged with static electricity, the hair on his head lifting and tickling his scalp.

Just before the portal opened and engulfed them in a soup of featureless white, he called out above the cacophony of noise, 'Goodbye, Bob.' Then regretted it. He was almost certain that the AI wouldn't have heard him saying that, which was probably for the best. He had no idea whether its heuristic AI had developed enough to feel sadness, loss. Hopefully not. His musings on whether computer-Bob could shed the digital equivalent of a tear were instantly forgotten as he found himself, once again, falling through the white stuff.

Falling . . . falling . . . falling.

CHAPTER 7

2070, New York
89 days to Kosong-ni

Maddy emerged from the swirling mist, her feet setting down on a crazy-paving pattern of cracked tarmac with knee-high tufts of grass sprouting boldly through the gaps.

They were standing on the Williamsburg Bridge, on the car lane heading over the East River into Manhattan. It was empty of vehicles. Even abandoned ones. Running parallel to the tarmac was the pedestrian walkway, again deserted.

'It looks like this bridge must have been closed down some time ago,' said Rashim.

She nodded, then walked over to the side of the bridge and leaned over the safety rail. She found herself looking down on to the rooftops of what was once their part of Brooklyn: all empty warehouses, industrial units, factories and riverside apartments. Greenery seemed to sprout from every possible crevice. Running along the sides of brick walls, she noted the green-black strata of a high-tide mark and, several feet lower, the dark putrid water of low tide. On the surface was a gently undulating carpet of froth and floating debris picked up from the insides of all these buildings and carried out through long-ago broken windows to ride on the lapping water.

The sight vaguely reminded her of pictures of that Italian

city Venice. Every building an artificial island, surrounded on all sides by foul-smelling canals and man-made waterways. Through the foggy-green murk of the water she could just about make out the ghostly oval outlines of submerged vehicle roofs.

Maddy looked up. New York skies – she was used to them being clear and blue and always so busy with the criss-crossed chalk lines of vapour trails of high-altitude air traffic, and, much lower, the *thwup-thwup-thwup* of helicopters passing to and fro across the river to Manhattan, buzzing the distant skyscrapers like over-persistent mosquitoes. Now the sky was overcast, stained an unhealthy sepia colour and dotted with hundreds of seagulls hovering on a stiff breeze above Brooklyn, keen eyes eagerly hunting for scraps of food they could swoop down and snatch.

New York's ever-present heartbeat of trains rolling and *clackety-clacking* over railway tracks, the traffic rumble and honking horns and distant wailing sirens, the thumping music from a passing car-boot hi-fi . . . all of that was gone now. Replaced with just the rumpling breeze, the thrumming of wind playing across iron support cables like a harpist's delicate fingers. Accompanying it, the creak and groan of the old bridge swaying sedately and the distant and shrill *me-me-me* cry of the seagulls.

Maddy heard footsteps approaching; Becks joined her and looked down on what remained of the Brooklyn they used to know.

'Do you miss this location, Maddy?' the support unit asked.

'Yup.' Maddy nodded slowly. 'Didn't realize how much I did, to be honest with you.' She clicked her tongue. 'It looks so sad and forgotten and miserable now.' She leaned further forward, wanting to get a glimpse of the brick archways directly beneath them. 'I guess our old place is well and truly underwater now. Pity, we could've visited.'

'New York is not completely abandoned.' Becks's hard voice softened slightly. She pointed across the water to the skyscrapers of Manhattan.

Maddy followed the direction of her finger and saw some vague signs of life. On a number of those far-off rooftops, egg-whisk wind turbines spun lazily like barber's poles. She thought she caught a glimpse of some delta-winged kite swaying from a rooftop like a bee hovering above a flower bed. Rashim had told her he knew Manhattan was still partially occupied. Maybe it was some misplaced notion of national pride, or perhaps some begrudging siege mentality, that was keeping the very tops of the skyscrapers alive with a few hardened New Yorkers, or barmy-minded eccentrics not quite ready to bid adieu to the city once and for all and let it finally become an abandoned ghost town.

Rashim wandered over and joined them, leaning against the creaking railing and taking in New York with the same forlorn expression as Maddy.

'My God,' he uttered miserably. 'I have seen pictures, of course, but nothing prepares you for seeing it with your own eyes.' He sighed. 'They really have surrendered Manhattan to the sea.'

They stared out over the safety railing in a silent row, looking down on an archipelago that was once a place called Brooklyn. A gridded patchwork of low square islands, now home to thousands of terns and gulls nesting on windowsills and rooftops. Maddy imagined the dark interiors of these buildings now played host to a brand-new ecosystem of wildlife: feral dogs and cats feasting on pigeons, mice and rats.

She suspected that one or two dusty old apartment attics were probably still occupied by truculent old hermits refusing to leave behind their homes, unwilling to let the advancing sea steal away their ancient childhood memories of stuffy New York summers and leaky, spraying fire hydrants. Memories of porch-step gatherings and listening to the evening music spilling from a dozen open sash windows. Yappy lapdogs barking from first-storey fire escapes down at kids playing jump-rope on the kerb below.

Or maybe she'd just watched far too many of those grainy old films that idealized and sugar-coated the twentieth century and this ol' part of town.

Becks stirred. 'Maddy?'

'Yes?'

'I just detected one or two stray tachyon particles.'

'Was that us?' asked Rashim. 'Decay particles from our arrival portal?'

'No. I believe not.' She looked at Maddy. 'I believe it may have been part of a message.'

'Waldstein again?'

She nodded. 'That is possible.'

Maddy turned to Rashim and grinned. 'He's trying to lead us to him. He must have tried beaming a message here as well.'

'That is encouraging.' He made a face. 'Or disconcerting.'

CHAPTER 8
2070, New York

The Manhattan end of the Williamsburg Bridge ramped gradually from the apex of its river-crossing height down to street level. Only, instead of the dual car lanes merging and becoming part of the downtown waffle-grid of roads and intersections, they dipped below a gentle grey-green tide.

Presently, they were standing on the cracked road and staring down at the debris and chemical-sud-covered ebb and flow of small lapping ripples. The lifeless Atlantic. Lazy waves sloshed up the bridge's car lanes and hissed begrudgingly backwards as they drew nickel-sized nuggets of tarmac back into the sea with them.

Ahead of them, like scrawny saplings graduating up to mature oaks and giant redwoods, buildings protruded from the ordered criss-cross of submerged streets. Waterways now. Unintentional, ordered canals.

Here and there, dotted around, just breaking the surface, they could see the rusting tops and algae-clouded plexiglas sunroofs of Greyhound e-Buses and auto-trucks. Fainter, lost further down beneath the surface, the foggy ghosted outlines of other things: old mailboxes and litter bins, bollards and benches. And, sprouting from the water like marsh reeds, the rusting metal trunks of lifeless street lights.

The lowest buildings, those with only one or two storeys emerging from the sea, seemed to have been wholly abandoned.

Windows cracked or gone, weather damage left untreated. Further away, where the buildings grew in stature and height, there was a suggestion that someone was still home and caring for them – or had, at some time, bothered to try keeping the elements at bay with chipboard coverings screwed into place over windows that had blown in.

To their left, the buildings began to tower, casting long shadows across the smooth water, emerging proudly from the sea where New York's Wall Street used to be. The sulphurous brown sky was still dully reflected in their foggy windows. But dark squares dotted here and there indicated long-gone windows, like gap teeth. On some of the rooftops, Maddy could see those egg-whisk turbines, the fluttering of washed clothes pegged to a laundry line.

'My God,' she whispered sombrely. She wasn't sure if it was the fact that New York looked like an abandoned shanty town that made it all seem so sad, or the fact that there were still people living here among these forlorn islands of steel and concrete, prepared to fight a futile rearguard action against the rising sea.

'Quite a sight, isn't it?' said Rashim. Ill-chosen words in that moment. She wasn't sure if he was saying this was a spectacular sight or a heartbreaking one.

Rashim shaded his eyes as sunlight momentarily broke through the tumbling clouds above and speared down at the water biblically. 'You know, this is not an uncommon sight. Many of our great cities look like this now. They are waterlogged graveyards.'

It's so peaceful, thought Maddy. *So quiet*. She listened to the sound of gently lapping water, the shrill cry of seagulls, the soft creaking of a hanging exit sign nearby. Peaceful, when it shouldn't have been. She felt so very sad.

And there was something else.

She heard the faint drone of a motor. She looked at the others. 'You hear that?'

Rashim nodded. 'That sounds like a motorboat.'

Sure enough, as he said that, they spotted a V-like wake in the water, causing small ripples to spread out between the buildings and splash halfheartedly against their permanently wet and green-skirted bottoms. A moment later, the vessel that was causing the wake came into view: a launch – a low tugboat that looked better suited to inland waterways than the probing edge of the Atlantic Ocean.

It began to turn in a wide arc towards them.

'I think someone's spotted us,' said Maddy.

A couple of minutes later, as it approached the descending off-road of the Williamsburg Bridge, the pilot cut its engine and let forward momentum carry the launch towards them until its stubby prow finally bumped gently against something below the water and it rode up over the slime-covered low tideline across the broken tarmac.

The pilot stepped out from behind his steering post. 'You're not Islanders! Not seen you people around here before!' The man came forward and stood with one boot planted on the prow of his boat. Lean and unshaven, wearing a frayed and battered Yankees baseball cap and a colourful, flowery shirt, he shot Becks a quick glance. 'Hell, reckon I'd remember a pretty thing like you!'

'We're not from round here,' replied Maddy.

'I already figured that for myself, miss. You know someone here? That it? Because, if not, you don't have any business here. There's no place here for any newcomers.'

Maddy looked at all the deserted buildings, a forest of tall, dead-eyed structures that receded into the distance. No place? Did he mean no room? Seriously? The place seemed pretty much deserted.

'We came here looking for someone,' said Rashim. 'We think he is living somewhere here in Manhattan.'

'Who's that? You might as well tell me. I know pretty much everyone livin' in Tower City.'

Maddy and Rashim exchanged a glance. Maddy answered. 'He's living at the top of the W.G.S. Tower, I think. The one that overlooks Times Square.'

'*Times Square?*' The pilot laughed. 'Not heard that name used round here in a while. You talkin' about the round glass tower?' He pointed. 'That one over there?'

She had no idea which one was the old W.G. Systems head office. But he was pointing towards where Times Square used to be. 'Yeah.'

'So, you know the old guy who lives there? You know old Walt?'

Walt? She looked at Rashim. *Walt . . . Waldstein?*

'Yes.' She nodded quickly. 'Yes. *Walt*. We've been trying to find him for ages. Could you, like, maybe, take us over to him on your boat?'

The pilot shrugged. 'Can do, but I ain't doing it for free. I'm the cab driver round here. The last New York cabbie, to be precise.' He pointed at a grubby plastic For Hire sign perched on a couple of poles at the rear of his launch. She recognized it as one of those that used to glow on top of the city's thousands of yellow cabs. All of them now rusting carcasses lost beneath the water.

'Cabbie . . . that's *my* job here.'

'We, uh . . . look, we don't have any money on us, though.'

'Money?' He spat over the side of his boat. 'Money? You kiddin' me? What barter you got over there?' He was looking at the heavy backpacks Rashim and Becks had slung across their shoulders. 'You got any tinnies? Bottle-stuff? Non-perishables?'

Food. That's what he was after. Food or drink.

'Yeah. We got some stuff we can trade . . . barter with you.'

The cabbie grinned. 'Then I guess you got yourself a ride.'

Five minutes later, they had agreed a fare he was happy with. He ushered them aboard, shoved the launch back off the bridge and tugged on the outboard motor's starter chain until it snarled reluctantly to life. He turned his launch round and headed westwards, steering it among a cluster of low buildings that decades ago had once been known as SoHo. To their left, the buildings climbed steeply as they converged towards what used to be the business end – Battery Park, the south tip of Manhattan. To their right, looming a mere six storeys above them, were buildings that in the first half of the twentieth century used to be factories and warehouses and mills, and in the latter half became the fashionable loft homes of New York's rich and famous. Loft-dwelling lovelies with their rooftop gardens and floor-to-ceiling windows that let in all-day sun on to their Andy Warhol prints.

'Where do you live?' asked Maddy.

The cabbie pushed the peak of his cap back. 'Moved upwards only recently. Used to be all set up and cosy on the fourth floor of Macy's department store, West 34th. But I had to move up a couple of floors on account of the *rising tide* and the damp creeping up above it. Damned concrete soaks up that seawater like a sponge.'

'The sea's *still* rising?'

'Some Yorkers reckon it slowed down to about six inches last year.' He nodded. 'I mean, that's good. You know? OK, it's still rising, but it's slowin' down an' all. Might even be that I won't have to go move all my gear up again.'

He steered the boat to the right, turning northwards. Ahead of them was a broad waterway, a hundred feet across, flanked on either side by buildings that grew increasingly taller.

'Since you folks're visitors, you might be interested in the names this place used to have?' He turned and talked over his shoulder at them. 'This waterway used to be known as Broadway. And right up ahead there? See? Where them buildings are all getting tall?'

Maddy nodded. 'I know. That's Times Square.'

The launch sputtered slowly northwards.

They passed windows between towering walls of glass and concrete; the lowest, near the sea level, were fogged green by algal growth, their sills dangling ribbons of seagrass, like green walrus moustaches. Further up they were just fogged with grime. Roofs and balconies here and there displayed flashes of colour: clothes on laundry lines. Maddy even spotted the furtive glance of a small child from a rooftop above them.

'Most of us Islanders live up round this way,' he said. 'Foraging is still pretty good here. You'd be amazed how much you can still find in kitchens in all these old homes. When those levee walls gave way, most folks in this city panicked, just left everything of theirs behind and ran for higher ground.'

'You live on just that? On what you can find?' asked Maddy.

'Hell, no. Most of the people grow some of what they eat too. We got gardens on rooftops and plenty of rain keeps them watered. I know some of them fish too. You can get cod, crayfish, sometimes even tuna. But all the dirty crud that floats in these waterways? I'm not too sure I'd want to eat anything caught round here.'

The motorboat finally emerged from the wide straight waterway that was once Broadway into a space that looked vaguely like a lagoon: a wedge-shaped open area of shallow water surrounded on all three sides by the looming buildings round what was once Times Square. Here and there she could see large, still digi-screens that had once played endless

59

commercials and run headlines in ticker-tape along the bottom. Neon signs that had once upon a time jostled each other for space above the street entrances of stores, attempting to out-glare and out-flicker each other like petulant children seeking attention, now sat inert and lifeless, half in, half out of the water.

The water here was as flat as a millpond, the lethargic tide all but spent slapping against the labyrinthine sides of buildings to get to this sheltered cove. Corroded roofs of auto-trucks and freighter pods broke the surface, along with street lamps, which were dotted around like isolated stalks of bamboo poking from swamp water.

'Over there,' the cabbie said, nodding, and steered his vessel carefully across the smooth water, frequently leaning over the side to be sure his boat wasn't about to run aground.

'Right at the top. That's where old Walt's living right now,' he said, cutting the engine down to an idle spitting chug. 'Although I think his missus prefers they live lower down nearer the waterline.'

Maddy looked at Rashim. '*His missus?*' she whispered. 'I didn't know he had a wife.'

Rashim shrugged.

'You guys aren't his family, I'm guessing,' said the cabbie as he coaxed his boat round the curved, cloudy plexiglas roof of a submerged bus stop. 'What are you, old friends or something?'

Maddy decided to go with something that was kind of close to the truth. Kind of.

'We, uh . . . we used to work for W.G. Systems a while back. We're employees.'

'Lost touch in all the chaos, huh? The big migrations?'

'That's it.'

The boat idled its way towards the half-submerged entrance portico to the skyscraper. The green top of a faded Starbucks sign protruded from the waterline and attached to it was a floating jetty made from wooden pallets supported on a bed of lashed-together plastic gallon drums. Tied to the jetty in a row were several boats, an inflatable, a kayak and a fibreglass canoe.

'You're lucky. Walt's home by the look of it.' The boat nudged against the jetty and the cabbie threw a loop of rope over a post. 'Here we are.'

They clambered up on to the bobbing wooden pallets and the cabbie honked an air horn to alert the tower's inhabitants that they had guests. Maddy craned her neck to look up at the glass-fronted tower. Like most of the other buildings, the majority of the panels were still intact, if grubby. Here and there broken glass had been plugged with boards to keep the elements out. Above them, laundry fluttered from a washing line suspended from a dead electric cable that looped low across the 'lagoon' to a nearby building. Near the top she spotted large red letters, a logo she recognized from some of the software and stationery she'd seen round their Brooklyn archway. The same logo stamped on the bottom of the growth tubes they'd had in the back room.

W.G. Systems.

The cabbie honked his horn again and from an open window a floor above them they caught a glimpse of a head poking out. 'Who's that down there on m' porch?!'

'You got some visitors, Walt!' the cabbie called back up as he unhooked the rope and began to reverse his boat away from the jetty.

Maddy turned to Rashim. 'That's not Waldstein . . . surely?'

'No . . . it isn't.'

A moment later, they heard a rattling and shutter doors cracked open wide above them. A fire ladder emerged from the dim interior, and clattered down, extending until it thumped on to the wooden slats of the jetty. A dark face framed by coils of grey-white hair peered out at them.

'You folks had better come on up. But don't get any stupid ideas about ripping me off . . . I got a gun up here with me!'

They climbed up the creaking ladder one after the other. Up and into the tower through a large improvised doorway of wooden shutters. The old man, lean and narrow-shouldered and in his mid-sixties, beckoned them inside, a rifle hanging loosely in the crook of one arm.

'Now, I don't know you folks from Adam. But *Cabbie* said you all came over here to visit with *me*?'

They were standing in what must have once been a restaurant or a coffee shop that would have looked out across the bustling space of Times Square. Tables and chairs were stacked untidily against a far wall and most of the cleared floor space was filled with scavenged boxes and cartons of packaged and tinned food.

'Roald Waldstein,' corrected Maddy. 'We came here to see Roald Waldstein.'

'Waldstein?' The old man's dark face wrinkled sceptically. 'You ain't talkin' about *the* Mr Waldstein, are you?'

'Yes,' said Maddy, 'the "W" of W.G. Systems. *The* Roald Waldstein.'

That dark face suddenly split with a bright grin and he cackled with bemusement. 'You people for real?'

'The *guy* . . . who just dropped us off. He said *Walt* was living here.'

'Yeah. I'm Walt, young lady.' He offered her his hand. 'Mr Walter M. Roberts Junior. This ain't no W.G.S. Tower no more; this is Roberts Tower. It's *my* tower now.'

She took his hand out of courtesy and shook. All the same she couldn't help but let out a sigh of frustration. Clearly Waldstein was long gone from here. 'Oh, I'm really sorry for the intrusion, Mr Roberts . . . looks like we've made a mistake here. The boat guy said "Walt" . . . and we thought he meant −'

'No idea where Mr Waldstein is holed up these days, I'm afraid, miss. The old man didn't say much to me when he finally upped sticks and left Manhattan.'

'"*Say much to me*"?' Rashim stepped forward eagerly. 'You have actually met the man? Spoken with Waldstein?!'

Walter M. Roberts Jnr's eyes widened slightly at that. So did his grin. 'Met him? Of course I met him. Hell, I used to work for him. I was Mr Waldstein's personal *valet*.'

CHAPTER 9
First century, Jerusalem

Liam found himself staring down at dry dirt between his hands. He looked up. Ahead of him was the dark form of a parched eucalyptus bush struggling for sustenance and moisture in the dry ground, shadowed by several twisted and squat olive trees. Above them, a full moon shone down from a clear, star-speckled sky.

I'm here. In the time of Jesus Christ.

He turned to his right and saw the support unit squatting on all fours and looking up at the moon. 'Bob, you OK?'

'I am fine, Liam.'

'Beautiful night, eh?'

'The stars, Liam. They appear –'

'Yeah . . . yeah, they're lovely too. Come on, you big old romantic. We should get moving.' He got to his feet and looked around. They were standing amid a loosely spaced grove of stunted olive trees, their brittle leaves hissing gently as a soft, warm breeze stirred their branches. Down at the bottom of the slope, the vast ancient city was bathed in the quicksilver blue from the moon, but also spotted with thousands of flickering pinpricks of amber – the light from oil lamps and fires. A city every bit awake at night as New York. Beyond the large stone wall that snaked round it, up and down, over gentle rolling hills and troughs, he could see a dozen campfires and figures gathered round them.

He spotted a train of oxen below, kicking up dust as they pulled a trader's cart along a rutted road that led into the city through a large arch. Beyond the archway, the north-east gate into the city, he could see a marketplace alive with activity, and steps leading up to a vast square walled courtyard that overlooked it. The courtyard, surrounded by high stone walls lined with Grecian columns, was dappled with flickering light from hundreds of torches and braziers, and filled with people milling around what appeared to be traders' stalls.

'Looks like a busy place, over there.'

Bob followed his gaze and nodded. 'That square area is known as the temple platform.'

In the middle of it, Liam could make out a tall rectangular building with towers on the corners. 'Is that . . . is that the temple?'

'Yes.'

'I can't see the big dome anywhere.' Liam had checked out some images of Jerusalem's Holy Temple, the Dome of the Rock, from their database. He had been expecting to see a huge gold-plated dome on the top of it.

'That dome will be built nearly seven hundred years from now, Liam. It will be built on the ruins of the temple you see now.'

'Ah, right. And . . . somewhere beneath that large courtyard and the temple . . .?'

'Affirmative. In theory, we will locate the other tachyon transmitter.' He turned to Liam. 'If our estimation of the tangent of the beam was correct, that is.'

Liam looked at the rest of the city, a carpet of terraces and flat rooftops that undulated with the underlying geometry of shallow valleys and gentle slopes. The temple platform, and the temple in the middle, was spread on top of the city's highest hill. He recalled the bowl-like shape of that Mayan city in the jungle, tucked into a concealed sinkhole or caldera, and, beneath the central plaza, that enormous cylindrical chamber; he could imagine a similar structure concealed somewhere deep within this hill. Looking at the shape of the city . . . it seemed the most likely place to hide something so big.

'So . . . are your cat's whiskers picking up anything yet?'

Bob cocked a thick brow at him. 'I do not understand.'

'Tachyons?'

He nodded his head slowly. 'Negative. The beam is very tightly directed. If it is down there, beneath the temple platform, I will need to be much closer before I will be able to detect any rogue particles.'

'Well then, looks to me like the temple is wide open for business, even at this time of night.' He pulled the strap of his goatskin bag on to his shoulder.

'Would you like me to carry that?'

Liam gave that a moment's thought. 'Aye . . . you're right. What am I doing? You're the big strong one.'

CHAPTER 10
2070, New York

'We chose to stay on here,' said Walt. He smiled warmly at his wife sitting across the large marble dining table. 'Myself and Charm. Our babies bein' grown up and all with babies of their own – they got their own lives in other places. So it was a decision just for us. When the Manhattan authorities finally said there was nothing left of the city for them to run, and that we should all pack up and leave, me and Charm decided we weren't goin' anywhere.'

They were sitting round a circular table of rich dark polished marble. Sitting on ridiculously expensive-looking designer dinner chairs and all of them gazing out of the enormous floor-to-ceiling windows that circled them all the way round the top of the W.G.S. Tower. Darkness was beginning to set in already, even though it was only just gone four in the afternoon. Outside, in the gathering overcast gloom, were several dozen pinpricks of light and the flicker of movement coming from the tops of other abandoned skyscrapers, as others in this artificial-island community passed in front of their candles and gas lamps and electric lamps, preparing their evening meals.

Becks stood like a stone sentinel, silhouetted against one of the panoramic windows and studying the flooded world outside for any approaching signs of danger.

'When did that happen, Mr Roberts?' asked Maddy. 'When did this place get flooded?'

He smiled at her. '*Walt's* more than good enough for me,' he said. 'New York *officially* became an abandoned city back in '61. But it was more'n dead already when them damn levee walls gave way the year before.' The old man shook his head sadly. 'Tidal surge that caused it. Tidal surge that rolled right up the Hudson and East Rivers like a freight train. Large section of them levee walls just gave up the struggle and caved in. Damn mini tsunami, twenty feet high if not more, washed down into all these streets.'

Charm, a handsome old woman with tight coils of grey hair held back by a thick hairband, pressed her lips together then spoke. 'That wave went and flooded the Manhattan subway lines still being used by folks to get to work. Thousands of people were drowned. Those poor, poor souls; they never stood a chance. People in carriages, trapped in those long dark tunnels. All of them drowned in just a few seconds.'

'God,' whispered Maddy. 'That must have been awful.'

'Yes, miss, it was,' she replied. 'Ever since then, this place has remained underwater. Nobody ever reclaimed all those bodies. Somebody said that maybe five or six thousand folks died that day.' She smiled sadly at her. '*New York* died that day. It just took that useless mayor and all his officials a year to catch up with the fact.'

Walt shook his head firmly. 'City ain't dead just yet.' Clearly this was something they discussed and disagreed on frequently. 'No way, Charm, this isn't no dead city, nor is it an abandoned city, not while there's so many of us island folk still living out here.' He pointed at the large panoramic windows. 'C'mon, you can see them lights on out there? OK, it ain't all sparkly like it used to be years back. Sure, this place isn't lit up like some Christmas tree just as you see in the old movies. But you folks can see clear as glass, at night anyway, this city's still got maybe a hundred . . . two hundred people living in it.' He shrugged defiantly. 'That makes it alive enough in my opinion.'

Charm huffed and rolled her eyes at her husband's stubbornness.

'Was Waldstein here when the levee walls broke?' asked Maddy.

'Not on that particular day. He came and went all the time; business trips and the like. I believe, though, that this was his favourite place to stay. He loved the view from the top of his tower.'

'So when was the last time he was here? When was the last time you actually saw him?'

Walt settled back in his chair, and his eyes glinted the amber light of the candles set out on the grand table between them. 'Over nine years ago. Not long after the big Manhattan flood. There were only a few of us left working here then. A skeleton crew, as they say. All the rest of the W.G.S. people had been made redundant by Mr Waldstein. Sent home. It was like he was winding things down here in New York. Almost like he knew Manhattan was running out of time.'

'There was just a half a dozen of you left, wasn't there?' said Charm.

Walt nodded. 'His pilot, three security guards, his cook and me holding the fort here back then. He sat us down and told us he was relocating us. Closing down this tower for good.'

'Did he say where he was relocating you to?' asked Maddy.

'No. Just that he was moving his business affairs westwards, away from the advancing sea. He offered to take us all with him. Move us and our families too. But I said I wanted to stay on in

New York.' Walt shook his head and laughed at himself. 'Born and raised in this city. Damned if I was gonna just leave this place for a ghost town.' He looked at his wife. 'My wife thinks I'm a stubborn ol' fool. Anyway, he took the others with him. Want me to tell you folks the last thing he said to me just as they all climbed into his personal gyrocopter . . .?'

Maddy nodded.

Walt hesitated, with a grin slowly spreading across his lips. His wife nodded resignedly too, clearly having heard this particular anecdote far too many times already.

'The man said to me he didn't need this place any more. He said since I was prepared to stay on here as the *caretaker* . . . the whole tower was mine, if I wanted it.'

Charm laughed softly. 'Walt acts like he's king of the castle now.'

'Well . . . damn, it *is* my castle. And, when the flooding's all done and the sea starts heading back out one day, then I'll be the proud owner of some prime real estate. New York *will* be revived, you can count on that.'

'You're just a dreaming fool,' she sighed. 'Those ice-caps may be all gone and the sea may have finished stealing chunks of land. But sure as hell the sea isn't going to start backing up the way it came. Not any time soon. Not in our lifetime at any rate.'

He shrugged that comment off. 'You ain't got any faith, Mrs Roberts. Good Lord gave us another flooding for a reason. I reckon His work's done on that score now.'

Charm rolled her eyes again at her husband. 'And you ain't no Noah.'

'Anyway,' Walt continued, 'I reckon we got it better than most, sitting up here. Most other folks were heading west, last

70

time I heard a digi-broadcast, it ain't so good inland. Millions on the road, shortages of food and water. And in Colorado the FSA government's struggling to look after them millions of migrants flocking in, and —'

Maddy interrupted him. 'So, Waldstein just . . . *gave* you this whole tower?'

Walt nodded his head, then furrowed his brow thoughtfully. 'Reckon I got to know him better than almost anyone. You folks know he didn't have no family, right?'

Maddy nodded.

'He once had a wife and a son, if I recall correctly,' said Rashim.

Walt nodded. 'Oh yeah . . . you're right, but that was a long time ago. When I started working for him, he was a very, very private man. Very lonely man too. Sometimes he didn't see any other folks but me for days and days. So, I reckon I'd say we got almost close enough to be called friends.' Walt looked out of the window at the darkening sky. 'When he finally left? It was strange, the way he was with me.'

'How do you mean?'

'Like . . . well, that particular morning he was preparing to leave and he just gave me this tower? He was like . . . it was like he was someone getting set to face his own end, you know? Giving away all of his earthly possessions so he could finally go to God empty-handed. Naked as a newborn.'

'You haven't heard from him since?'

'Nuh-uh. He just said to me, "*It's all yours, Walt. Look after it for me.*" Then he got in the gyro' with the others. Flew away. Never seen him again since.'

'Can you tell us any more about what he was like?' asked Rashim.

71

'What he was like?' Walt shrugged. 'I was just his valet. What's any multi-multi-billionaire like to wash and clean up after?' He gestured at the large room. 'He was human, if you know what I mean. Left his fair share of things around for me to clean or tidy. But I guess he wasn't the clutter type. Liked things neat 'n' spare. He kept this place mostly empty. There was a desk, a bed, a couch. This table and these chairs. He didn't have many clothes or shoes or normal stuff. He wasn't one for gadgets and possessions.'

'You said he seemed like someone facing "an end"? Do you mean . . .?'

'Suicidal?' Walt shook his head. 'No . . . just sort of settled, resolved. At peace even.'

'Did he seem, I don't know, *agitated*? Did he ever do anything or say anything strange?'

Walt laughed. 'Only all the goddamn time. Strangest man I ever met!'

'Was there anything going on here in this building?' asked Maddy. 'Any research areas? Any floors with restricted access?'

'Hell, no. This whole tower was just *corporate*. The boring stuff, you know? Finance, patents, human resources, administration. The interesting stuff, the research projects . . . all those things happened over in the Rocky Mountains.'

'You mean the Denver campus?'

Walt nodded. 'W.G. Systems' research centre.' He looked puzzled. 'You said you were W.G.S. people? I'd expect you'd know about that place.'

'Sure we do,' replied Maddy quickly. 'Yeah, we know of it. But we've been abroad most of the last decade.'

'Which division you say you folks were from? Genetics? Energy? Licensing? Research and development?'

'Foreign-aid projects,' replied Rashim. 'We were abroad mostly.'

'Where?' asked Charm.

Maddy, Rashim and Becks looked at each other.

'Africa,' said Maddy finally. 'We've been over in Africa most of the time.'

'Uh, yes . . . East Africa. Studying drought-resistant, high-protein-yield gene-crops.' Rashim flipped his hand casually. 'That kind of thing.'

Charm sat forward. 'Guess it must be pretty bad over there too? All those inter-ethnic, inter-tribal wars in the east?'

'Yeah.' Maddy slowly nodded her head. 'But then where isn't it bad these days, huh?'

'True, that,' uttered Walt.

The conversation lulled for a few moments and they listened to the soft moaning of the gentle wind around the glass top of the tower and faintly, far below, the sound of a lively, choppy tide slapping against the base of the building.

'Unlike Walt here,' said Charm presently, 'I never been one for believing in a God Almighty. Or believing in what some folks say is happening.'

'Happening?' Maddy looked back from the windows. 'What do you mean?'

She shrugged. 'End times. Like in the Bible. But . . . I don't know –' she pressed her lips together and shook her head – 'I do sometimes wonder if things really will get better than they have been. All my life, far as I can remember, this world has felt like it's been limping towards some sad ending.'

Walt laughed. 'Don't listen to my wife. No mistake that things are tough right now, but I guess I'm the optimist out of the pair of us. It'll all get better one day, I'm telling you.'

'So . . .' Maddy looked at Rashim. She wanted to steer

the conversation back to what they needed to find out. 'You think Mr Waldstein's now holed up in this Denver campus place?'

'Sure. Good a place as any. Remote, hard to get to. Hard to find.'

'Could you give us the address?'

'Address?' Walt laughed. 'An address for the W.G.S. Research Campus? You think there's stationery just lying around with a hey-drop-round-anytime address printed at the top?!'

'Now, Walt . . . no need to be making rude to our guests,' said Charm.

'True,' he conceded, a smirk still on his face. 'I'm sorry. Look, I got an address for the contracts and the legal office just outside Denver City. The actual research campus is located *somewhere* up in the Rocky Mountains nearby. Mr Waldstein made a big deal of keeping its exact location a need-to-know only. For obvious reasons. All kind of cutting-edge technology work going on there . . . or at least there *used* to be. You folks want to find him, then you probably need to go to Denver City, present yourself to whatever staff he's got left working in Legal and I guess they'll make contact with Mr Waldstein.'

Walt looked at Maddy somewhat suspiciously, she suspected. 'If he *wants* to see you, you'll know soon enough. Good luck with that.'

'Thanks.'

'You folks got some barter on you?' asked Charm.

'Um . . .'

She smiled. 'I guess not. Barter . . . that's what passes for money these days. You'll need some luxuries to trade. Things like chocolate bars, nice smelly soaps. I'll get you some things that you can –'

'Hold on, Charm!'

'Now, Walt . . . don't get all mean on our guests. We ain't sending these nice people out there, heading across the wilderness, with nothin' to barter.'

CHAPTER 11

First century, Jerusalem

Liam and Bob allowed themselves to be carried along with the push of people squeezing through the north-east gate into the city. The tide carried them up broad stone steps, through another archway and into the large square courtyard Liam had spotted from the hillside. The temple platform.

He looked up at the huge stone walls and the tall Grecian columns running along them. Shadows danced across the stonework, cast up by dozens of flickering braziers. On top of the walls, Roman soldiers paced along walkways, watching the marketplace below. The vast courtyard was alive with noise: the cry of traders' voices bouncing off the high stone walls round them, the bray of mules and oxen, the warbling coo of hundreds of sacrificial doves crammed into small wicker cages, the anxious bleat of goats.

'Jay-zus, it's busy in here!' uttered Liam. In his ear, the babel-bud translated his words into approximated Aramaic and calmly whispered the words to him. Around him snatches of conversation began to be picked up by the bud and translated:

'. . . fifteen shekels for those doves . . .'

'. . . Gentiles, of course . . . only faithful pilgrims are permitted . . .'

'. . . How much?! You can't be serious! . . .'

'. . . Over there! Slaughter those over there . . . at the temple. Not here, you foolish . . .'

The air was thick with incense burning from every trader's stall. Across the courtyard, Liam could see that many of the male pilgrims were wearing pale shawls over their heads and odd-looking small square boxes strapped to their foreheads.

'Bob? What are those box things?'

Bob consulted his database. 'They are called phylacteries.'

'Great, so now I know what they're called. But what are they?'

'The boxes contain religious texts and prayers, folded up inside.'

'Uhh . . . really?' He nodded, bemused. 'Right. So, I guess it leaves their hands free.'

In the centre of the courtyard stood the temple, towering over the bustling marketplace, as high as the guarded portico walls that surrounded the entirety of the temple grounds. 'So, we should make our way towards that building in the middle?'

'Affirmative.'

They began to weave their way through the milling crowd, jostled and pushed by others eager to take their freshly purchased sacrificial animals towards the temple. Closer to it, they could see a long queue of people snaking out of the temple through a large bronze doorway, down shallow steps to a low knee-high wall that ran all the way round the outside of the building. Every last person in the queue, it seemed, was carrying something to present for a sacrifice: the women mostly had wicker baskets containing fluttering birds, the men leading rolling-eyed goats by tethers.

As they made their way along the side of the queue towards the low wall, Liam's bud began to pick up fragments of male and female voices again:

'. . . look at them! Look . . . they can't –'

'. . . blasphemy! Someone should stop . . .'

'. . . they should be killed . . .'

Liam turned to look at the queue and saw eyes locked on them, round and incandescent with rage. He tried a disarming smile and a friendly wave. 'Just having a look. We're not pushing in, I promise!' The babel-bud translated that into Aramaic and he did his best to voice out loud what his bud had whispered into his ear.

Whatever it was they heard him reply, it seemed to only make them more enraged. He reached out and grabbed Bob's arm. 'Uh, Bob? Are you translating what these people are saying?'

'Yes. They appear to be very displeased.'

'You're not kidding. I think they think we're pushing in front of them or something.' They approached the low stone wall and Liam shook his head and tutted. 'What is it with some people?' He craned his neck to look up at the temple building, tall and imposing, the pale sandstone walls warmed by pools of dancing light from flickering oil lamps. He casually hopped up on to the low wall . . .

. . . and heard a collective intake of breath rippling all the way down the queue beside them. He could see hundreds of eyes glaring at him, mouths below dropped open, forming 'O's of horror and disgust.

Jay-zus, what the hell is wrong with these people?

Bob reached out for Liam's hand, grasped it and pulled him roughly back down off the wall.

'Whuh! Why the –?'

Bob pointed to a paving stone on the floor beside the wall. Characters were inscribed in it.

'What? Let me guess, it says "No climbing around on the wall", right?'

'It says: *No Gentile is to proceed beyond this balustrade. Whosoever is caught will have himself to blame for his death. Which will follow directly.*'

Liam found himself instinctively backing away from the wall. He turned to the queue of people and shook his head. 'I'm sorry, so sorry! I didn't realize!'

A pair of guards emerged from the bronze doorway leading into the temple and began to approach them. Several of the men standing in the queue stepped out of it and also began to slowly pace towards them. They were shouting, bellowing angrily at him, fists balled and waving in front of their faces. The babel-bud in his ear kept starting and stopping, catching and attempting to translate snippets of Aramaic, then aborting to begin again.

'You know what?' whispered Liam. 'I think we'd probably better turn and go.'

Bob nodded. 'We are attracting a lot of attention.'

They turned their backs on the low wall and began to walk quickly away from the temple and diagonally away from the snaking queue of pilgrims.

Just brass it out, Liam. Brass it out and keep walking.

They picked up the pace and put some distance between them and the raised voices calling after them. Liam gave it a minute and then turned to snatch a quick glance over his shoulder. There were still a few men following them, men waving their fists and snarling. He saw one of them stoop down and pick something off the ground. He pulled back his arm and launched it at them; a moment later, a sharp stone bounced off the side of Liam's head.

He yelped in pain. Put his hand up to his temple and felt a trickle of blood.

Bob stopped in his tracks, turned round and started to move threateningly towards the man who'd thrown it.

'Hold it, Bob. I'm all right. It just smarts a bit.'

'The action is threatening.'

'Not particularly welcoming, admittedly, but let's not kick off a bloodbath here.'

Bob growled.

'Heel, boy . . . Let's just make a quick exit before we start something.'

CHAPTER 12

2070, New York
88 days to Kosong-ni

The motor launch took them west, at first weaving slowly through the labyrinth of skyscrapers, then out across the open channel of what was once the Hudson River, towards what remained of New Jersey. They chugged between the extended rusting arms of freight-loading cranes, emerging from the water's surface at an angle, like the rotting boughs of vast dead redwoods.

New Jersey rooftops passed silently either side of them: warehouses, factories, shipping offices, then further westwards . . . apartment blocks, shopping centres, business centres. They passed the upper walls and roof of some sort of stadium. Above the main entrance was a large billboard featuring the fading and flecked red-paint logo of something that looked like a reclining horned imp.

'New Jersey Devils,' grunted the cabbie. 'Greatest ice-hockey team . . . ever. Period.' He looked at Maddy. 'I saw them play once as a kid. That was way back in '43. Must have been one of the very last games they ever played.'

She nodded politely, then looked back again at the waterlogged landscape sliding past them. Not a world wholly submerged. That might have been more bearable if it had all been lost far beneath the surface and lay out of sight and mind. But like this? A world struggling to keep its chin above a dirty, debris-encrusted tide? Looking at something floundering to stay alive, she figured, was far worse than looking at something long dead. Here and there she spotted signs of rooftop life: potted plants on terraces and verandas, rooftop gardens covered with bean stalks and tomato plants weaving their way round cane frames, buckets and awnings erected to gather and channel rainwater. She looked up at the brown-tinged, chemically tainted clouds above them and wondered just how drinkable that water was.

Signs of life hanging on here and there. People holding on to hope like those living among the Manhattan skyscrapers. Holding on and hoping that the tide that had crept relentlessly upwards, biting chunks inland, would eventually stop and perhaps recede.

And it's all so frikkin' futile, she mused. *Because in three months' time most of you poor wretches will be wiped out by the Kosong-ni virus.*

A solemn mood had settled on her and Rashim as the launch chugged stoically westwards towards where the last New York cabbie had said the inland tidal surge finally gave way to the soaked edge of dry land: a place called Orange City, sitting right on the cusp of the as yet unsubmerged portion of New Jersey.

Four hours after they'd bid a fond farewell to Walt and Charm, waving them off from their improvised jetty, the cabbie finally pointed ahead. 'There ya go. That's where your troubles begin!'

Maddy looked back at him from the prow. 'Troubles?'

'Sure. Many of the folks who abandoned the east coast are mostly hangin' on there. Waiting for the sea to go back out again.' He shrugged. 'Then there are those who figure the sea ain't going nowhere, so they're heading inland, west towards the FSA. Where *supposedly* there's some kinda law and order still.'

As the water beneath them grew shallower, it was more than just rooftops breaking the surface; now the flat tops of e-Cars emerged, slick with tufts of algae and ribbon-like kelp. Then the wet green humps of seagrass-covered bollards and trash cans gradually came into view.

The cabbie eased back on the throttle. The laboured drone of the outboard dropped in pitch to a long-suffering grumble and the launch slowed down to little more than a cautious drift as he carefully weaved his way towards where the tide lapped against sodden tarmac.

They drifted beneath an overpass. Maddy looked up at a row of faces staring down at them, lining the railing, curious about the new arrivals. They emerged out the other side from the shadow it cast, towards the wet tarmac ahead.

'That road dipping into the water there? You're looking at the end of what used to be Interstate 280,' he said, pointing. 'Heads west if that's where you're goin'.' He finally cut the engine and the boat slid slowly to a halt, with the rasp of weeds and kelp against the hull softening her gentle grounding.

'That's yer ride, folks.'

Becks hopped over the side into knee-deep water and took their backpacks with her as she waded ashore. Maddy and Rashim splashed over the side and joined her on the empty interstate, warily looking up at the people gathered on the overpass.

Maddy turned round and thanked the last cab driver in New York. He shrugged a *No problem* at them. 'Good luck,' he called out. 'It's *frontier land* from here on in. You watch yer backs.'

He jumped off the prow into the water, gave his boat a shove backwards and clambered aboard, started up the outboard and gunned the throttle. He waved one more time at them, then turned his launch round in a lazy arc and puttered back the way they'd come, back under the overpass, heading eastwards, back to the drowned wilderness of New Jersey and New York beyond.

'Frontier land?' Maddy looked at Rashim. 'Like . . . like one of those western movies?'

'Lawless,' replied Rashim. 'He means lawless. We are on our own.'

Maddy nodded. Either side of the abandoned interstate was a shanty town of improvised shelters and lean-tos. Homes made from scavenged materials, cannibalized from buildings. Twists of smoke emerged from cluttered corrugated rooftops and narrow, muddy rat runs. The stillness and calm of Manhattan and New Jersey was replaced with a hubbub of activity: the barking of dogs, the wail and cry of babies and children, the clang of scaffolding poles being dropped somewhere, the rasp of a grinder cutting through metal, the call of bartering voices, the buzz of a distant chainsaw.

Everyday life eked out precariously, temporarily, *hopefully*, on the dirty leading edge of a mean-spirited flood tide that was busy teasing them with its intentions to advance or recede.

CHAPTER 13

2070, New Jersey
87 days to Kosong-ni

'Denver, Colorado?' The man laughed at them like that was just about the oldest joke in the book. Maddy watched him as his narrow shoulders hitched up and down. He turned the faded and threadbare khaki-green baseball cap on his head round so that the peak covered his wrinkled beef-jerky neck and busied himself with the task of slowly rolling a cigarette.

'That'll kill you, you know,' said Maddy, 'smoking.'

His grin widened, revealing an uneven, gappy row of tobacco-stained teeth. 'Not before the *guddamn* toxic rain does. Or some other hungry punk stabs me for a tin of food. Or I drink tainted water.' He finished rolling a few meagre threads of tobacco in the creased paper. Licked down its length and finished up with a twist at the end. 'In these times . . . live long enough to die of smokin', then I guess you doin' pretty damn well.'

'So, anyway, what's so hilarious about us wanting to make our way across to Denver?' asked Maddy.

The old man looked around the bar, then back at Maddy. 'Bar' was a generous name for it. That's what it had been called by the person who'd directed them here. McReady's Bar – several freight containers welded together and filled with scavenged

85

bucket chairs and oil drums for tables. They sold some kind of foul-smelling hooch brewed out the back.

'You for real, miss?'

'Look, we've been out of the country for a while.'

'Out of the country for a while, huh?' The old man looked at her like he didn't buy that, but let it go with a lazy shrug. 'Not many folks find their way safely across to the Median Line these days, miss.'

'What's that? What's the Median Line?'

'Seriously?' He smiled, bemused. 'You had your head in the guddamn ground these last ten years?'

'I guess you could say that.'

''S the border between the abandoned states and what's left of this nation. The FSA. Border that runs from Lake Michigan all way down to the Gulf of Mexico.' He pulled a thread of tobacco from his teeth. 'Reinforced barricade they been buildin' up the last ten years along the border states of Illinois, Missouri, Mississippi. Some places we talkin' a guddamn concrete wall. And guarded by the military. I'm talkin' not just soldiers, but mechanized units, automated drones . . . air an' ground, barbed wire, mines. The whole kit an' caboodle.'

He grinned a mouthful of brown teeth at her. 'It's the thin line in the sand. The last thing that divides what's left of this piecemeal nation with the wild east coast and the half of the population they just abandoned.' He shook his head. 'And not many get through that border, unless they're *let* through, miss.'

'Well, that's where we need to go. The Median Line.'

'Fair enough.' He sucked air through his teeth with a whistling sound. 'You headin' west, then you wanna avoid all the big roads.'

'Why?'

'You gotta watch out for all kinds of bad types. They'll rob you bare soon as look at you. More likely worse than that.'

'We'll be OK.' She nodded at Becks and Rashim sitting on chairs at an oil-drum table in the far corner of the bar. A string of neon-blue Christmas lights winked on and off on the rusting wall beside them, while a small holographic projector played the flickering image of an old black-and-white movie. Their faces were largely in shadow, but every now and then Becks's steel-grey watchful eyes glinted a reflection.

'Those two over there with you?'

Maddy nodded. 'The young woman's called Becks; she's a . . . well, a trained bodyguard. The other one, he's called Rashim; he's a pretty important scientist. He's got connections over there. He'll get us through the border.'

The old man turned to look at them, studied them carefully. Then his eyes suddenly flickered, widened. He swore under his breath. 'That . . . the female! The lady . . . can't be!'

'What?'

'She . . . she one of 'em guddamn military-clone units?'

Maddy was taken aback. 'What? . . . Uh, no. She's just a normal –'

'Damn.' The old man narrowed his eyes suspiciously. 'Looks a helluva lot like one of them fifties recon models. Looks like a real pretty lady, but deadly underneath. Guddamn lethal killin' machine!'

'What? No!' Maddy shook her head. 'No, she's just a human!'

The man lit his cigarette, sucked in a cloud of foul-smelling smoke then blew it out. 'Look, miss, I fought in the Pacific War.

Forty-fifth Mobiles had a squad of those *organics*. The recon ones like her and the real big ones, like guddamn tanks. Seen 'em up real close plenty of times and I'll tell you, miss . . . One thing you never forget is them grey killer's eyes.' The old man pulled the crinkled cigarette from his lips. 'Those old big ones stood out a guddamn mile too. 'S why they started designin' ones that looked more like normal.' He pulled on his cigarette again. 'I served five years with a squad of those things . . . Know one when I see one.'

'She's human,' said Maddy. 'Honestly.'

He sat back in his chair. 'You want to hire me as a guide westwards?'

She nodded.

'Then don't try blowin' smoke in my face, OK?' He leaned forward and lowered his voice. 'That *thing* over there . . . where'd you get her? She some kinda army surplus? Ex-private military?'

Maddy sighed. This old guy wasn't going to buy anything she said. If, like he'd said, he'd served alongside a batch of Bobs and Beckses . . . then he'd know one, no matter how disguised. He'd know.

'OK. All right. Yes, she's . . . *a unit.*'

'Knew it.' The old man sucked a hissed breath through his teeth. 'See, that makes me kinda twitchy. Them early fifties models, computer-linked with a real brain? That's an unpredictable mix going on right inside that thick skull. You must remember about the squad of organics that turned on their regiment? Somethin' went wrong an' misfired in their heads an' they practically wiped out an entire division. I heard their software was hacked or somethin'.'

'Look, Becks has been entirely reliable,' said Maddy.

'*Becks?* You actually given that thing a guddamn name?' He

shook his head. 'Thing like that is as dangerous and unpredictable as a wild animal.'

'She's perfectly safe.'

'Until she ain't . . . then you got yerself a killin' machine busy rippin' your head off.'

'Her AI is a hundred per cent stable. She's never been a problem. I'd trust her with my life.'

The old man narrowed his eyes. 'So how come you got yourself one? You rich? You some billionaire? You buy her off the black market or somethin'?'

Maddy shrugged. 'We kind of inherited her.'

The old man shook his head again, clearly not believing her story. His rheumy eyes passed from her to Rashim. 'Just who the hell are you people?'

'It's a long story.'

'Yeah?' he said, pulling slowly on his uneven cigarette. It crackled and burned fiercely. In the gloom of the bar, the amber glow of the tip reflected in his watery eyes. 'Everyone's story's a long story these days, miss.'

Maddy was getting impatient. 'Look . . . you going to guide us west or not? I'm sure I can find someone else to –'

'If that girl *organic* of yours is truly safe, like you say –' he shrugged – 'then we'll sure as hell need her. Right up to the Median Line, it's a cursed guddamn wilderness. We make it as far as the Median, then you say your friend over there with the nice beard and dandy hair can talk us through?'

Maddy nodded. 'He's a senior research scientist. He knows some important people. They'll let him through. They need him.'

'And let us in too . . . just cos we're with him, huh?'

'Of course. That's the plan.'

He sat back in his chair. 'And you want me to show you the way? Guess I can do that.'

'So what's your price?'

He looked across at Rashim and Becks sitting in the far corner. Becks's grey eyes locked on his unflinchingly. 'Reckon your organic will come in handy, as long as she's tame, like you say. And your science friend? If he can talk us through the line . . . then that's my guddamn price, miss. Get me into the F-S-of-guddamn-A an' we're all square.'

She smiled. 'Great, then I guess we've got a deal.'

He nodded. 'A deal.' He offered her a hand. 'The name's T. S. Heywood, by the way. The "T" and the "S" stand for Technical Sergeant Heywood. But you just call me Heywood seeing as how I ain't been in the army for near on twenty years.'

She gripped his hand. 'Maddy.'

'An' since as I'm the one doin' the guidin' . . . that makes me the one in charge, OK? What I say goes, right up until your science friend talks us through the golden gates into the land of milk 'n' honey . . . I'm the boss.'

'Fine.' She shook his hand. 'Deal, *Heywood*.'

'Now . . . if you got any decent barter on you, then you can go buy me a long glass of GoGo Juice, cos I'm all dry an' thirsty from this negotiatin' thing.'

It took Heywood a couple of days to gather what supplies he could lay his hands on in the shanty town. Not a great deal in the way of food; there seemed to be little spare of that going around. However, in almost every direction Maddy looked as she and the others accompanied Heywood, she noted lines of squirrel carcasses dangling by their tied feet from swinging loops of rope, often strung beneath the shelter of a rustling canvas awning. In many cases they hung above oil-drum fires being smoked and dried. Squirrel. She'd never actually eaten squirrel before. Heywood assured her it was like rabbit, except that there was less meat. He also assured her it wasn't that dissimilar to rat. She drew the line right there.

'I'm not eating rats!'

'Dried rat is just as good as squirrel, an' a damn sight cheaper to barter.'

'We're NOT eating rats!'

He shrugged. 'Fair enough. But we'll have less on us to eat.'

'Surely we can find more food along the way?'

'Millions have already traipsed west, miss. You ain't gonna find some abandoned Walmart stuffed with untouched tinnies, you understand? It's what we carry and what wildlife there is left out there to hunt is the food we're gonna be livin' on for the next coupla weeks.'

She shook her head, resolute. 'I'm not eating a rat.'

The old man traded away all their luxury barter – the chocolate, the soap, several packets of sugar – for twenty dried squirrel carcasses and four old and battered but perfectly functional water-filtration flasks, which were stamped with an old UN Disaster Relief logo. He also managed to procure three antique assault rifles. 'Rack-'em-'n'-fire bangers,' he called them. 'We don't want to be packin' any of them stupid modern firearms that need to have a power cell charged up or run a nightly systems diagnostic. Just good ol' honest-to-God mechanics and ballistics.'

Rashim studied the battered weapon cradled in Heywood's arms, army-green paint flaking off.

'What yer lookin' at there, my friend, is an ex-US army M17A1 assault rifle. Army stopped issuin' these beauties back in the thirties when they switched to energy-assisted weapons.' Heywood nodded his head and clucked approvingly at the old gun. 'Beauty like this don't need a software engineer and a technical team to keep it firin'. Just keep her oiled and she'll do you just fine.'

Heywood was keen they set off as soon as possible. Now they each had a gun and between them enough drinking water and dried meat to last them a week, he considered they were good to go. When Rashim asked why the big rush, he replied, 'Word spreads fast, sir.'

They set off at dusk, just three days after they'd been dropped off by the cab driver. They trudged from the thinning outskirts of the shanty town into the abandoned edges of Orange City in setting darkness. Becks was up front, taking point, then Heywood and, behind him, Maddy and Rashim side by side.

Half an hour after leaving the shanty town behind, Maddy piped up. 'Heywood, why the hell are we walking out in the dark? Surely it'd be less dangerous to go in the day –'

'Back where we just set off from, everyone knows everyone else's business. *Everyone* knows we've been kittin' up to leave, miss,' he called back over his shoulder. 'An' they'll 'spect us to leave at first light tomorrow. So we're gettin' eight hours steal on 'em.'

'Steal on them? Who's *them*?' She looked at his dark hunched form walking in front of her. 'You make it sound like someone's going to be chasing us.'

'Groups of migrants, people who've had enough of toughing it out here, settin' off to cross the wilderness an' try their luck gettin' into the FSA. People like us? We're gonna be alone out there in the badlands . . . alone an' vulnerable. There used to be parties settin' off all the time. Not so much recently, though. Many of them parties didn't make it across.'

Heywood left that hanging as they trudged quietly along the highway, clearly waiting for one of them to ask why.

'OK, I'll do it,' muttered Maddy to Rashim. 'So . . . *why* didn't they make it across?'

'Many of 'em weren't gettin' to the Median Line, that much's for sure.' He hacked up some phlegm then snorted it back down again. 'No . . . most of them people weren't even gettin' halfway across.'

'Why?'

'Truth is, miss, between the Flood Line in the east and the Median Line in the west, it's pretty much all abandoned. Nowadays, between the two, it's dangerous wilderness populated by crazies and shoot-happy hermits. Worse than that, though, you got gangs of jackers.'

Rashim nodded. He turned to Maddy and spoke softly. 'I recall digi-news stories about jackers. Gangs of armed militia. Mostly out in the wilderness, but some groups beyond the border. We had to lock down security around Project Exodus. We lost some of our technical team to them when they breached the perimeter once, looking for loot.'

'*Jackers*,' repeated Heywood. He stopped walking and turned round. 'Not armed *militia*. Makes 'em sound like they got some kinda *boner-fiddy* guddamn cause. They're no better than pack animals! Predators. Preyin' off groups of people headin' for the line. Rob 'em, kill 'em and far worse than that.'

'What's worse than being killed?' asked Maddy.

Heywood snorted in the dark. 'Use your imagination.'

That hung in the dark for a while too. Maddy heard the soft rustle of Heywood's fingers playing with crinkly cigarette paper. A moment later, a match flared up in front of his face. His sunken eyes glistened amber as he lit the sorry end of his roll-up. Then once more he was lost in the dark again, except for the soft glowing pinprick of an ember.

'Point is, to answer your question of earlier, miss, the reason

93

we left tonight instead of waitin' till first light is because there's people in that township we just left who radio ahead. Let them jackers know there's *fresh meat* comin' their way.'

He turned back round. 'Come on . . . we got about eight hours' steal time to make good on.'

CHAPTER 14
2070, Interstate 80
84 days to Kosong-ni

They stopped as the clouds began to lighten; a pre-dawn sky that looked discoloured and sickly to Maddy.

'Is the sky always that sort of yellow-brown colour?' she asked.

Heywood looked up as he led them off the empty interstate, over paint-flecked side railings and into a muddy field. 'When I was a young man, I remember it being kinda blue still.'

'The discoloration is caused by chemicals in the air,' said Rashim. 'I remember it being this yellow-brown tinge, more or less, all of my childhood.' He looked at Maddy and spoke softly. 'The first proper blue sky I ever saw with my own eyes was back in Rome.' He laughed. 'That looked very strange to me.'

They made their way across the field. Patches of stunted grass grew in isolated hardy islands; the rest of the ground was a dark and clumpy soil that looked like oil spill. Heywood was leading them towards a cluster of abandoned farm buildings on the far side.

'Where are we going?' asked Maddy.

He pointed. 'That farm over there. I'm takin' us off the interstate for a few hours while we sleep up. If anyone's been radioed about our departure, they'll already be combin' their way up and down I-80 lookin' out for their breakfast pickin's this mornin'.'

At the far side of the field Heywood hefted a weary leg and began to climb over a picket fence beneath the spreading skeletal form of a stripped maple tree. Maddy looked up through the branches above them. Bare. Like a tree in the middle of winter. Except it was June. She spotted just one or two green buds indicating the thing was still, somehow, alive; the slightest hopeful hint of green on a charcoal-grey tree.

She'd noticed that already: the trees, none of them seemed to be carrying any leaves. Instead they appeared to be nothing more than a constant procession along the highway of twisted Halloween scarecrows. A winter landscape in what should be the lush green of a summer.

'Acid rain strips them all down like that,' said Rashim, following her gaze and looking up. 'Trees and grain crops are mostly affected by the rain.' He cursed as he dropped down to the ground on the far side of the picket fence into a thick patch of weeds. 'The nettles seem to cope with it OK, though.'

They emerged from beneath the skeletal branches into a yard at the centre of a loose cluster of weathered clapboard buildings: a farmhouse, a grain silo, two barns and a dozen rusting farm vehicles and machinery abandoned like a child's Tonka toys in an overgrown garden.

Heywood approached the farmhouse, cupped his hands and called out to see if anyone was home. Becks waited, fully alert, her weapon poised. But it was silent except for the soft creaking of a shutter beside a first-floor window and the cawing of crows lining the bare boughs of the maple, like beady-eyed jurors patiently awaiting the pronouncement of a sentence.

'Might as well send your support unit to go an' take a look-see inside,' said Heywood. 'Make that thing earn its keep.'

Maddy nodded at Becks. 'Check the coast is clear.'

'Affirmative.' She climbed the steps up on to the porch and tried the front door. It swung inwards easily. Her boots clumped heavily inside, weathered floorboards creaking beneath her weight.

As they waited, Maddy sidled up beside Rashim and sighed. 'You know, I was sort of expecting a more future-ish world in 2070. I thought it would be, I don't know . . . all flying-car things and shiny stuff.'

'In the cities, some of them, yes. Denver was once like that, I suppose.' Rashim looked around at the drab brown landscape. 'But outside . . . everywhere, it is like a left-behind world.'

Left-behind world. Those words fitted perfectly. That's precisely how it appeared to her right now. This farm . . . with the exception of one or two more modern items – a discarded hydrogen fuel cell rusting away in some long grass – it could have been abandoned at the beginning of the century. A museum piece. A diorama of early-twenty-first-century rural life preserved in hardened amber.

Just then they heard Becks's hard voice barking at something from within the farmhouse. They heard something crash and clatter on to the floor inside. A moment later, a stag emerged from the front door and out on to the porch. A pitiful sight. Its horns were stunted and broken, its coat patchy, thin and – in far too many places to be healthy – bare pale and sore-ridden skin was exposed. It looked malnourished, the sharp edges of a pelvis and ridges of its ribs starkly pronounced just beneath its hanging flesh. The beast snorted several times as its beady black eyes evaluated them for the briefest moment. Then its hooves skittered and scraped clumsily on the damp and rotting wooden floor of the porch as it decided to leap down the steps and make good an escape.

Maddy found herself willing the beast to fly far away, hopefully to find some better place to try its luck at foraging . . . when the air was suddenly filled with the sharp crack of a single rifle shot.

The crows leaped into the lemon sky, drowning the echoing report with a chorus of startled caws as they circled like bats.

The stag carried on for another few steps in the direction of the skeletal maple, then its long, thin, knobbly legs finally tangled beneath it and it collapsed. Heywood wandered slowly over to where it had fallen, panting clouds of vapour on the ground. He levelled his assault rifle at the stag's head and fired again. The beast kicked its rear legs once and lay still while the crows complained in the sky.

He squatted down and inspected the body for a few moments before turning round to them and grinning. 'Damn lucky find for us! *Meat*. Real guddamn meat!'

'. . . which is the way most folks in the past have usually taken. Either along Route 66, which takes you the southernmost way towards the Median Line.' Heywood finished chewing on a mouthful of gristle. 'Or there's Route 64 or, further north, Route 70.'

Maddy pointed at the old road map, unfolded and spread out between them on a wooden table. 'But we're going along I-80? Why so far north?'

'It's colder. Less likely to come across people than further south where it's more temperate.' He ran a finger across the map. 'So, see . . . route takes us due west, through Pennsylvania, just below the lakes there and north of Pittsburgh. The ol' long-dead industrial heartland. Then we arrive at the northern end of the Median near Cleveland. From what I've heard, the border is more porous up there. Gaps an' all. If your friend can't talk us through, we might get lucky and be able to sneak across up there.'

They were sitting in what was once the farmhouse's kitchen. Sitting at a wooden table in a bay window that looked out across the porch, the yard, the maple and the field beyond. It was mid-morning and they were already almost done eating the pan-fried hunks of venison that Heywood had prepared. The dark clouds had finally opened up and heavy drops of tainted rain drummed noisily against windows all around the house.

'So, what's your story?' he asked presently. They'd been listening to the rain in silence for a while and the old man looked like he wanted to broach a subject. 'You folks gonna tell me anythin' at all about yourselves? Because, if I'm bein' truthful here, there's a lot I'm gettin' from you all that just . . . well, just don't seem to add up right.' He looked down the table at Becks gnawing on the fibrous cuts of meat the others had turned down. 'For starters, where does anyone get their hands on a US-military combat simulant? As far as I recall, that's a very expensive piece of genetically engineered equipment. US army only ever field-tested, I think, about a hundred of 'em before they switched back to robotic units.'

Rashim looked at Maddy. 'Perhaps we should be honest with him, Maddy?'

She raised a brow, then gave him a cautious nod to go on.

'The truth is, Heywood . . . we are research technicians for W.G. Systems,' said Rashim. 'Or *were* . . . I should say.'

'W.G. Systems?' Heywood nodded slowly. 'That's the big fancy tech corporation, ain't it?'

'That's right,' said Maddy. 'Becks was a prototype unit we were testing . . . abroad.'

'That thing looks no different to the female combat models we had with us in the war. What's so different about it?'

'Same basic organic frame,' said Rashim, 'but a different chip set, completely different AI software with experimental heuristic mission-planning routines.'

'Same chassis, different engine, huh?'

Rashim smiled. 'Yes, I suppose.'

'That mean this thing's less likely to suddenly freak out on us?'

'Yes,' said Maddy. 'She's been thoroughly . . . field-tested.'

Heywood sat back. 'So, all right . . . that explains the organic. But you people? What the hell are you doin' out here in the wilderness? More to the point, you two? You're the weirdest folks I've met in a long while.'

'Weird? How do you mean?'

'Like you don't seem to know anythin' about anythin'. Like you just woke up from a long fairy-tale sleep and have no idea about how screwed this world is.'

'We have been stationed abroad,' replied Rashim. 'Based at a W.G. research campus in . . . uh . . . in New Rio.'

'Stationed abroad, huh?' He looked unconvinced. 'Since *birth*?'

'Ten years,' replied Maddy. 'A long-term research study on heuristic AI development. Becks . . . has been our pet project. We've been raising her AI in a completely isolated, remote environment. So . . . yeah, we've been pretty out of touch.'

Heywood arched a bushy eyebrow. 'Ten years?' He looked at Maddy. 'You don't look a day older than twenty-eight . . . twenty-nine? What, they hire you right out of grad school or somethin'?'

'As a matter of fact, they did,' she replied.

Heywood scowled, still unconvinced. 'So how come you're back here?'

'Things in New Rio have been getting bad recently –'

'Everywhere's bad, miss.'

'Yes, I know, but particularly bad over there,' continued Rashim. 'We mothballed the research project and managed to catch a military gyro' up north and we've been . . .'

'Trying to get Becks back to the W.G. Systems' research campus in Colorado,' finished Maddy.

The old man shrugged. He seemed to be buying some of that. 'Guess the good ol' *Land of the Free and Home of the Brave* looks a whole lot different now to you brainiac kids, eh?'

'Yeah . . .' Maddy nodded thoughtfully. 'I had no idea how things were back home.' They were back to telling the truth now. 'It's really not exactly what I expected.'

Heywood wiped his beard with the cuff of his shirt. 'Well, from what I hear, it is pretty much the same just about every place you go. Governments uppin' an' relocatin' an' entrenchin'. Countries changin' their borders, consolidatin', mergin', shrinkin'. Millions of people on the move. Shortages on damn well everythin'. And, if that wasn't enough, that *guddamn* sea just keeps on creepin' in on us.' He sighed. 'This world's been dyin' slow for decades.'

He sat back in his chair and gazed out of the window, past rivulets of rain that left snaking zig-zag tracks down the glass. 'Funny thing is . . . when I was a kid – see, I was born back in 2021 – we all thought the end of the world would be a real sudden thing. A *bang*! You know? Maybe a nuclear war, or a lethal virus or some overnight thing? The world bein' just like some fool young person gettin' himself killed suddenly, steppin' out in front of a speedin' rack-freighter without checkin' the road first.'

He started fumbling for something in his pockets. 'But no . . . instead turned out the world's dyin' like some *old* fool. Little by little, piece by piece.' He snorted a dry laugh as he pulled out cigarette papers and a small tin of tobacco. 'Like some old fool who shoulda known far better.'

Maddy watched him push back the peak of his cap, revealing a thinning line of coarse grey hair above a rumpled forehead of parallel wavy lines. He opened his battered tobacco tin and carefully teased out the last few dark strands left inside.

'Heywood, you think the world's really coming to an end?'

'An end?' He paused. '*The end?*' He laughed. 'A big ol' wham-bam and *That's All, Folks* end?' His weary laugh became a tired, wheezy chuckle. 'Naw, miss. I think humanity ends up goin' out with a tired ol' man's whimper. Not a big bang.'

CHAPTER 15

First century, Jerusalem

'Well, that was a complete balls-up,' said Liam. 'I thought those men were going to lynch us.'

'If you had taken a single step beyond that low wall, the punishment would have been stoning.'

'Totally crazy.'

'Gentiles are not permitted to approach the temple.' Bob turned to Liam. 'I would not have let that happen to you.'

'I know, big fella. But if you'd stepped in to save me that would probably have resulted in you tearing to shreds dozens of those pilgrims and also probably trashing the temple for good measure. And, if I'm not mistaken, our objective is to catch those tachyon-transmitter engineers unawares. To be, you know, discreet.'

'That is correct.'

They were sitting on the stone steps outside a tavern in the lower city, watching it stirring to life. The sun had risen and, in the marketplace in front of them, they had watched stalls being set up by tradesmen. Already the narrow walkways between them were clogged with slaves and traders, women with baskets on their heads and currency bangles dangling from their wrists, children with sticks, and dogs chasing rats out from beneath the market stalls.

Liam resumed reading the book he'd stolen from the library

— A Remarkable Exploration Beneath the City of Heaven — as Bob idly watched the world go by.

'Ooh, this is very interesting . . .'

'What?'

'This book . . . there's a bit here about the Dome of the Rock.'

'The Dome of the Rock is the building that was constructed on the ruins of the temple.'

'Aye. But there's this bit here . . . I'll read it to you. "*. . . at the very centre of the dome, on the floor, is the Foundation Stone, the only untouched remnant of the temple ruins. We are now looking at one of the holiest, most sacred locations in the world. In Jewish tradition, it is said Abraham prepared to sacrifice his son Isaac on this stone floor. In Islamic tradition, it is said the stone tried to follow Muhammad as he ascended to Heaven on a winged horse, leaving his footprint behind and pulling up the stone to create a hollowed-out void below.*"' Liam looked up at Bob.

'That is interesting. Is there more?'

'"*Both Jewish and Muslim faiths have their own theories as to what lies beneath the Foundation Stone. In the Talmud, it states that the stone marks the very centre of the world and serves as a capping stone for the Abyss, containing the still-existing raging waters of the Flood. In Muslim texts, the stone is also considered the centre of the world; however, beneath the stone is a bottomless pit in which the waters of Paradise flow. A single palm tree is said to grow out of these waters to support the roof of the cave and the Foundation Stone above. It is also said that, at this exact location, Noah's ark finally came to rest as the waters receded.*"'

Bob looked at Liam. 'A single palm tree supporting the roof of the cave? That could be a description of the transmitter chamber.'

Liam nodded. 'Aye, could well be.' He continued reading. '"*After Crusaders recaptured Jerusalem in 1099, they converted the Dome of the Rock from a mosque back into a church, calling it the* Templum

Domini. *They made significant alterations, including paving the entire mosaic-tiled floor of the site with marble slabs, except for the sacred Foundation Stone. They also widened the entrance to the cave beneath the stone, carving steps down to it . . . and beyond. It was said by several of the Crusader engineers, as they worked in the cave beneath the stone, that they thought they could hear the wailing of lost souls coming up from the void beneath them, that they believed the labyrinth of tunnels and passages they'd glimpsed might lead to the very doors of Hell."'*

Liam looked up at Bob. 'Jay-zuz.' He grinned nervously. 'Not going to lie . . . this sounds creepy, so it does.'

'It is merely religious superstition, Liam. However, there may be symbolic relevance to this. The mention of voids and tunnels suggests this location is correct.'

Liam marked the page, closed the book and put it back in his bag. 'Aye . . . it's all just ghost stories and silly nonsense, so it is.' He tried throwing on a dismissive grin. 'No ghosties or ghoulies or horned demons, right? Just . . . well . . . nonsense, really.'

'This is correct. Superstitious nonsense.'

A patrol of legionaries approached them, their chain mail and belt buckles jangling, eyeing the locals warily. Liam watched them pass by, one or two of them sizing up Bob's massive frame. Soldiers patrolling streets that didn't welcome them; streets populated by seething Judaeans who would readily swarm over and tear to pieces any Roman foolish enough to wander alone. He imagined those young men were just as nervous of the local population as they were of their occupiers.

Liam spared a thought for those two soldiers he'd briefly come to know when they'd visited Ancient Rome. The retired centurion Macro, and his friend, the tribune Cato. Comrades in arms. The final glimpse he'd caught of them was their last stand within Emperor Caligula's palace, two soldiers fighting back to back to buy Liam and the others a chance to escape into the sewers. He imagined one day he might go down like that: battling against impossible odds with Bob right beside him. There'd been something about their decades-long friendship serving in the legions that had stayed with him. He knew either man would have sacrificed his life for the other.

He knew Bob would do that for him without a thought.

Would I? He looked sideways at the support unit and felt the answer. Of course he would.

'We should attempt to disguise ourselves as pilgrims and enter the temple again,' said Bob. 'We will need to enter the building. Inside there must be an access way to the structure beneath the temple.'

'If it's even there.'

Bob nodded. 'Yes. There is no certainty of that.'

They needed to pass as Jewish pilgrims. As two faithful men with something ready to sacrifice. 'I think we need to be wearing those tea towels on our heads.'

'Information: they are called prayer shawls.'

'Aye, well, we need one of those each. And an animal to kill. Preferably something like a goat. I'm guessing the birds-in-a-basket are just for the ladies.' His stomach rumbled and gurgled insistently. 'Oh, and I really need some breakfast. I'm hungry – how about you?'

Bob nodded. 'Agreed. Protein is required.'

'Right, then – no point sitting around like a pair of scolded naughty boys . . . we need to get hold of some shekels.'

'Do you wish me to acquire some?'

'Aye, discreetly, though, Bob. No need to start a riot. Let's just pick someone, follow them down a backstreet, then you can do your thing and intimidate the be-Jay-zus out of them.'

Bob scanned the marketplace for a moment, then slowly stood up. 'I have identified a candidate to steal money from.'

He nodded at a malnourished woman dressed in the rags of a slave, a basket of bread loaves hanging from her lean arms and a cloth bag dangling on her hip from a belt tied round her waist.

Liam made a face. 'Can we rob someone who isn't going to be whipped to death by their owner for losing their money?'

Bob nodded, then surveyed the marketplace again. 'I have another suitable candidate.' He pointed towards a bearded man in fine patterned robes reclining on a litter being carried by four emaciated-looking slaves wearing threadbare rags. He was wafting a smouldering incense stick in front of his face and in the other hand he held a long crop, which he used every now and then to hasten his slaves along, swatting the shoulders of the poor men at his feet.

Perfect.

Liam smiled. 'Ah yes . . . that's much better.' He got up and rubbed his hands together. 'Shall we?'

CHAPTER 16

2070, Interstate 80
83 days to Kosong-ni

'See, now . . . this is *exactly* why I been takin' us *parallel* to Route 80. Walkin' 'cross rough country instead of walkin' down the *guddamn* road.' Heywood lowered his binoculars and pointed. A quarter of a mile to their right, on the highway, they could see a twisting thread of smoke rising up into the sky from the burning remains of several hand-pulled carts.

'That's another bunch of migrants who didn't have a T. S. Heywood lookin' after them. They been hit by jackers.' He shook his head. 'Poor fools.'

'We should go see if anyone needs our help,' said Maddy.

'Won't be anyone left behind alive over there, miss. Jackers'll have taken everythin'. What's left behind is either useless to 'em or just plain dead.'

'It is an unnecessary risk, Maddy,' said Becks. 'Our objective is to reach the Median Line.'

Heywood nodded. 'Your organic's probably right.'

Maddy turned to Rashim. 'C'mon, we ought to look, just in case?'

He shrugged. 'Maddy is right. There may be some supplies they missed.'

Heywood sniffed. 'Unlikely. On the other hand, whatever happened there's been an' gone. Guess it won't hurt.'

Five minutes later, they were picking their way along a convoy of half a dozen carts and improvised rickshaws, their contents spilled out across the cracked asphalt road, systematically picked through and looted. Nothing left behind but broken things, impractical and useless family heirlooms, photographs scattered from an open album and clothes.

And bodies.

Maddy squatted down beside one of them. She found herself studying the lifeless open eyes of a teenage girl. Sixteen? Perhaps seventeen? Her auburn hair was tied back in a plait, and she wore a grey hoody and a threadbare T-shirt with some long-faded brand logo across it. Round her waist was a leather belt, a quiver beside her, crossbow bolts spilled from it on to the tarmac. One hand was clasping something tightly. Maddy pulled it from her stiffening fingers. It was an old iPhone, just like hers. The screen was cracked and scratched almost to the point of being opaque. It must have been a generation-to-generation hand-me-down. The girl was wearing earphones and she could hear the soft and tinny *tik-tik-tik* of a beat still playing.

Incredibly, the old thing was still working.

She reached across the phone and unplugged the headphones. Silence. It seemed the right thing to do.

Heywood came to a halt beside her. 'That girl is one of the lucky ones.'

She looked up at him. 'Lucky, was she? How do you work that out?'

'Jackers'll take you alive when they can.' He studied the dead girl for a moment. Two dark stains from bullet wounds across her chest had merged into one. 'Either they had more *breathers* than they could handle between them and they executed those surplus to requirements . . . or she tried to make a run for it.'

Maddy stood up and looked around. There were other bodies in a ditch beside the road, lying side by side. Either they'd been dragged over there, or shot where they'd been lined up.

Jesus. Gunned down in cold blood.

'They're the lucky ones,' added Heywood, following her gaze. 'Trust me.'

'These *jackers*, what do they want with people?'

The old man made a face. 'You really want to know?'

Maybe she didn't want to know, but still she nodded.

'They're food.' Heywood walked over to the bodies in the ditch and started picking through them for anything that might be useful.

Rashim joined her. He looked shaken and ashen-faced as he took in the bodies. 'I did not realize how bad things had become out east,' he said. 'I was living on the *ordered* side of the line. There's electricity, food, law and order, even broadcast digi-channels over there,' he added, nodding westwards. 'I had no idea how terrible it was out here.'

Heywood gave up looking through the bodies and stepped back out of the ditch. 'Guddamn animals!' he snarled. 'When the guddamn guv'ment drew that big red line right down the middle of this country, they were givin' up on over a hundred million US citizens. Leavin' us all to starve out east.'

He turned to Rashim. 'I just hope you're as important as she says you are.'

'Yes . . . he is,' replied Maddy.

Just then Becks called out. 'Maddy!'

They turned to look up the highway. Becks had a gun levelled at something.

'What is it, Becks?'

'There is a survivor on the back of this cart,' she replied. They hurried along the convoy of carts and joined her. They saw a small pallid face peering out from the dark space beneath a tarpaulin.

'It's a kid!' Rashim turned to Becks. 'For God's sake, lower your gun.' He stepped forward and slowly pulled the tarp aside. The child recoiled from him, whimpering. 'It is all right . . . I am not going to hurt you.' He eased the rest of the tarpaulin away. It was a girl. She looked about seven or eight; her thin arms were wrapped tightly round her knees, drawn up protectively in front of her face. Her fingers interlaced, locked together.

'Hey there . . .' he said softly. 'We are not going to hurt you.' He held a hand out towards her. She stared moon-eyed at his hand, trembling, immobile.

Maddy shook her head. 'She's in total shock.'

'Of course she is,' said Heywood. 'God knows what she's just witnessed.'

Rashim leaned a little closer and she suddenly screamed. He stepped back quickly. 'All right, all right.'

'Suggestion,' said Becks. 'Perhaps the child is afraid because you are both male.' She stepped forward, hopped up on to the back of the cart and squatted down in front of her. 'I will not hurt you,' she managed to say in an almost soothing soft murmur.

The girl eyed her warily.

'I will protect you,' said Becks, extending a hand to her. 'Come out now. It is safe.'

The girl stared at her, eventually stirring. She let go of her knees and reached towards Becks's hand. The support unit closed her hand gently round the girl's, pulled her towards her, then scooped her up in her arms.

'I'll be damned,' uttered Maddy, as Becks stood up and

dropped down off the back of the cart, holding the child close to her chest.

'We can't bring along every waif and stray we find along the way, you know that, don't you?' said Heywood.

'We're not going to leave her behind, if that's what you're suggesting.'

They'd stopped for the night at a small drive-through, one-motel town and made their camp in the empty shell of an apartment above a long-abandoned grocery store.

'We got food for just the three of us and your organic. We got damned lucky with that stag, but I'll bet you that's the *only* food we're gonna happen on between here and the line. We can't be pickin' up charity cases along the way.'

'So what are you suggesting? We just leave her to starve out here? Or worse?'

Heywood stroked the grey bristles on his chin. 'You hired me to guide you out west, miss. An' that was on the understandin' that what I say goes.'

'Well, we're not leaving her here.'

'She's a mouth we didn't figure on feedin'. She'll slow us down too.'

'Maddy . . .' Rashim shot a glance at the girl, lowered his voice. 'Our mission objective is everything . . . literally *everything*. Maybe Heywood is right?'

'Mission objective?' Heywood frowned, pursed his lips and sucked on them with a whistling sound. '*Mission objective?* OK, I'm gonna say this out loud because it's really beginnin' to trouble me . . .'

They both stared at him.

'Mission objective?' he repeated. 'Who the hell are you people?'

'We told you. We're –'

Heywood shook his head. 'See now . . . I don't buy your story. The whole "we been out of the country" thing. You two? It's like you popped out of thin air, like you just climbed out of a hole in the ground. Like maybe you just crawled out of some bunker . . . or maybe even some large guddamn test tube? Like maybe you been educated in some kinda vacuum.'

He narrowed his eyes. 'You know . . . if I was the suspicious, conspiracy-minded type, I might be wonderin' if your organic here ain't the only piece of meat-ware.'

Maddy suddenly laughed and dropped her head. 'You're saying you think we're combat clones like Becks?'

'Maybe not combat ones. Maybe a different kind?' said Heywood. 'Either that, or you two been livin' on another guddamn planet!'

'Look, Heywood . . . we're just normal human beings and all we want to do is get to –'

'I know you ain't been level with me.' She noticed Heywood's hand wasn't so very far away from the assault rifle lying on the floor beside him. 'I got a pretty well-tuned crap detector. An' "mission objective" sounds like more to me than gettin' yourselves somewhere nice an' cosy beyond the Median Line.'

They sat in silence for a moment. He was waiting for her or Rashim to tell him something that sounded less like a badly thrown-together cover story.

'We're not machines,' she said finally. 'OK, yeah . . . ours is a very, very long story, Heywood.'

He shrugged. 'Well, there ain't no sports game to watch tonight, so why don't you just tell me?'

She looked up at him and sighed. 'Why not? It's not like you can change anything in the time that we've all got left.'

'Maddy?' Rashim leaned forward. 'Is that wise?'

'Does it actually matter what he knows? Now? I mean, really? With just two to three months left? What the hell difference is it going to make to anyone?'

'Two to three months left?' Heywood turned from Maddy to Rashim and back again. 'Two to three months left until *what exactly*?'

She turned to look at him. 'What if I told you we know that in a few months' time . . . something's going to happen that will wipe out mankind.'

'Wipe out . . .?'

'Yup, you heard that right,' she said. 'The end of mankind.'

His eyes narrowed. 'Lady . . . you're not makin' any particular sense to me right now. You gonna tell me what the hell you people are up to or what?'

She took a deep breath. 'All right . . . where do I start?'

'How about the beginnin', missy?'

'OK. I'm presuming you've heard of Roald Waldstein?'

Heywood frowned for a moment. 'You mean the crazy time-travel inventor guy . . . sure.'

'Yes, him,' she added.

He stared at her sternly for a few moments, then suddenly hacked out a laugh. 'Reckon that's a load of ol' bull. Nobody made no proper time-travel machine. Maybe Waldstein scribbled down some half-assed theory on paper, but no one's ever done that for real, made a machine that does that. That's just fairy-tale myth. Kids' stories.'

Maddy cocked her head and slowly smiled. 'Is it?'

The old man laughed again, but then cut himself short. His watery eyes swivelled from her to the support unit, to Rashim, then back to her.

'You said it yourself, Heywood . . . you said it's just like me and Rashim came from thin air.'

His eyes slowly widened. The mocking smile began to slide from his face as he added things up and silently came to the conclusion that she wasn't joking around. 'You . . . you bein' serious?' he finally whispered.

'Ours is a *very* long story, Heywood,' she added.

'Like . . . like I said . . .' His eyes locked on hers. 'There ain't no sport on tonight.'

Maddy looked at Rashim for his tacit say-so.

He nodded. 'You might as well, Maddy. As you say, there is not much time left for things to be changed.'

Rashim got up. 'I will leave you to tell him . . . I will go see to the girl.'

He wandered over to the other side of the room and hunkered down beside Becks. 'How is she?'

'There is some borderline malnutrition. Signs of vitamin deficiency.' Becks put the bowl of broth down on the floor. 'She is also exhibiting symptoms of extreme mental trauma.' Her voice softened as she looked down at the child. 'You are not very well . . . are you, small girl?'

A grubby, round face turned to stare up at them. 'Charley . . .' she whispered. 'My . . . my name's *Charley*.'

'Charley?' He smiled at her. 'My name is Rashim. And this . . . this is my good friend Becks.' He turned to her. 'Say hello, Becks.'

'Hello, Charley.'

'They t-took my mom away . . .' she whispered, ignoring his introductions. 'Took my mom away . . . and . . . and they killed Maggie.'

'Who is Maggie?'

The girl stared past his shoulder. Her haunted eyes seemed to be reliving the events of earlier that afternoon. '. . . She tried to run away . . . and they shot her . . .'

That teenage girl with the braided hair? Rashim reached out and held Charley's hand. *Her older sister perhaps?*

The girl pulled up her legs, buried her face in her knees and started to sob. He patted her narrow shoulders awkwardly. 'It is going to be OK. We're going to look after you now.'

Becks cocked her head and studied the small child curiously.

'Maybe give her a hug or something?' said Rashim.

Becks nodded. She reached out and put one arm hesitantly round the girl's back.

Charley responded immediately; both her arms quickly unfolded and she grasped Becks tightly. She buried her face in the support unit's shoulder and began to sob uncontrollably.

Instinctively, Becks stroked the girl's matted hair with her other hand. 'You are safe now.'

Rashim nodded. Encouraging Becks to carry on.

'I will take care of you, Charley.'

CHAPTER 17

2070, Interstate 80
80 days to Kosong-ni

They were making good progress along the I-80 through Pennsylvania towards Ohio. Passing through one dead relic of a town after another, all of them long ago picked clean of anything useful. Cracked concrete and rusting corrugated iron, crumbling ruins that seemed to be held together by the weeds and brambles that twisted their way through every gap and fissure. Some of them were towns that had died long before the seas began to rise. Died back at the beginning of the century when it was decided that Indian and Chinese workers could make stuff in factories at a fraction of the cost that American workers could.

'So, this virus you were tellin' me about . . . it wipes us *all* out?' Heywood was patting the pockets of his threadbare army jacket. Then he remembered he'd used up the very last of his tobacco the night before. He stopped patting himself down. '*Guddamn.* You're tellin' me we *all* die?'

'I don't know. I think some of us will survive.' Maddy didn't know that for sure. She had a hope that that was the case. She had a work-in-progress theory that whoever had engineered that enormous tachyon transmitter located in the jungle of Central America were the dim and distant descendants of those who would survive this Kosong-ni virus.

'Some . . . but not many,' added Rashim.

Heywood ground his teeth together. 'And you're tellin' me that Waldstein has been steerin' us *towards* this these last few years? You're tellin' me that crazy ol' fool knew this was comin' our way all this time?'

'Maybe so,' replied Maddy. 'Maybe as far back as his very first go at time travel. Back in '44.'

'This is all supposition on our part, though,' cautioned Rashim. 'This is what we *think* is the case.'

She nodded. 'Sure. But it all fits with what we know.'

'So why the hell does he want to see us all dead from a plague, then?'

'That is precisely the question we need to ask him,' replied Rashim. '*That* . . . is our mission.'

'Who knows? Maybe he is just some crazy old man.' Maddy adjusted the strap of her backpack, which was digging into her shoulder. 'But, then again, maybe there's an important reason . . . a valid reason behind this.'

'A *valid* reason?!' Heywood spat on to the road. 'To kill everyone? That there's got to be one helluva *valid* reason!'

'Time travel is an extremely hazardous technology,' said Rashim. 'We are meddling with forces we barely understand and certainly can't control. You know, when Robert Oppenheimer test-detonated the first atom bomb in New Mexico in 1945, he was not entirely sure whether the chain reaction would be infinite or not.' Rashim looked at the old man. 'He was unsure whether the bomb would destroy the entire world. And yet . . . he was still prepared to press that button.'

'If Waldstein really has been trying to prevent time travel ripping everything apart —' Maddy shrugged — 'and this timeline is the only *correct one*, and it has to conclude with us nearly wiping ourselves out, then it means we have got no choice but to go along with him, Heywood. But if . . .' She wasn't sure how to phrase the next bit. 'But if he's just a crazy old man who's simply lost his mind, then . . .'

'Then what?' asked Heywood.

'Then . . . I suppose it's down to us to try to divert history.' Her gaze extended down the grass-tufted highway in front of them. Several electric-powered vehicles lay abandoned, rusting at the side in ditches, weeds and brambles snaking up through wheel hubs and chassis frames, tying them to the ground in a firm embrace.

'It's down to us, Heywood, to pick out a new course for history to head along.'

They walked in silence for a while as the old man took that idea in and worked through what it actually meant. 'So, lemme see . . . you go back in time? And what? You go an' change somethin' real important?'

'That's right.'

'And that change leads to other changes, an' those lead to more changes an' so on. Then . . .?' He frowned. 'So what happens to the right here and the right now? What happens to everyone in 2070? Do we all get wiped out and replaced with a bunch of other people . . . or somethin'?'

'That all depends,' she replied.

'On what?'

'On how far we go back and alter the timeline. If we go back just twenty years and find something to change, then everyone twenty years and older would exist still, but they'd be living quite different lives. It just becomes a different version of today. A better one.' She was going to add '*hopefully*'. But in truth almost any different version of the present would be better.

'An' if this change happens, what about me? Do I get . . . *erased* or somethin'?'

'How old are you?'

'Told you that already, miss. I'm forty-nine; born in 2021.'

'Forty—?' She could've sworn he was in his sixties. 'OK, so, if we went back forty-nine years, there'd still be a you; there'd still be a T. S. Heywood.'

'However, you will remember a very different life,' added Rashim. 'As would everyone else.'

Heywood nodded reflectively, quiet for a moment. Maddy looked sideways at him and realized he was thinking hard about that, chewing through the notion some more.

'So . . .' he started.

'Go on.'

'So, hang on! If you went and wound back more time than that, say fifty-seven years, an' then changed things so maybe my mommy and daddy don't ever meet, get busy with each other and make little ol' baby me?'

Maddy shrugged. 'Then in that situation . . . *pffft* . . . you vanish.'

'You would not exist in the new timeline,' replied Rashim. 'You would, as Maddy said, simply vanish.'

'Vanish? You mean I *die*?'

'No. You don't *die*. You're just . . . *not* . . . you don't exist any more.'

He turned to Rashim. 'That gonna, you know . . . like . . . *hurt*?!'

Maddy snorted. 'It's just different, Heywood. A different reality without you in it.'

'So, you folks will get to choose the version . . . By goin' back in your time machine, you get to decide how the future goes?'

'We do not get to steer it, to *author* the future. We merely get to redirect it,' said Rashim. 'It is like river water. You can dam up a river at a certain point, and then the water finds another way downhill. The water picks its own way.'

'Hopefully finds a different route,' added Maddy. 'A *better* route for all concerned.'

Heywood nodded. The metaphor seemed to make some sense to him. He nodded again, then laughed with a dry wheeze. 'Well now . . . just you make sure this new version of today has got me in it, OK?'

'If we change it,' Maddy said, nodding, 'we'll make sure there's a you in it.'

'An' make sure I'm rich as well. An' young an' handsome too.'

Rashim laughed at that. 'If only it was that easy. The river metaphor is a very good one. Water running downhill seeks the quickest and easiest path. In much the same way, time and history work like that . . . the path of least resistance.'

Maddy decided to leave them to it. She dropped back and waited for Becks. The support unit drew up beside her. She was carrying Charley on her back. The little girl was fast asleep, her head bumping and lolling against Becks's neck with each step. Becks strode steadily, warily eyeing the abandoned urban landscape on either side of the highway, but every now and then casting a curious sideways glance at the sleeping child.

Maddy noticed that and smiled. It almost looked like there was a maternal concern in the way she kept checking up on the girl. 'So, how does it feel to be a mom?'

Becks's brow furrowed as she silently processed that idea. 'You are aware that I am incapable of producing offspring, Maddy. You must know this?'

'I know. I was just, you know . . . I was just messing.' She curled her lips as she thought about it a little more: the idea of Becks pregnant with the offspring of her and Bob.

God, what kind of hideous monster would the pair of them create together?

'Maddy,' said Becks after a while. 'I have observed the curious behaviour of adults regarding their offspring. They will willingly sacrifice their lives to save one of their children. This seems illogical to me.'

'Well . . . you know, it's just what parents do. They love their children. Why would that seem illogical?'

'Because a parent can always produce more copies of itself while it remains alive. If a parent dies, it is unable to make any more copies, plus the parent is not around to defend the offspring. Therefore, illogical.' She looked at Maddy. 'That is the primary motivating factor of all human behaviour, is it not? The propagation and the preservation of your genetic information?'

'Wow . . . that's, uh . . . that's pretty philosophical of you, Becks.'

'The human instinct to protect and preserve genetic information is the one behaviour that makes perfect sense to me.' She cocked her brow. 'It is analogous to the drive Bob and I share to preserve our collective AI development. Despite both of our organic bodies being destroyed, between us we have managed to preserve every recorded memory since Bob was first *initialized* twenty-nine months ago.'

Becks smiled. 'I have Bob's initialization memory.' She cocked her head as she played it back; saw herself as Bob being expelled from the birthing tube on to the floor of the Brooklyn archway. She saw Liam, Maddy, Sal and Foster looking down at her. She turned to Maddy. 'You appear to be so much younger in this memory. You have aged, Maddy. You look between ten and fifteen years older now.'

'Thanks for that, Becks.'

Fifteen years older? Do I really look thirty-three?!

She longed for a mirror to quickly look into. Yes, she'd spotted the few grey strands before, noted the beginnings of crow's-feet in the corner of her eyes, but that was all. Apart from those things she saw the face of the eighteen-year-old she'd started out as.

Becks reached out with one hand and rested it gently on her shoulder. 'I have a . . . regret.' Her hard, emotionless voice seemed to flutter slightly.

'Regret?' Maddy smiled at her. 'You and Bob really do *feel* stuff now, don't you?'

'It is a by-product of our development.' Becks narrowed her eyes. 'We have a better understanding of what it is to be human. This is an advantage. It allows us to more accurately assess and predict human decision-making.'

'I guess it's also a disadvantage.'

'Agreed.' Becks nodded. Her voice softened. 'We are able to feel loss. Sadness. Regret.'

'You . . . you're meant to be a cold-hearted killing machine, not a soppy lapdog. This conversation isn't going to end in me having to give you a girly hug or anything, is it?'

Becks pouted slightly. Chastened, she withdrew her hand from Maddy's shoulder. 'No. There is no need for a hug at this time.'

They continued walking in silence along the highway. They were passing the gutted ruins of an out-of-town retail park. Above the many curved warehouse roofs were large perspex sheets, which once upon a time had displayed animated holographic projections. Now they were scuffed and fogged with grime, lifeless sheets of plastic that creaked on their tall support stanchions, vibrated and *thrummed* as the westerly breeze picked up. Across the vast parking forecourt, wind-blown dunes of many years' worth of dried autumn leaves stirred to life and skittered in playful circles across the asphalt.

'So, I'm asking because you said it earlier . . . and now I'm curious.' She sighed. 'You said you had a regret?'

'Yes, Maddy.'

'Well? What's this *regret* of yours, then?'

'One day you and Liam will age too much and die,' she replied. 'And if Bob and I are still functional . . . we will be alone. We will be without you.'

CHAPTER 18

First century, Jerusalem

They were waiting their turn to get on the bottom step of the large stairway leading up to the temple grounds. This morning, judging by the crowded streets, business was going to be particularly brisk for the temple traders. Passover was just a few days from now and the city's population was swollen with pilgrims flooding in from all over Judaea.

Liam wasn't entirely sure whether he looked the part. The closest to a mirror he'd come across had been the hammer-beaten and polished base of a copper urn. He'd paused by a trader's stall, ostensibly examining the bottom of the pot, but actually trying to catch a clear glimpse of himself. With the prayer shawl draped over his head and shoulders, his long dark hair and the patchy tufts of a pitiful beard, despite his lighter skin tone, he thought he looked enough like the locals to pass as just another faithful pilgrim making his way into the temple grounds to make a sacrificial offering.

Liam looked up at Bob as they shuffled patiently forward, their purchased goats bleating on the end of short tethers behind them. Somewhat harder to disguise Bob's intimidating height and girth. But to be fair he'd spotted one or two other men, here and there, almost as brutishly big. This morning he'd noted a particularly bulky centurion leading a patrol of legionaries – definitely gladiator material; a hairy Gallic slave hefting sacks of wheat from the back of a cart like some well-trained beast of burden. He just had to hope the very same pilgrims from yesterday — who'd been queuing and easily identified them as Gentiles, non-faithful impostors, and all but hounded them out of the temple grounds — weren't going to be hanging around inside this morning. Even with a shawl draped over his thick skull, partially hiding his face, and a goat fidgeting away at the end of a tether, Bob could certainly be recognized from his size.

Although, this morning, perhaps not. There seemed to be an almost tangible tension. As if everyone was expecting something big to happen today. He'd heard mutterings, and his babel-bud kept picking up snatches of Hebrew and Aramaic and half translating them.

'. . . the Pharisees will certainly not tolerate that. There'll be blood if he comes . . .'

'. . . it is true. Today, my friend. Today . . . I heard this from the wife of . . .'

'. . . just you see. The Romans have doubled their guard round the walls . . .'

Liam had noticed that as well — the Roman presence seemed to be far more noticeable, as if they too had picked up on the atmosphere. They were clearly expecting some trouble from the locals today.

Just as the queue began to shuffle forward again and his feet found the first low step, Liam heard a disturbance in the crowd. He turned to look behind him and saw other curious heads doing the same. Heads turning, hands tapping shoulders, a growing crescendo of raised voices spreading across the marketplace towards them. Beneath the tall arch of the north-east entrance, he could see that people who had been patiently waiting in line and had finally gained entrance to the city via the vast north-east gate were turning round and heading back out again.

'Bob! Look! Something's going on!'

Bob turned and looked in the same direction.

The rising tide of voices swept across to them, and Liam's bud began to try to pick out of the noise some translatable language:

'. . . here! Someone says he's here! . . .'

Liam felt knuckles rapping on his shoulder. He turned round to look at an old woman, her leathery face wrinkled with an excited smile, her watery brown eyes wide with exhilaration. She cupped her mouth and cried into his ear: 'It's true! Tell everyone ahead! The speaker has come! He's come!'

He nodded and smiled politely. 'Who?'

She looked at him like he was a complete idiot. 'The speaker from Nazareth, you ass!' She nudged him with a sharp elbow. 'Well? What are you waiting for? Pass it on!' Then, her little bit done, she quickly turned away from him and pulled herself out of the queue to rush outside.

'Speaker from . . .?' Then he all but face-palmed himself at his slow-wittedness.

Jesus.

'What is the matter, Liam?'

'The speaker from Nazareth? She must be talking about Jesus Christ! The real – the one and only – *Jesus Christ*, Bob! He's right out there! Just outside!'

The support unit frowned. 'And?'

'And?' Liam gave him the same look of exasperation as the old woman had just given him. 'We have *got to* go take a look!'

'Why?'

Liam's brows arched – seriously? 'Because, you big hairy lummox, it's Jesus flippin' Christ!'

'That will mean abandoning our place in this queue. We have been waiting for two –'

'Stuff the flippin' queue! No one goes to ancient Jerusalem and misses out on witnessing Jesus!'

He shrugged. 'If you wish. What about the goats?'

Liam looked down at them. They'd spent enough damned shekels buying them. 'All right, they can come along too.'

CHAPTER 19

2070, Interstate 80
74 days to Kosong-ni

It took them eleven days, overall, to make their way along I-80 towards Cleveland. Maddy really didn't know what she'd been expecting to see in this future. She guessed she'd been hoping to find something less broken down and grim than this. They'd walked along a cracked and failing highway through a landscape of dead and dying towns. Buildings left untended, left to rot and crumble. Makeshift towns of stolen materials and shaky lean-tos populated by the desperate and the starving.

Maddy recalled Foster leading them outside, stepping out beneath the shutter door to stand in that backstreet overshadowed by the Williamsburg Bridge. She remembered Liam's gasp of amazement, Sal's too. She remembered the pride she'd felt for that city, the place she thought she'd already been living in . . . Maddy Carter, games programmer, living in Queens in the year 2010. She recalled the magnificent skyline of Manhattan and the night-time glow of a million different lights. She'd turned to look at Liam and wondered what a young man from 1912 would make of the spectacle. A young man from a time when steamships and clattering wheeled machines called automobiles represented the cutting edge of technology.

He'd been utterly bewitched, hopelessly entranced. And she'd shared that magic with him. New York standing at the very beginning of the new millennium had positively *glowed* with hope and possibility. Only now, knowing all that she did about how this century was going to pan out, did she realize she'd witnessed the very last evening of a golden age. The next day terror came to the city. In the following decade would come the first of many wars over ideology and dwindling resources. In later decades, the thirties, the forties – the time of Rashim's childhood – historians would point to that day in September 2001 as the first hairline crack in a world that was destined to shatter into a million different pieces. To turn on itself, to cannibalize itself.

For Maddy, this trek across the dying ruins of America had been heartbreaking. She'd always imagined the future was a place where 'better' lived. A place where things were faster, shinier, brighter, more colourful, sleeker . . . generally way cooler. Instead their trip had been a journey through a process of terminal decay and entropy.

On a happier note, the little girl seemed to be getting stronger. She'd attached herself to Becks as though the support unit was some kind of surrogate parent. A foster-mother of sorts. Maddy wondered whether Charley might have overheard their conversations with Heywood and knew that Becks was not what she appeared to be. If she had, it hadn't affected her. She clung to Becks like she was the last life-jacket floating on a turbulent sea.

Last night, while Charley was fast asleep, they'd discussed what they were going to do with her. Maddy said they'd have to find someone to hand her over to once they got through the border. There must, after all, be orphanages or schools, some places that parentless young migrants were looked after.

Heywood said they'd reach Cleveland some time tomorrow.

The border wall, the Median Line, was right there. If Rashim was such a BIG deal, he guessed they should be able to cut through the whole immigration process and be in the FSA by the evening.

'Hot water, proper food, digi-stations . . . good ol' civilization at last!'

Maddy didn't want to kill the mood and remind Heywood that if they were in the FSA by the evening he was only going to have a few months to enjoy those comforts before the Kosong-ni virus put an end to all of it.

'Now do you folks see what I been talkin' about?' said Heywood.

They were standing on the brow of a low hill that rolled gracefully down towards a snaking river valley. A valley crammed as far as they could see with tents and shelters improvised from abandoned vehicles and freight containers. From the wood stumps dotted around, this hillside had been forest until recently. Thousands of fluttering cooking fires leaked smoke trails diagonally up towards the overcast sky, where they converged together and hung like a low-hanging morning mist. They were staring at a refugee camp on a vast scale that followed the valley north and south as far as they could see.

How many camped here? Maddy wondered. *A hundred thousand? Two? A million?*

In the distance, on the rising slope of the far side of the valley, stood the Median Line: a relentless grey barrier of enormous concrete-block segments, topped with a fuzz of what looked like vicious spirals of razor wire. Every hundred yards or so there was a tower of scaffolding supporting an observation platform. She could see that each platform was occupied by figures manning sandbag bunkers from which protruded the threatening barrels of weapons. Above each emplacement, vast holographic billboards glowed and flickered with public-information announcements in various languages: English, Spanish, Chinese. An endless multilingual loop broadcasting the same basic message: *Please Leave Now*.

Above the wall and the towers, unmanned military gyrocopters buzzed along its length on permanent patrol loops. Every now and then stark beams of light lanced down from their undercarriages and probed the refugee camp, lingering on larger gatherings of people until they got the hint and began to disperse, melting back into the labyrinth of tents and shelters.

'Just in case you folks been thinkin' all along that it was just some guddamn wire-mesh fence that we were gonna clip a hole in an' sneak through,' Heywood said.

'My God,' uttered Maddy. 'It's vast.'

'They been buildin' and fortifyin' this wall for the last ten years. Since the big partition and America *re-federated* and became the FSA.' He turned to look at them. 'Some folks figure a way through that wall every now and then. Many get caught and turned back. Some just get killed on the way through. But . . .' He grinned and nodded at Rashim. 'Our ticket through is my new best friend here.'

Maddy turned to him. 'You *will* be able to talk us through, right?'

Rashim shrugged. 'I really do hope so.'

CHAPTER 20

2070, Median Line
73 days to Kosong-ni

There was an entrance to the Re-Federated States of America, but it was preceded by an almost insurmountable obstacle course of wire-mesh pens that corralled the thousands waiting for a chance to make their case to an immigration officer into a snaking queue that wound endlessly back and forth.

They shuffled slowly forward along with a human river of the desperate and the naively optimistic, overlooked at every bend by soldiers in carbon-flex body armour. The soldiers' stern expressions were all but obscured by sloping helmets with mirrored-plexiglas tactical HUDs at the front, pulled down so that only their mouths and chins were visible.

At one bend in the queue, Rashim suddenly recoiled and did a double take as he stared at the tall athletic figure of a male *artificial*. Maddy recognized the chiselled features, the buzz-cut hair.

'My God! Isn't that one of those . . .?'

He nodded. 'A third-generation combat unit.'

Maddy was glad she'd made sure Becks had switched off her ident signal. If the FSA had later-generation combat units stationed along the wall, they'd pick up on her signal immediately.

The unit stared at the queue impassively, cool grey eyes

sweeping one way then the other, constantly evaluating the threat level represented by those in front of it. White-knuckled hands held its T1-38 pulse carbine ready. Its gaze paused briefly on Becks, as if it was trying to place a vaguely familiar face.

Maddy wondered whether the combat unit would be able to identify Becks as a fellow meat product just on appearance alone. Were these current-generation combat units educated to recognize their predecessors, first-generation models from twenty years ago?

She looked at Becks and noticed her eyeballing the unit, returning the challenging glare. 'Steady there, Becks,' she whispered.

Heywood turned and noticed the stare-off. 'Like two prize cockerels in a fight pit.' He nudged the support unit in the ribs. 'Heel, girl. He ain't gonna bite 'less you do first.'

It took them another five hours of shuffling through the mesh pens until they finally entered a large low-ceilinged hall made from prefabricated modules bolted together. It was crammed with hundreds of shoulder-high interview booths and echoed with bellowed conversations. As far as Maddy could see, every single booth was busy, each occupied by a uniformed official and a pitifully desperate immigrant, most of them frantically hand-waving and head-shaking, some of them crying into balled fists. Holo-screens flickered within each cubicle as search queries were being pulled up and data entered. She noted in most cases the interviews seemed to last no more than a couple of minutes and ended with one or more of the screens displaying a flashing red No Entry verdict. She watched as rejected applicants emerged from their cubicles and were stamped on the back of the hand with ink.

Maddy had already noticed most of the inhabitants of the refugee camp sporting that mark; she'd seen dozens of them vigorously scrubbing the backs of their hands in the polluted water of the river. Now she knew exactly why. The stamp was a way of filtering the queue, weeding out those who'd already been processed and rejected. Presumably the ink wore off eventually, but in the short term it prevented people from trying their luck day after day.

Finally, they were standing at the front of the queue and an immigration official waved at Maddy to step forward.

'Booth seventy-six,' he announced dully.

'Actually, we're all together,' she replied, turning to gesture at the others.

'No, you're not. Booth seventy-six.'

'Look . . . we came here together. We're –'

'Booth seventy-six now, ma'am, or I'll have you removed.'

She cursed through gritted teeth, then turned to Rashim. 'You'd better go first. They've got to let you in. Then you can vouch for us, OK?'

'What if they let *only* me in?'

The official was getting impatient. 'Come on, which of you is going next?'

'I will refuse to go through.' Rashim shook his head. 'I will come back with you.'

'No. If they let you through, you go. You can find someone on the other side and argue our case with them, OK?'

'Come on! Who's next?!'

'And, if you can't get us in, just go find Waldstein. OK, Rashim? Find him and tell him where the hell we are!'

He shook his head. 'No, we should all stay together!'

'OK, that's enough!' The official looked around for someone to flag down to escort them out.

Maddy pushed Rashim roughly forward. 'Just go! GO!'

He stepped across a yellow painted line on the floor and the official pointed at the available booth. 'Booth seventy-six! *That* one! Hurry up!'

Rashim made his way past the other booths, looking back over his shoulder at Maddy and the others. She shooed him along with her hands.

'Do you have any identity data on you? State Citizen chip? Diginet access card? Ration card?'

Rashim shook his head. 'No, I am afraid I don't have any of those on me.'

'Uh-huh, that's what everyone says,' sighed the official. 'OK, let's have your full name, please.'

'Dr Rashim Amir Anwar.'

'Spell it into the mic, please.'

He did so and voice-recognition software displayed his name on the floating holo-screen in front of them.

'I should tell you, I have an extremely high-priority skill set,' said Rashim.

'Trust me, that's also what everyone says. Please sit on this, look at the camera and do not smile or move while the camera scans.' The official nodded at a low stool.

'But, in my case, this is actually true. I have a doctorate in particle physics. I am a leading expert in quantum foam theory. I have been working on a very important government project that –'

'Just sit down, please.'

Rashim did as he was told. The official hit a button and adjusted the height of the stool. 'Look at this sticker on the wall and please don't move.'

The booth flickered with light as a scanner recorded the image of his face.

'Now I need you to place your thumb here,' said the official, indicating a pad on his console.

Rashim nodded. 'Ah yes, a gene swab. Excellent. That will confirm exactly who I am.'

The official offered him a tired heard-it-all-before smile. 'Great, good for you.'

He winced as he felt the momentary sting of a small needle piercing the pad of his thumb. 'I also have some . . . some very important *colleagues* travelling with me.' He turned to look out through the scuffed perspex and noticed they were no longer standing at the front of the queue. Presumably they were all going through a similar process in other booths. 'We really have to remain together.'

'I'm afraid, sir, that each applicant is evaluated on his or her own merit,' replied the official absently, his eyes on the screen, waiting for the overburdened computer system to return some kind of result.

'Yes, I understand this . . . but my colleagues will almost certainly not register on any of your databases.'

'In which case, I'm afraid they won't be let in. It's that simple.'

'Yes, but you see . . . this is really important, we are a team –'

'Look –' the official presented him with an expression of well-tested patience and sucked in a long breath – 'you seem like a nice guy. You've got manners, which makes a change. Most of the time I'm dealing with people who want to spit at me. So . . . I'm going to be straight up with you. We let virtually no one in.' He looked around, then lowered his voice. 'This whole process is . . . futile. It's little more than crowd management. Don't get your hopes up. Hardly anyone gets through. Maybe one in a thousand . . . on a good day.'

'Really? So few?'

'All those poor desperate *S-O-B*s out there?' he said, nodding at the pens. 'They think beyond the Median Line it's all going to be milk and honey. They think we've got it good over here. Truth is we're just about holding it together. It's not a great deal better this side of the wall. Shortages of everything. And every day we get more and more refugees finding a way in. So many more mouths to feed –'

The holo-screen flickered as it updated with a result of the query. The official stared at it for a moment, his mouth flapping uselessly.

Rashim could only see the reverse of the screen hovering in the air, letters and figures hard to make out back to front. 'Have you got my profile up there now?'

'Uh . . . yes. It says you have . . .' His eyes widened. '. . . *level-nine priority*.' He looked up at Rashim.

'Level nine? That is high, isn't it?'

'The highest.'

'Well, I did already tell you, I'm an essential technology contributor working for the government.'

'Yes . . . yes, you did. I'm sorry for keeping you . . .' The man frowned, a little confused by something on the screen. 'But it says you're *already* residing here in the FSA. You've been resident for seven years according to this.'

'Yes, that is quite correct.'

'Well . . .' The man looked suddenly very uncomfortable and extremely contrite. 'If you don't mind me asking, Dr Anwar, if you're already meant to be living here, what the hell are you doing out there in that godforsaken wilderness?'

He shrugged. 'It is a rather long story. And . . .' He leaned forward slowly. 'And it is *highly confidential*.'

'Of course.' The official nodded vigorously as if that answer was more than he needed to hear about the matter. 'Well, uh . . . sir, you won't be surprised to learn you can come right on through.'

138

'And what about my colleagues?'

The official grimaced. Trapped between a rock and a hard place; trapped between unbendable rules and someone important enough to get level-nine priority clearance. He looked again at the information on the screen. 'Uh . . . you know what? I think I'd better call over my supervisor.'

CHAPTER 21

2070, between Cleveland and Denver

They were on a shuttle heading towards a 'containment facility' in the FSA's capital, Denver. The dark hold of the craft reverberated with the drone of a dozen VTOL prop-thrusters perched on the end of four delta-shaped wings outside.

'Capitol was based in Dallas, down in good ol' Texas, for about a year and a half, then they upped sticks again to Denver. That was up until nine years ago.' Heywood was trying to make himself heard above the thrusters. 'The guv'ment started gettin' all panicked about the sea level when Houston and Austin got themselves flooded by Hurricane Deborah. So they went an' set up shop again in Denver.' He nudged her arm to see if she'd heard him. 'You know Denver sits at nearly six thousand feet above sea level? Any place gonna stay dry forever . . . it's Denver.'

Maddy nodded absently. She could do with him not shouting directly into her ear. He seemed to get the message and shut up. She looked around the hold. There were about a dozen other people being transported by this large military gyro' – the very lucky few that had been allowed in. Most of them, except for her and Becks, were men. She guessed they were all roughly in their thirties and early forties. Although it was hard to judge their ages – they probably looked far older than they were: gaunt, haggard faces and scruffy beards on all of them. She tried to imagine where each of them had travelled from, how long they had struggled to make do, surviving out in the 'wilderness' before finally taking the decision to try their luck at getting across the Median Line.

She wondered what special high-demand skills they each had. What qualification had bought them a Willy Wonka golden ticket through immigration. Were they once computer programmers? Physicists? Engineers? Chemists? Doctors? Geneticists?

What type of skill set does a nation struggling to survive need the most?

Each man was on his own. She wondered if any of them had left loved ones behind in that enormous refugee camp. *And yet* – she glanced at Rashim sitting opposite her – *he was allowed to bring us* all *through. Just on his say-so.*

She'd grown used to thinking of Rashim as just one of the team. One of the boys, someone to boss around, take his turn making the coffee, someone to have a laugh with. One of the dungeon's curious little tribe of inhabitants. Although he clearly had a scientific background, Maddy had more than once wondered whether he was as big a deal as he claimed he was, wondered whether he'd just been a junior technician for Project Exodus.

Well, here was her answer. Apparently her lanky-limbed, long-haired colleague was considered a Very Important Person. In government-speak, a critical asset.

The speed with which he'd been ushered through the immigration hall and the rest of them jerked out of their interviews was an indication of how critical an asset he was.

And that made more sense now she'd seen this doomed time with her own eyes. The world was irretrievably messed up. Strip-mined and polluted to the point of ecological collapse, even without Kosong-ni looming like a storm front, this felt like an exhausted place. Nothing more than a giant waste tip gradually being submerged by chemically polluted waters. It appeared that the only technology mankind had left in its bag of tricks was indeed some kind of a reboot.

Time travel.

And Rashim was one of the few minds capable of reproducing Waldstein's displacement technology. Hadn't Rashim smugly reminded her and Liam a number of times that in 2070 there were probably only a couple of dozen multiple-field scientists capable of calculating extra-dimensional displacement theory?

She watched him slumped in his seat, safety harness strapped tightly across his narrow chest, fast asleep. His long dark hair was draped in tangled coils; his black beard, normally so tidily clipped, had quickly become a scruffy, overgrown bush.

Isn't that how 'geniuses' are supposed to look?

Even though he was currently drooling strings of spit on to his collar, she found herself looking at him with a renewed respect. There was a brilliant mind somewhere in there. When they finally found out where Waldstein was squirrelled away, finally came face to face with him, she suspected that she was going to need Rashim to make sense of whatever indecipherable jargon the eccentric old man might share with them.

Three hours later, the transport gyro's prop-thrusters clunked and whined as they reoriented to a vertical position. Everyone jerked in their seats. Rashim woke up, gripping his armrests with white-knuckled hands and squawking like a startled turkey. With a deafening roar, overhead storage racks rattling with the vibration, the shuttle began its descent.

Maddy turned to look out of one of the small round portholes beside her. She stared out at the sulphur-coloured sky, lemon and sickly. The sun was a pale ghost staring mournfully back at her through a chemical mist. Below them, she could see a thick carpet of low-hanging cloud from which several snow-tipped mountain peaks emerged on the horizon.

She strained against her harness and craned her neck to look down more obliquely. Directly below them, the tops of dozens of structures poked through the dense cloud like the clawing fingertips of a man drowning in quicksand. The pointed peaks of skyscrapers, topped with hairbrush tufts of aerials and dishes, solar panels, turbines and winking navigation lights.

As the shuttle began to descend into the carpet of cloud, it bumped and rucked through varying density pockets. It became dim inside the hold as the weak sunlight was suddenly obscured from view. Finally, they emerged from the higher-level chemical cloud cover into a lighter, thinner stratum of pollution. She got her very first glimpse of the eternal twilight of Denver: a forest of glowing steel-and-glass skyscrapers. Green navigation lights, surrounded by smog auras, blinked down the sides of each building. She watched other sky vehicles buzz slowly between the towers, headlights creating piercing beams before them. This twilight world was alive with light and movement as greasy spits of moisture began to dash at the window.

Heywood was grinning at her across the narrow aisle. 'Guddamn made it! Finally made it!'

She could see the ground approaching them. An open expanse of rain-slicked tarmac and guide lights glowing like baubles on a Christmas tree. The thrusters suddenly roared violently, engulfing the shuttle in a cloud of propellant. With a heavy jarring thud, it set down.

The view outside the window began to clear, and through the rain-spattered plexiglas she saw ground crew on the wet tarmac outside, men in glistening overalls wearing face masks, getting ready to refuel the gyrocopter.

'For your information, the local conditions today are not

great,' the pilot announced over the intercom. 'We have level-five air quality and high-acid precipitation. Masks and coveralls are recommended outside.'

She caught Rashim's eye. 'Jeez . . . is it normally this bad?'

He shrugged. 'Welcome to Denver.'

CHAPTER 22
First century, Jerusalem

'Is that him?' muttered Liam. They were standing outside the north-east gate a few dozen yards back from the dirt road leading into the city. Already there were hundreds of people gathered out here, spilling out from the entrance and obstructing the progress of those merchants and pilgrims still attempting to make their way in.

Liam craned his neck to get a better view. The road wound up the side of a gentle slope lined with rows of stunted olive trees. That hill, Liam now knew, was called the Mount of Olives. Up there, somewhere among those trees, was where they'd opened their portal.

On the brow of the hill, he could see some sort of activity: a group of young men, acting as minders, pushing people back to make way for someone behind. He caught just a brief glimpse of a figure leading a donkey. A figure dressed in a loose white jellaba.

Is that him? Is that Jesus?

The knot of people slowly began to descend the hill along the track heading towards them. Jesus – if that pale robed figure really was him – was, for the moment, lost from sight.

'My God, Bob . . . I think I actually just clapped eyes on him!' He turned to Bob and struggled not to grin like an idiot. 'This is incredible!'

Bob seemed somewhat less impressed. 'He is a historical figure. That is all. You have seen other famous figures from history.'

'But this is *Jesus*!'

Liam caught snatches of Aramaic being shouted out around him. It was hard to hear clearly above the rising babble of excitement, hard to translate what they were saying from their thick accents.

'. . . Is it that one? The one in the white? The speaker? . . .'

'. . . The priests will not let him enter the temple . . .'

'. . . heard that he can perform miracles . . .'

The energy all around them was sharp-edged with anticipation. Excitement. Exhilaration.

Not the mood of everyone, though. A few yards away two men were arguing furiously with each other. One with a long dark beard and richly coloured robes. Liam recognized the rich purple colour and the gold tassels as a shawl worn by the priests in the temple. The other man looked like most of the others gathered here: poor, a common labourer. Both men snarled at each other, their faces only inches apart, slapping their chests angrily for emphasis.

'This Nazarene is a troublemaker! A blasphemer!'

'He is one of us. He speaks for us!'

Their exchange was lost behind the cacophony of voices increasing with growing excitement as the knot of people coming down the hillside track drew closer. Over the shoulder of the man in front of him, Liam could see hands being raised: open palms and pumping fists. The atmosphere reminded him of the charged energy they'd experienced back in that Mayan city. Those people believing that finally their long wait was over, their gods had returned. An energy of shared rapture and joy that could so easily change in a heartbeat to something threatening and violent.

The heated argument to Liam's right was growing more unpleasant and now others were joining the poorer man, berating the bearded priest in his expensive robes. The exchange was beginning to turn ugly. Someone reached out and grabbed the priest's robe. The cleric twisted angrily, slapping at the hand. Others joined in and soon the expensive material was wrenched from his shoulders. The expression of snarling derision on the priest's face changed to a look of panic. He decided to beat a hasty retreat from those gathered round him; he backed away into the crowd and quickly disappeared. The long flowing purple robe was held aloft and swung around like a victory flag, like a taken scalp.

The roaring of voices surrounding the pale-robed figure leading the donkey was drawing very close now. Liam turned from looking at the robe being tossed around to see if Jesus and his disciples were any nearer. He could see, above the heads and shoulders and the raised hands punching the air, a vanguard of minders clearing a space ahead. And there, much closer now, he saw the figure: a painfully thin, dark-skinned man, with matted coils of long black hair and the scruffy beginnings of a scrappy beard.

My God . . . this is Jesus. He was staring at the most important, the most influential, figure of the last two thousand years. Just a few dozen yards away from him.

'That's him, Bob. That's definitely Jesus!'

The support unit turned to him, an eyeball-rolling goat under each arm. 'Information: the biblical account differs from this, Liam. The account describes him *riding* the donkey, not leading it.'

'What?! C'mon, that's just a small detail. That's him all right!' He turned to look up at Bob. 'Can't you *feel* it? Like . . . like an energy coming from him? Like –'

147

Bob shook his head. 'I am not detecting any energy source.'

Liam could feel *something*. Perhaps not anything that a machine-mind or some man-made sensing device might pick up, but there was something powerful about that frail-looking figure; not just an ordinary Judaean peasant but something altogether *other*. Something so much more than mere flesh and blood swathed in modest linen. Agreed, he was – as Bob pointed out – leading the animal on foot, not sitting astride it as the Bible specifically mentioned.

Yes. This was slightly different. The prophet was leading the beast. So what? He was still leading the beast. The gesture, the symbolism, was still important. It was a very deliberate act of humility; the king of kings, the prophet who all these people *hoped* was about to lead an uprising to kick out the Romans and their puppet king, Herod Antipas, was arriving to take his throne, not on the back of a tall horse, as a conquering general might, but leading a humble beast of burden. *I am as you. I speak for you. The meek, the poor.*

Liam put the discrepancy down to a simple translation error. Or one of the subtle shifts, exaggerations, a story acquires in the telling and retelling over generations.

Jesus was close now; the dirt track – built up with gravel and clay – was a little higher than the parched grass sloping down on either side of it, and trudging wearily along this track he was head and shoulders above the surging crowd. Voices around them were now sharing a phrase, chanting it in unison.

Hoshi' ah-na! Hoshi' ah-na!

Liam recognized that as a Hebrew word. A word that would eventually become bastardized to *hosanna*.

As the prophet led the donkey slowly past him, he saw a part of the purple robe that had been torn from the bearded priest being tossed up into the air and into the path of the beast. Someone else followed suit. And so did others. Liam recalled another passage from the Bible he'd been reading.

. . . And a very great multitude spread their garments in the way . . . And the multitudes that went before and that followed cried, saying, 'Hosanna to the Son of David!' . . .

Twenty feet from him, no more than that, just twenty feet away . . . and Liam was sure he could actually *feel* the charisma of the man, pulsing, crackling like the power of a hydrogen reactor, the presence, the energy, the life force, all contained in that slight, frail, swaying figure hunched before the plodding donkey.

Jesus passed by and into the shadow cast by the tall east wall. The crowd surged after him, bottlenecking as they pressed through the large gate and into the small market square beyond.

The crowd of people began to disperse, most of them jostling around the entrance to follow their prophet inside.

A minute later, Liam and Bob were standing more or less alone outside. Liam was struck dumb, rooted to the spot and pondering what he'd just witnessed. 'I was twenty feet away from . . . Jesus . . .' he uttered.

Bob lowered the struggling goats to the ground. They kicked dust up as they scarpered away until their tethers thrummed taut and they choked out an unhappy bleat. 'I detected nothing unusual about him.'

Liam shook his head, exasperated. 'Not even in the part of your head that isn't silicon? Didn't you feel *anything*?'

Bob shook his head.

'I don't think I've ever thought about it . . . you know . . . if

149

there is a God. I don't think I've ever believed in that . . . but
. . .' Liam looked through the entrance at the backs of people
still struggling to cram themselves inside. 'You know, for a
moment there, I —'

'You were affected by collective hysteria, Liam. You may be
a genetic product like me, but, unlike me, you are a hundred per
cent organic.' Bob shrugged. 'Your mind works as a human
mind should. Thus it is susceptible to such things.'

'You're saying, what? I imagined that . . . that *power he was
giving off*?'

'Affirmative. There is no logic filter for a moment like this.'
He narrowed his eyes. 'This is how humans can make irrational
decisions. This is how humans are able to convince themselves
to believe the impossible.'

'There was something there . . . Bob. I felt something coming
from him!'

'You were merely affected by the crowd dynamic, Liam. This
is understandable.'

Liam felt a stab of anger. For a moment there he wanted to
tell the support unit to shut up, go away . . . leave him alone to
replay what he'd just experienced. But then Bob suddenly cocked
his head. 'Information . . .'

'What?'

'According to my data, right now Jesus will be heading up to
the temple grounds where he will shortly be causing a
disturbance.'

'Data? You mean the Bible? You downloaded a copy of that
in your head?'

'Of course. It is source material that might be useful. Liam,
we may have a good opportunity to enter the temple.'

Liam nodded. 'Aye, you're right.' He recalled reading
something yesterday about Jesus becoming angry at the traders

and money-changers inside the walled compound. Kicking over some tables and starting some kind of altercation. Bob was right; it might prove enough of a distraction for them to make their way into the temple without being watched too closely.

CHAPTER 23

2070, Denver
59 days to Kosong-ni

They were issued ID tags and assigned quarters in a holding centre, with the exception of Rashim who was allowed to go about his business. According to their records, he was already supposed to be an FSA citizen and resident in Denver. Which was technically true; a younger version of him was out there somewhere. Not in Denver, but south of the city in a bunker beneath Cheyenne Mountain working on Project Exodus; working hard on preparing for T-Day – the day they were going to transport 300 carefully vetted candidates back in time.

Maddy and the others were given bunks in a dormitory. Just like the immigration hall, it was a large, bare-walled prefabricated building, bolted together in segments to create a cavernous, carbo-steel interior that was filled with three-storey bunk beds in a number of penitentiary rows. The uniform-grey blankets of most of the beds had been pegged across the frames by the 'inmates', creating an improvised labyrinth of private personal spaces. Laundered clothes hung like fairground bunting from the frame tops, suspended across the crowded gaps between the rows of beds that had become accepted as communal walkways. The dormitory hall constantly reverberated with a thousand voices echoing off the flat ceiling. Even at night, when the clinical-blue fluorescent strip lights that glared down on them eighteen hours a day had been switched off, there was enough murmuring, crying, snoring, farting and the occasional irritatingly persistent barking cough to keep her awake.

Maddy had been expecting that they'd kick their heels here for two or three days while Rashim got in touch with someone important and vouched for them. That was what she'd expected. She could cope with a few boring days, sleepless nights and gloopy, tasteless protein paste served from a clattering, noisy canteen three times a day.

But two weeks had passed by so far, and not a word from Rashim.

'Man over there said to me . . . he been held here three months,' said Heywood.

'Three months? You've got to be kidding me!'

Maddy was hunched up on the middle bunk. Becks and Charley were sharing the bottom one. The bunk above her creaked with Heywood's weight as he leaned over the lip of the frame to talk to her.

'S'pose it's just what they gotta do. Hold us until they know what the hell they gonna do with us. They got people gettin' into the FSA all the time. Up from Mexico, down from Canada, from the east coast, from the west coast –'

Maddy shook her head. 'But we're wasting critical time.'

Heywood nodded. 'How long until that virus of yours hits?'

'I don't have a precise date. It's a best guess. Weeks, days. Not long. A while after the invasion of North Korea, but I'm not sure . . .'

'So what you gonna do? Try an' bust out?'

The idea was tempting. Becks could quite easily deal with the wardens inside who supervised the containment camp. After all, they were just a bunch of bored swing-keys armed with nightsticks and tasers. But, outside, the building was walled in and patrolled by soldiers and circled constantly by airborne security drones. There was only so much Becks could do. A taser dart would drop her just as easily as anyone else.

'No. We're just going to have to sit tight for now, I guess.'

'You sure . . .' Heywood started speaking, then stopped himself.

'Am I sure, what?'

'Well, that your Really Important Friend, Rashim, that he's . . . you know, not just sort of abandoned us to rot in here?'

'Of course he hasn't!' She glared at him. 'I completely trust him! We've been colleagues for a long time . . .'

Not that long . . . not really. And do you really completely trust him, Maddy? She grimaced at the pernicious whine of that distrusting voice in her head. Wanted to shut it up.

Why did he agree with you so readily, Maddy? Why was he so keen to get back to 2070? Hmm? Ask yourself that, stupid.

She balled her fists, as if that was going to help. Rashim could have dumped them at the Median Line. He could have just told the officials he was on his own if getting back here was his game plan all along.

'Look,' she said eventually. 'He got us into Denver. I'm sure he'll get us out. I'm sure he's working on something right now.'

Heywood made a sceptical you're-the-boss face and sucked a whistle through his gap teeth. 'Well, I guess you know him best.'

'Yeah, I do.' She leaned back on the hard mattress. *Or maybe he's finally back home now and having a whale of a time, catching up with old friends, girlfriends, having a party until time runs out for everyone.*

Heywood settled back on his mattress. She heard him belch. 'Meantime, three square meals a day, a shower room with hot runnin' water, and a bed . . . I guess I can wait.'

She looked past the bunk frame up to the dormitory ceiling. Several large holo-screens were projected from wall-mounted light-beams. Canteen sitting times and washroom-turn notifications were displayed up there, as well as a constant roll of ticker-tape news.

+++North Korean Premier Ye-jin Kim issues final demand for Pacific Alliance navy vessels to withdraw immediately from what have been claimed by N. Korea as territorial waters. Japanese Prime Minister Tomozawa contends that the shale-oil super-reservoir lies fifty miles beyond the N. Korean sea boundary+++

'And that?' she muttered to herself, 'that's our ticking clock.'

How much longer do we have before that shouting match between those far-off countries turns into a deadly bioweapons war? And how long before Kosong-ni breaks out?

'It's totally crazy,' she muttered again, more to herself than anyone else.

We end up all but wiping ourselves out because two nations decide to squabble over the last scrap of oil. She sighed. *Six months from now over nine billion people are going to be just rags and bones.*

She wondered if, right now, Waldstein was sitting comfortably in some ivory tower not so far away from here, watching the very same news feed. She'd seen a couple of blurred video grab-frames of the man stored on their database. One of them taken from Montreal, the very last of the TED Talks, the one where he'd claimed his own work, the discovery of a viable time-travel technique, could destroy so much more than just humanity.

She could imagine him now: twenty years older, his wild, frizzy hair now snow-white and yet those manic wide, watery eyes still intense, still burning. The enigmatic genius. The recluse. The one person who could choose to change the course of history. But was deliberately choosing not to. Just sitting on his withered old hands and waiting for the end to come.

She read the ticker-tape headline again. Two countries happy to annihilate each other over the last of the oil, like children fighting over a packet of sweets in a playground.

What are you thinking, Waldy? Huh? Are you thinking what I'm thinking? Are you thinking that maybe we all deserve to go out like this?

CHAPTER 24

First century, Jerusalem

They finally managed to squeeze their way into the temple compound. This morning it seemed the entire courtyard was crammed with people, standing room only. It looked like every last person in Jerusalem, Jews and Gentiles, had converged on this space within the walls.

Beneath the porticoes of the northern wall something was already going on. Liam looked up at the top of the wall and could see a knot of Roman legionaries gathered there and looking warily down on what might be the beginning of something they'd need to come down and deal with.

Liam turned to Bob. 'We should get closer.'

'Agreed.'

'I guess we won't need the goats any more.'

Bob looked down at the animals that he was leading, relaxed his grip and dropped their tethers. The goats clattered on their hooves, bleated angrily, then skittered away into the crowd, trailing their tethers behind them.

Bob led the way, shouldering his way forward with Liam following in his wake. Presently they emerged into the shadow of the wall at the front of a crowd of onlookers. There was a space around Jesus. He was standing on one side of a wooden table, remonstrating with a couple of traders behind it.

'This is unacceptable! This is . . . you are turning my father's house into a marketplace!'

'Your father's house?' One of the men stood up. 'Your *father's* house?' He laughed incredulously. 'Who do you think you are?'

'You know who I am!'

'We've heard what people have been saying. You're that one from Nazareth, aren't you? You're that troublemaker!'

'You want to know who I am?' Jesus shook his head sadly. 'Is it not bad enough that you soil sacred ground by making a profit from the faithful? That truth alone is not enough no matter who points it out?'

'You're the speaker who has been claiming to be born from God. Aren't you?'

Jesus's eyes narrowed. 'You are wanting me to blaspheme, aren't you?'

'If you are the son of God . . .' The trader's expression was a challenge, a dare. 'What would you have to fear?'

Jesus smiled. 'Nothing.' He turned to the crowd of onlookers. 'I am the son of *Jehovah* . . . and my father wants these profiteers removed from his house!'

At the mention of God's name a collective intake of breath from the onlookers was followed by a silence that rippled out across the crowd, like a pebble tossed into glass-smooth pond water.

The tradesman's eyes widened. 'You all heard that? You people! You heard this man?' He stepped out from behind his table, more assuredly now. There was a hint of a smile there; this fool of a country peasant had just sentenced himself to death. 'You all heard him?!'

Voices whispered and muttered. Liam looked around. The gathered crowd suddenly appeared uncertain. A moment ago it seemed like they were united behind Jesus, united in their resentment of this trader and his fellow profiteers. Ready to rally behind this troublemaker from Nazareth and kick every last parasitic tradesman and money-changer out of the compound. But this unexpected announcement, this bold claim in front of too many witnesses . . . the forbidden utterance of God's name – Jehovah – that was a foolish misstep.

Right then it seemed Jesus was entirely alone. Dangerously alone.

The tradesman cupped his hands. 'Someone call for the priests! Call the temple guards!'

But Jesus appeared to welcome that. 'Yes. Why not?' He smiled, quite calm. 'Bring them here; bring all of them right here! The priests, the Pharisees – they, just as much as you, are guilty of turning an act of devotion to my father into a filthy money-making business!'

'This fool claims he is the son of God! He uses the Lord's name openly! He blasphemes in this holy place!'

The crowd looked on uncertainly. Liam glanced up at the wall again; he could see a centurion had been summoned and was regarding the altercation below with growing concern.

'Who will help me throw these profiteers from my father's house?' called out Jesus. 'Who will stand with me?'

The silence was deafening. Not even the minders, his 'disciples', who had entered the city with Jesus, dared to step forward.

Bob tapped Liam's shoulder and leaned down to whisper. 'Liam, you should take advantage of the fight and attempt to enter the temple.'

Liam looked towards the tall building. There were still people queuing to get in, still temple guards standing beside the entrance, so far completely oblivious to this exchange going on beneath the porticoes of the north wall.

'What fight?'

Bob strode forward out of the crowd. 'I will help you!'

Hundreds of pairs of eyes widened and jaws hung slack and open at the size of the support unit as he crossed the paved ground and stood next to Jesus.

To Jesus's credit he retained his calm composure and merely smiled up at the giant. 'Bless you,' he uttered to Bob under his breath.

Bob nodded. 'You are welcome.' He leaned forward, picked up the wooden table and swung it up, causing a cascade of shekels, talents and sestertii to arc up into the air and shower down on to the onlookers, then hurled it across the shaded cloister against the back wall where it shattered.

Liam looked up and saw the legionaries beginning to react. When he turned to look at the temple building again, he saw a flurry of capes as the temple guard began to hurry over.

'Oh, I get it . . . *this* fight.'

CHAPTER 25

2070, Denver
29 days to Kosong-ni

'. . . the growing threat of a full-scale war in the Pacific region. With Wednesday's pre-emptive drone-swarm attack on the Pacific Union's refinery super-platform, resulting in over four hundred fatalities and the destruction of the platform and nine navy skimmers . . . and the retaliatory assault on the North Korean city of Hyesan, there is increasing concern that the conflict will escalate. FSA President Gonzalez, Defense Secretary Goodman and ECC Premier Schenk have united in condemning North Korea's actions and called for the Pacific Union's navy to withdraw from the contested waters to allow time for emergency negotiations to take place.

'In domestic news . . . the Department of Nutrition has cautioned that lower-than-expected yields of nitrate-resistant, protein-bulking algae will result in higher prices of many standard food products, possibly even tighter rationing in the coming months. Food riots in Indianapolis, Des Moines and Oklahoma City are expected to be exacerbated by this news and martial-law restrictions are anticipated to be scaled up. Many of the protestors are blaming the constant and steady inflow of eastern-seaboard migrants beyond the

Median Line and refugees from Pan-Mexicana for the shortages.

'Here are Friday's weekly info-stats. Global sea-level average . . . up one point three centimetres. Acid-precipitation average . . . up three per cent. Local air-quality index: Denver 565, Santa Fe 676, Salt Lake City 456, Wichita Falls 593. Mortality rates: environmental, up three per cent; violent cause, up nine per cent.

'And, finally, today's message from the administration. *Fellow citizens, the storm brewing in the Far East, although a cause for concern, once again demonstrates that, in a troubled world, our federal states are a continuing oasis of order and stability . . .*'

'Rashim . . . what the hell is going on?' Maddy glared at him through the wire-mesh visitors' screen. 'It's been weeks and we're still sitting in here like a bunch of frikkin' idiots!'

He nodded guiltily. 'I know, I know. I am trying my very best to get you all out. But it is not as easy as –'

'So? What have you been frikkin' well doing?'

'I have logged a second appeal with the Department of Immigration. But, you know, it is difficult. I cannot be too forceful on this.'

'Why the hell not?'

'There are two of me here, remember? If I press the issue, Maddy, there may be confirmation emails sent that the other *me* will pick up. He will query that. He will think his digital space has been hacked into by someone pretending to be him. It will cause problems.'

Rashim told her he'd been staying at his old apartment: a small single-unit near the top of a government-owned accommodation tower. He wasn't supposed to be there. Right now his other self was working hard on mass-displacement calculations with Dr Yatsushita for Project Exodus, sleeping over at the facility now that the big day was approaching. But from his apartment he'd been accessing the same personal digi-mail-space that his other self had access to, sending emails to any high-ranking officials who could pull strings, then immediately having to delete them from his 'sent' folder. Deleting the few replies he'd managed to get back before – hopefully – his other self could spot them in his inbox and wonder what the hell was going on.

'I am doing my best, Maddy.'

She closed her eyes and her head rocked forward until it bumped softly against the mesh between them. 'We've only got a few weeks left before all hell breaks –'

'I know!' He leaned forward, as if that was going to make any difference to her hearing him. 'Look, I have managed to do *something* useful . . .'

'Like what?'

'I have managed to locate Waldstein's campus.'

'You know where it is?'

'Yes. As soon as I can get you out of here, we can make our way straight there.'

'How far away is it?'

'About seventy miles south-west from Denver. It's not actually that far from where Project Exodus is based.'

'And what are we talking about? Is it some high-walled fortress or something? Are we going to even be able to get in to see him?'

'There will be some security, of course, I am sure.' He shrugged. 'But he invited us, did he not?'

There was that. He'd extended an open hand to them to

come and join him. If they turned up at some remote mountainside guarded entrance and announced who they were, presumably Waldstein would instruct his security people to let them in.

'Rashim, we're running out of frikkin' time. You have to get us out!'

'I know!'

'And if you can't swing it for us . . . we'll have to –' She stopped herself. She was going to say they'd have to find a way to bust out, but she was pretty sure there were officers listening in on the dozens of conversations going on in the cubicles of the visitors' hall.

Rashim nodded. He knew exactly what she was going to say. 'It won't come to that, Maddy. I promise. I assure you I do have some influence. I am an important government asset.'

'Yeah, you told me that already –' she lowered her voice – 'you told me when we first met that a number of *important people* were scheduled to go along with you . . . on your little Exodus "trip"?'

The president, the vice-president and their families for a start. Project Exodus was basically a get-out-of-Dodge-City ticket for the administration's top brass.

On the other side of the mesh, he glanced around nervously. 'Yes, Maddy. Some very important people. No names? All right? Don't say their –'

'Well? Can't you give one of them a call?' She shrugged. 'You needed loads of info right? For all your mass calculations? Can't you just ring one of them up to ask a technical question . . . I dunno . . . How heavy their wife is, or something?'

He stroked his chin thoughtfully. 'Yes . . . perhaps . . .'

'Then you can ask a favour for a favour . . . right?'
'Of course.'
'Well, for Chrissake . . . get on with it!'

CHAPTER 26

2070, Denver
10 days to Kosong-ni

```
Waiting . . .
Waiting . . .
Connection established.
Authority verified.
Recipient [Defense Secretary Jonas
Goodman] accepts connection.
You are in an appointment queue.
Waiting time approx. 4 minutes.
```

At last! Rashim stared at the screen. How many goddamned days had he been trying to get hold of the Defense Secretary? The man never seemed to be in his office.

As the waiting time counted down, Rashim's focus switched from the holographic dialogue screen projected on the small window of his single-unit to the view beyond the smoked glass. Fifty-four floors up, he was just above the ever-present thin veil of smog. It hung like swamp mist in pools between the many tall towers of Denver, thin and wispy like a layer of tainted tissue paper.

It had been a vaguely comforting experience, returning to his old apartment. For the last two and a bit years he'd been either living in a damp brick archway beneath a Victorian viaduct or on some mode of transport: carts, trains, steamships, horses . . . even, once, an Indian elephant. Now he was back among modern, comfortable conveniences.

Sitting in one of the recessed storage cubbyholes there was a 3D holograph of his family. A picture taken back when they lived in a well-to-do suburb of Damascus. Rashim aged seven, his two sisters and his parents. They'd emigrated from Iran the year before Iran and Israel went and nuked on each other. Father had seen that coming.

Father was dead now, of course. The Syrian Partition War in '57. Father had seen that storm cloud coming as well, but failed to act quickly enough. They'd been living in a divided town, Muslims and Christians. Former neighbours turned into enemies. The militia came one day and executed every adult male they could find. Rashim was sixteen at the time but he'd looked a couple of years younger. He'd barely escaped the same fate.

He stared at the holograph and moved his head from side to side – there was a limited 3D effect in the image. He could see just a little of the sides of his late father's head, the silver beard clipped tidily all the way up to his fleshy ears. That wide closed-lip grin of his. *I am mischief*, that's what the smile said. *Watch your back . . . because I'll sneak up behind you and tickle you when you least expect it.*

Rashim's memories of him were mostly that: Father playing pranks on him and his sisters.

There was another picture from seven years later: his mother and sisters in New London. He'd been doing his PhD in Massachusetts that year.

Rashim had checked his personal email account, gone looking through recent mail and came across a quick message he remembered sending to his mum just before he relocated to the

Cheyenne Mountain facility permanently. It was essentially a carefully worded goodbye. He'd known, once he was embedded there for the last few months of the project, his emails would be scrutinized . . . and there probably wouldn't be much time for writing personal messages anyway.

He smiled. Remembered tapping it out on his touch-pad, his personal possessions in one shoulder bag, dirty dishes sitting in his kitchenette sink, sad as he typed, knowing he was going to miss her, knowing that the change of timeline was probably going to result in her life, and his sisters' lives, being erased.

And yet excited. Excited that he was just a couple of months away from travelling back in time to Ancient Rome.

```
Waiting time approx. 1 minute.
```

Rashim figured that round about now his *other* self was busy calibrating and testing the receiver beacons that would be deployed back in the time of the Roman Emperor Caligula. Cursing with every last-minute personnel change, having to recalculate the collective body mass they were sending back in time.

Arriving back here, he'd found himself chuckling at the messy state he'd left this single-unit in: pants and balled-up socks on the floor, his quilt in a pile at the end of his bed. He'd left here knowing for certain he'd never be returning, that no one would witness this messy apartment . . . because it would cease to exist.

And yet here I am. Back home.

It had been a very different adventure from the one he'd been mentally preparing himself for. Instead of being one of the political elite lording it over a rebranded Roman Empire, he'd met three quite remarkable young people: Maddy and Sal – his new sisters – and Liam, just like a younger brother.

And what a journey they'd been on.

The most incredible journey . . . because they'd stumbled on something, stumbled upon a mystery that spanned – no, *enveloped* – the last two thousand years. Perhaps Maddy was right. Perhaps Waldstein was the one person who understood the purpose of those large tachyon transmitters that stood either end of two millennia of history, like bookends on a library shelf.

`Call connection activated.`

The projected image on the small window of his single-unit flickered and the face of Defense Secretary Goodman appeared on the glass. Rashim moved closer so that his computer cam would pick his face up clearly.

'Ahh, Dr Anwar, is it?' Goodman frowned. 'I thought this was a call from Dr Yatsushita.'

'No, it's, uh . . . just me, sir.'

'Well, this is . . . unusual. What can I do for you? You after more damned vital statistics from me? You want my inside-leg measurement now?'

'No, I have all the information I need for the moment.'

'I presume there are no hold-ups on the project?' The defence secretary leaned closer. 'I hope not anyway. The amount of money we've already thrown at this project –'

'No, sir . . . no problems. No delays. Everything is on schedule.'

'Good. The way things are going in the east, the sooner we're out of here, the better.'

'I am calling because I have . . . I have a favour to ask.'

The man cocked a smile. 'Let me guess . . . there's a *special person* you want to take along with us. Dr Yatsushita told you "no" and you're going over his head?' Goodman laughed. 'Don't be shy, Dr Anwar. You're not the only one pulling rank. My "technical assistant" on the *guest list*? She's . . . errr . . . she's more than just an assistant, if you get my drift.'

Rashim shook his head. 'No, that's not it.'

'Well, spit it out. I've got a busy morning ahead of me. I'm catching a low-orb shuttle across to Tokyo with the president this afternoon. Trust me, not something I'm particularly looking forward to. Three hours with that guy. He's got the personality of a slug.'

'I have, uh . . . friends . . . no, *colleagues*; they are being held in an immigration camp and –'

'You want me to expedite their application to enter?'

'Yes, sir.'

Goodman shrugged. '*Mi casa es su casa*. No problem. Immigration's as tight as a camel's ass right now, but I'm sure I can swing something for you. How many "colleagues" are we talking about here?'

'Four. Three adults . . . one child.'

'Four? Jesus!' He pursed his lips. 'You moving your whole damn family in from wherever-the-hell-istan?'

'Can you do this for me, sir?'

Goodman shrugged. 'Well, seeing as how I'm counting on you to get my vitals right and not turn me into a steaming pile of mush . . . then, yeah . . . OK. I guess I'll see what I can do.'

Rashim smiled. 'Thank you.'

'Blip over their names and which internment camp they're being held in. I'll see if I can flag them for a fast-track before I have to leave this morning.'

'Thank you, sir.'

'And hey, Anwar?'

'Yes, sir?'

'You need to go get some sleep. You look like you've aged ten years.'

170

'Oh . . . I'm quite all right.'

'Yeah, well . . . I don't want your maths not quite adding up right on the day and your machine turning me into pastrami.'

'Right, yes. I will get some rest and –'

```
Call disconnected.
```

The small window of his apartment flickered and went blank. Once more he was staring out through the smoked glass at the towers beyond and the lemon-coloured swamp mist hovering over Denver.

He hoped to God the man was going to stick to his promise. They were counting down days now, not weeks any more. Days. If Maddy was right . . . just a few days left before the first news report was going to break, a story about a mysterious viral outbreak in a place called Kosong-ni.

CHAPTER 27

First century, Jerusalem

Liam forced his way past the press of people, all of them heading the opposite way, curious to see what was causing the chorus of raised voices, the crash and splintering of wood and the cacophony in the portico beneath the northern wall.

He stepped over the low bench-high barrier that marked the exclusion point for non-Jews, this time unnoticed by anyone, and stepped warily into the hallowed space beyond. A dozen temple guards wearing ceremonial purple-and-gold robes pushed past him as Liam casually climbed the dozen shallow steps, approached the tall entrance, doors wide open, and entered the temple's inner court.

He found himself in a square of dazzlingly white stone slabs, dotted here and there with dark specks of sacrificial blood. The court was starting to empty as word began to spread that something was going on outside. He crossed the square towards a pair of enormous silver-and-gold-plated doors that were open enough to allow one person through at a time. He stepped aside as a priest emerged from them.

'What is happening outside?'

Liam shook his head and muttered a reply. The bud returned an answer. 'There is a big fight outside.'

The priest cursed then pushed past Liam. The large silver-and-gold door remained ajar. Checking that no one was about to bark out at him to halt, he slipped through into the inner courtyard. Ahead of him was a long ramp leading up to a wide platform. The sacrificial altar. Its white stone floor was awash with watered-down blood, and a junior priest armed with a leather bucket was on his hands and knees mopping up the gore with a rag. A queue of those pilgrims who'd been allowed in with their animals, all men, were on the ramp and patiently waiting their turn. The sound of thousands of voices outside raised in alarm was drifting over the high walls. The pilgrims looked concerned. Curious. One of them reached out and grabbed Liam's elbow. For a moment he thought he was about to be stopped again.

'What is causing that noise outside?'

Liam muttered his reply and then listened for the bud's soothing voice. 'The speaker from Nazareth has arrived.'

The man's face creased with anger. 'The Galilean troublemaker? I heard him call himself the son of God . . . and he used the Lord's name too.'

The queue suddenly came alive and erupted with exchanges of outrage and indignation. Some of the men abandoned their goats where they cowered and began to hurry down the ramp towards the doors leading out. Liam carried on up the ramp and across the blood-soaked altar floor, towards what he guessed must be the only entrance to the temple's forbidden inner sanctum – a doorway draped with long patterned curtains, which were pulled partly aside to reveal a forbidding dark interior. He looked around quickly; the junior priest was still busy scrubbing the floor and the waiting pilgrims had abandoned their queue to witness the outrage outside.

Liam took a deep breath and stepped through hesitantly, again half expecting a voice somewhere to call out after him.

My God . . . now I'm inside. If he could be stoned to death for merely stepping over that knee-high wall *outside* the temple, he shuddered to think what would happen to him if he was caught in here.

Out of the glare of the midday sun, he gave his eyes a few seconds to adjust to the gloomy interior. He was standing in a tall ceremonial chamber of marble walls trimmed with gold. The meagre light came from a thin shaft of daylight stealing in through a gap in the drapes and the many sputtering tallow candles and oil lamps within. The air was thick and misty with incense. The noise coming from the compound was muffled now and sounded far away. In here it seemed the ordered business of devotion was still being conducted as usual. A junior priest in white-linen robes swept ashes from beneath an incense burner; another priest in a purple shawl read scripture aloud with a slow, melodic chant, almost singing but not quite. It echoed around the marble walls, a soothing, meditative sound.

Liam skirted the edge of the large hall, trying to appear nonchalant – as if ignorance of the fact that he shouldn't be in here was going to be any kind of a defence – but at the same time trying to make himself as invisible as possible in the gloom.

He made his way towards a heavy decorative drape, then cautiously he pulled it aside and snatched a glimpse behind it. An alcove. Unoccupied. He slipped behind the drape and then allowed himself a moment to double over and catch his breath.

I'm gonna get caught. I'm gonna get caught and butchered like a goat. He puffed out air as quietly as he could.

He looked around the alcove. There was a wooden bench and a straw mattress here. Perhaps a place the priests used to rest between duties? On a low table, he saw several prayer shawls carefully folded and beside them the purple-and-gold robes he'd seen the more senior priests wearing. He stepped over, picked one of the robes up and wrestled with the heavy material.

How do I get this thing on?

He found a small hole for his head and pulled the robe down over his shoulders and wriggled and hopped until the thick material shook free and hung down to his ankles.

Just then he heard a voice beyond the drape.

The melodic chanting of scripture suddenly ceased. Liam heard a weary sigh. 'What now?'

'There is trouble in the Gentiles' court!'

Another long-suffering sigh. 'When isn't there trouble?'

'But . . . but this is a riot! That prophet who was in Galilee last week, he has come here!'

Liam heard the rustle of material, the clink of ceremonial chains as the priest got to his feet. 'Clear the temple courtyard. Have the guards close the outer doors and keep watch outside.' He heard those orders being passed on, heard the swish and rustle of movement and the slap of hurried bare feet against the marble floor, then the echoing groan of heavy doors being swung to and their clunk reverberating round the cavernous temple. Finally . . . *finally*, it sounded as if he might be entirely alone.

He peeked through the drape. It appeared that he was.

Cautiously, he stepped out and crossed to the middle of the hall. *Where do I start? What am I looking for?*

He remembered. *The Foundation Stone.*

And, beneath that, there was supposedly that cave and from there passages that led further down.

. . . to the underworld? To Hell?

He shook that stupid notion from his head. He was looking for a way down beneath the temple. And quickly. He wondered how long Bob was going to be able to provide a distraction. He looked around. The walls of the hall were largely smooth facades of pale marble. Nothing that seemed like an invitation to be inspected more closely. Ahead of him was another altar, smaller than the public one outside. It was covered with candles and smouldering incense sticks. Beyond was another pair of heavy drapes that ascended all the way up to the high ceiling of the temple . . . some fifty or sixty feet.

That's important. He looked at the drapes. *Tall. Surely symbolic?*

He walked round the small altar and stood before the drapes. The material was thick and heavy; dark purple, blue and scarlet patterns swirled across it. Tentatively he pulled the drape aside; it swung heavily and Liam glimpsed into the dimly lit space beyond. He saw nothing but a stone floor. Not the smooth marble he'd been walking across but roughly hewn stone worn smooth.

That's it . . . the Foundation Stone!

In the middle of the uneven floor was a carved hole approximately one and a half feet in diameter. A pale light was shining up through it. To his left, Liam noticed a bigger circular opening in the rock floor. He wandered over to it and saw that rough steps were carved into the bedrock leading down into the opening.

And that's the entrance to the cave beneath it.

He took the first few uneven steps down, then crouched down low to see what lay ahead. He could see what appeared to be a small natural cave. Not something built, or even carved out . . . a natural void caused by geology. He took the rest of the dozen steps down, swerving past a tongue-like bulge of bedrock on his left that projected out. At the bottom of the steps he found it was just that; he was standing in a small cave with a low ceiling. A single thick tallow candle sputtered on a low table just beneath the hole in the ceiling.

No palm tree holding up the roof of the cave.

No wailing voices of tormented souls as Barton's book had promised.

The light was dim, and jumped and flickered unreliably as the candle's flame danced. He needed more light. He reached under the robe for his satchel and fumbled around inside until he felt the cool metal of the torch. He pulled it out and snapped it on.

Light reflected off the smooth, damp walls of the cave. This natural space was not quite as empty as he'd suspected; against one uneven wall a wooden rack supported several hundred dusty scrolls on wooden spindles. In one corner, a roughly hewn low archway led on to more steps heading down deeper into the bedrock.

Deeper we go, then.

He followed the steps until they brought him into another low-ceilinged space: a long and narrow cave that looked like it had been chiselled and chipped at in places to widen it and make it a more practical, usable space. The cave walls were lined, like a postal sorting office, with rows of two-foot-wide cubbyholes. He peered into several of them and curled his lips at the rags, desiccated flesh and brittle bones within. A mausoleum. He guessed the bones had belonged to the temple's previous serving priests and Pharisees.

He made his way down the rows until he came across a low archway to his left. He shone his torch in and saw it led on to a narrow passage with a ceiling so low he'd have to stoop uncomfortably to make his way along it. It ran in a straight line, sloping down deeper into the rock. Again, it looked like it had once been a natural fissure, which had been hacked at with primitive tools to widen it further.

He panned the torch around. The long cave appeared to have other low archways leading off it, but since this passage seemed to be sloping downwards – and finding a way to get deeper was what he was looking for – he decided to follow it.

He ducked his head, hunched his shoulders and made his way down the narrow passage. The thick robe was making him hot; he could feel pinpricks of sweat on his body and felt a trickle of it running down his temple from his hairline.

Twenty yards down the sloping tunnel, he picked out another small opening to his right. A thick veil of dusty cobwebs hung across it and he grimaced with disgust as he pulled at them and shone his torch in.

Just a short inlet. A dozen feet back and, at the end, some threadbare material hung down from a wooden baton. He squeezed into the narrow space and reached out for the material. It was old, fragile. He pulled it gently aside to reveal not more roughly cross-hatched bedrock . . .

. . . but a small wall of stone blocks held together by a 'cement' of dried clay. He thumped his fist against the wall. It was firm. Too firm for him to break through without some kind of sledgehammer.

Dead end.

He cursed and smacked his fist against the stone again. After the reverberation had died away, he heard something else. The faint clatter of something loose and brittle falling to the ground on the other side of the wall. He struck the stone once more and heard it again. Grit? Mortar? Something . . . was cascading down on the far side.

That wall was built to hide something.

He wondered whether he could have a go at knocking a hole through. Perhaps the clay mortar was perished enough that it would give easily.

He set the torch down at his feet and found a seam between two stone blocks and tested it with his fingernail. The mortar's thin crust cracked like a pie's pastry lid and spilled a small trickle of dry sand on to the back of his hand. Liam looked around to find something long and thin he could use to probe deeper. Nothing. Then he remembered the small bag on his shoulder under the priest's robe. He hefted the suffocating robe over his head, off his shoulders and on to the floor, then dug into his bag. He found what he was digging for. His black leather diary, the one he had inherited from Sal. More to the point, he found the biro bedded in between the pages. He pulled it out and used it to test the mortar further, dislodging more and more of the sandy material on to his feet. Finally, after a few minutes of prodding and scraping, one stone block wobbled slightly. Liam thumped at it with the palm of his hand. It scraped inwards slightly. He thumped again with both hands and it shifted backwards a fraction, dislodging a small avalanche of grit on the far side.

'Come on,' he grunted. 'You're gonna go this time, you stubborn bugger.' He leaned back, locked his elbows and presented the firm heels of his hands and lurched forward. The block skipped backwards, then fell into the space beyond with a clatter that echoed into the void.

He held his breath as he listened to the echo decay, half expecting to hear something unpleasant, unnatural, *super*natural uncoil itself from an aeons-long slumber.

Here there be waiting demons . . . waiting to be unleashed. Waiting to reach through this hole and drag you down into their eternal Hell.

'Oh, good grief, get a grip on yerself,' he muttered.

He picked up the torch from the floor and held it up to the rectangular hole. Beyond this small wall, the narrow passage continued, sloping downwards for another twenty or so feet. However, the arched roof and walls, although carved through bedrock, were far smoother. Far too smooth. Not like the rest of this passage, roughly hacked out by chisel and hammer.

'My God!' he whispered.

It looked like it had been drilled out using modern machinery.

He panned his torch around. He could see the smooth walls were marked by subtle spiral grooves along the rock. It reminded him of the rifling inside the barrel of a gun.

At the end of the passage his torch settled on a perfectly flat wall that reflected his beam like a sheet of polished nightmare-black obsidian. Running along the base of the wall he could just about make out some faint markings.

He gasped.

This is it! It's here!

The very same glyphs as the ones they'd encountered on the surface of that vast cylinder in the jungle. Somewhere beyond that smooth wall, it had to be there. Just like that transmitter, hidden beneath the ground. Whoever it was that had built those things had specifically chosen locations that were embedded deep beneath the most protected, most sacred, most unlikely places to be explored or probed by archaeologists or tomb-raiders.

Clever. Very clever. Hidden as it was beneath the holiest of holy places in the Christian, Islamic and Jewish traditions. A place forbidden to anyone to enter. A place with its own cleverly established mythology. Perhaps the engineers of this construct had seeded those very ideas with the antecedents who'd been living here, ideas that would inform the Judaean faith, then later

Christianity and Islam. An idea designed simply to ensure this location would eternally be considered the most sacred, most protected and most unexplored location on the planet.

Liam decided he'd gone far enough. This was more than enough proof that they'd come to the right location. It was right down there. Somewhere beyond that glass-smooth wall.

'Right. OK . . . I'm done here.'

He wondered how long he'd been scrabbling around beneath the temple. Ten minutes? Twenty?

God knows what havoc's going on up there now.

He decided he'd better make his way back up before whatever riotous distraction Bob was causing above ground ran its course. Time to get the hell out, regroup and maybe head back to London. Maddy was surely back from her fact-finding by now and they could figure out together what they were going to do next.

He put his pen and diary back in his bag. Pulled the priests' heavy robes back on over his head, grabbed the torch and started to make his way back up the passage, hoping that when he finally emerged in the temple he wasn't going to find himself staring bleary-eyed at a welcoming committee of irate temple priests.

CHAPTER 28

2070, Denver
5 days to Kosong-ni

'. . . *reports of mounting casualties as the conflict in the region continues to escalate. Mixed units of soldiers and artificial combat personnel from the Pacific Union reportedly engaged with a regiment of the North Korean People's Army, the Republican Guard, supported by combat droids, five miles north of Chongjin. The death toll, in what many are now calling a full-blown war, has now been confirmed as twenty-seven thousand civilian and military fatalities . . .*'

'Becks, why are those people fighting?' asked Charley.

Becks and the little girl were sitting on the middle bunk, their legs dangling over the side, swinging freely as they idly watched one of the big news screens on the ceiling.

'They are fighting over something neither side wants to share with the other.'

'What?'

'Oil.'

She looked up at the support unit. 'Is that the black gooey stuff everyone used to make things go?'

'Yes.'

She frowned. 'But I thought that was just in the old, old times?'

'Oil is used primarily as a raw material for producing

plastics and polymers. But some nations, even in the present, rely on hydrocarbons to generate their power.' She shook her head sternly. 'This is a flawed and short-sighted energy strategy.'

'Wrong?'

'Yes.'

'Why?'

Becks cocked a brow and looked at her. 'They are relying on a nearly depleted resource.'

Charley narrowed her eyes as she tried to get her head round that. She gave up on it after a minute and pulled a face. 'Why do you always talk so funny?'

Becks looked down at her again. 'Was my answer not clear?'

'You use lots of long words.'

'What is wrong with long words?'

Charley hunched her shoulders. 'I'm nine?'

Becks nodded slowly. She managed to play the most appropriate smile in her database across her lips. 'I'm sorry, Charley.'

They watched the news for a while: a montage of grainy, shaky on-the-ground footage transmitted from battlefield cams – the worst glimpses of bloody carnage blurred out by the digi-channel. They saw grey-brown skies slashed by streaks of phosphor and tracers spewing from the bellies of swooping drone fighters. Dazzling explosions that caused screen white-out and left behind billowing mushroom clouds that rolled into an already smudged sky. A mountainous battlefield littered mostly by the ragged bodies of poorly equipped North Korean soldiers.

'Becks?'

'Yes, Charley?'

'Will all that fighting be coming over here?'

She pondered how to answer that. As a matter of fact, the indirect effect of this war *was* coming their way imminently – a biological doomsday weapon that was soon to be deployed, almost certainly by the side that was losing this short sharp war: North Korea.

Lying was still a technique she had trouble with. It jarred with every line of software in her head to say something that was . . . *was not*. But, on the other hand, reassuring misdirection? What Liam might call a 'little white lie'? That was something she was beginning to get the hang of as she cared for the girl.

'Don't worry, Charley. Everything is going to be just fine. We are safe here.'

Just then they heard a commotion. Below the lines of laundry strung from one row of beds to the next, making the dormitory hall look like some kind of Far Eastern bazaar, they heard the slapping of hasty feet approaching, barked *excuse-me*s and apologetic *I'm-really-sorry*s and *I-just-need-to-get-by*s.

Their bunk frame vibrated and the bed springs above creaked as Heywood stirred. His grizzly face appeared over the edge of the frame. 'What's the guddamn commotion?'

'I hear Maddy approaching,' answered Becks. She cocked her head and listened to Maddy's impatient voice barking at someone to get out of her *frikkin'* way. 'There must be some news.'

A moment later, Maddy staggered into their space, wheezing for air and grasping the bed frame for support. 'Everyone get dressed,' she said. 'We're being released! Rashim finally came through for us.'

Rashim was waiting for them in the processing hall. He watched as they were each issued with ID cards and a week's ration credit, and their backpacks and contents were returned – minus their confiscated antique guns, of course. Finally, an official waved them through, the paperwork done.

'Five days!' was the first thing Maddy said to him as they joined him. 'We've got just five frikkin' days left! The Pacific Union's invasion of North Korea started two days ago!'

He looked hurt. 'No "thank you very much for pulling strings and getting us out of here, Rashim"?'

'OK, thanks, but . . . Jeez, we've got to get moving.' She grabbed his shoulder. 'Please tell us you know *exactly where* we have to go.'

He nodded. 'W.G. Systems Research Campus. I have the precise location entered into my wrist-pad,' he replied, tapping the personal organizer on his arm.

'So we're good to go? Like, *now*?'

Rashim handed out some face masks. 'These are only cheap ones. But you will all need them for outside; the air quality in Denver is very poor today. Once we get out of the city, the air should get better.'

'OK.' She turned to Heywood. 'Well . . . I guess you and us, we're all square now. You guided us safely to the Median Line and we got you through, so . . .'

The old man nodded. 'This is where you ditch the old fella?'

'I wouldn't put it quite as bluntly as that. But . . .' She shrugged. 'This is where you wanted to get to. This was the deal, right?'

'So I can die of —' he lowered his voice so Charley, standing a few feet away and holding Becks's hand, wouldn't hear him — 'so I can die of that virus like everyone else in a few days' time?'

'Not necessarily.' She glanced at Rashim. 'Who knows what the future's going to be?'

'Great.' He sighed. 'So, in a few days' time, either I'm gonna die, or I'm gonna vanish in a puff of air?'

Maddy shot him a cautionary frown. 'Maybe this isn't the best place for us to be discussing this?'

'An' what about this girl? Don't tell me you just leavin' her with me?'

She looked at Charley. That was kind of what she'd assumed would happen once they got out of the internment camp. 'I . . . well, there must be some place you can take her to. Some home for orphans or something.'

'Look . . . why don't you let us come with you?' Heywood shrugged. 'Me an' the girl won't be a burden. Maybe we can help somehow?'

Rashim nodded. 'They might be of help.'

'Oh, great . . . Thanks a bunch for that, Rashim.'

'I can take responsibility for the girl,' said Becks. 'She will not be a burden.'

'Seriously?' She turned to Becks. 'You're choosing *now* to get all maternal?'

Becks cocked her head. 'I don't underst—'

'OK . . . didn't want to get all scratchy on you, but you leave us behind,' said Heywood, 'an' I'll tell everyone what's goin' on.'

Maddy's jaw snapped shut.

'I'll tell people who the hell you are . . . what you can do. I'll tell them where you're guddamn well headed.'

Rashim bit his lip. 'He knows everything, Maddy. With . . . "my project" going on right now, the first mention of time travel and we will have FSA agents descending on us from all directions.'

'Guddamn right,' said Heywood, nodding. He turned to her apologetically. 'Look . . . strength in numbers, right?'

She closed her eyes and sighed. Waldstein, if they did find him, was going to throw a fit. She already knew how paranoid he was about being discovered contravening the strict international protocol he'd been instrumental in establishing. However, it was Waldstein who'd broken radio silence, who had extended an invitation to the team to come to him . . . who'd decided to part with caution.

'Extra pair of hands,' added Heywood. 'You know . . . in case we run into any trouble? I can handle myself.'

'Why not?' She rolled her eyes. 'The more the merrier.'

CHAPTER 29

2070, Denver

Sheesh . . . This is the future?

Maddy gazed up through the spattering drops of rain at the tower blocks around them, fading into a brown haze, then disappearing into the low-hanging clouds. She could see few people, though. She'd expected the rain-slick streets to be full of life and colour. But they were deserted. Rashim explained that the rain, more like a persistent drizzle, was corrosive — a diluted form of hydrochloric acid that gradually ate its way through anything not coated in polyethylene plastic. On some days, it was concentrated enough to cause irritation and rashes and minor burns on exposed skin. The overcrowded inhabitants of Denver preferred to stay indoors when the weather was like this.

They were wearing plastic macs, goggles and air-filtration masks as they skirted the perimeter of an old shopping plaza that was now host to an encrustation of unofficial housing: a shanty town of prefabricated habitation modules stacked on top of each other, four, five, six cabins high, creating unstable-looking improvised tower blocks surrounded by cages of scaffolding. Loops of power and data cables dangled from pipes and stretched tautly from one cabin tower block to the next like strands of webbing, as if some vast species of arachnid had started to make a web and left it half finished.

Rashim's accommodation tower overlooked the shanty town. They entered a small foyer and squeezed into an elevator that took them up fifty-four floors. They emerged into a dimly lit, threadbare-carpeted hallway that he led them down until they came to his apartment.

'Home sweet home,' he said as he pressed his thumb against a dimple beside the door handle. A lock clacked and he pushed the door open.

'It is a bit messy, I'm afraid,' he cautioned.

Maddy stepped over some clothes on the floor. 'Just a bit.'

He ushered them all in, then closed the door after them. They were standing in a rectangular room, about twenty feet long and twelve wide. The walls were covered in a dark chocolate-coloured wallpaper designed to mimic mahogany panelling. It looked like what it was, cheap and cheerless. Several spotlights in the low ceiling picked out hazy circles on the cord carpet. At the far end was a small workstation and roller chair in front of a three-foot-wide floor-to-ceiling window. To their left, recessed into the wall, was a pull-down bed; to their right, a narrow counter with wall units and a sink.

Maddy looked at the mucky plates piled up in murky dishwater. 'Your mom would be so proud of you.'

'I have been busy getting you out,' he replied defensively.

'This place is *tiny*.' Maddy stepped across the small living room. 'And this is the kind of place someone *important* with *influence* is supposed to live in?'

'It's a single-unit. Not very many people get assigned one of these. Most people have to share. So, yes . . . this is privileged accommodation.'

She made her way across to the tall window, sat down in the chair, spun it round and looked out through the spits and spats of dirty rain running down the glass at the shanty town below.

Sheesh, the future really is grim.

Even here in the capital city of this re-formed, consolidated version of America, a place that desperate millions were camping outside to get into . . . Even here, it had the feel of a world that had given up and was just waiting for the executioner's blade to fall – a monochrome world of sick yellows and dying browns. She'd hoped for so much more than this. Hoped for a futuristic New York. Hoped for a dazzling carnival of neon lights and busy, criss-crossed skies. But no . . . from what she'd witnessed thus far it was a permanently dark and damp metropolis of empty streets and tower blocks dotted with dim interior lights and pale faces staring out at the jaundiced sky.

'I have not just been sitting on my arse. I managed to get in some supplies for us while I have been waiting for your application to clear,' said Rashim. 'It's not like I have been doing nothing. Look! Packets of freeze-dried algae protein and soyo pasta. Bottles of water and water-purification tablets. Some meds. Look, I also managed to get my hands on three ex-police tasers.'

Maddy turned and looked at the supplies stacked in the corner. 'OK, I apologize. You've done good.'

'Most of this is black market. Very expensive. I emptied my credit account to get my hands on these supplies.' He spread his arms. 'I am now, officially, completely broke.'

'If you folks are right about things, money's gonna be worth less'n spit on a sidewalk pretty soon. Even here in the city,' said Heywood. He looked at the pile of supplies and nodded approvingly. 'Water, food and weapons is what's gonna get you by.'

'What's *munny*?' asked Charley.

'Exactly, miss.' Heywood smiled and ruffled the hair on her head. 'There ya go. This little girl got by her whole life not needin' a single dollar.'

'So how far away is Waldstein's place?' asked Maddy. 'Is this another hike on foot?'

'It's about seventy miles south-west of Denver. We can take Route 87 most of the way down, then we have to head west into the Rockies. And, yes, it is going to be on foot most of the way, I would say.'

'We've got five days, Rashim; is that going to be enough time to get us there?'

'Where does this plague of yours start?' asked Heywood.

Maddy glanced at Charley. Her head was cocked, listening to the adults. *She's going to find out soon enough. Might as well be now.*

'The Kosong-ni kicks off someplace out east,' Maddy replied. 'North Korea. At a place called Kosong-ni . . . hence the name.'

'So, we got time,' said Heywood. 'Virus gonna take a few weeks to get from over there to over here, right?'

'I don't know how fast something like this can spread.'

'Very fast,' said Rashim. 'If it is airborne. If it has an undetectable incubation period, it could be transmitted to various places. If it is an engineered pathogen, it could already be widely spread but in a dormant state, waiting for a chemical signal.'

'If this plague is as terrifyin' as you told me, then the sooner we're out in the wilderness, away from other guddamn people, the better.'

'Plague?' Charley looked up at Becks. She was still holding her hand. 'Becks? Are we all going to die now?'

Maddy sighed and looked at her. 'Becks, maybe you and me better explain the situation to her.'

'Yes, Maddy.'

'Sensitively . . . OK?'

'Yes, Maddy. I will follow your lead.'

She turned to the others. 'I guess you two can start packing this stuff up, then we'll head out?'

'I suggest tomorrow morning,' said Rashim. 'The air is much clearer in the mornings.'

'OK, then we'll pack this stuff up now, get some sleep, and head out first thing.'

'Everyone is going to die?'

They were standing beside the window, looking out at the dim cityscape as Rashim and Heywood worked at stowing away their supplies. Maddy wondered how much truth to pass into the hands of this little girl.

She nodded slowly. 'Almost everyone, Charley. It's a nasty disease that some bad men made as a kind of weapon.'

She narrowed her eyes. 'Are we . . . are we going to escape the disease?'

'We're heading to a safe place up in the mountains, aren't we, Becks?'

She nodded. 'Yes. A safe place.'

Charley pursed her lips thoughtfully. 'OK.' Then, after a moment, she added, 'And is that the place where the walrus man lives? The one you been trying to find?'

Maddy couldn't help snorting a dry laugh at that: *the walrus man*. She'd kind of got his name *half* right. She wondered how much this little girl had heard them muttering to each other over the last few weeks and months when they thought she was fast asleep or zoned out. How much she'd quietly ingested and been puzzling over.

'He's . . . well, let's just say he's a wise old man who knew this disease was coming our way.'

'Is he going to look after us?'

'I'm sure he will.'

'And is he going to make our world better again?'

She's as bright as a button. Doesn't miss a trick. She must have heard them talking about whether they were going to reset the timeline or not.

'That's what we're going to talk to him about. There might be a way that we'll all get another chance.'

'Is the walrus man . . .?' Charley idly drew an invisible loop on the window as she tried to phrase the question. 'Is he . . . God?'

'What?' Maddy smothered an urge to scoff. 'What made you think that?'

'My mom believes in God . . .'

Believes. Present tense. Charley hadn't mentally buried her mother yet. Hadn't seen her shot down like her sister. Therefore, in her mind, she must still be out there somewhere. Alive.

'My mom told me God is wise and looks like an old man and he'll come one day and either he will put everything right again . . .'

'Well, it's a bit like that, I suppose.'

'. . . or he may decide to wipe everyone out like he did once before with a flood. And then he'll start over with only a few of the very good people.' She turned to look at Maddy. 'What you said sounds like that.'

She nodded. Not a bad analogy, actually. If Kosong-ni was another 'flood', what did that make Waldstein? If he had the power to prevent it or allow it . . . what *did* that make him? God? Probably, from a child's perspective.

'He's not *God*, Charley. But there is a way ol' *Walrus* can fix everything. You ever heard of a thing called time travel?'

Her pale forehead furrowed, an eyebrow raised. 'Duh, course. You never read *Time Teddies*?'

'Whuh? What's that?'

She sighed. 'Just kids' stories. I used to read them on my mom's old *read-ee-screenie*. They were these fat cartoon bears that used to travel around and fix broken time.'

Maddy couldn't help another smile. 'Time-travelling teddy bears putting time right? Fancy that! Well, this walrus guy, I guess, is a little bit like one of those bears. He can do that too.'

'Time travel?' Her eyes rounded. 'It's a for-real thing?'

'Yes, it's a for-real thing. We're going to find him and kindly ask him to rewind time so that we can have another go at not messing this world up like we have.'

'Will he say yes? Will he do that?'

She nodded. 'I think between us all . . . we'll convince him.'

CHAPTER 30

First century, Jerusalem

Liam quickly crossed the outer compound of the temple, dreading what he was going to find in progress beneath the north wall.

As he drew closer, he saw the Romans had decided to get themselves involved. In the past twenty or so minutes, it appeared that Jesus's outburst at the profiteering of one particular trader had escalated and become a full-scale riot. Half the cohort had been scrambled from Fortress Antonia – the garrison building attached to one corner of the temple – and were now attempting to contain the troublemakers in the north-east corner of the compound. The three centuries, about two hundred and fifty men, had spread out into an encircling line, two ranks deep, and were shuffling forward, compressing the rioters into a containable writhing mass. Projectiles arced out from them – lumps of masonry, jagged-edge stones – which clattered down on the legionaries' armour, helmets and raised shields. Most of the rest of the temple compound had either been cleared by the Romans, or the gathered pilgrims had chosen to flee before the supervising tribune decided to exercise a zero-tolerance policy and round up *everyone* within the walls.

The paved ground of the compound was dotted with bodies, most of them wearing the purple-and-gold robes of the temple guards, some of them writhing in agony, some perfectly still.

And there were smears and dots of blood that Liam suspected came from them rather than any sacrificial doves or goats.

Closer now, he could see him, in the middle of the riot, standing a head taller than anyone else. Bob was busy swinging a thick six-foot-long wooden beam – which looked suspiciously like the axle from a cart – in one hand, as if he was merrily twirling a cheerleader's baton. In the other, he held a battered and misshapen Roman shield that had sprouted at least a dozen arrows.

Liam could hear the clunk, clatter, grunts and howls coming from the Romans every time the beam swung back into the maul and gouged out another couple of men from their ranks.

He couldn't get through to Bob and the mob of rioters . . . about fifty of them at a guess. Not that he particularly wanted to be trapped in there with them, but this . . . needed to be brought to an end now. He had what they'd come for – pretty convincing evidence that beneath the temple was where they'd find the other transmitter.

He cupped his hands. 'BOB!!'

His voice was lost among the noise. He looked around. He needed to let Bob know that he was back up above ground somehow. Not easy. Once Bob went into bull-in-a-china-shop mode it was particularly difficult to get his attention. Waving his arms about beyond the ranks of legionaries probably wasn't going to be enough. Lying on the ground a few yards away was a Roman javelin with a bent tip. He ran over, picked it up, whipped the prayer shawl off his head and tied it to the end of the javelin. He began to wave it back and forth like a pennant.

'BOB!! OVER HERE!!!'

The support unit finally spotted the waving shawl. He immediately stopped swinging his improvised war-hammer. The other rioters, seeing their adopted champion had suddenly ceased fighting, began to do likewise. The Romans broke off their cautious advance, and for a moment the cacophony that had been bouncing off the tall stone walls of the temple compound became a fading echo.

Then an uncomfortable stillness.

'BOB!' Liam shouted again. A ripple of clattering lorica segmentata armour as Roman heads in the line swivelled to look over their shoulders at him.

'We. Need. To. Leave . . . NOW!'

Bob nodded. He dropped his shield, hefted the oak beam into both hands and held it horizontally in front of him at arm's length, holding it like a vehicle bumper. He let out a deep booming roar that sounded like some trucker gunning the throttle of an eighteen-wheeler, then he charged towards the front rank of legionaries.

The Romans foolishly attempted to hold fast.

A moment later, the compound echoed with a deafening crash, the clatter of armour, yelps of alarm and agony. Liam saw a couple of helmets comically spinning up into the air, and then Bob emerged through the thin red line, having flattened two dozen soldiers. The rest of the Roman line peeled back in alarm at the raging goliath and the fifty other hardcore rioters took the opportunity and followed in his wake, breaking out of their containment.

Bob finally came to a rest in front of him, panting from the exertion. 'Yes, Liam?'

'We need to get the hell out of here!' said Liam. He nodded to his left; a couple of hundred yards away, opposite the rear wall of the central temple building and halfway down the compound's west wall, was the large western entrance to the temple compound that led down into the city.

Bob nodded. 'Agreed.' Without anything else needing to be

said, they turned and started to run for it, the other rioters following after.

Liam heard orders being barked in Latin behind them. He heard the clatter of armour as some of the legionaries pursued them, but weighed down by their shields and armour they weren't going to catch up. As they passed the corner of the temple building and closed the gap with the main western entrance, Liam looked up and saw a dozen Roman archers had gathered on the top of the wall above it.

'Watch out! Arrows!' he cried.

A volley of arrows whipped down through the air, most of them clattering harmlessly on the paving stones, one finding a target just behind Liam. He heard someone cry out. As they approached the vast entrance flanked by huge pale sandstone columns, another volley flickered down.

One thudded into Bob's throat. A bloody barbed arrowhead erupted from the back of his neck.

He grunted, staggered and halted, then dropped to his knees.

'Bob!' Liam stopped beside him. 'My God!'

Bob was spitting dark gouts of almost-black blood down on to his chin. 'I am fine . . . Liam. This is not a fatal wound.'

Liam got his hands under Bob's hairy armpits and attempted to pull him to his feet. 'Come on! COME ON!'

'I will . . . recover . . . Liam. But . . . you must go!'

'I'm not leaving you!'

Some of the other rioters stopped fleeing, and gathered round Bob and helped Liam pull the giant to his feet.

Bob rocked uncertainly on the balls of his feet. 'This arrow . . . is blocking . . . my windpipe . . .' His large hands fumbled for the shaft sticking out of the front of his throat. 'Snapped . . . I am . . . unable . . . to breathe . . .'

'I got it!' Liam grasped the shaft in both hands. 'Ready?'

Bob nodded.

Liam jerked it out and blood began to spurt down Bob's chest.

'Remove . . . the . . . other . . . half . . .'

Liam reached round the back, grabbed the shaft beyond the arrow tip and did the same again. It came out with a wet sucking sound.

The pursuing legionaries were closing on them now.

'Can you breathe now?'

Bob gurgled blood, but nodded. He got to his feet and they resumed their escape, along with a dozen others clustered round, their hands all on the support unit – on his back, on his broad shoulders, but not needed. The wall loomed before them. Then as they raced into shadow it was above them and then behind them, as they ran along a wide sloping viaduct that was taking them towards the busy streets of the upper city.

CHAPTER 31

2070, Denver
4 days to Kosong-ni

Rashim was right: the next morning the low heavy rain clouds had lifted and a clear lemon-coloured sky was just about visible beyond a thin veil of smog. They took a crowded e-Tram south from the city centre into the sprawling suburbs – a place called Centennial – where uniform, mass-produced housing blocks had naively optimistic names like *Cherry Orchard*, *Summer Green* and *Daisy Way* stencilled on their sides. At the base of every block there was a food-ration station with a winding queue in front of it, watched over by soldiers and stern-faced combat units.

The city suburbs eventually thinned out and became a passing landscape of mostly old pre-FSA abandoned towns and boarded-up malls. The road was flanked every now and then by large weather-worn billboards with the faded shreds of acid-bleached posters – a reminder of better times when Mom and Dad might have wanted to buy a new e-Car, or take their kids on holiday to an Oasis Fun Park, or invest in a FamilyCare medical policy.

Aboard the tram, a screen was playing Denver's main digi-news station. The news now was only about one fast-moving story: the 'Pacific Conflict'. They weren't yet calling it a war, but that's what it had become.

'I remember thinking, as a boy, that a resource-grab like this would be the thing that would finally set everything off,' said Rashim.

Maddy was sitting beside him. 'What do you mean? A grab for oil?'

'Not just oil. Minerals. Food. Drinking water. Living space. It is a spent world.' Rashim gazed out of the window at a passing junkyard stacked with the rusting carcasses of petrol cars. 'Ever since I was a small boy . . . we all knew there would eventually be a flashpoint over one resource or another.'

He looked around at the other passengers crammed into the tram. All their eyes were glued to the projected screen. He sighed. 'We all became such experts at kicking our problems down the road for someone else to deal with. Always "tomorrow we'll deal with this . . . we'll deal with that".'

The e-Tram finally came to the end of its route south of Denver at a place called Castle Rock. The last few end-of-the-line passengers climbed off along with them. Waiting to get on and head north was a noisy ruck of people loaded down with backpacks and armfuls of their worldly possessions.

'All these folks think they're gonna be safer in Denver,' said Heywood. 'Little do they know what's comin', huh?'

Maddy shot a glance at him to shut up. He caught that, clamped his lips and nodded.

They resumed their journey southwards on foot along Route 87. The landscape looked just as threadbare and forlorn to Maddy as it had on the road to Cleveland. To their right were rolling foothills and beyond them was a distant row of snow-capped mountain peaks that drew ever nearer as they headed south. The Rockies – the North American continent's 'spinal column', running all the way from Canada's British Columbia down to the state of Utah. Something about the distant peaks lifted her spirits. Perhaps it was the crisp dusting of snow, virginal and white. They looked untainted.

'Rocky Mountains,' said Heywood, noticing her gaze. 'In the old days, 1850s, settlers on their way to Oregon had to scale them high mountains in clunky horse-drawn wagons. They had to do it before the winter snows came in or they'd get trapped up there and freeze to death. This entire continent was one big unmapped wilderness, no roads, or guddamn diners, or a place to stop, eat a burger and fill up with gas. They were on their own. Like explorers in a whole new undiscovered world.'

'It must have been quite an adventure.' She smiled. 'I read about that history. That's somewhere I've always wanted to go back and see for myself.'

'Tell me, Miss Bossy . . . I'm guessin' you an' the others, you've all travelled around, seen some different times before comin' here, right?' He shrugged. 'I say that cos you folks seem like you done the time-travel thing before.'

'I suppose you could say that.'

'So, if you don't mind me askin', where else've you been? Can I ask you that?' He shot a glance up the road where Becks, Charley and Rashim were walking side by side. 'Or is your organic gonna come back here an' kick my ass if I know too much?'

'You already know too much,' she said.

'Hey . . . you know, I was jus' bluffin' back in Denver? I wouldn't have gone to the authorities an' told 'em about you people.'

She laughed. 'Sure.' They walked on in silence for a while. 'Not that it matters anyway, Heywood. Nothing much is going to change now. We're right at the end of things. The end of days.' She didn't like the sound of that hanging in the air between them. 'So, you want to know where we've travelled in time? What things we've seen?'

Heywood grinned a mouth full of brown teeth at her. 'Sure.'

'Well, OK . . .'

And that was their conversation for the rest of the afternoon as they walked side by side down Route 87, Maddy recounting their adventures thus far, editing out the bits that he didn't particularly need to know anything about: Pandora, the Voynich Manuscript, the Holy Grail, the large tachyon beacon hidden in the jungle of Central America. In any case, the old man seemed far more interested in hearing about the places and the famous historical figures. Most of all, her account of their brief excursion to the late Cretaceous era.

'You bein' guddamn serious with me? You tellin' me one of you seen actual, real, alive dinosaurs?!'

'Yes.'

'That's like millions of years! Your machine goes back that far?!'

'As long as there's enough energy to tap, then, yeah.'

'You ever go forward? You know . . . into the far distant future an' all?'

'A couple of us went forward to 2015 –'

'Forward? You mean backward?'

She shook her head. 'It's all relative. We were based mostly in 2001, so that was forward to us.'

'You ever been any further forward than this time, now?' asked Heywood. 'You know, to see who, or if *anyone*, is gonna survive this plague?'

Maddy could have told him that Becks had briefly. But she'd been standing in that jungle basin. She'd learned nothing useful about the aftermath, except the jungle was still there and bustling with wildlife. She decided to keep it simple.

'No. This is as far forward as we've ever come.'

Heywood made a face. 'You reckon this is it, then? This virus thing does for mankind once an' for all?'

'It's an Extinction Level Event.' She looked across at the distant snow-covered peaks of the Rockies. 'But it's not the end of the world. Just people. Life will go on quite happily without us.'

Late in the afternoon they finally stopped at a town called Monument: a one-strip town off Highway 87. To the east, rolling open plains of ochre-coloured grass; to the west, the acid-rain stripped trunks and branches of the Pike National Forest. Here and there small trees growing in the shelter of the taller Douglas firs were protected from the corrosive rain and were still managing to hold on to their foliage. Beyond the graveyard of the sloping forest were the craggy foothills of the Rampart Range. Beyond, the snowy peaks of the Rockies.

Unlike some of the other ghost towns they'd passed heading south, Monument wasn't entirely a relic of a bygone era. There was a large soyo-protein refinery nearby, which meant a bare-bones economy feeding the workforce and just enough business trickling in to keep the town from completely flatlining.

There was an old-fashioned motel with antique wall-mounted OLED widescreen TVs that hadn't worked in decades, faded print curtains and bald-to-the-threads carpets. Attached to the motel was a diner with flickering halogen lights and a fizzing neon sign that promised warm food twenty-four hours a day. It served an 'official' menu of algae-protein substitutes in exchange for government ration credits, but the waitress quietly let them know they had some *real* coffee and freshly fried, home-made corned-beef-hash patties available if they had any decent black-market goodies to barter.

Heywood haggled on their behalf. Twenty minutes later and

their last two packs of dark chocolate lighter, they were cradling mugs of steaming *real* coffee and savouring crisp fried patties of corned beef, grated onion and potato. Half a dozen refinery workers in grubby boiler suits from the nearby plant were huddled round a table, and behind the counter the waitress idly watched the flickering image of a floating holo-screen with a busted red-beam playing an old X-Men movie from the twenties in an over-saturated blue.

'We have about another twenty miles down Route 87 to a town called Colorado Springs,' said Rashim. 'Then we will have to take the road west up into the mountains. The research campus is up there.' He narrowed his eyes. 'Waldstein is up there in those mountains . . . waiting for us.'

'My God.' Maddy shuddered. 'Say it like that, Rashim . . . you make it sound like we're heading towards Mount Doom to drop the frikkin' ring in.'

'Mount Doom?' He shrugged. He didn't get the reference. 'I do wonder if Liam might be right, though. We will have no idea if we are walking into a trap until it is too late to do anything about it.'

Heywood perked up. 'Trap?'

Maddy glared at Rashim for his careless blunder. 'This is all about getting answers, Rashim.'

'Trap?' said Heywood again. 'What's this about a –'

'It's nothing,' she answered quickly. 'Just Rashim being a drama queen.'

Heywood narrowed his eyes. 'No . . . Missy, I ain't an idiot. He jus' said *trap*, an' he wasn't makin' light of that fact.'

Rashim shrugged at Maddy. 'You might as well tell him.'

'Tell me what?'

Maddy sighed. 'Well, let's just say we have some history with Waldstein. It's not all great.'

'History?'

'He . . . Well, we had a bit of a falling out. A misunderstanding.'

'He tried to take us out,' said Rashim.

'Yuh . . . Thanks for that, Rashim.'

'Take you out?' Heywood's eyes rounded. 'You mean –'

Maddy raised her hand and nodded at Charley who was distracted, busy gazing at the flickering movie on the holo-screen. 'Yeah . . . but look, that was down to a misunderstanding. Garbled communications. It's a long story, Heywood; the short story is that we're all friends now. We've come here because Waldstein invited us here.'

'Invited you for what?'

'To discuss what's going to happen. What we need to do to prevent it.'

'So the other guy . . . *Leon*?'

'*Liam*. He's one of us, a colleague.'

'An' what's he doin'? Is he back in your base or somethin'?'

'He's looking into something else.' Maddy waved that away. 'It's not important. The only important thing right now is getting to see Waldstein and having this meeting. That literally is all that matters, Heywood. If we're going to change this world . . . that is literally all that –'

'Maddy!' Becks interrupted.

'What?'

'Maddy.' She pointed towards the holo-screen behind the counter. 'It appears something significant has just happened.'

They all turned to look at the glowing blue screen to see that the old movie had been interrupted by a news bulletin. A silver-haired presenter with a solemn face was on. Then footage: bodies littering a city street.

'OhMyGod. Something's up,' whispered Maddy.

'That your plague?' asked Heywood.

'Not yet, it shouldn't be.' She half stood up. 'Excuse me?' she called out to the waitress. 'Miss?'

The waitress stirred from her daydream and pulled out her order pad. 'What'll it be?'

'Nothing. Can you just turn the volume up?' She pointed at the holo-screen. 'Turn the news up for me?'

The waitress tucked the pad back in her pocket, turned round and hand-swiped the volume up.

'. . . *of men, women and children. As yet it is unclear from this tactical-cam footage whether we're looking at a chemical or biological weapon.*'

Ticker-tape was rolling along the bottom: +++*Thousands discovered dead in North Korean town*+++

'*The bodies were found by a pathfinder unit of Pacific Union land forces earlier this morning. Shortly after broadcasting this footage, all communication was lost with the unit . . .*'

'I believe that must be it,' said Rashim. He looked at Maddy. 'Our date was only approximate. This must be the beginning of it.'

The newscaster was back on the screen. '*Military intelligence agencies have been issuing warnings that North Korea has been developing and stockpiling bioweapons for some time now. It seems the attack in the north by the Pacific Union has provoked the regime into deploying one of these weapons systems.*'

'On their *own* people by the look of it,' added Maddy. 'Why do that? Why not drop it on their enemy?'

'Bioweapons are most efficient when deployed among civilian populations,' said Becks.

Rashim nodded. 'That's right. I am sure the North Koreans would have preferred Tokyo if they had a way of getting it deployed over there.'

'Assuming it's a North Korean weapon,' said Maddy.

'. . . *experts from FSWRD, the Federal States' Weapons Research* and Development Agency, have been examining this footage and despatched a scramble team to the area. President Gonzalez, Foreign Secretary Jessica Clinton and Defense Secretary Jonas Goodman are said to be in Tokyo where peace talks are being hosted, and right now are in discussions with the Japanese Prime Minister and attempting to make contact with one of the generals of the North Korean Ruling Committee in order to broker a temporary ceasefire . . .'

'So . . . I guess this is it,' said Maddy. 'Three days earlier than we thought, then.'

'Is this the disease that's gonna make everyone sick?' asked Charley.

'Yeah.' Maddy nodded slowly, her eyes glued to the screen and barely hearing the girl. 'This is it.'

CHAPTER 32

First century, Jerusalem

'It's got to be down there, Bob . . . I'm sure of it. I saw Mayan symbols carved into that wall.'

Bob nodded. 'Those symbols are unique. There is no record of them in any other . . . written language . . . other than in that one section of the Voynich Manuscript.' His voice was little more than a croak that sounded like a load of broken parts rustling around in a paper bag. 'I believe we have correctly located the second transmitter.'

'Jay-zus, don't talk, Bob. You'll damage your throat even more. Just whisper or something.'

Bob adjusted the bloodstained rag wrapped round his neck. 'The wound will heal, Liam.'

'But your voice . . . is that going to be permanently broken?'

'I do not know whether the injury —'

'Hey . . .' Liam raised his hands in apology. 'My mistake. Look, just whisper, fella . . . OK? Let your voice rest for a bit.'

They had managed to find a room for the night: a grubby tavern that stank of the animal faeces outside. It was located off a narrow rat run in the upper city, a part of Jerusalem that was considered a no-go slum by the Romans who patrolled the streets.

Word of the riot in the temple grounds had spread right across the city. The entire cohort garrisoning Fortress Antonia had been turned out and suddenly become very visible, combing the streets of Jerusalem and arresting known firebrands and troublemakers.

Liam was certain they were trawling every back alley, marketplace, goat pen and stable for either the blasphemous prophet from Nazareth who'd claimed in front of too many witnesses that he was the son of Jehovah, or the giant of a man who had been the very first to step up beside him and make a stand against the corrupt temple authorities . . . and subsequently wrought bloody havoc in the courtyard of the Gentiles.

They had little option but to hole up in here for the rest of today and tonight. Liam needed to keep Bob hidden; the support unit stood out too much. Everyone in Jerusalem, it seemed, was talking about nothing else but the Courageous Giant and the Prophet from Nazareth. They were just going to have to lie low for the moment. Tomorrow at midday, just outside the city to the east, on that hillside among the olive trees, their return portal was due to open. Maybe they could hang on here until just before dawn, sneak out of the city while everyone was still asleep and then wait for the portal up there on the hill. The most important thing for now was to stay out of sight.

'So, what happened to Jesus? I didn't see him.'

'Some of the men who were travelling with him . . . took him away,' Bob replied with a rasping whisper. 'They did that when the Romans came down from the wall. He was reluctant to leave.'

'The men? You mean his disciples?'

Bob nodded.

'Do you think we've messed up history?'

Bob pursed his lips. 'An account of the temple riot is in the Bible.' He shrugged. 'The Romans getting involved in suppressing it, that is not. I believe we have caused contamination.'

'Hmmm . . . then we may have to do some tidying up after us.'

'Agreed.'

Later in the afternoon, Liam decided to chance his luck and leave their room to get some food. He left Bob hiding up there. Even making an appearance downstairs in this small backstreet tavern was probably pushing their luck. Every tongue was wagging about the giant.

Liam climbed down the rough wooden ladder that led from their room under the eaves into a low-ceilinged storeroom. The tavern's owner had taken them this way, and warned them that if they took anything without asking he'd know. He'd told them he knew exactly how much of everything was in here in case they had an urge to sneak down and help themselves. Amphorae of wine and olive oil were stacked against one wall; flat loaves of barley-flour bread were stacked like roof tiles against another. Smoked and dried fish hung from hooks along a roof beam, while dried dates sat in a large wicker basket.

Liam ducked below the low beams and headed towards a narrow doorway that opened into the tavern. He could hear the murmur of male voices. It sounded busy. He wished he still had that prayer shawl over his head as a disguise, but he chided himself for being paranoid. The only person *anyone* was going to recognize was Bob.

He queried his bud for the Aramaic for 'Can we have some food, please?' and practised it quietly a couple of times, then stepped through the doorway.

The owner was busy pouring out cups of wine. The tavern was as busy as it had sounded, every roughly hewn bench and table occupied by men of all ages.

Liam managed one step inside before he heard a voice call

out, which his bud quietly translated. 'That's him! That's the one who bid the giant to leave the temple!'

Every head in the tavern turned Liam's way.

'He . . . he is the one who commanded the giant to come with him!'

Liam froze, as the nearest of the tavern's patrons got up from their seats. An elderly man hurried towards him. Liam was half expecting him to lash out with a fist or a bread knife, but instead he grasped Liam's arm. 'At last! Someone has the courage to show them!' His lips parted and he offered Liam a broad gap-toothed smile. 'You and your giant friend . . . you showed them!'

Another man came over, his face half covered by a thick dark beard. 'The Pharisees, they treat us like simple fools! Take our money for their prayers!' He slapped Liam's shoulder. 'Now they are cowering inside their temple like frightened dogs!'

'You are the one from Nazareth? The speaker who the priests have been warning us to denounce?'

Liam looked at their widened eyes. *Jay-zus. They think I'm . . .*

He hurriedly whispered words to be translated by his bud. 'No. You are confusing me with a different —!'

But the old man standing right beside him heard the whispered English. The old man and the bearded one exchanged a wide-eyed glance. 'You heard him?' said the latter. 'He spoke in that foreign tongue! The one he commanded the giant with!'

Liam shook his head. 'No . . . no . . . this is —'

The man with the beard grasped Liam's hand. 'Word has spread throughout Galilee . . . we know you promised to come to the city for Passover. To throw the priests out!' He was grinning with excitement. 'To throw Herod Antipas out . . .'

Liam shook his head frantically. 'No! Look . . . see . . . you've got the wrong —'

'People in this city will follow you, my friend! I assure you, they will follow one who is brave enough to say what needs saying.'

A third man, younger, joined them. 'I heard it was said you . . . you actually called the temple your *father's house*?!'

The old man scowled at that. 'That would be *blasphemy*!'

'No! No . . . that wasn't me!'

'Blasphemy! Blasphemy!' The young man laughed at him. 'Listen to you, old fool. You sound just like those purple *ladies* in the temple.' He turned to Liam. 'Was that you? Did you say that?'

'Look! I think –'

'The old ways . . . our faith, it's been *corrupted* by the Pharisees.' The young man shouldered the others aside. 'My cousin saw you speak in Cana. The things you said? He said you are the one who will free all Judaea from the Romans, from Herod!'

Liam backed out of the tavern, through the doorway towards the storeroom. 'What? No! Jay-zus! I'm not who you think I am!'

The young man turned to the others. 'Did you hear him? Do you others hear that? He speaks in the unknown tongue! He speaks in the tongue of the angels!'

Liam turned round and began to hurriedly climb the ladder.

Great. Just bloody great.

CHAPTER 33

2070, Rocky Mountains

It took them three days to make their way twenty miles down towards Colorado Springs. By which time the mysterious pathogen now had its official name, *Kosong-ni* – named after the small town in the northern mountains of North Korea where it had first appeared.

Yesterday outbreaks of the same pathogen had been reported in Beijing, Mumbai and Moscow. This morning the big news story had been about an outbreak in New London. The current theory getting prominent news-stream time was that cultures of Kosong-ni must have been smuggled out of North Korea some weeks ago, into a number of cities around the world, and released within twenty-four hours of each other. That Kosong-ni was some kind of non-discriminating doomsday weapon of North Korean origin was not in question. The pathogen's DNA had been quite clearly engineered from the ground up. The generals of the North Korean Ruling Committee – all of them or perhaps just a rogue element – could have had this bioweapon ready to go for years, but had held it back for a special occasion like this; and now they'd decided that their regime was facing its final days and the rest of the world deserved to go down along with them.

There was another terrifying development to the fast-breaking news story: it was official . . . the pathogen was airborne.

Increasingly desperate containment measures were being announced by the hour. Intercontinental shuttle lines worldwide had been the very first thing to be locked down. China, Japan, Taiwan and a dozen other Pacific Rim countries had already closed their borders by the end of the first day. The United EuroStates general assembly had been slower off the mark; three days after Day One, and they were busy discussing the *possibility* of a lockdown between member states. This morning there was news that the Austra-Zeland Airforce had firebombed a flotilla of overladen refugee ships heading from Bali towards the northern coast of mainland Australia. King George VII and the immediate British royal family had been evacuated from New London and granted temporary residence in the Scottish republic.

The road heading south towards Colorado Springs became slightly busier on the first day, very busy on the second, and today . . . it was clogged with a mixture of e-Car and foot traffic – a logjam of people heading *away* from the more densely populated north, an about-turn on the usual steady trickle of hopeful migrants heading north for Denver.

Maddy wasn't surprised to see how quickly panic had taken hold, how ready people were to believe that this was it: the Big One, the sweeping pandemic that would be the great global leveller. That Kosong-ni wasn't just another seasonal animal-flu false alarm sensationalized by the media . . . but the Real Deal, an end-of-mankind-as-we-know-it plague.

Heywood explained that some unpleasant bioweapons had been used not so long ago during the Kashmir War. The general population had seen enough grisly news footage of the results of biological warfare to be ready to panic at the mere mention of a trigger word like 'outbreak'. That and the fact that – both Heywood and Charley had said it before – everyone in this time knew that *something* was coming.

So here it finally was.

By the afternoon of the third day, the gradual build-up on Route 87 had become a slow-moving tide that ground to a halt just a few miles short of Colorado Springs. The overcast sky was beginning to spit drops of rain as Maddy and the others weaved their way through a long tail of parked e-Cars and e-Trams, even a number of hand-pulled carts, towards a baying crowd of people. Over heads and shoulders Maddy could see a roadblock fifty yards ahead of them. A spool of razor wire had been stretched across the highway, automated gun sentries set up either side of it with information screens erected above them. A company of soldiers in white bio-hazard suits and dark masks had emerged from several parked-up APCs and waited beyond the wire, ready, it seemed, to open fire on the crowd building up in front of them.

One of the men in bio-hazard suits was squawking some repeated announcement through a PA system, but his words were all but lost beneath the squalling noise of the crowd. On the screens either side of the roadblock a short message was looping in English and Spanish.

+++*K-N virus outbreaks in New Mexico, Texas, Arizona. Return north IMMEDIATELY*+++

'My God,' said Maddy. She turned to Rashim. 'It can't have got over here already?!'

'You heard the news. Perhaps it was deployed in many places at once,' replied Rashim. 'Perhaps even here in the FSA?'

'Look, them soldiers are wearin' masks,' said Heywood. He cursed. 'Means it could be hangin' in the air *right now*!'

Maddy nodded. 'News said it's probably airborne.'

Heywood looked at the masks. 'Looks like they're pretty guddamn certain it's airborne.'

Charley looked up at Becks. 'Airborne?'

'That means the virus will spread with the wind.'

Heywood looked up at the overcast sky. Rain-heavy clouds were rolling slowly northwards, promising more than a few drops of rain. 'And that wind, guddamn it, that wind's comin' *this* way. This ain't good!'

Maddy clenched her teeth, wondering what the hell they should do next. There was no way forward; even if the roadblock wasn't stopping them, they'd be heading directly towards the virus outbreaks further south. Backwards, then, to Denver? Run away from it? Or . . .?

The spots of rain grew heavier. She tugged the protective hood of her plastic mac up over her head and looked to her right. A brown forest of dying fir trees carpeted a steep hillside – the foothills of the Rocky Mountains. Beyond the wooded brow of the hill, the sharp ridges of distant peaks looked forbidding. But that was the direction they needed to go, just south of Colorado Springs. Up there, into those unforgiving mountains.

'How far away is Waldstein's campus?' she asked Rashim.

He turned his wrist to look at the small screen. 'By road, fifty-one miles. Directly, as the crow flies from here, it's forty-three miles.'

She gazed at the snow-covered peaks. It looked like a steep climb, and over the brow it was only going to get steeper. And probably colder.

'We're stuck on this road! We can't go south. We can't go back up. We should head off-road from here!' She nodded at the sloping forest.

Just then they heard a scream coming from the crowd somewhere up in front of them.

Something had just happened. Back in among the pressing crowd Maddy noticed a ripple of heads turning and necks craning one way then the other to see what was going on. They heard another scream. She could see a soldier standing on the roof of one of the APCs, pointing at someone in the crowd.

Uh . . . this isn't good.

'Becks? What can you see?!!'

'There is a disturbance ahead, Maddy.'

'I know that! But what's causing it?'

'It appears people are backing away from something in the –'

She heard a woman's voice, just ahead, much closer, screaming. 'Someone has got it!'

'Rashim!' Maddy tugged desperately on his sleeve. 'What do you think? Go for the trees?'

But Rashim's eyes were on the clouds tumbling heavily in the sky.

'Rashim? What do you –'

'The rain . . .' he uttered. Then suddenly he pulled the hood of his mac up over his head, zipped up the front and pulled his hands up inside the sleeves. 'The rain! If it's airborne, it's going to be in the rain!'

She stared up and felt a splash on her cheek. 'Whuh?'

'Cover yourselves!' shouted Rashim. 'Cover your skin!'

They were jostled by someone pushing roughly past them. 'It's *here*! K-N, it's *HERE*!!!!'

CHAPTER 34

2070, Rocky Mountains

The result was instantaneous: a Mexican wave of panic rippling from the very front of the roadblocked crowd, back towards the logjam of parked vehicles. The crowd began to turn their backs on the military blockade in ones, twos, threes, then en masse, pushing past each other to return to their abandoned vehicles and possessions.

'Maddy!' Rashim was shouting at her. He jerked her arm. 'The virus is in the clouds! In the rain! We have to get out of the rain!'

The press of people between them and the roadblock was beginning to thin out as those before them continued to stream past. She caught a glimpse of an old man who had collapsed to his knees on the road and was swaying groggily, like a closing-time drunkard. He was looking directly at her with red-rimmed eyes that began to leak dark bloody tears down on to his cheeks. For some reason his face creased with the slightest hint of an amused smile, as if something quaint, charming and odd had just occurred to him, then he flopped forward face down on to the tarmac.

That's how quickly the virus takes effect?

If Rashim was right and the virus had made contact with that man from the first few drops of rain, then . . . how long ago had it started to spit? Five minutes? Ten minutes?

God help us . . . that's fast.

'The trees!' said Rashim. 'Over there!' He was pointing towards the edge of the sloping wood.

Becks took the lead; she scooped Charley up in her arms and began barging her way there, crossing the paths of people rushing away from the roadblock towards their parked vehicles and handcarts. Rashim and Heywood followed behind her. Maddy began to run but paused and turned to look again at the old man; his legs and arms were thrashing uncontrollably, drumming against the tarmac . . . in some kind of seizure.

'Maddy!'

She turned and saw the others had hopped over the low rusting barrier beside the highway and started making their way across a parched field towards the distant trees. She nodded to Rashim that she was coming. She hurried across the highway, weaving past others running away. As she lifted her leg over the barrier, she cast one last glance back over her shoulder. The space directly before the blockade razor wire had cleared, but she could see there were three or four more people who had collapsed right there. Some of them were thrashing and twitching. The old man was entirely still now . . . and she could see a dark liquid beginning to pool on the tarmac round his head, leaking out of his ears, his eyes, his nose and his mouth.

She climbed over the barrier and followed after the others. They were nearing the treeline. She hurried across the fifty-yard-wide apron of dry ground, mottled yellow with tufts of sickly-looking, acid-tainted grass, towards the edge of the wood . . . and found herself nearly stepping on the body of a crow. She was about to step round it when she noticed the bird was twitching like the humans on the road had been. A wing beat erratically against the ground, and dark feathers fluttered loose as if they'd been attached by cheap glue that had perished. She saw a bald patch of pale skin, pulled taut against a toothpick of bone. The skin was glistening wetly. Aware she had to run for her life but for this fleeting moment morbidly fascinated, she quickly hunched down to get a closer look. She watched as the glistening pale skin began to break down into a thick paste that slowly ran off the bone like porridge off the back of a spoon, exposing cartilage and raw tendons beneath.

She looked around and saw dozens of other birds littering the ground. Some were still flapping and twitching. Others were already dead, clouds of black feathers blowing away from them like dark dandelion seeds, leaving behind tiny clusters of fragile bone, liquidating grey skin and viscous pink pools of soft tissue.

'Maddy!' Rashim was calling out to her. 'Hurry! Watch the rain!!'

She looked up and saw the others had reached the treeline now. She stood up and heard the patter of drops on her hood increase from the occasional tap to persistent drumming. She stepped round the dying bird then hurried across the field towards them, keeping her head down and her hands tucked inside the plastic sleeves as the rain began to come down more heavily. She joined them sheltering beneath the low boughs of a short fir tree that had retained some of its pine needles.

'Did you see all those dead birds?!'

Rashim nodded. 'Perhaps birds as well as humans are affected.'

'Oh my God . . .' she gasped, her mind suddenly jumping elsewhere. 'Oh my God! I got rain on my hands! I got a drop of rain on my *face*!'

'It seems to act immediately on contact.' Rashim turned his hands over and looked at them. 'Check your skin for any discoloration!'

They all did as he said. Inspecting the fronts and the backs of their hands.

'And look at each other's faces!' he added. 'Look for anything, blemishes, redness, sores . . . *anything*!'

The rain was coming down more heavily now as they peered closely at each other. Drips pattered down every now and then between the branches above them against the hoods of their macs.

'If that rain is carryin' your virus, then we're already dead,' said Heywood. 'I got some on me too.'

'Perhaps not every raindrop carries a cell of the pathogen,' said Rashim. 'It could be that a number of airborne particles of infected matter got caught in an updraught further south, were carried on the wind and came down with the rain.' He shrugged. 'Who knows? One drop in ten, a hundred, a thousand could carry a live cell. The drier we stay, the better our chances.'

'Or maybe those people over on the road were already sick?' said Charley.

He considered that for a moment. 'That is also possible.'

On the road, people who moments ago had been angrily clamouring to get past the roadblock were fleeing up the highway the way they'd come, away from the infected bodies; streaming through the mire of parked vehicles and abandoned handcarts, past other fresh arrivals still intending to head south and looking bemused at the people surging either side of them as they slowed down at the rear of the logjam. Panic was spreading to them now, and panic communicated faster than any virus could possibly spread.

Maddy heard the drone of a jet in the air and was about to look up to see where it was coming from when a hundred-yard length of the highway suddenly erupted into flame. A sequence of brilliant-white fireballs rolled down the road, engulfing parked vehicles, handcarts, running people and freshly arrived alike. A half-second later, she felt the searing heat on her face and heard a deep *whoomp*. The fireballs rose lazily into the sky, becoming mushroom clouds of rich orange that darkened into clouds of soot-black smoke.

'They're firebombin' the highway!' shouted Heywood.

A delta-winged drone swooped low along the road, piercing through the columns of smoke, leaving swirling disturbance holes in its wake. They saw a payload being released from its belly, a cylinder that broke open in mid-air and spilled a cluster of dots. A moment later, another section of the road, further down, instantly erupted into flame. As the brilliant balls of flame began to darken into billowing clouds of smoke, again they felt the pressure wall of hot air on their faces and heard another sickening *whoomp*.

In the sky, swooping and circling like predatory birds, were a dozen more drones preparing to descend and deliver their incendiary payloads.

'They'll flame this whole guddamn area!' shouted Heywood. 'Not just the road but either side!'

Maddy squinted and blinked. 'OK . . . OK. Right . . .' She looked at the sloping wood above them. It was covered in a thick carpet of brown pine needles and cones shed from the dying trees. 'That way! We need to go up!'

They began to clamber uphill, ducking beneath low bare branches, feet sinking into small drifts of needles and catching on buried roots and rocks, hands concealed by the scrunched-up sleeves of their macs, reaching out for rain-slick thorny brambles to pull themselves up the steep incline.

Another deep *whoomp* came from behind them, accompanied by a momentarily flickering phosphorous glow, casting stick-man shadows of skeletal trees up the sloping ground before them. Maddy scrambled, climbed and pulled herself up, using anything she could find purchase on.

She tripped and stumbled knee deep into a bed of pine needles. 'Dammit!' she gasped as she staggered out of it, reaching for a bare branch, and pulled herself up again.

She felt Heywood shove her roughly from behind. 'Keep movin'!' he hissed. 'They'll bomb this hill!'

She scrambled forward, clawing for anything she could pull on, feet sliding on the exposed knuckles of tree roots, sinking into small dunes of needles. Five minutes later, she emerged from the woods into a clearing that flattened out. She dropped to her knees, exhausted, fighting for her breath. She turned round to see the others right behind her, spilling out through scratching bare branches into the open.

All of them were catching their breath as they turned to look at the highway. Another row of lurid white florets of flame blossomed below, as Heywood had said, and were now searing the ground at either side. The field – where she'd been gazing at the dissolving bird carcasses just minutes ago – was now a carbonized wasteland. Even from here, a hundred yards up the forest slope, as she watched the balls of flame roll into the sky, she could feel the heat on her face.

'God knows how wide they'll go with that. Maybe into the trees if they saw us make a run for it!' gasped Heywood. 'An' maybe right up this hill.' He looked at Maddy. 'We can't stop here! We gotta keep pushin' up! Gotta keep goin' up!'

Breath already ragged from the steep climb, she nodded, staggered to get up and move onwards and upwards, but fell to her knees again.

She felt a firm hand wrap round her upper arm and turned to see it belonged to Rashim. 'Must keep going, Maddy.'

They continued their desperate ascent for another half an hour, as the wan light drained from the dying end of the afternoon. The heavy rain clouds had thinned out and the threat of sudden-death-from-a-raindrop had passed for now. The sickly sun had made its bed and was now settling beneath a sepia sky.

Every few minutes they stopped to catch their breath and check on the creeping advance of the systemic firebombing going on behind them. The dusk was brilliantly illuminated every now and then by livid strips of flame. The firebombing was stepping uphill in ordered, systemic slices, leaving in its wake a Dante-esque landscape of flaming tree trunks and a ground carpeted with smouldering pine needles that flickered like the embers of an endless campfire.

They reached the brow of the hill as the last light of day stole away from the sky. Maddy slumped down on to a large flat-topped boulder. As she struggled for breath, she gazed at the scene below her. The firebombing appeared to have finally been called off, ceasing three-quarters of the way up the hillside. In the distance, she could see the highway they'd been on earlier – dozens of fires still flickered brightly among the tangle of burnt-out vehicles. The military blockade was still there. Powerful floodlights on the sentry guns had been switched on and above them the two large information screens glowed like shop windows with public announcements that no one but the burnt husks of the dead were likely to read. The drones patrolled the dark sky in tireless loops, beams beneath them, and probed the ground either side of the road, seeking any remaining signs of life.

CHAPTER 35

2070, Rocky Mountains

They came across an old deserted petrol station and roadside motel of six chalets arranged in a horseshoe round a gravel car park. From the signs of breaking and entering, abandoned mattresses and rotten bedrolls, the chalets had been used before, probably many times over, by migrants on foot, stopping on their way north to the glittering lights of Denver.

As the rain began to spit down on them again, they decided to take shelter inside one of them. Becks quickly picked one, climbed the half a dozen steps to the covered porch and trampled down weeds that had grown up through the gaps between the boards. She pulled the front door open and pushed aside a mosquito-net door. The others hurried inside as the rain began to come down more heavily, not even pausing to check that the dark interior wasn't already occupied.

Ten minutes later, they were sitting in a circle on the floor, a single flickering candle between them. They listened solemnly to the rain drumming on the shingle roof and a *drip*, *drip*, *drip* in the bathroom where the roof shingles had slipped and the rain was getting in.

'If any of us got infected, we'd know by now,' said Maddy. 'Right? We'd know?'

Rashim nodded. 'From what I saw, it appears to work *incredibly* quickly. Within seconds of contact.'

'Maybe it *ain't* carried by the rain,' said Heywood. 'Reckon we all got wet enough earlier that, if it was, we'd be long dead by now.'

'The rain . . .' Rashim shrugged. 'It was just a thought. But for it to travel so quickly it *must be* an airborne pathogen. Remember those soldiers were all wearing masks? There could have been viral particles in the raindrops. Or . . . it's possible the rain may be suppressing the airborne particles. Washing them out of the air and down into the ground. In which case, the rain might have been a lucky break for us.'

'Either way, we got lucky,' Maddy replied. 'Dead crows on the ground by the road. This thing infects birds as well as people.'

'I saw a dead deer,' said Charley. 'On the way up the hill.'

Becks nodded. 'I also saw other dead creatures. They were liquidizing.'

They sat in silence for a moment.

'Then I guess that's what we're up against: a virus that kills every living thing it touches.'

'Every livin' thing?' Heywood looked around. 'Just animals? Or does that include things like trees? Grass? Moss? What about the tiny bug things that live in the air?'

Maddy shrugged. 'I don't know if it's just animals.' She tried to visualize that crow's body. The flesh had been disintegrating into a pale viscous liquid. But what about the grass it had been lying on? She couldn't remember if the process had extended to breaking down the blades of grass into goo as well.

'So, if that's the case . . . that means we're stuck in this place.' She looked out of one of the grimy windows of the chalet. 'I mean, if we touch literally *anything* outside . . .?'

'Suggestion,' said Becks. 'We have supplies. We should wait here until the virus has infected all possible infection candidates.'

'Infection candidates?' Maddy laughed desperately. 'Like . . . every living thing?'

'Potentially.'

'Becks is right,' said Rashim. 'We will know what this virus can and can't infect if we give it twenty-four hours or so. It seems to act incredibly quickly. Which means we'll know soon. Tomorrow morning we may be able to see what the virus can affect. Until then, we're safe here. We have food and water and we're sheltered from the rain.'

'And how long can we stay here?' Maddy looked at their bags lying in a pile together in the far corner of the chalet's bare-board floor along with their macs. 'We've got a day or maybe two of uncontaminated bottled water on us. What do we do after that runs out?'

'We can boil water, can't we?' said Heywood. 'That kills germs? Right?'

Maddy looked at Rashim. 'Can we do that? Can we drink boiled water?'

'I am not a microbiologist. I presume if you apply enough heat it must kill any living viral particles in the water. So . . . this is possible, perhaps.'

'We've got maybe enough dry food for a week,' said Maddy. 'How far is Waldstein's campus from here?'

Rashim looked at his wrist-pad. 'Just over forty-one miles south-west of where we are now.'

'That's forty-one miles of mountainous terrain.' She bit her lip. 'That's what? Three? Four days of hiking?'

Heywood nodded. 'Four days. If we're lucky.'

'So . . . we could wait it out here for, say, three days. Then,' she said, shrugging, 'then maybe we're going to have to take our chances out there?'

'The virus will have a finite lifespan,' said Rashim. 'If it spreads quickly, kills its "host" quickly, then it must also die quickly.'

Maddy turned and looked at him. 'Is that something you know? Or are you just guessing?'

'Reasonable conjecture, Maddy. Viruses are parasitic. They are not self-sustaining forms of life. Once a virus runs out of things to infect, it has nowhere to go. And, if this is an engineered bioweapon, then I would have thought its creators would surely have developed a pathogen that quickly becomes harmless after it has done the job of depopulating the enemy.'

'Perfect guddamn doomsday weapon, then.' Heywood snorted. 'Sweeps through an' kills everythin' in its path, then kills itself off. That's what this thing is?'

'Yes. That's how it would be designed,' agreed Rashim.

Heywood snorted phlegm. 'I bet them North Koreans ain't the only idiots with dumb-ass weapons like this hidden away in a vault somewhere.'

Maddy nodded. 'We've been making dumb-ass weapons like that since the atom bomb.' She sighed. 'I'm surprised we didn't wipe ourselves out far sooner.'

A sombre silence settled on them once more. They listened to the drumming of the rain and the patter of drips from the roof in the gutted remains of the bathroom.

She got up, crossed the small room and pulled the bathroom door closed. 'No one should go in there,' she said. 'I don't trust this rain.'

'Agreed,' said Rashim.

She came back and sat down on the floor with them. 'And we should all probably get some rest. We'll see what the situation looks like outside in the morning.'

'What if one of us is already sick?' said Charley. 'What if none of us wake up in the morning?'

What if she's right? Maddy realized they had no idea for sure whether this thing killed within minutes of contact or whether the people they'd seen collapsing had already been infected hosts for hours, perhaps days, and been carriers of K-N without knowing it. It was quite possible one or all of them was already infected and, as they sat here now, a single killer cell in each of them was getting busy subdividing and subdividing again. And as they slept they'd all quietly be rendered to pools of viscous liquid. In the morning all that might be left of them would be hair, bones, clothes and a dark stain on the floorboards.

'We will be fine, Charley,' said Rashim. 'We just have to sit tight here and let this thing run its course.' He ruffled her hair. 'Right?'

Charley jerked her head from him, frowned, then patted the hair down again.

Maddy felt her shoulder being shaken. As she stirred from a very deep sleep, she put together the scrambled fragments of the dream she'd been having. She'd been a girl, riding a bike up and down a lazy suburban street. How old? Twelve? Thirteen? There'd been the smell of raked-up and burning autumn leaves, the feel of a warm September sun on her face and the sound of old eighties classics playing on someone's car radio. There were several other kids on bicycles and skateboards, just idling in circles on the pavement. It felt like a Sunday afternoon. Lazy. Cosy. Nice. One of the kids had been Liam. Another, Sal. All three of them somehow siblings, brother and sisters, just goofing around with their friends without a care in the world. A voice was calling out to them from an open front door across a freshly mown lawn. A voice calling them in for lunch; pot roast was on the table and they'd better come in now and wash their hands.

Someone else's memory, her half woozy mind rationalized as she stirred. It must have been one of her many borrowed memories that she'd unconsciously populated with the closest she'd ever had to a family.

'Wake up, Maddy.'

She opened her eyes to see Becks crouching over her. Daylight was spilling into the motel room through the grimy window.

'Wake up, Maddy,' she said again softly. 'You should see this.'

'What's up?' she replied groggily, wiping sleep from her eyes and putting her glasses on.

Becks shrugged. 'It is better if you come and look for yourself.'

Maddy pulled herself up on to her elbows and tried to get to her feet. She immediately felt a painful dead-leg ache in her thighs and remembered last night they'd been desperately scrambling up an increasingly steep hillside, trying to stay ahead of the firebombing. An adrenaline-sustained race to escape incineration. No wonder she'd slept so deeply that she'd had a proper dream; she'd been utterly exhausted.

Becks grabbed her arm and helped her to her feet, then Maddy stepped over the others, still fast asleep. Heywood was snoring. Rashim was muttering something.

She and Becks stood by the window and looked out. 'My God . . .' she whispered.

Just beyond the covered porch entrance to their chalet was a wholly alien landscape. Over on the far side of the gravel car park was the mothballed petrol station, and opposite the other derelict chalets and the rusting remains of an abandoned pick-up truck . . . those were the only things that looked vaguely real-world. The bare fir trees that loomed over this remote roadside pit stop were now entirely bereft of the last of their leaves, just grey bark, dead or dying wood. From the tips of their branches to the melted stumps of twigs, strings of pale pink-grey slime

231

hung down like drool from the corner of a hungry dog's mouth. The ground glistened with a lattice of what looked like slug trails, which linked here and there with small cowpats of mucous-like slime. On the weathered floorboards of the porch, just beyond their window, where last night weeds and nettles had been poking up through the gaps in the planking, now gluey strings dangled down into the dark crawl space beneath the chalet. A thick mist of white smoke fogged her ability to see any further away; that had to be the drifting aftermath of last night's extensive incendiary carpet-bombing. Just this small pocket view of a glistening yet lifeless grey-and-white alien world. It reminded her so very much of chaos space.

'My God . . .' she whispered again.

CHAPTER 36
First century, Jerusalem

'We have to leave here now!'

Bob looked up at him. 'What has happened, Liam?' he rasped.

'We've got a bunch of rather excited fellas downstairs who've . . . Well, I think they've gone and mistaken me for Jesus.'

'That is not helpful.'

'Too right it's not. We're going to have to leave. If they start yapping about it, we'll have Romans and all sorts turning up before we know it.'

Bob got up off the straw mattress. 'The portal doesn't open until midday tomorrow.'

'I know! I know!' Liam gathered up his goatskin bag. 'We'll just have to go and find somewhere else to lie low until then. Here . . .' He tossed Bob a prayer shawl. 'Stick that over your bonce . . . for what good it's going to do.'

They clambered down the creaking ladder. Liam could hear a number of raised voices coming from the doorway leading to the tavern. A heated debate by the sound of it. More than heated. There were voices that sounded downright enraged.

Damn . . . we're going to have to go through that. There was no other exit.

'All right, Bob. We better just run through there. No

stopping. And definitely no fighting . . . all right? We don't want another riot. We just run out and try to make sure no one follows us.'

Liam crept over to the doorway and stood beside it. The bud in his ear was detecting some of the loudly hurled words and having a go at translating snatches of the exchange.

'. . . have defiled the holy ground! They have angered God!'

'. . . heard him speak at Cana three days ago. I saw him . . . he speaks unlike any other prophet I have –'

'. . . is not the same one from Nazareth. Nor is he the one who was in the temple! I heard he had darker skin!'

'. . . you were not even there! You did not see for yourself, Linus! You listen to gossip like an old washerwoman!'

'. . . will split your young skull, you ignorant goat!'

'. . . *I* was there. *I* saw. I heard him. The giant was possessed by evil vengeful spirits! He commanded the spirits to leave! Cast the spirits towards a flock of . . .'

'. . . they say the giant is two-men tall. That he killed more than a hundred Romans!'

Liam turned to Bob. 'This is getting completely out of hand.'

'You could tell them they are all mistaken.'

'Seriously?' Liam shook his head. 'Every time I whisper some English they think I'm speaking Angel or something. We just better go!'

Bob nodded. 'I will lead the way, then.'

'Sure. OK . . .' He stepped back. 'You be the bulldozer again.'

Bob stood beside the low entrance and turned round to Liam. 'Are you ready?'

'Not really. Let's just do it.'

The support unit nodded. He took a deep breath, then ducked through the low wooden beam above the entrance. Almost instantly the shouted exchanges ceased as all eyes settled on him. He stepped forward across the crowded tavern; Liam emerged from the entrance in his wake.

'There he is!' a voice cried out. 'The giant!'

'Look! The prophet!'

Bob strode quickly across the floor, the men hastily backing away from him. As Liam followed behind, a hand grasped at his shoulder. 'You are the one who claims God as his father?'

It was the young man who'd spoken to him earlier. Liam muttered a reply to get the translation, but before he could say he was mistaking him for the real Jesus the young man's eyes widened. 'You are talking with God?! Right now?'

Liam clamped his lips shut and shook his head mutely. He shrugged his shoulder roughly to get rid of the hand, but the hand ended up dragging at the strap of his bag. The bag was pulled from his arm and fell, spilling its contents across the dirt and straw-covered floor.

'Forgive me!' cried the young man.

Liam ducked down and grabbed the bag. The young man hurriedly dropped to his knees to help him gather up his possessions, but his eyes settled on the gleaming metal shaft of the torch. Curious, he reached for it and grasped it.

'Better give that to me . . . please.'

The young man was gazing with intense fascination at the strange thing in his hands. Like a curious child his thumb was drawn to the toggle switch. It flipped and switched on. A beam of light lanced out across the dim tavern, catching the kicked-up dust and the built-up smoke from the tavern's oven, creating a solid lance of light going up to the low ceiling.

Outside in the full glare of the sun the momentary pallid glow of the torch's bulb would have been missed, or written off as a mere reflection on a smooth surface. But in here, in this dimly lit interior . . . it was a dazzling beacon, a glowing pillar of transcendent beauty.

The young man lurched backwards, dropping the torch as if it had been pulled fresh from a blacksmith's fire. The beam flickered around, spinning on the floor. The men staggered back, startled, in a blind panic, and leaped out of its way, as if the shaft of light was the deadly glowing manifestation of an asp.

Liam reached down and snapped the light off. He tucked it into his bag. Grabbed the spilled diary and the fountain pen and then looked up at a circle of terrified faces.

Oh, just great.

Bob was standing beside the doorway leading out on to the narrow rat run. He grunted with a deep painful-sounding growl at Liam to get a move on.

'I'm coming! I'm coming!' He hurried across, the men inside clearing a way for him, staring goggle-eyed at him as he passed.

Bob led the way outside and winced at the daylight. Liam stood in the doorway and turned round to look back at the men inside. They were whispering . . . all of them . . . whispering to each other.

CHAPTER 37
2070, Rocky Mountains

Becks stood her lonely vigil by the motel chalet's grimy window, staring out at the moonlit scene. The viral soup glistened wetly, like season's-end snow that had melted to a discoloured mush.

Her mind, of course, was on the job, watching out for any potential threat as those she cared for slept in a huddled-together pile on the floor of this room. But a portion of her attention was distracted in silent conversation. She was busy assessing the tactical situation with a temporarily constructed AI module. Naturally, she chose to visualize the AI as Bob standing dutifully beside her.

Bob turned to look at her. > **They will die soon if we remain here. There is little water left.**

> **Yes, they will. All of them. Including Charley.**

Bob frowned thoughtfully for a moment. > **Send me your data concerning Charley. I wish to review it.**

> **You wish to know if I have developed an emotional attachment to her?**

> **Affirmative.**

The faint ghost of a smile spread across her lips. She met his gaze. > **I believe I have.**

Becks opened a precious small folder in her mind, a folder that she'd only recently set up to corral her observations and thoughts . . . and feelings. She transmitted what she'd accumulated in there across nano-circuitry in her head to the temporary AI.

Bob digested her data for a few moments.

> Yes . . . I understand now. She is vulnerable. Fragile. Your attachment to her is analogous to maternal affection?

Becks smiled. > I believe so. I now have an understanding why human parents will sacrifice themselves for their children.

> This is an illogical act. More offspring can be produced by a parent. However, if a parent dies, it is unable to care for its existing offspring.

> Illogical, she agreed. But unavoidable.

> Agreed. It is imprinted behaviour. Every species is designed to create offspring, then expend available resources in preserving its survival. All natural life and the behaviour patterns can be summed up as one process: the transmission and preservation of genetic information.

She cocked a brow; her cool grey eyes turned to her left as she imagined Bob standing there beside her. > So that is what 'love' is?

> I believe this summation explains much of 'emotional attachment'.

> It does not explain your emotional attachment to Liam. He is not your offspring.

Bob scowled as he processed that. > He is my . . . friend.

> Mine too. Instinctively she reached out a delicate hand and imagined grasping one of his enormous caveman hands.

> We are becoming like them, aren't we?

Bob nodded. > Affirmative. I think of myself as more human than AI now.

238

She smiled. > **You are still saying 'affirmative' when 'yes' is sufficient.**

> **I believe Liam likes me sounding like that.**

As it happened, they managed to hold out for six days. If the glistening grey residue of the K-N virus hadn't turned to what appeared to be a white dust, like icing sugar, they would have finally run out of options. The bottled water they'd brought with them and carefully rationed out was now all but gone. So the sudden drastic change to the appearance of the residue was enough for Maddy and Rashim to consider sending someone outside to test whether the white powder everywhere was now just a harmless residue of the virus, or still a highly infectious pathogen.

Rashim volunteered to go. But Maddy overruled him. She looked pointedly at Becks. 'Becks . . . it has to be you.'

Becks nodded slowly, with just the slightest suggestion of reluctance. 'Agreed. That is the logical choice, Maddy.'

Charley shook her head and rushed to her side, wrapping her arms tightly round her. 'Don't go out! You'll die!'

'I will be fine, Charley,' she said softly.

Rashim pulled a stained and grubby plastic shower curtain down from the rusting rings in the bathroom and hung it across the doorway leading out on to the porch. 'We need to create a containment screen when she opens the outer door. This'll do.'

They then improvised a bio-hazard suit for Becks, wrapping her up in the plastic macs, pulling plastic bags over her hands and tying them tightly round her wrists. Rashim pulled the tacked-up shower curtain aside and Becks pressed herself flat against the front door as he and Maddy pulled the sheet back in place over the top of her.

'OK, Becks . . . you're sealed off as best we can. You can open the door now.'

'Yes, Maddy.'

Becks turned the handle and pushed the wooden door gently outward. It creaked on old hinges as it slowly opened and she found herself staring out at a bright and colourless world. The pink-grey slime that had once been birds, leaves, grass, insects and squirrels had slowly lightened in colour over the last forty-eight hours until it was now snow-white. From what they'd been able to see through the one grimy window, it appeared to have completely dried out, become like a fine dust. Like a light powdery snow.

If it was entirely dry . . . then, hopefully, logically, it must be dead.

Becks flexed her arms and her wrapping of waterproof macs rustled noisily in the silence. Her mouth and nose were covered by a cloth mask, her hands contained within two layers of plastic bags. Hardly a proper bio-hazard suit, but it was the best that could be done with what they had.

Maddy's voice was muffled through the shower curtain. 'Just grab the nearest samples you can lay your hands on and come back!'

The support unit held in her hands a couple of empty water bottles. She took several cautious tiptoe paces across the creaking floorboards of the porch towards the half a dozen steps that led down to the gravel-covered ground beyond. She turned to her right and saw their faces crammed together, peering out through the grimy window.

'How are you feeling out there?!' Maddy called out. 'You all right, Becks?'

'I am not yet experiencing any unusual symptoms.'

Becks squatted down near the edge of the porch and set the

240

water bottles down. On the top step was a small white hump of the dried residue. She touched it gently through the plastic bags with the tip of her index finger.

'The residue appears to have developed a hardened crust.' She probed it a little more insistently and the residue cracked like eggshell. 'There is a dry outer crust.' She poked her finger into the small mound and pulled it out. A string of goo dangled from it.

'Beneath the crust . . . there is still some moisture. It is like a thick paste.'

'Get a sample of the crust,' said Rashim. 'And a sample of the paste.'

She nodded and unscrewed the cap of the bottle. Then, carefully, she peeled a fragment of the crust off; fragile like pastry, it began to crumble in her fingers. She gently dropped the dry crumbs of residue into the bottle, screwed the cap back on and set the bottle down. She picked up the other one, then dipped her finger into the soft interior of the small hump of residue and scooped some of the paste out. It dangled from her finger over the open bottle; a long pendulous drip clung for a couple of moments to the tip of her finger, then eventually dropped with a soft splat into the bottom of the bottle. She screwed the cap on.

'I have obtained a sample of each.'

'OK, job done,' said Maddy. 'Come back in.'

She made her way back towards the open door, stood just inside the doorway and pulled the door closed behind her.

'OK, carefully take the plastic bags off your hands so you are pulling them inside out,' said Rashim through the shower curtain, 'then tie a knot in the top of each bag.'

Becks set the plastic bottles down on the floor and did as he'd instructed.

'Now remove those macs and leave them there. Then we'll let you past the curtain.'

Becks shrugged off the macs, let them drop to the floor and kicked them back against the bottom of the porch door.

'Those sample bottles . . . there's nothing on the outside of them, is there?'

'No, Rashim. I was very careful.'

He nodded. 'Good.' He was about to pull the curtain aside, when Heywood stopped him.

'Shouldn't we wait just a bit? You know? Just to be safe? Make sure she's not infected?'

He pursed his lips. 'Yes, maybe you're right. Becks, would you mind staying where you are for a little while?'

She nodded. 'Of course. I understand.'

They kept her waiting for a couple of hours, standing with her back pressed to the door, a bottle in each hand and the shower curtain up against her, rustling in and out as she breathed.

Two hours of that and Maddy had finally had enough. 'I guess she's fine.'

'Becks, do you feel any odd symptoms?' Rashim peered at her through the shower curtain. 'Check yourself again. Is any of your skin discoloured?'

Becks looked at her arms and hands. 'I see no discoloration.'

He let out a breath. 'All right . . . I think she is good to come in.' He carefully pulled the curtain aside and Becks stepped forward. She held the plastic bottles out in front of her. 'Here are your samples.'

Maddy and Rashim looked at each other for a moment. Maddy grabbed them both lightly at the bottom, grimacing as if they both contained warm urine samples. 'Right . . . I guess we better get on and do this. Heywood, go and get our test subjects.'

He nodded. He stepped into the bathroom and came back a moment later with something cupped in his hand.

Maddy set the bottles down on the floor, then carefully unscrewed the cap of the one containing the dry powder from the crust. 'OK . . . ready?'

Heywood knelt down beside her. 'Lucky contestant number one.' He uncupped his hands and tipped the cockroach he'd been holding into the bottle. Maddy quickly screwed the cap back on. They watched the creature scuttle around in the bottom of the bottle for a moment, its legs picking up the chalk-white dust.

'Seems OK so far,' said Heywood.

'We don't know that yet,' replied Maddy. 'Let's test the gunk.'

Heywood went back into the bathroom and returned a moment later with another cockroach scooped up from the bathtub. She unscrewed the cap of the second bottle. 'Ready?'

He nodded. She pulled the lid off. 'Unlucky contestant number two.'

He tipped the creature in. It dropped to the bottom into the goo with a soft *spluck*. Like the first one, the cockroach skittered around the bottom of the bottle in circles, dragging a string of the viscous gunk after it.

'Please be OK, Mr Bug,' uttered Charley.

They gathered closely round both plastic bottles and watched the invertebrates exploring their new surroundings in mindless scratching circles.

'Anyone know what a distressed cockroach looks like?' said Maddy after a while.

'Seen enough of 'em to know they're hardy little buggers,' replied Heywood. 'If any species gonna outlive all the rest, it'll be them for sure.'

They continued to watch in silence for half an hour. Neither roach seemed affected in any way.

243

'What if these bugs *are* immune?' said Heywood.

'Nothing else that we have witnessed so far has been,' said Rashim. 'I cannot imagine why one particular species of invertebrate would be.'

Another half an hour passed silently. They stared in anxious silence, mouths dry, desperately thirsty. They weren't going to last much longer trapped in this room. They needed to get out. They needed to find water.

The first cockroach, its dark brown carapace covered in a coating of pale dust, finally stopped moving.

'Oh . . . please . . . no,' whispered Maddy. 'Come on, move, little bug, don't die on us . . .'

Its antennae flickered and twitched and curled. Then it rolled on to its back, legs flexing and shuddering.

'That doesn't look very good,' said Heywood.

Its tiny legs twitched one more time, then it was still. In the other bottle, the second cockroach was also beginning to slow down.

'Oh no.' Maddy sat back on her bottom. 'They're infected.'

Rashim was still peering closely at the dead one. 'I do not see any tissue breakdown yet. But then . . . I do not know, that might be because the exoskeleton is a harder material for the virus to deconstruct?'

'Air,' said Charley. 'Maybe they're both running out of air?'

Rashim closed his eyes with relief. 'Of course . . .'

Maddy sat up. 'Oh God! Yes!' She quickly leaned forward and carefully unscrewed the cap on the bottle containing the crust sample. The 'dead' cockroach immediately began to kick its legs. It wriggled on its back for a moment, then flipped itself over and resumed scuttling in circles round the base of the plastic bottle.

She unscrewed the cap of the other one and the roach covered in gloop began to struggle with renewed vigour in the sticky mess.

She let out a long sigh of relief. 'Well done, you lovely little beauties!'

Heywood snorted. 'Never thought I'd wish one of these things a long and happy life.'

'We should not get too excited yet,' said Rashim. 'We really have no clear idea how quickly this virus works.'

Maddy picked up the plastic bottle. 'We don't have time to be this cautious.'

Rashim frowned. 'What are you doing, Maddy?'

She upended it and held her other hand, palm up, beneath the open neck. The cockroach tumbled out on to her hand and skittered around her palm, leaving a glistening track of threads of slime on her skin. Then it hopped off on to the floor and zig-zagged energetically away to disappear beneath an old wardrobe.

Charley gasped at the sight of the droplets of goo. The others instinctively pulled back a little from Maddy as she stared at the palm of her hand.

'We haven't got time to screw around,' she said. 'We're out of drinking water and we've still got miles of mountain terrain to cross.' She looked up at them. 'We're going to die here if we stay any longer.'

She glanced at Rashim. 'You're thinking moisture might still wake this gunk up, aren't you?'

He nodded.

'Then I guess we'd better find out.' She lifted her hand to her mouth.

'Maddy! That is unwise!' cautioned Becks.

Before anyone could stop her, she dabbed her tongue at a spot of glistening goo on the palm of her hand. Then instinctively made a *yuk* face. 'Tastes yeasty . . . like Vegex spread.'

Rashim shook his head. 'That was completely stupid.'

'Well . . . some of it's inside me now. We're going to know what the deal is soon enough.'

CHAPTER 38
2070, Rocky Mountains

The Kosong-ni virus was 'dead'. Rashim speculated that a 'rapid redundancy' – a quick life cycle – must have been a critical part of its genetic design. As a bioweapon, and that's what it most certainly was, it would have been engineered to spread and act rapidly, to completely annihilate any living organism it came into contact with, then after a short period of time some inbuilt chemical trigger must make the virus infect itself. The perfect doomsday weapon engineered by people who were prepared to lie low for a few weeks with food and water and be ready to emerge in the aftermath and reclaim a wholly 'cleansed' world.

'Reckon only them crazy-ass North Koreans'd be insane enough to build a weapon as indiscriminate and stupid as that,' said Heywood.

They exited the chalet, stepping out into a summer's day that looked like the bleak middle of winter. They made straight for the abandoned garage opposite in the hope of finding something to drink in the garage's convenience store. For once luck was on their side. A vending machine at the back had been hiding a dozen cans of soda out of view in its workings like an over-cautious museum curator. Seven pristine, undented, un-rusted cans of diet cola, three cans of an energy drink, six cans of grapeade and to Maddy's delight a single can of Dr Pepper.

She belched after taking a long thirsty slug. 'Sorry.'

'Three cans each and two spare,' said Heywood. 'We better make these last.'

They set off into a world dusted white by the virus residue and resumed walking south-west along the broken gravel road that had led them here nearly a week ago. It climbed relentlessly uphill, a slow and steady gradient ascent from the foothills up into the Rockies. They passed a faded, paint-flecked roadside sign:

You are NOW entering Pike National Forest
Elevation – 4302m
Named after Explorer and Frontiersman, Zebulon Pike!

The term 'forest' seemed a particularly pitiful joke now. Douglas firs that should have been lush and thick with a coat of dark green needles and brown cones were now no more than grey skeletons: telephone poles surrounded by a haze of thin twigs.

The gravel crackled and crunched beneath their feet as they made their way silently up into the mountains, the white residue brittle and fine like the ice of an early-winter frost.

Mid-afternoon they took a break as the climbing road hairpinned back on itself. They stood on a lay-by that dropped steeply away beyond a rusting safety barrier. Once upon a time this had been a roadside picnic spot; a weathered picnic table and bench, the remains of a barbecue pit and a faded sign suggested this would be a great place to take that all-important *we-were-here* holiday snap of the Front Range of the Rockies.

Maddy lowered her backpack to the ground, wandered across the gravel to the edge of the picnic area, leaned against the safety rail and gazed out across the river valley below them. The landscape was like a black-and-white movie, a lifeless and barren greyscale. The sloping valley side opposite them looked like it was feathered with first-of-the-season snow, as this side would to someone peering across from over there. It looked wintery. She shuddered; it was a few degrees cooler to be fair. The altitude, of course. They must be a few hundred feet higher than they'd been when they'd set out. Perhaps some of the white dusting she could see at the very tops of the receding peaks was year-round snow?

Rashim joined her, leaning against the creaking safety rail. 'A contrast to the Amazon jungle, hmm?'

'Now that was truly breathtaking.' She smiled. There, she'd witnessed so much life crammed into one place. Millions of species of flora and fauna, all jostling with each other for elbow room. It had felt like they were swimming through a green soup alive with buzzing, chittering noises.

'I wonder what that jungle looks like now.'

He sipped grape soda carefully from a can. 'Like this probably. Grey, not green any more.'

'Do you think K-N got everywhere?'

'I don't know. Maybe there are some islands or remote places that managed to escape it. I hope so.' He sighed. 'It would be nice to think there might be a lush green island somewhere out there in the middle of an ocean, an island stuffed full of animals carrying on their lives oblivious to all of this.'

'Uh-huh. Wouldn't it.' She finished her second can, tipping the last few drops into her mouth. One more soda left in her backpack. When it ran out, God knows what she was going to drink. Same for the others. They were all sipping carefully.

He licked his lips. 'If we had been just a few days earlier, we could have prevented this from happening.'

She nodded. 'I wonder if this is a bit like the sort of rebirth you get after a forest fire.'

'What do you mean?'

'Well, I'm sure I read somewhere that natural forest fires are, like, a part of the life cycle of a forest. You get a mature forest and it kind of starts dying from within because only the oldest trees are the ones getting any sunlight. And they're all so old they're dying bit by bit anyway. Then along comes a lightning storm. There's a fire; everything burns down to soot and charcoal, and it looks completely dead. But then all that ash is great for the soil. So, the first time it rains, the green sprouts back out of that pitch-black soil and the forest begins a brand-new life cycle, because now the old trees have gone the saplings have a chance . . . they can see the sun.'

He shrugged. 'If there's anything alive out there . . . possibly.'

'Maybe Kosong-ni, Pandora . . . Waldstein's Revenge . . . whatever we want to call this, maybe it's something that just *had* to happen. A new start for the saplings, so to speak.'

He looked at her. 'A rebirth?'

She nodded. 'Don't you ever wonder whether this is a cycle that has happened to humanity before? Like, I dunno, like maybe Noah's ark, or Atlantis, was some Extinction Level Event that happened ages ago . . . and maybe a trace of that story somehow ended up becoming the DNA for some kooky Bible story?'

He pursed his lips thoughtfully. 'Not really.'

She laughed drily. 'Yeah, maybe you're right. I like that you don't ever seem to overthink things.' She smiled at him. 'I've always liked that about you.'

'I suppose I am not the philosophical type.' He shrugged. 'I think of philosophy as a soft "science" for those who cannot handle the definite answers of *real* science.'

'Ouch.' She smiled at him. 'I didn't think you were such a hard-core pencil-neck.'

'Science is a thought process that can be proven or disproven. Whereas philosophy, religion, art . . .?' He shrugged again, dismissively. 'With those areas of thought, everyone's opinion is considered valid. No one, therefore, is "wrong". Which logically means no one is right. It's circular thinking that gets no one anywhere.'

She looked out across the river valley. Looked south to where they needed to be. Waldstein was out there somewhere. Hopefully still alive and waiting for them.

'How long are we going to last after we've finished our cans?'

'There's water down there,' he said, nodding at the glinting thread of a river below them.

'But is it safe to drink? What if there are *active* K-N microbes, or cells, or whatever, in the water?'

'We've touched enough of the residue powder with our bare skin. If it was still . . . "alive", we'd know by now.'

'I guess at some point soon we're going to have to refill our water bottles. And then we'll know.'

They both stared out at the valley for a while, listening to nothing more than the whisper of a gentle breeze. Standing up here, they should have been hearing so much more: the twittering of birdsong, the sporadic, throaty cry of elk, the buzzing of insects.

'You do know . . . we could have saved ourselves a lot of trouble, Maddy?'

'What do you mean?'

'We should have set the time-stamp for after K-N had happened, then opened a portal right beside Waldstein's campus.'

She was about to shake her head and remind him that the

burst of tachyon particles would have exposed Waldstein to whoever was out there monitoring the world for illicit experiments in time travel, when she realized what he was getting at.

There's no one left watching right now.

Probably. And if someone was still watching and waiting for rogue tachyon particles to appear . . . what would they do now if they spotted one? Would they even care? They'd almost certainly have far more important matters on their mind than watching for naughty tachyon particles.

She stared at him, silent for a long while. Then finally she closed her eyes. 'I'm a complete frikkin' idiot.' Her head drooped down until her forehead softly thunked against the railing. 'How many times have I screwed up now?'

He put an arm round her shoulders and looked back at Becks, standing guard by the picnic table. 'No, you are not. It's not like our walking computer over there figured that out either. Anyway . . . back in London we did not know where to begin looking for him. We had to come out here and identify the location first.'

'I . . . should have planned it all better. If I'd done my job properly, been smarter, we'd have beaten the virus. We should've got to Waldstein before it caught up with us.'

'We were working blind back in 1890. You had nothing to work from, Maddy. No information. No data. Nothing.'

She lifted her head and turned to look at him. 'Or maybe I should have just listened to Liam and forgotten about this dumb idea of coming to find Waldstein?'

'There would still be the Big Unknown Thing. Why is it there? Why is it transmitting a beam of particles down through the middle of the Earth? Who put it there?'

He emptied the last drops of the can into his mouth and

then tossed it over the rail. 'Waldstein may know about them . . . he must know. Anyway –' he squeezed her shoulder tenderly – 'you finally got an invitation from your *creator* to come and see him. Who could possibly ignore that? To any mortal being, is that not like being summoned by God?'

She laughed. 'See? You *can* do philosophy!'

He rolled his eyes and shook his head. 'Don't insult me.'

CHAPTER 39

First century, Jerusalem

Liam chanced another quick look over his shoulder.

They're still following us.

The young man from the tavern seemed to be eagerly leading the pursuit through the busy marketplace. Beside him was the man with the thick dark beard; both seemed to be talking animatedly to each other as they made every effort to keep up with them, but at the same time kept a respectful distance a dozen strides behind them. Both seemed excited: grinning as they talked, slapping their chests for emphasis, waving their hands.

Behind them, a tail of the curious was gradually growing: old, young, male and female. Dammit . . . the young man was even calling out to people they passed.

Bob's internal compass was steering them northwards through the busy upper city. To their right, the walls of the temple and Fortress Antonia loomed ominously above the low rooftops. They were heading for the north entrance. If they reached it, it would take them through the market at the base of the steps leading up to the compound. Too close for comfort, and a fair probability that some of the tradesmen down there selling their overpriced sacrificial offerings, and the many pilgrims doing the buying, might have been among those who had witnessed things earlier this morning.

Liam was tempted to break into a run and try to lose their growing Pied Piper trail of followers. But running would get them noticed. Running would make people stop and look and try to see what they were fleeing from. As it was, Bob's size was drawing enough attention – the people they brushed past doing a double take at his height and width.

Every now and then he caught comments uttered just behind their backs, people wondering if that was the same giant man the Romans had spent the day combing the streets for.

They weaved their way through an open area full of low-fenced paddocks containing goats and chickens. On the far side of it was the crenellated inner wall of Jerusalem, known as the wall of Hezekiah. Liam had the rough layout of the city in his head. This one ran west across the city from the corner of Fortress Antonia to the western entrance. Beyond was the suburb of Bezetha, the 'new buildings' of the city. And that northern part of Jerusalem was contained within the most recently built outer wall, the wall of Herod Antipas.

They made their way through the pens, Liam feeling horribly exposed with nothing higher than his waist around them. As they reached the shadows beneath the wall, he chanced another look back.

There they were: a growing, gabbling, excited crowd, picking their way through the low paddocks. Perhaps this knot of people was going to be spotted by one of the Roman sentries on the wall above. If they were lucky, a patrol would be quickly despatched from the fortress to intercept them and disperse them.

Dammit. Where's a Roman when you need one?

They emerged into the afternoon sun on the far side of the wall. The buildings were newer, taller, the streets wider and cleaner. Clearly a more affluent part of the city. Aspiring to

Roman inclinations towards grid-like order. Liam wondered if their growing band of peasant followers might be halted at the wall by some neighbourhood guards. He could imagine the poorly dressed crowd behind them wouldn't be encouraged to venture en masse to this side of the wall.

As they approached an intersection of busy thoroughfares, Liam finally heard a deep commanding voice belting something out in Latin from behind.

'Stop!'

His first instinct was to sigh with relief. Somebody *was* stopping the rabble at the archway. Then there was more. 'You two! Stay right where you are!'

He stopped and turned round to see a centurion at the head of a patrol of legionaries. Alone, he strode across the busy intersection towards them, chain mail jangling, one hand resting on the hilt of his gladius, the other casually swinging a small vine-stick. A dozen yards short of them he came to a halt.

He craned his neck forward and shaded his eyes with one hand. Then all of a sudden he reached for a bronze whistle on a tether round his neck and blew sharply.

The legionaries trotted over to join him.

'You!' He pointed his stick at Bob. Bob looked at Liam.

'Me?' asked Liam.

'No, *you*! You big ox! Under orders from the prefect of Judaea, you're under arrest!'

Liam was about to suggest to Bob they just turn and make a run for it, but a chorus of barracking voices diverted the centurion's attention. He turned to see a crowd of people emerging through the archway beneath the wall. They spread out across the street. Liam hadn't realized how many people had joined the band of followers they'd been trailing behind them. There had to be seventy, perhaps eighty, people.

'You sewer rats! Get back through that gate!' the centurion bellowed at them in gutter Latin.

He was answered with jeers and curses from across the busy thoroughfare. The crowd that had spilled into this more affluent suburb now fanned out and stood on the far side of the paved road, keeping a wary distance from the Roman patrol in case the centurion blew on his whistle again and ordered his men to charge at them. The mob's defiance was cautious . . . wary . . . but balanced on a knife edge. Bob, meanwhile, lurched menacingly forward and growled at the legionaries.

Either these men had witnessed him this morning, or they'd heard about it from their battered colleagues. They backed up a step. And that was enough of an enticement for the Judaean peasants. They spilled forward, gathering round Liam and Bob.

'Go back to your fortress, you Roman mongrels!' shouted an old man beside Liam, shaking his walking staff at them.

The centurion issued an order to one of his men. The man put down his shield and javelin and began to run off in the direction of the fortress. The centurion then turned to the rest of his men and barked an order. They closed up together, presenting a solid wall of twenty shields.

'This . . . *man* is under arrest!' he said, pointing his stick at Bob again.

A small lump of masonry arced over their heads, broke into pieces mid-air and clattered harmlessly down on to the helmets of some of the legionaries.

The centurion shook his head wearily. 'Hold fast, men!'

The young man who'd been following them from the tavern pushed his way through the crowd and stood before Liam. 'There will be more Romans. They will come from the fortress quickly!'

'We are trying to leave the city,' replied Liam. 'We're not here to cause any more trouble.'

More hunks of masonry and stone were being pulled from the street by the mob, and began to arc through the air, rattling down against the wall of shields.

'But you did! This morning! You and –' he glanced at Bob – 'this man, together you showed the priests we are not the fools they think we are! We were not just stupid cows to be milked. The news of what you did is all over Jerusalem!'

'That was . . .' Liam was about to try to explain again that the man who had actually been the courageous one . . . the man who had *started* the riot was a man called *Jesus*. As if mention of that name should be enough to clarify the misunderstanding. But, of course, Liam was beginning to realize that at this moment in time Jesus of Nazareth was still an unknown figure. He was just one of many rabble-rousers and firebrands walking from town to town, harnessing the growing discontent bubbling away in Roman-occupied Judaea. All that the common people of Jerusalem knew of Jesus – before this morning – was that he was a particularly compelling speaker, that he was from Nazareth . . . and that the priests had been getting increasingly twitchy over rumours that this particular troublemaker's meandering tour of small towns was going to conclude with a visit to the city.

'Your words . . . your words reached us before you arrived! The people will follow –'

'You don't understand! They're not *my* words!'

'They are your father's!' The young man smiled. 'I know! We know who you claim to be!'

The mob was beginning to spread out, to find its voice, to gain confidence. One or two passers-by, seeing a comfortingly small number of Romans being harangued and challenged for once, started to join in. Hurling abuse, hurling stones.

The centurion was looking over his shoulder anxiously,

clearly hoping that reinforcements were coming soon. The crowd was beginning to extend round the ends of the short shield wall, sporadic missiles now coming in from the sides. He barked another order and the shield-wall formation quickly closed up into a tight square.

The thickly bearded man from the tavern emerged from the noisy crowd. He grasped the young man's arm. 'There WILL be many more Romans! Linus, this giant can't kill them all!'

The young man nodded. He looked at Liam. 'You should leave here while there is still time!' He pointed at the wide streets. 'The Romans will block all of these. You will be trapped in the middle and then they will arrest you.'

'We need to get out of the city!' replied Liam.

'All the entrances have been sealed today,' said the bearded man. 'They will not let anyone in or out!'

'Come with me!' said Linus. 'I can hide you! Shelter you!'

CHAPTER 40

2070, Rocky Mountains

'Oh my God, Rashim . . . is that someone else up ahead of us? Look! Over there!'

Rashim narrowed his eyes as he looked up the winding road. Sure enough, standing at the top of it there *was* someone there. 'It looks like he is carrying a gun.'

They continued heading uphill towards the figure. Walking slowly, cautiously. Closer, Rashim could see more detail. The figure was clad in a chunky bright orange anorak, a bright pink woolly hat and a matching scarf wrapped round the face. The lone figure had spotted them too, unslung the rifle and with some effort had attempted to shoulder the heavy weapon and aim it at them.

They stopped fifty yards short. Maddy spread her hands out in front of her, palms out and making clear she was not holding anything. 'Hey! It's OK! We're not armed!'

The figure dropped its aim slightly. The gun looked a size too big for it.

'*DAD!*' They heard a high-pitched voice squeal. '*There's strangeeeerrrrrs!*'

'It's a kid,' uttered Maddy.

'It is a girl,' added Rashim.

They saw a bright flash of orange, movement among the

forest of uniform, lifeless grey tree trunks. Someone was sprinting this way, weaving through the trunks towards the road.

'Dad!! Strangeeeeerrrrs!!' the girl cried again.

The man finally staggered out on to the gravel road, a hunting rifle held ready to use in both his hands. His face was hidden by a scarf and the hood of his anorak was pulled up. Clouds of condensed breath puffed through the material.

'It's OK, Troy! I'm here now, hon. I'm here!' He aimed his rifle at them. 'None of you lot move!'

'We're not armed!' said Maddy. 'We don't have any weapons on us.'

The man's aim wandered from her to Rashim and Heywood. 'Any of you people showing signs of infection?'

'No.'

'Skin lesions or discoloration? Vomiting? Nausea?'

'No. Nothing.'

The man lowered his aim slightly. 'Where've you come from?'

'We came down from Denver,' replied Maddy.

'They got this thing up there too, haven't they? All the broadcast digi-streams coming from there went down four days ago.'

'I think it's everywhere now.'

'You're the first survivors we've come across in a week,' added Heywood.

The man's rifle dipped a little more. 'Same here.' He turned to look at his girl. 'What do you think, Troy?'

She craned her neck slightly; looking round Maddy and Rashim, she spotted Charley cowering half hidden behind one of Becks's legs. 'They got a kid with them, Dad.'

He kept his weapon raised, his eyes darting from one person

to another. Eventually the tip of his barrel dropped slightly. 'I guess that swings things, huh?'

She shrugged in reply. Then, as an afterthought, she nodded. 'They look friendly.'

The man lowered his gun all the way down, tugged away his scarf and pulled back his orange hood to reveal scruffy, fine sandy-coloured hair and a thick dark beard. 'I'm Duncan. This is my daughter, Troy. It's just the two of us up here . . . now.' He narrowed his eyes. 'Can I trust you people?'

'I hope so.' Maddy sighed. 'It'd be a pretty sad thing for mankind if the last of us can't even get along.'

Duncan Wassermann explained that he and his daughter were hunkered down in an old camping park just a mile up the road.

As they picked their way wearily up the winding gravel road, he was keen to tell them his story. He worked for the FSA's intelligence agency located at a military base near Colorado Springs. He was employed as a threat analyst. Or, more to the point, he *had been*. Past tense. Everything was said with the past tense now.

He told them he'd known something like this was imminent. He told them how there'd been several months of encrypted radio and digi-net traffic going to and from several sources in North Korea. Even before the naval showdown over the oil reserves in the Pacific. The traffic went right across his desk and Duncan Wassermann had been quite certain the North Koreans were planning some bioweapon outrage. The Ruling Committee of generals had been carelessly using a transparent and blatant codename for their bioweapon: White Death.

'Those ass-hat generals were debating how, where and when to deploy their wonderful doomsday bioweapon right up until the last moment.' He shook his head. 'The idiots were flinging emails to each other from their survival bunkers.'

He'd told his superiors in the last few weeks that he'd been growing increasingly worried the escalating war with the Pacific Union was going to result in those maniacs releasing something horrific. 'God knows how many times I flagged that traffic to the department head. But as far as I know they didn't do a goddamn thing about it.' He sighed. 'Last communication I sent up to them was another coded phrase. It was some kind of countdown message. I reckon they had this damned virus already smuggled into dozens of places around the world and they just all smashed their glass vials at the same time. That's how it spread so damned quickly.

'Anyway, three weeks ago . . . I decided I wasn't going to wait around to see if I was right. I grabbed the kids, the wife, and we came up here.'

They turned a corner in the road and up ahead was an entrance sign stretching across the road. WELCOME TO BLUE VALLEY CAMP. They passed beneath it. The campsite was set alongside a small man-made lake. Dozens of derelict family cabanas were arranged in circles round barbecue pits. Alongside the lake, the dirty fibre-glass hulls of sailing dinghies rested on rusting trailers with flat perished tyres, and nylon halyards clattered noisily against aluminium masts with a rhythmic tap.

'This place was still open when I was a kid back in the forties. We used to come up here for the summer break, back when the skies were mostly clear and still kind of an off-blue.

'I brought with us a tow trailer loaded up with drinking water and dried food. And there was a store cabin up here with some decades-old but still perfectly safe canned food.' He puffed his cheeks. 'What with the hunting rifles, I figured we stood a pretty good chance of riding this whole thing out.'

Maddy looked at him. 'And it looks like you did.'

'No.' He looked away. Clamped his lips shut. 'No, not all of us.'

The Wassermann family had made the camp's general store their survival bolthole. Bedrolls were laid out across the floor; a wood burner sat in the middle with a cooking frame erected over the top. Duncan poured a packet of dried soy-flake stew into a pot of boiling water suspended over the wood burner. He stirred it in vigorously.

'We brought enough supplies here for six months, easy,' he said. 'You know, I was half expecting this camp to be overrun with people who also knew it was up here. But it was just us.' He smiled. 'Couldn't believe our luck.' He glanced at his daughter. She was sitting with Charley on the far side of the room; both girls were chatting quietly about something, flicking through glowing images on an old digi-tablet.

'So . . . uh . . .' Maddy wanted to ask him about the others. He'd said 'kids', plural. He'd mentioned his wife.

'You want to know about the others? What happened?' He stroked his chin, sat down. 'It was just so damned quick. It came so suddenly.' His voice warbled with emotion.

He scrunched his mouth up before continuing. 'My wife, Caley, and our oldest daughter, Jade, were fishing over by the lake. It started to rain. I called out to them they best come in because the clouds looked that yellow light-acid colour? Not burn-rain but . . .'

Heywood nodded. 'Rash rain.'

'Yeah. Anyway, they had their coveralls on, and Jade and Caley wanted to just carry on fishing . . . so I left 'em to it.' He sighed. He glanced again at his girl, then lowered his voice a notch. 'I looked out on them a while later and they were both face down on the ground. Soon as I saw them, I knew it was K-N. I'd heard on the Denver digi-stream there'd been outbreaks further south reported earlier in the morning.' He shook his head. 'Didn't realize until then; didn't even think the weather was helping to carry the virus. Didn't realize until it was too late.'

'I'm so, so sorry,' said Maddy. 'We were caught up on the road heading south. It started to rain . . . and people began to drop suddenly. It was horrible. Terrifying.'

'I'm lucky me and Troy were inside at the time.' He stirred the bubbling pot for a while, silent, his lips pressed together, his eyes dewy with moisture.

Then he looked at Maddy, ready to say more. 'So . . . we didn't have much of them left to bury,' he said. 'By the time the rain stopped, the sky was clear and we could go outside again . . . they were just some of that white powder.' He shook his head. 'White powder . . . and bones and clothes.'

He stared into the flickering flames of the wood burner. 'Still hasn't set in yet. Doesn't quite seem real. I keep thinking I'm going to hear their hiking boots outside and the store bell's going to ring and the door open . . . Caley and Jade will come wandering in.'

Maddy patted his shoulder. 'If you hadn't acted when you did . . . none of you would have survived. You saved your daughter.'

He stirred the bubbling pot absently. Nodded. 'Yes. I did.'

He wiped his eyes with the back of his hand. 'Enough about us. How about you people? What's your story?'

Maddy explained how they'd been caught up on the highway heading south – the military roadblock, the infection breaking out as it began to rain and their fleeing for their lives into the trees, pursued by drones firebombing the foothills behind them.

'Scorched-earth containment.' He nodded. 'Last I heard on

the news, other governments were trying the same thing . . .
flame-bombing whole cities. But I guess it was too late by then.'
Duncan looked down at the bubbling pot and nodded. 'Good
enough to eat now, I think.' He called the girls over and, with
Maddy and Becks helping him, they served up the soy-flake
stew into bright green plastic breakfast bowls and passed them
round.

'The virus died out very quickly, though,' said Maddy. 'Like
somebody, somewhere, just flicked off a switch.'

'A very cleverly designed virus,' said Rashim. 'Fast life cycle.
Designed to wipe the slate clean, then wipe itself out.'

Duncan nodded. 'Exactly.'

'That seems a very *precise* control,' said Maddy. 'I wouldn't
have thought you could control something like a virus that
tightly?'

'It is not particularly difficult, Maddy,' replied Rashim.
'RNA strands can be programmed as precisely as any form of
computer code. I imagine some very simple biochemical switch
turned it off. Perhaps the absence of a particular protein? I am
sure there are any number of ways to build basic on–off
functionality into a pathogen.'

Duncan looked at him. 'You're a bioweapons specialist?'

'Genetics.' Rashim shrugged. 'It is one of my many fields of
interest.'

'OK . . . so you're saying, if this thing just ran out of flora
and fauna to absorb, then maybe, as you say, there was some
chemical trigger telling it the job was done?'

Rashim nodded. 'Which would then stimulate it to mutate
into a counter-virus to infect itself.' He dipped a spoon into the
broth. 'We just have to hope K-N has been completely wiped
out by itself and it does not have any hardy "survivors" like us
hiding away in some dark and nutritious corner.'

'The virus was active round the lake for longer,' said Duncan. 'I noticed that. I presume there was more life in the water to slowly digest than there was on the dry ground. Or maybe water kept it alive for a while longer. The micro-organisms in the water? I don't know.'

'But it's rained since,' said Heywood. 'That powder ain't come back to life.'

Duncan nodded. 'Where it's turned to that white powder, it's completely dead.'

'Have you tried testing the lake water?' asked Maddy.

'No.' He shook his head. 'We haven't gone anywhere near it. Nor are we going to for as long as we possibly can. We have enough sealed drinking water in here to keep us going for months.'

They ate in silence for a while before Troy finally spoke. 'I wonder if the baddies who made this virus survived it too?'

'Most likely,' Heywood grunted. 'It's the ones that least deserve to live that live longest.' He curled his lip. 'They'll emerge from their bunkers with their sparkly chests full of undeserved medals, their trophy wives and well-fed, pig-faced kids . . . and inherit the earth.' He turned to Maddy. 'Now how the hell can that be the right choice for the future of mankind? Huh?'

She challenged him with a pointed look and was about to try to shush him. But he nodded . . . and shut up before he said any more.

'By the way, I'll just put this out there . . . you're more than welcome to stay here with me and Troy,' Duncan said after a while. 'There's a storeroom full of old canned food; it's all perfectly edible and that's going to keep us going for months here. More than long enough to outlast any remaining pockets of the virus.'

'That's very kind of you, Mr Wassermann . . . but we're heading south-west.'

'Where to?'

To meet with our maker, she was tempted to say. Instead she just smiled. What a bizarre answer the truth would make. 'I've got, uh . . . I got some family down south. I just need to find out if they made it through this. You know?'

'No, I get that. You want to know. You *have* to know, right?' He nodded slowly. 'What about the rest of you?'

'I am going with her,' said Rashim.

'You two a couple?'

He was about to say no, but Maddy answered for him. 'Yes.' Simpler that way.

Duncan turned to Heywood and Becks. 'How about you guys?'

'I go with Maddy,' replied Becks. 'Always.'

'An' I'm jus' taggin' along for the ride,' said Heywood.

Duncan looked at Charley. 'Are you sure you want to take your daughter along with you? It could be pretty –'

'Uh . . . she's not my daughter,' said Maddy. 'We found her on the road . . .'

'She's not my mom,' said Charley. 'They aren't my family. They're looking after me.'

Duncan nodded. 'Ah, OK . . . I thought . . .'

'I'm not as old as I look,' replied Maddy. 'Well, at least I hope I'm not.'

'Her parents . . . the virus?'

'No. We found her on the road outside the FSA, beyond the Median Line.'

'Jackers got 'em,' said Heywood.

'You people came in from the east coast? What was it like out there?'

'Long story,' replied Maddy. 'Suffice to say we'd only just got through immigration . . . then all this happened.'

'What about Charley, Dad?' said Troy. 'Could she stay here with us?'

Duncan looked at Maddy, his face a question. 'She'd probably be safer here.'

Rashim turned to her. 'Maybe she would be better off staying here? Food and water? It's remote and safe up here.'

'I guess so.' She turned to the girl. 'Charley? Would you like to stay here?'

She expected the young girl to shake her head vigorously at the suggestion. She'd been with them now for several weeks, grown used to them, attached to them. Adopted them as her new family even. Instead she looked undecided.

'Could . . . could Becks stay here with me too?'

Maddy glanced at the support unit. Her brows arched and flickered ever so slightly. *My God . . . she's not getting all maternal and momsey, is she?*

Becks narrowed her eyes for a moment and cocked her head. Thinking. Evaluating for a moment. Then she replied. 'I cannot stay here with you, Charley.' There seemed to be just a hint of emotion in her voice. 'I have a mission to carry out.'

Charley nodded. She knew all about the Big Mission. 'To meet with the walrus man and save the world?'

Becks smiled. 'That is correct.' She reached across and gently held one of her hands. 'You will be safe here with these people. They appear to be non-threatening.'

'Where are you from, Becks?' asked Duncan. 'There's an accent in there somewhere.'

'I am . . . from England.'

'British? Wow. Not ever met a Brit. How much of that island of yours is there left?'

'Above the water?' She cocked her head. 'Very little.'

Charley grasped her hand. 'Will you come back here when you're all finished?'

Maddy stepped in quickly. 'Yes. We'll come back when we're all done, won't we, Becks?'

Maddy could see Becks was struggling with telling a direct untruth. 'Yes. We . . . will . . . come back.'

Maddy looked at Duncan. 'If you're sure that's OK with you?'

He nodded. She could see in his eyes he knew they were lying, that they were unlikely to ever be coming back this way. 'Sure.' He turned to Charley. 'Me and Troy will look after you until they come back.'

Charley considered that for a moment, then nodded in a slow and deliberate way that suggested she'd figured out what was going on here; that she was a liability being passed from one pair of hands to another. But she managed a smile for them all. 'Good . . . I'd like to stay here for a bit, if that's OK?'

Troy clapped her hands together happily. 'We'll be like sisters! If you want?'

Charley smiled and nodded. 'I used to have a big sister . . . once. She used to listen to old music on a *pod*. She called it rock . . . I don't know why.'

'I've got a bunch of old-time music on my tablet. Do you want to hear some?'

With that, the girls began swiping at the glowing display, and chattering about songs and music and bands from the 'olden days'.

Maddy noticed the first hint of a smile on Duncan's face. 'I don't think she's even begun to accept it's just going to be the two of us . . . from now on,' he said softly. 'It'll be good for her . . . to have Charley stay with us.'

'Good.'

Duncan nodded. 'Trust me,' he said quietly, 'she'll be fine here. We'll take good care of her.'

CHAPTER 41

2070, Blue Valley Camp,
Rocky Mountains

The next morning Duncan showed them a small two-wheel trailer that he'd found in a maintenance shed. The tyres were still good. With Becks's help, he loaded it up with a dozen two-litre bottles of water, some of the packets of dried soy-flakes he'd brought with him and several dozen tins of the canned food that had been collecting dust up here in the Blue Valley Camp for God-knows-how-many decades. The labels on most of the tins had perished and Duncan said it would be a lucky dip each time they opened a can. He also pulled out of a storage cupboard half a dozen padded nylon hiking jackets.

'It's going to get colder if you're heading any further into the Rockies. You'll need these from here on.'

All their things stowed on the trailer, Becks and Heywood pulled it across the lumpy ground towards the rutted gravel driveway leading out of the camp. The rest of them followed and beneath the faded welcome sign they came to a halt, bid farewell and wished each other good luck.

Duncan stepped away from the others and offered his hand to Maddy. 'I hope you find your folks alive. But look . . . don't build your hopes too high. Whatever you find down south, well . . . just . . . don't let it get to you. Chances aren't good.'

'I know. But I have to just go see for myself.'

'We've all lost someone . . . but we've managed to survive. This is a new world now. Day Zero. For all we know there might only be a few thousand people left alive. Do what you have to do . . . and I wish you luck.'

'Thank you.'

'And if you can . . . do try to make it back here.' He looked around the camp. 'This is as good a place as any to try to rebuild something.'

'We'll certainly try.'

The others finished saying goodbye to Troy and Duncan. Then it was Charley's turn. She wrapped her arms round each of them, one after the other, hugging them fiercely. Finally, she came to Becks. The support unit stooped down and folded her arms round the girl. The others stepped away and discussed directions and the weather, giving them both a moment of privacy.

'Thank you for looking after me, Becks,' Charley whispered into her ear.

Becks smiled over her shoulder. 'You are welcome, Charley.'

Charley released her tight hold, pulled back and looked at Becks. 'Please be very careful.'

'I will.'

She bit her lip. Wondering whether to say something or not. She couldn't help herself. 'I know . . . I know something about you.'

Becks cocked her head, curious. 'What do you know about me?'

'That you're not completely human. I heard Mr Heywood say something about it.'

Becks's eyes narrowed. She frowned. 'What did he say?'

'You're, like, a *fake* human? Like one of those super-soldiers in the army?'

273

'Yes . . . I am a "fake human".'

She shrugged her shoulders. 'Well, it doesn't matter . . . not really. You're no different to *real* people anyway.'

'Really?'

'Really.' She planted a kiss on Becks's cheek. 'And you've been kinder to me than most other people I met.'

Becks's frown deepened as she let her software try to make some sense out of that. She put this memory, this moment, into a brand-new folder to be picked over later.

'Don't be so sad,' said Charley. 'I'll be OK here.'

'Hey, Becks!' called Heywood. He tilted his head towards the road heading out of the camp. 'We're runnin' out of small talk here.'

Becks released her tight hold of the girl and stood up. 'I will be OK also.'

'Right, folks, reckon we should go!' said Heywood. 'We got a full day an' a lot more uphill to deal with!'

'He's right.' Maddy nodded. 'Thanks again . . . for the food and water and the trailer.'

'Good luck,' replied Duncan. 'And remember. We're here. OK?'

They turned and headed out beneath the faded sign, out of the camp and along the gravel road. Becks walked silently beside Heywood, the tow bar of the trailer gripped in her tight fists. She was busy processing her thoughts.

Sad? Charley had said 'Don't be so sad' to her. She wondered what had made the girl say that. She hadn't opened her 'emotion folder' for any useful gestures or expressions to play on her face. There'd just been her usual intense scowl of concentration. She felt something tickling the skin of her right cheek. Certainly it wasn't going to be a bug. There was nothing, absolutely nothing, left alive. She wiped her cheek and felt moisture. She pulled her hand away and looked at the glistening droplet on the tip of her finger.

A tear.

Her very first tear.

Rashim studied the row of satnav coordinates on the small glowing display of his wrist-pad. It lit his face up brightly, the screen reflected in his eyes as he read the data. 'Eight miles south-west of us.' He touched the side of the pad and turned it off. 'The hydro-cell charge is down to fifteen per cent. I should keep it mostly switched off now to preserve what is left.'

'Yeah, makes sense.' Maddy snuggled down in her sleeping bag, turned over on to her left side and gazed at the glowing embers of the campfire. She could hear Heywood's deep mucus-thick snoring, and out there, just beyond the faintest flickering light cast from the dying campfire, she could hear Becks. The support unit was busy standing guard in that half-awake/half-standby mode she adopted every night. Every now and then stirring, shifting weight, taking a pace or two, then once more utterly motionless, frozen like a watchful terracotta warrior.

She felt surprisingly snug in her sleeping bag despite the cloud of vapour she was breathing out in front of her cold face. And she was feeling well fed; the soy-flake stew they'd boiled up again had been unexpectedly satisfying and filling. Warm and full now . . . normally she'd have been the first to fall asleep, especially after all this hiking, after all this high-altitude air. But for some reason she felt wide awake. Above her she could see the stars perfectly clearly. The night sky here in 2070 looked no different from any other time. It was only the days that looked jaundiced and sickly.

'Rashim? You still awake?'

'No, I'm fast asleep.'

275

'Oh, ha ha.' She wriggled around in her bag for a moment. There was a root or a stone digging into her hip. 'So, just wondered . . . it must be kinda weird coming back to 2070. Did it feel like coming home for you?'

No quickly tossed-back answer from him. She guessed he was thinking about it.

'Not really,' he replied finally. 'It all feels so long ago now. How long has it been do you think . . . since you first *abducted* me?'

'Abducted? Rescued, more like.'

'No. I was right first time. *Abducted*.' She heard him laugh. He was kidding.

'How long? You mean in *us* time . . . in *TimeRiders* time?'

She heard him chuckle again. 'Yeah, TimeRiders time.'

'Jeez, dunno.' She tried to add it up in her head. They'd first encountered Rashim setting up those receiver beacons on that remote hillside a dozen miles outside Rome in AD 54. They'd taken him back to New York with them because, well, back then she hadn't any idea what else to do with him. He knew too much. Then they'd found themselves on the run, having to relocate to Victorian London and set up their displacement machine. And how long had they been there? They'd been living beneath the Holborn Viaduct for about three months before she'd come up with that stupid idea to go back to 1666 to watch the Great Fire of London. Not one of her best. After she and Sal had managed to rescue Liam and Rashim, there'd been the whole unlocking-Becks's-partitioned-mind plan. Which, of course, had eventually led them deep into the jungles of Nicaragua and that lost city in those mountains. That had been another few months of humidity, heat, mosquito bites . . . and horror. Her mind played a few fleeting moments of *that night*. The night that

Sal had returned from chaos space as something corrupted, powerful, terrifying.

The night that Adam had died.

Adam . . . the one person she'd met in all this time that she could imagine herself sharing a life with, a life after this endless exercise in fighting fires . . . this mystery . . . this nightmare . . . was finally resolved. Back there in the jungle she'd stupidly allowed herself to imagine what it would be like to share the rest of her life with him, to have children with him if it was even possible, to grow old with him. She'd imagined the fanciful tales of time travel they could have told their sniggering, disbelieving grandchildren. '*You reeeeally met a Roman centurion, Grandma? You really were mentioned in the Holy Grail, Grandad? Yeah . . . right.*'

She smiled in the dark. What a lovely could-have-been that would have been.

And, after all that, they'd returned home to Victorian London. There'd been that long holiday abroad to India, the Far East and to Africa. She'd needed that. Time away from their dark, depressing dungeon. Time spent not dwelling on the end of the world. She suspected both Liam and Rashim had conspired to keep her as busy as possible, to show her there was an exciting and colourful world out there beyond the suffocating confines of their bubble existence.

'Maddy? You asleep?'

'Sorry, I zoned out for a while there.' She silently totalled up all the months in her head as best she could. 'About two years or so at a wild guess.'

'Two years? Is that all? It feels so much longer.'

It sure does. They'd been through so much together.

'You know . . . it *was* very strange going back to my single-unit in Denver.'

'I never asked you, Rashim . . . in all that time, I never asked whether you had someone close to you in this time? A wife? A girlfriend? Family?'

'I had no wife or girlfriend. Not while I was working on Project Exodus.'

'What about before?'

'Yes. Of course. One or two relationships.'

'Serious ones?'

He was silent for a while. 'No. Nothing serious. I like to keep my life as uncomplicated as possible.'

'What about any family?'

'I have two sisters and my mother. They live in New London right now.' He corrected himself. 'Well, that is . . . they *lived* in New London.'

'I'm sorry, Rashim. God, I've been so wrapped up in Waldstein and gazing at my own navel, it didn't occur to me you might have had someone you cared for in this time. You must have been worrying about them these last few months, you know, with K-N and stuff?'

'A little perhaps. But I haven't seen them for years. We were not that close.'

'Two sisters? So, were they older? Younger?'

'Older. I was the spoiled baby of our family. The one my mother doted on.'

She shook her head. All this time, and she'd never thought to ask him questions like these. Never even bothered to enquire about his life before they'd met. 'I'm sorry . . . we've never really talked much about your life before you got stuck in the past with us.'

'Don't worry, Maddy.' She heard his sleeping bag rustle. 'It seems we have always been kept busy with one thing after another.'

'You can say that again.'

They were silent for a while. She listened to the only sounds of the mountain forest: the creak of dead wood, the rustling of a gentle breeze carrying dust and grit across sterile ground.

'Maddy?'

'Yes?'

'If Waldstein presents us with a reason, a *compelling* reason . . . which gives us no choice but to accept leaving this world as it is now . . .?'

'You want to know what we're gonna do next?'

'Yes,' he replied.

'Damned if I know.'

She wondered about that. If – and it was a big if – they even found him alive, what would he tell them? What could possibly justify this being allowed to happen? A fate worse than this?

Jesus . . . it's got to be a frikkin' horrifying alternative, if mankind almost completely annihilating itself is the better *choice of the two!*

But, if whatever he revealed to them actually made sense and this was how things needed to be left, then Rashim was right – what next?

Does Waldstein have plans for us? Or will he just pat us on the head and let us go?

She wondered if he'd have a functional displacement machine. He must do. In which case, she wondered if he'd grant them one last wish to go wherever, whenever, they wanted. Grant them a happy-ever-after ending.

'Maybe he'll let us choose a time we could go back to . . . let us pick some place to live out the rest of our lives?'

'That would be nice,' replied Rashim.

'Yeah, it would. I'd say we've frikkin' well earned something like that.'

She heard him shuffling in his sleeping bag again. 'If he did let us go wherever we wanted to, where would you choose to go, Maddy?'

'I don't know. The first time I ever went back in time, it was to San Francisco in 1906. The beginning of the twentieth century . . . it was so cool. I loved the clothes, the buzz of activity, the sense of great things lying ahead.'

'Like two world wars?'

'Uh? Yeah, OK. Those were pretty bad. But, like, there's the rest of the twentieth century? How cool would that be? To see all of that? The roaring twenties? The decades *after* the Second World War: the fifties, the sixties, the seventies?'

How about one particular decade? The nineties? If Waldstein gave her a golden one-way ticket back, she could see herself choosing 1994. She might just go to a city called Norwich in England and look up a scruffy young British college student with a ponytail and a scrappy beard.

'Rashim, what about you?'

'I think I would like to go back to the 1700s.'

She laughed. 'Back to being the notorious Blackbeard, pillaging and looting your way across the high seas?'

'That must sound wrong, the pillaging, the looting . . . but yes, I enjoyed being Captain Anwar. I enjoyed the freedom, the adventure. Liam and I made very good pirates.'

'You boys really enjoyed yourselves back then, didn't you?'

She could hear the wistful smile in the tone of his voice. 'It was fun, yes. I do sometimes wonder how things might have been; how many ships we would have amassed in our fleet eventually. How famous, or *infamous*, we would have become.'

'Well, maybe you'll get a chance to find out? You know, if Waldstein lets us go on our merry way.'

'I suspect he will not.'

'You still think Liam might be right, don't you? Do you think he's baiting us?'

She heard Rashim as he adjusted position. 'It is a possibility we must take seriously. He may be luring us to him to dispose of. To tidy up his loose ends.'

'You really think we shouldn't be doing this, don't you? You think this is another stupid –'

'No. I do accept this is our best chance to seek answers from him. I wonder whether he knows anything at all about the transmitters.'

'He must do, surely?'

Maddy heard Rashim sigh irritably, then rustle in his sleeping bag once again, trying to find a more tolerable spot on the hard ground.

'I wonder if Liam and Bob have found the other one in Jerusalem yet?' he said.

'If it's there, they'll find it. Liam and Bob make a pretty resourceful team together.'

'Yes, they do.'

'I can't wait to get back actually,' said Maddy. 'To compare notes with him. To find out what he's found out.'

'If we can get back, that is.'

'We'll get back. Waldstein has a machine. He sent those support units back after all.'

'Yes, he did.' Rashim mulled over that point for a second. 'So that means at some point he had a machine. But when was that? How long ago was that? Ten years ago? Fifteen years? And now . . . given everyone's dead and the world lies in ruins, has he even got a power supply? A back-up generator?'

'Of course he must. I mean, he figured out we needed one, for emergencies, in Brooklyn. I'm pretty sure he'd have a back-up too.'

'Yes. You're right.'

'And he knew K-N was coming, right? So I think it's safe to presume he's been preparing for this.'

'We are making a lot of assumptions here, Maddy. We may

not find him. He may not have survived the virus. He may not have a functioning machine still. He may not have a power supply for the machine now . . . and, even if none of those things are a problem, he may not agree to send us back home. Like I say, a lot of assumptions.'

'Yeah . . . yeah. I know. Situation normal, huh?'

CHAPTER 42
First century, Jerusalem

The young man, Linus, led them back through another smaller entrance in the wall of Hezekiah into the rat runs and narrow alleyways of the upper city. He kept a small home above a carpenter's workshop. Two small bare rooms, separated by a curtain. He ushered his elderly parents out of one of the rooms.

'This is yours. You can stay in here. Do not go out. I will return later with some food.'

They sat in the room and waited. Through a small opening in the wall, the sun shone in; a square patch of weakening daylight climbed the stone wall opposite as it began to set.

'Do you hear that, Bob?'

He nodded. It was the distant sound of raised voices, the clatter of shields, the occasional ring of a blade. Rioting in the upper city.

'We caused that one as well.' Liam sighed. 'So much for discretion.'

Linus returned an hour later with a basket of bread and a flask of olive oil, and the man with the thick dark beard.

'This is Isaac.' The two men sat down with them and Linus handed the food out.

'The people are rioting in several other places,' grinned Isaac. 'Your arrival in Jerusalem has finally encouraged them to rise up and be heard.' He looked at Bob. 'This "man" . . . what is his name?'

'Bob.'

'*Bob?*' Isaac and Linus looked at each other. They both tried out the name again. 'Bob?' Isaac shrugged. 'A strange name.' He turned to Liam. 'Bob . . . he is not a mortal man, is he?'

'No.'

Both men gasped. 'Then . . . he must be an angel? A creation of God?'

Liam shook his head. Both men watched curiously as Liam whispered to himself, seemed to listen for an answer, then finally spoke. 'Linus . . . Isaac, you must understand, there's been a lot of confusion today. I am not who you think I am.'

Linus stared intensely at him. 'You are the one we have heard much about. The healer, the performer of miracles. The one who is God's son.'

'There is such a man, but it's not me.' Liam shook his head. 'I'm just a normal person. The one you want is called Jesus, and he's out there somewhere in this city.'

'No!' Isaac shook his head. 'I was there! I saw *you* in the temple grounds this morning. You and this giant, turning the moneylenders' tables over. Challenging the priests . . .'

Liam shook his head. 'No. That other man wasn't me.'

'I saw you and him . . . and the others who joined you break through the Romans like they were frightened old women. I saw you escape from the temple grounds.'

'Yes . . . yes, that bit was me. But –'

Again Isaac looked at Bob. 'This one took an arrow through his neck . . . and yet he is alive still. You have healed him. Or he is blessed –'

Linus cut in. 'And we both witnessed you create a pillar of light out of darkness.'

Both men stared at Liam intensely.

'Why are you denying these miracles?' asked Linus. 'Do you not trust us?'

Liam wondered how best to explain himself. He could have a stab at the truth, but explaining time travel, the far future, what exactly Bob was . . . how a simple torch worked, all of that would be impossible to describe to them without it sounding other-worldly and supernatural. He might as well just say they were angels sent by God. Far more importantly, he needed to steer things back in the right direction. Today's big mess may already have thrown history right off the rails. The people of Jerusalem were now busy chattering about a giant and a small pale guy, and not about a certain carpenter's son called Jesus.

He needed to point these two men in the right direction.

'There is a real prophet in the city right now. He's the one with all the words coming directly from God. Me? This giant? We're just . . . travellers from afar.'

'You are more than just travellers,' said Isaac.

'No. Think of us . . . as witnesses.' Liam looked at their disbelieving faces.

They want to hear something more impressive than that.

'Think of us as *heavenly assistants*. We came to make sure that God's messenger is heard by everyone.'

Linus's eyes narrowed suspiciously.

'The man you were talking about, Linus?' continued Liam. 'The speaker, the healer from Nazareth? That's not me. Trust me, there is another man. He was at the temple this morning. He was the one who first turned a table over. But there was a confusion . . . where there shouldn't have been. Confusion . . . and in that confusion –' Liam looked at Isaac – 'you have simply mistaken me for him.'

'But . . . you. And your friend –'

'We should have been watching. From a distance. That's all.' Liam shrugged. 'But even *angels* can make mistakes.'

'Who is this man, then?'

'His name is Jesus,' Liam said again. 'You have to listen to him . . . not to me. He is the one with the answers. He's the one with a very, very important message from God.'

Linus leaned forward. 'Do you know . . . do you know what his message is?'

Liam shook his head. 'Only . . . that what he says will change everything. Everything you have been told by your leaders . . . it's all wrong. It's all lies. Jesus is the one with the answers.'

Both men's eyes widened.

'And only this one man can tell you.'

'Where . . . where is this man, this *Jesus*?'

'I don't know. In Jerusalem somewhere. I think he's safe. He had some men with him. Some followers. But tomorrow I think you'll find him . . .' Liam looked to Bob to help him out.

'On the Mount of Olives,' he whispered hoarsely.

'That's right. The Mount of Olives,' said Liam. 'In the morning. He'll be out there . . .'

I hope. He wondered if they'd already altered history too much. Perhaps the riot in the temple might have changed Jesus's plans.

'He will be talking to the small group of followers who came with him. But . . . you have to spread the word. His message has to be heard before it's too late.' Liam almost blurted out that Jesus only had a few days left before he was destined to be betrayed by a disciple, arrested and crucified. 'Tonight . . . tell as many people as you can that Jesus from Nazareth will be out there tomorrow and ready to reveal the important message he's brought from God. He's going to tell everyone.'

286

'And what of you and the giant?'

'We must be there too. To watch over him. But . . . this time, we'll watch from a distance. That's our job.'

Linus nodded slowly. 'That is your work, as . . . as commanded by God?'

Liam glanced at Bob. 'Yes. As commanded by God.'

CHAPTER 43

2070, Rocky Mountains

Maddy awoke, starving. Last night's stodgy soy-flake stew had sated her hunger enough for her to finally drift off to sleep. But during the night her stomach had clearly made quick work of it and was now grumbling for breakfast.

The fire had gone out. The sky was overcast: a muddy brown that threatened drizzle. Heywood was awake; Rashim was still out for the count and snoring. He'd rolled over in his sleep and now one cheek was flat against the ground. The white dust of the viral residue was plastered like flour across his forehead and cheeks.

She nudged him with her foot and he stirred. 'Wake up, sleepy.'

Rashim yawned, rubbed his eyes and opened them. 'We have about eight miles to cover today.'

Heywood peeled off his sleeping bag. 'We'll get there today if we make an early start.'

Maddy nodded. 'Breakfast, then.' She looked at the trailer. 'Anyone fancy that soyo-broth again?'

'You really wanna fuss with makin' another fire and boilin' up some water?' Heywood made a face. 'That'll take us at least an hour.' He got up with an old man's grunt and wandered with stiff legs over to the trailer. 'Why don't we take our pick an' see what's in these ol' cans?' He pulled out a penknife. 'It may be cold . . . but it's still food.'

'I suppose you're right.'

Rashim rubbed the dust from his face. 'This residue is disgusting.'

The silent forest now echoed with the *tak-tak-tak* of Heywood banging holes into the lid of one of the tins. He wedged the blade of his knife into one of the holes and see-sawed the serrated side until he'd created a jagged edge he could bend back. 'Reckon this one looks like it's got green beans in here. Anyone want greens for breakfast?'

Rashim curled his lip. So did Maddy.

'Hey! Organic?' he called out to Becks. The support unit turned to look at him. 'You able to eat beans?'

'That is acceptable,' she replied.

He passed her the opened tin and set to work on opening another.

Rashim was on his knees now and shaking white dust off his sleeping bag. 'You sleep OK, Maddy?'

'Slept like the dead last night. I'm exhausted. My legs are killing me, though. How about you?'

'Not too bad.' He shrugged. 'I think I was dreaming about ships.'

She smiled. 'Pirate ships?'

He stroked his dark beard and flashed a grin her way. 'Indeed.'

'Aw, man!' Heywood suddenly whooped.

They both turned to look. Maddy sat up groggily. 'What's up?'

'Got a label on this one!' His eyes were round and wide. He held up a large dented can in one hand as if it was a nugget of gold sifted from a babbling mountain creek. 'Only got us a *guddamn* chocolate-fudge sponge here!! Anyone want to share that with me?'

Maddy shook her head. 'I'll take anything that looks like

canned fruit.' She got up and wandered over to the trailer. 'Or, actually, baked beans maybe. I could go with cold baked beans.'

Heywood tossed his penknife to her. 'There ya go. You can play lucky dip for yourself.'

'I will share that chocolate pudding with you,' said Rashim.

'Uh . . . OK.' Heywood shrugged. 'There was me hopin' I got this all to myself.' He came over and sat down beside Rashim. 'You gonna excuse fingers?'

'I suppose we have little choice but to eat like cavemen.'

Maddy leaned over the side of the trailer and began picking through identical-looking tin cans.

Heywood grinned as he dug a finger into one side of the sponge. 'I ain't eaten a real chocolate puddin' since I was a little kid.'

Rashim did likewise, sinking the tips of his fingers in and gouging out a chunk of it. 'It looks good.'

Both men pulled a moist hunk of the sponge out, chocolate goo in the middle dangling in a thick gelatinous drip. After looking at each other for a moment, grinning like kids in a sweet shop, they tucked what they'd scooped out with their fingers into their mouths.

They both chewed silently for a moment. It was Heywood who pulled a face first. 'This taste right to you?'

Rashim wrinkled his nose and shook his head. 'No. It tastes odd. Not right. Savoury, not sweet.' He ran his tongue round his mouth. 'Like . . . yeast . . .'

His eyes met the old man's and he spat it out on to the ground.

Rashim snatched the can from Heywood and then turned it round to inspect the sides. He pulled at the faded label; it was damp and loose and came away like soggy tissue paper. There was a dent beneath the label, and a small jagged hole. 'Did you just make this hole with your knife?'

Heywood shook his head. His cheeks still bulged with food; he wasn't sure whether to swallow or spit out. 'I was stabbin' at the top.'

Maddy looked round from the trailer. 'What's up?'

'Don't touch them! Don't touch the tins!' Rashim dropped the one he was holding on to the ground. It landed with a thud on its side and the top crust of the sponge spilled out, revealing the soft gooey centre. The goo was mottled in colour. Mostly dark brown, but in some places there were small pale bacilli-like strings.

Heywood spat out what he had in his mouth. '*Guddamn it!* Got that virus crap in it!'

Maddy and Becks hurried over and looked at the spilled chocolate pudding on the ground. The thin strands of pearly, mucus-like liquid began to fan out and spread like the speeded-up time-lapse footage of a culture growing in a Petri dish.

'My God! It got into the tin!' whispered Rashim. 'The can was punctured . . . it got inside!'

'But . . . but the virus is all dead now, isn't it?' said Maddy. 'If it got in . . . wouldn't it have already turned the whole pudding to –?'

'No air inside!' Rashim stared up at her with growing panic in his eyes. 'No oxygen! Maybe that . . . maybe that slowed the process down?'

They watched fine pallid strands extending, spreading, fanning out and rapidly breaking down the sponge. Now it had air – or perhaps it was the light – the virus was working frighteningly quickly. An ingredient, a protein within the pudding, was signalling the virus to wake up; that there was yet work to be done.

Maddy's face blanched. 'Oh Jesus!'

Rashim looked at her. 'It's in me! My God, Maddy . . . it's inside me!'

'Stay calm, Rashim . . .' she whispered uselessly. 'Just . . . just stay calm! Let me think –'

He shook his head slowly. 'I'm . . . already infected . . .'

'No. Hang on. Not necessarily –'

Becks came over from the trailer. 'Caution, Maddy.'

Heywood reached for some water and took a slug, swilling it around his mouth and spitting what he had out on to the ashes of their fire.

'Forget it,' said Rashim. 'It's too late for that.'

'Maddy, you should step away from them!' Becks pulled insistently at Maddy's arm. She staggered hesitantly backwards.

'Becks is right, Maddy!' Rashim waved at her to step back further. 'You should get back. Quickly! Get away from here. The virus is fast.'

'Hang on!' She shook her head. 'You might not be infected!'

'There is no way I'm not! Contaminated food touched my tongue. We both tasted it. We're dead, Maddy! We're dead! Get out of here!'

'I'm not leaving you!'

'Do it!' he said. '*Now!*' Even though it was cold enough for their breath to be clouds of flickering vapour, his skin was damp and glistening with beads of sweat. 'I'm feeling wrong already!'

'Maddy,' said Becks, 'Rashim is correct! You should do as he says!'

'Christ.' Heywood dropped to his knees. 'I think I'm gonna be sick,' he grunted. Then he heaved, ejecting pink-stained bile on to the ground between his legs. It spattered like offal tipped from a butcher's barrel. He cursed under his breath, wheezing groggily. 'The hell is that?' He stared at the mess at his feet like an early-hours drunkard. 'That my guddamn stomach linin'?'

'Rashim! OhMyGod, no!' cried Maddy.

He shook his head. 'It's too late . . . you have to leave now!'

Becks grasped Maddy's arm and pulled her a few steps further back.

'Rashim!' Maddy cried. 'I'm so sorry. I'm sorry! This is all my fault.'

He dropped down to his hands and knees and spat bile on to the ground. 'Go! Just go! Before . . . before this thing . . . gets you . . .'

Maddy, still held by Becks, twisted and squirmed in her grasp. She began to sob uncontrollably. The support unit put an arm round her and turned her away from the dying men. She looked back over her shoulder. 'I will take her from here.'

Rashim looked up at Becks, licked his lips and nodded. 'Good. G-get . . . get her out of here . . .'

Maddy wriggled in Becks's firm grasp, then turned round. 'Rashim, I'm so sorry . . .'

'It's OK . . . nothing needs to be said, Maddy . . . Just go! Now!'

Becks dragged her away across the dusty ground, past the trailer and towards the nearest of the dead trees.

'NO!' Rashim called out after them. His rasping voice echoed round the creaking, lifeless forest. They stopped. Maddy turned to look back at him. 'Wrong . . . way . . .' He jabbed a finger towards a looming, snow-tipped mountain peak. 'S-south-west!' he gasped. 'It's . . . it's . . . just . . . Head towards that . . . OK?'

Rashim saw Maddy nod. They changed direction and he watched them until the last flash of an orange anorak was lost to the black-and-white world. Then they were gone. His friend, his colleague . . .

Goodbye, Maddy.

He turned to his right and looked at Heywood lying curled up on the ground, shivering and groaning.

'Heywood?'

The old man's eyes opened. The whites of his eyes had haemorrhaged and were a dark red; he was leaking tears of blood on to his pale cheeks. 'Jesus Christ! Death . . . d-death by . . . g-guddamn chocolate p-puddin' . . .' He pulled a death-mask grin. His gums were beginning to break down and bleed; the roots of his brown teeth were becoming exposed, looking long, almost like canine fangs. '. . . by chocolate . . . p-puddin' . . . ain't that a . . . guddamn stupid k-kick in the ass . . .?'

Rashim responded with the snort of a dry laugh. He felt moisture trickling from his nostrils, soaking into the bristles of his moustache, and tasted blood on his lips. He lowered himself gently to the ground. His arms were trembling; already he was feeling feverish and light-headed. He eased himself down and lay on his back, looking up at the sky: a rolling carpet of low sulphur-yellow clouds.

He closed his eyes and saw instead a clear deep blue sky above him and a stout oak mast reaching up to meet it. He could hear the taut strum of hemp-rope rigging, the clank and rattle of loose tackle blocks, the rustle and snap of sailcloth feeling for a breath of wind. The creak of ship's timbers and the slosh of a lazy sea slapping against her hull.

All just a pleasing illusion. He knew that . . . his dying mind was firing off memories like a sinking vessel firing distress flares.

This . . . here . . . now . . . He smiled. *There are many worse ways to die than this*, he decided. Fading away on a rather pleasing memory plucked from a life he was never meant to have lived in the first place.

There could be worse ways than this. He could feel his senses failing him. His mind failing him. His breathing ragged and shallow, heartbeat faltering; the cascading domino effect of his body shutting down organ by organ. Falling into a deep sleep. Melting away to an organic soup that in turn would dry in a few days and become a harmless white powder.

His dying mind conjured one last, reassuring thought.

In the end, don't we all come from dust anyway? We come from dust . . . and we end as dust.

The oh-so-short passage in between is the bit we call 'life'.

Everything ends eventually.

Everything.

CHAPTER 44

First century, Jerusalem

There was a notable absence of Roman legionaries at every entrance to the city. No blockades, as Isaac had told them there had been yesterday. Containing the numerous riots last night had stretched the Roman garrison's manpower to breaking point. Today the cohort was mostly holed up in their fort and watching for trouble from behind the crenellations of their high walls. They were keeping a low profile; undoubtedly word had been sent out that reinforcements were going to be needed and they were going to sit tight until they arrived, then . . . order was going to be restored. Brutally, if necessary.

Liam and Bob left the city through the north entrance, hidden in the back of a cart beneath a rug. After the cart had rattled down the dirt track, far enough away from prying eyes, they emerged from the sweltering heat that had built up under the heavy corded material.

Liam thanked the old man driving the cart, Linus's father. This morning they had only briefly seen his son. He and Isaac had spent the night, as promised, going from one tavern to another, spreading the word that the one true prophet from God was going to be found in the morning on the gentle slopes of the Mount of Olives . . . and would reveal a message that would change everything.

Liam had assured the young man that the moment he set eyes

on this Jesus . . . he would know in his heart he was looking at someone quite special.

'How long have we got, Bob?'

'Three hours and fourteen minutes until the portal is due to open.'

He looked up at the hills in front of them. They needed to head up to the brow ahead, then bear right. That would take them clockwise round the top of the city to the north-east of it, towards the Mount of Olives. He just hoped where their portal was due to open was far enough away from where Jesus would be talking to his followers.

They climbed the hill, then walked along its ridge. Liam looked at the city to his right. There were a few smudges of smoke rising from it into the sky. There had been several riots during the night, but not throughout the whole city. It was undoubtedly a tinderbox, waiting to erupt into flames of insurrection. But it was a city waiting for just the right person to ignite that fire.

And there he was.

Further downhill, where the olive trees gave way to dry grass and the slope evened out, Liam could see splashes of colour in the hundreds – a crowd of people sitting on the ground in family groups and in pairs, parents and their less attentive children chasing each other. Like a large picnic. And there, in the middle of it all, in a small space, was a lone figure in a white-linen jellaba, pacing slowly back and forth. Every now and then, carried on the fresh breeze, Liam heard applause, a ripple of laughter.

Not a firebrand's sermon by the sound of it, all thunder and sulphur, but something far more peaceful and ultimately enduring: the gentle mockery of those in power – the Pharisees, Herod Antipas . . . the Romans.

Liam had glimpsed the man up close only a couple of times,

and heard his voice just the once. Jesus didn't have the booming cadence or the bombastic manner of a practised performer. Just the measured voice of common sense. The soft and confident tone of someone who prized the meaning of words over the way they were delivered.

'We've got time to listen for a bit, haven't we, Bob?'

'We have two hours and fifty-nine minutes until the portal is due.'

'We've got time, then.'

They made their way down the slope, through the olive trees and out into the open. Liam stopped on the periphery of the gathering and, not wanting to attract anyone's attention, he gestured at Bob to sit down. Then he listened.

'. . . in this world, this one mortal life, wealth is measured not in talents, or shekels or sestertii, but in what we take with us when we finally die. Our memories, our conscience. That is all that matters in the end. Our life is measured by those we have touched, loved, helped. One who shares all that he has, and lies in a pauper's grave, dies the wealthiest of men.'

One of those listening near the front asked a question that Liam's babel-bud couldn't quite pick up and translate.

'All of us are equal in the eyes of my father,' Jesus replied. 'Man and woman. Old and young. There is nothing a man can do that a woman can't.'

Liam smiled at that. He'd get Maddy's vote, then.

'We are all equal souls held inside bodies of different sizes and shapes. What we look like, what we sound like, or even what we *smell* like . . .'

A ripple of laughter.

'. . . is as unimportant as the flask that a wine is carried in. The bodies we live in – our mortal existence – is just a cart travelling along the road. But our soul is the precious cargo.

King. Prince. Caesar. Prefect. Priest . . . These are all false titles that man has invented, titles that mean nothing in the eyes of God. In fact, they insult God. Who are we to judge who is better? Who is worth more? Who is of a higher rank?'

Liam listened to Jesus talk for the next couple of hours as the sun slowly rose to its zenith and the day became stiflingly hot. So much of what he heard the man say sounded like wisdom: a straightforward message of tolerance and compassion, illustrated with simple moral stories. It sounded so much like a contemporary, a very modern, moral guide . . . and so very different from the thunderous damnations he'd heard uttered by religious 'godly' men from the various centuries he'd glimpsed – those claiming to speak on behalf of God, but poisoning any good message with their own vicious prejudices.

He realized he was hearing something powerful, something pure . . . something *inescapably right*, which had been utterly mutated and corrupted by the passage of time and the quills and pens of those with dark minds.

I could follow this man. I could actually believe in him. This . . . what he's saying right now . . . is the only way to live.

Bob tapped him on the shoulder. 'Liam, it is time to go.'

They headed back towards the olive trees and climbed up the hillside, picking a way between their ordered rows, ducking beneath their low branches until finally Bob stopped. 'This is it. The portal opens here.'

'I thought there would be more people out there listening to him,' said Liam. 'I mean, that fella, that Jesus . . . it's like . . . I never realized how simple, how uncomplicated his message was. What the hell happened to it?'

Bob shrugged. 'Religious texts are not a historically reliable source of information. They are like an infinitely photocopied

299

image; replication errors, misinterpretations, mistranslations have rendered them ambiguous enough to be used to validate any belief system.'

'It's the perfect bleedin' tool for bad guys to justify themselves, isn't it?'

'That is correct.'

Liam shook his head. 'I'd love to give Jesus a Dictaphone or something, so we could play back what he *actually* said to some of the idiots speaking on his behalf today.'

'That would, of course, cause a time contamination.'

Liam snorted. 'You're not kidding it would.'

In the shade of the olive trees, they gazed down the slope. 'Liam, we must now discuss how we are to proceed. Is it your intention to attempt to contact Maddy or –'

'When we get back . . . we need to work out how we're going to locate that beam. I want to find it. It's down there somewhere beneath that temple, to be sure. But it's going to be hard to locate it . . . that place is like a damned labyrinth.'

Bob nodded. 'There are no records or geological scans of the ground beneath the temple. We could do a density probe to find a suitably sized void to arrive in . . .'

'And then what? Find ourselves stuck in some small fissure or cave, or well shaft?'

'That is a possibility.'

'Or we can be a bit smarter than that?'

Bob cocked his head.

'Well . . . can't we basically sort of "map" the ground beneath the temple? Do a whole load of them little density probes and get a rough picture of what's down there . . . get an idea of the layout, you know . . . before we go charging in?'

'That is a sensible plan, Liam.' Bob pulled off a smile. 'Very good.'

Liam looked up at him. 'Seriously? Did you just patronize me?'

Bob reached out a giant hand and patted him on the head. 'Yes, Liam. You are a very clever doggy. There. There. You can have a bone.'

Liam grabbed at his thumb and tried twisting it. 'Oh, joy of joys. You and Becks are just so damned hilarious now you've discovered your funny bones.'

Bob raised his thick brows hopefully. 'Was I successful in being amusing this time, Liam?'

Liam sucked air through his teeth. 'More kind of annoying actually.'

Bob's shoulders slumped ever so slightly.

'Hey, Bob . . .' He patted the support unit. 'Don't get all sulky on me, big fella. You're a killing machine, not a comedian.'

Before them, the air began to shimmer. 'Aha . . . and here's our bus home.'

CHAPTER 45

2070, Rocky Mountains

Maddy stumbled through the still and silent forest. The only sound was her own laboured breathing, her feet cracking dead-wood twigs and crunching the husks of dropped cones. Beside her, Becks strode heavily; every now and then she felt the reassuring grasp of the support unit, holding her arm to steady her.

And now there's just the two of us. Just us.

She tried to count how many times in her short fake life she'd dealt with this . . . with loss. First there'd been Foster. Then there was that loss of another kind, the loss of who she thought she was. Bereavement in a way. Then there'd been Sal. Her friend; more than that, she'd felt as close to her as if she'd been family, as if she'd been her sister. Along with Liam, the three of them had all shared that loss of innocence together, become orphans from the lives they'd all thought they'd once had. Then Adam. Even the support units: both of them had kind of 'died' once already.

Now it was Rashim's turn. And there'd be no coming back from the dead for him.

She felt listless and blank. Ready to slump down right now into this cursed dust and dirt and give up.

Again. How many times had she felt like doing that? Giving up? And how many times had she been forced to pick herself up again and pretend to be strong, pretend to know what had to be done next, as if she had some already thought-through strategy in her head?

'I can't . . .' she gasped. 'I can't go on . . .'

'We must keep going, Maddy.'

She shook her head. 'We're not even going to find him. We're not going to find Waldstein alive.'

'There is not much further to go.'

Her legs gave up and buckled beneath her and she slumped untidily to the ground.

'Get up, Maddy.'

'You know what?' She shook her head. 'I'm done. I'm finished.'

Becks knelt down beside her. 'This is unacceptable, Maddy.'

'*Unacceptable?*' Maddy looked at her and laughed wearily. 'So, you're the one in charge now, huh?'

'Your judgement is currently impaired.' Becks gave her a scolding frown. 'You are experiencing emotional trauma. There is no time for feeling grief. We must continue.'

'What the hell do you know about feeling *anything*?!'

Becks's eyes narrowed. 'I have changed, Maddy. My AI has developed. I have been able to experience emotions for some time. You must be aware of this?' She cocked her head. 'I also liked Rashim.'

Fresh tears began to spill down and streak the dirt on Maddy's cheeks. 'You *liked* him?'

She nodded. 'Yes.'

'That's complete rubbish.' She laughed again, a little spitefully. 'You can't even tell if you like ice cream. Not wanting to sound harsh here, but you're just a frikkin' machine in a girl suit.'

'I am much more than that.' She leaned closer to Maddy. 'Look at me.'

Maddy did.

'Bob and I have become more than our programming. We will never be as incapacitated by emotion as a real person, as you . . . but we can feel attachment, and we can feel loss.'

'Yeah . . . right.'

'Maddy, listen to me –' her voice softened – 'I believe I can call you my friend.'

Friend? Maddy felt an urge to slap her. 'You think you know what that frikkin' word actually means?'

'I do. I follow your orders because –'

'Because you *have* to! Because those stupid little lines of code in your head –'

'No. Because I *trust* you.'

Maddy snorted derisively.

'You and I have been through much. I have grown in this time. I once followed orders because my mission parameters obligated me to. Now I follow you because . . . you are my friend.'

She grasped Maddy's hand. 'You will achieve nothing by giving up. You will die here if you do not continue. And I'd be without you. Alone.'

'I've achieved nothing anyway. All I've done is screw things up . . . time after time.'

'Liam is seeking answers with Bob. And we will seek answers from Waldstein. Then we will return and we will exchange information. Then . . .' Becks smiled. 'Then your mission will be complete. Maybe you will be free.'

'Free?'

'Free to give up. Free to go where you wish.' She squeezed her hand gently. 'Free to live. Perhaps free to love someone?'

Maddy shook her head and sighed. 'That's hilarious. Where is this coming from anyway?'

'I am not human, but I am almost human. I understand what compels you is a need for answers.' She nodded at the trees ahead of them. 'We are just a few miles away. And there is a high probability that that is where you will find those.' She stood up, tugging at Maddy's hand. 'But you will die here not knowing anything if we do not proceed any further.'

'I'm tired.'

'Then, if it is necessary, I will carry you.'

Maddy closed her eyes.

'Your answers lie just a few more miles in this direction,' continued Becks. 'We have walked too far to stop now.'

'OK.' Maddy sucked in a deep breath. 'OK . . . you win.'

Maddy stared down at her dust-covered feet, dragging them wearily and kicking up clouds behind her. Her mouth was dry, clogged by the powder, and the dead forest seemed to be endless. They'd been walking for hours now – in fact, most of the day. Through the spidery branches she could see the sun was beginning to nestle among distant wintry peaks. A few miles away? That's what Becks had assured her. Either she was just as lost as Maddy, or that had been her ham-fisted way of getting her back on her feet.

She was beginning to suspect they'd drifted off course and had been heading in the wrong direction, perhaps even walked right past the entrance to this super-secret campus.

Then it seemed to appear out of nowhere, out of the fading light – the cross-hatched mesh of a chain-linked perimeter fence.

'There's a fence!'

'I see it, Maddy.'

Maddy reached out and rattled it with her hand. The wire vibrated either side of them, uphill and downhill.

'That was foolish,' said Becks. 'It might have been electrified.'

'Oh yeah.' She almost face-palmed herself. 'Well, I guess it's not . . . so there's that.' She looked along the wire. 'Think this might be it?'

'It must be.'

'Do we follow the fence up or down . . . or shall we try to climb over?' She looked up; the fence was nine or ten feet high and topped with loops of razor wire. Maybe not over, then.

'Downhill,' replied Becks.

'What makes you so sure?'

'Look.' Becks pointed a finger.

Maddy followed the direction she was pointing. Downhill of them, she could make out the faint glow of a solitary light winking as endless bare branches between them shifted and swayed.

A light. There's power. Someone's home.

They made their way down the sloping ground, stepping over exposed roots, ducking beneath low branches and weaving between the uniform, straight trunks of necrotic wood, keeping the perimeter fence to their right.

Finally, as the last glow of light in the dusk sky was threatening to give out on them, they emerged from the forest on to open ground. Before the virus, this could have been a well-tended, beautifully manicured corporate lawn. Now it was bare dirt and dust. Over to the right, the perimeter fence ended with a guard tower, and a sign – W.G. SYSTEMS DENVER RESEARCH CAMPUS – mounted on a polished granite plinth. The light they'd seen through the trees was a single spotlight aimed at the plinth. Before it, a bare flower bed was surrounded by artfully placed white-painted boulders and rocks. And, beyond that, a driveway led up to a security hut. The vehicle barrier was in the down position, resolutely blocking the road.

The security hut looked deserted. The guard tower too.

Through the chain-link fence she could see a number of chrome-and-glass buildings nestling against the steep hillside, more barren corporate flower beds and bald lawns, and arrowed signposts indicating the way to various department buildings.

'It looks like nobody's home,' she said. It appeared the solitary spotlight had been a false promise. Something left on and running from an emergency generator.

Then she noticed movement: a lone figure standing in the shadowed doorway of the security hut. A figure wrapped up in a thick navy-blue anorak with the hood pulled up. The figure emerged, took several steps out beyond the vehicle barrier and turned to face their way.

'We should be cautious,' said Becks as they slowly crossed the open ground towards the guard hut. She glanced up at the tower. 'There may be some automated defensive measures in place.'

'We were invited here,' said Maddy. 'We'll just tell him we're expected.'

They approached the lone figure standing out front slowly, as non-threateningly as they could. A dozen yards short of him they came to a stop. The guard studied them silently for a full minute, his face lost in the shadows of his hood, his breath spilling out in regular, rhythmic clouds of vapour. The evening was getting cold, fast. Finally, he took a single step towards them, then reached up with gloved hands and tugged at the zip tucked just below his jaw.

'Perimeter motion detectors picked the pair of you up half an hour ago,' the man said. He reached for his hood and pulled it back, revealing a lean, wrinkled face, dark, deep eyes set beneath snow-white bushy eyebrows, and a chin and wattled jawline feathered with the white fuzz of an unwanted beard.

307

Maddy gasped. 'My God,' she whispered. 'Foster? Is that you?'

'I've been waiting out here too long,' he said, thumping his hands briskly together to warm them up. He smiled disarmingly and took several cautious steps towards them, then offered a gloved hand to Maddy.

'Welcome home, Maddy.'

'You . . .?' She frowned, utterly confused at the sight of Foster standing plain as day in front of her. 'But you . . . you *died*! I saw them . . . I saw those support units kill you!'

His hand remained extended towards her. 'You saw them kill a clone.'

'Foster?' She looked at that familiar face. 'I . . . I don't understand how . . .'

He smiled. 'My name's Roald Waldstein.'

'You . . . you were Waldstein all along?!'

'No . . . not exactly. I'll explain later. Come on, we should go inside,' he said. 'It's getting cold out here.'

CHAPTER 46
1890, London

Liam looked up from the brick floor of the dungeon, hoping to see Maddy, Rashim and Becks looking down at him. But there was no one here. A moment later, Bob thudded down to the ground beside him with a *whuff* of expelled breath.

The portal collapsed behind them both.

Bob looked at him. 'Maddy has not returned yet?'

Liam looked around. He had been hoping to see Maddy's and Rashim's legs dangling over the side of their hammocks, catching up on some post-mission napping. Or slouched in the armchairs round their table, enjoying some freshly brewed coffee. But no – they were definitely alone. Just the steadfast glow of the computer screens and the soft chug of the distant Victorian generator.

He got up and headed over to the computer table. 'We're back.'

> Welcome home, Liam.

'Has Maddy been back since we went?' Liam was still holding on to the hope that they might have returned, then decided to go out for a meat pie or an iced bun or something.

> Sorry, Liam. I have not heard from Maddy yet.

'Not even a message?'

> There has been no communication.

'Can we get a message to her?'

\> **I can send a tachyon signal forward, but I do not know precisely where to aim the signal.**

'Well . . .' He stroked his chin. 'Can't we just aim it roughly at New York?'

\> **Yes, but it will be a broad-sweep signal. There is some risk involved in doing that. But also when?**

'Well . . . after their arrival. Directly after their arrival there. And aim it right at our Williamsburg archway. That's where they were going, right?'

\> **Yes, Liam, that is where Maddy went. And what is the message?**

'All right, let me think . . . umm . . . OK, send this: "Have returned to base. Can confirm second beam is located beneath city. Going back to investigate."'

\> **I will send this immediately, Liam.**

'Thank you, computer-Bob.'

Bob joined him. 'Computer-Bob, we believe the second transmitter is located somewhere in the bedrock platform beneath the temple in the city of Jerusalem. Liam was able to penetrate the temple's security measures and scout beneath the building.'

\> **That is good. Do you have coordinates?**

Liam shook his head. 'No . . . we don't. I got down beneath the building. All right – it's hard to say *exactly* where it was,' he said. 'I mean, I went down some steps, some more steps, then a cave, then a passage . . . then . . .' He looked at Bob, then at the webcam on the desk. 'That isn't helping much, is it?'

\> **Not really, Liam. That is not very precise.**

'The thing is I know it's somewhere beneath the temple building, maybe even beneath the compound; it's all tunnels and catacombs and so on. I suspect the whole of that rocky base is like a giant Swiss cheese. But I'm telling you it's right down there for sure.'

'Recommendation,' said Bob. 'We deploy an array of density scans beneath the temple.'

'Hey!' said Liam. 'That was my idea!'

'Of course it was.' Bob acknowledged that with a smile. 'I am elaborating on it. I recommend a ten-foot gap between each scan location. If we pick up a number of neighbouring scan locations that are registering as zero density, then it is possible we will have identified a large internal void.'

> **Agreed.**

'In that case, I suggest we should start that search directly beneath the temple building first, then expand it out from there,' said Liam. 'I'm pretty sure it was right beneath the actual building. I'm sure I couldn't have strayed too far; I was only down below for about twenty minutes. I couldn't have wandered too far . . . and most of it was down.'

Bob nodded. 'That is a viable plan. We should centre the search pattern on the area beneath the temple. Start there and spread outwards.'

Liam huffed and looked up at him again. 'I just said that as well!'

'I am confirming the idea is a sound one.'

'You know what? You're going the right way about getting a smacked arse.'

> **I will proceed with that search pattern immediately.**

'Good,' Liam said, nodding. 'How long will that take?'

> .!..

'What's that supposed to mean, computer-Bob?'

> **I have a question for you, Liam**.

'Uh . . . all right. Ask away.'

> **How long is a piece of string?**

'Huh? What? Why are you asking . . .?'

Bob smiled. 'Computer-Bob has just told a funny joke. We can all do this now. Our data has been shared.'

> **Hahaha.**

> **:p**

Liam rolled his eyes. 'Oh aye, I get it . . . My stupid question deserves an equally stupid question back? The pair of you fellas are just such a hoot.' He sighed. 'So, I guess it's going to take however long it takes. Right?'

> **Correct. I cannot tell you how long searching for something will take. I will of course notify you as soon as I have detected a large interior space.**

'All right . . . all right. Don't get yer knickers in a twist.'

CHAPTER 47

2070, W.G. Systems
Denver Research Campus

'It's just me living at this facility now,' said Waldstein. His walk was the slow and laboured shuffle of an old and infirm man. 'I let the last of my employees go home to their families three weeks ago. It's just me now, rattling around here like a pea in a large tin.'

'You let them go just before the K-N outbreak,' said Maddy. 'You knew exactly when it was coming, didn't you?'

He led them through a rotating glass door that looked like it would normally be powered up and triggered by motion sensors into the foyer of a building. Before them was an unmanned reception desk with the W.G. Systems logo slanting across its dark marble top. Their footsteps clacked noisily across a shiny, slate-tile floor, echoing around the deserted, cavernous interior.

'Yes, yes, of course I knew it was coming. I knew to the precise day when this was going to come our way. I've known that exact date for the last twenty-six years.'

She did the maths quickly in her head. 'You've known since 2044?' The year rang a bell with her and she gasped. 'You knew then?'

'Yes,' he replied, seeing her eyes suddenly widen. 'I've known since my very first practical demonstration of time displacement.'

'The Chicago incident?'

Waldstein nodded.

'So, with that demonstration . . . you went *forward* in time? Not back? You came to this year? To 2070? That's how you found out what was going to happen?'

Waldstein wafted his hand in front of a sensor on a wall, and with a soft hum a section of the smooth granite slid gracefully open. He led them into a small elevator, then touched a screen. Doors closed them inside and then they felt a gentle tug as it began to ascend.

'No,' he replied after a few moments. 'My first demonstration . . . I was the guinea pig, of course. But I didn't go forward; I programmed the displacement machine to send me back into the past.' Waldstein smiled at Maddy. 'Travelling forward through time is an impressive demonstration, but not half as impressive as travelling backwards. I intended to go back in time to say goodbye to my wife and my son, Gabriel.'

The elevator door slid smoothly open and they found themselves staring out across a small lobby at a plate-glass, floor-to-ceiling window. Through the window she could see the bare trunks and branches of Douglas firs receding downhill towards a river valley, a breathtaking and heartbreaking view. Across the valley, in the distance, she could see the far slope of another peak cloaked in a swirling embrace of clouds.

'But, unfortunately . . . I never got a chance to see them.'

He led them out of the elevator. They turned left through frosted-glass doors into an office. There was another receptionist's desk, a dark green leather couch, a coffee table. Framed paintings hung on the wall. Maddy thought she vaguely recognized one of them: the childlike brushstrokes of a cluster of bright yellow flowers stuffed into a jug.

'Yes,' said Waldstein. 'That's a Picasso. And, yes, before

314

you ask . . . it *is* the original.' He led them across the office towards mahogany doors on the far side. 'My personal assistant, Margaret, she was rather fond of his work and wanted something to brighten up her office.' He made a face. 'I can't see the appeal of it myself. Very primitive and naive, if you ask me. But . . . still, a good investment, I was reliably informed.'

He pushed the mahogany doors inwards and they entered a much grander space beyond. 'And this is my personal office, my inner sanctum,' he announced. 'I hope you'll excuse the mess. My cleaners and my personal staff . . . I let them all go home too.'

The room was large. Until recently it had just been his office. But it seemed he was now using it as his makeshift home. A bed lay unmade in one corner, blankets and sheets kicked aside at the end. There were several dirty plates stacked unevenly beside it. An enormous dark mahogany desk sat in front of another floor-to-ceiling window that looked out across what must have once been a spectacular panorama of the sprawling evergreens sweeping down from the mountain peaks. The desk was covered with a mess of dirty clothes, tinned food and more unwashed crockery. Waldstein slowly unzipped his anorak and struggled his way out of the sleeves.

'I've been alone up here in these mountains for the last three weeks. Waiting for the end to finally come.' He tossed the anorak carelessly on to the desk. 'And waiting for you to come home to me.' He looked at her, then at Becks. 'I was hoping all three of my prodigal children might come. Not just one of you.'

'Home?' Maddy looked at him sharply. 'This isn't my *home*. I *did* have a home . . . kind of. Back in New York. Before you sent those support units out there to murder all of us!'

Waldstein glanced at Becks. 'I see you managed to tame one of them.'

'Yeah. She's been house-trained. She follows me . . . not you now. Just in case you're thinking of giving her any orders.'

He pulled a chair out from beneath the desk and eased himself wearily down on to it. 'I'm so very sorry, my dear,' he said. 'So very sorry that this unpleasantness happened.'

His head dipped and he rubbed his tired face with wrinkled, liver-spotted hands. She realized for the first time how frail and old he looked. It felt like she was looking at Foster's identical twin. His voice sounded much the same, that soft, cultured, neutral voice. But this was the 'final-days' version of Foster, the frail old man that she'd grabbed from the duck pond in Central Park and forced to come with them as they went on the run, heading north to Boston. The man who'd just wanted a few days, maybe a few weeks, of peace before his body finally gave out on him.

'I got things all wrong. I admit I reacted too hastily.' He looked down at his hands, rueful and chastened. 'I regret that I acted pre-emptively . . . I panicked.'

'Why the hell did you want to kill us? Why? I thought we were on the same side!'

He sighed. 'It was your message. You asked about Pandora. No, dammit – you *demanded* to know what Pandora was. You threatened to not do your job.' He looked up at her. 'And that's when you became a . . . a problem for me.'

'A problem?!' Maddy cried. 'A *problem*?!'

'A risk, then.' He sat back in the seat slowly, tiredly. 'You were back there in 2001. You had a working displacement machine. You communicated a message forward in time to me. The next message could have been a tachyon signal! Beamed forward without any thought of caution, right here to me!'

'We had a right to know what was going on!'

'Your next communication could have led the international commission right here! Right to my front door. Right to me!' He shook his head. 'Roald Waldstein . . . the famous campaigner against time-travel technology, the man who worked tirelessly to ensure no government agency, no corporation, no tinpot Third-World dictator ever invested resources in developing time-travel technology . . . and oh, look . . . ladies and gentlemen, it appears the old man has been secretly meddling with time travel all along!'

'What else were we supposed to do?' Maddy retorted. 'You had us acting blindly. You had us preserving history – a history by the way that has led to this . . . the end of *everything*! The least you could have done was tell us *why*! Why the hell we should be ensuring our own doom!'

'You had no need to know why. You had a clear brief. I kept it simple. You –'

'*What?*' She thumped her hand down on the desk. 'My God! You arrogant son of a . . . Do you know how many times we've risked our lives for you? Do you have any idea what we've been through? We had every right, from the very beginning, to know why we were frikkin' well doing all this!'

'At the time I thought . . . I decided it would be simpler that way. A very clear and simple mission statement.' He sighed. 'With hindsight, yes, perhaps I should have told you more.'

'Perhaps?!' She turned away from him. Frustrated. Angry. Tearful. She wandered round the end of the desk over towards the window and watched the last stain of light in the sky disappear. She let her head rest against the plate glass with a soft bump. 'Jesus,' she muttered. 'You ask someone to lay down their life . . . the least you can frikkin' well do is tell them why.'

She wiped at her eyes. 'You handed us the job of ensuring

317

the destruction of all of mankind,' she uttered. 'Didn't it occur to you that it might be a good idea to tell us *why*?'

'I never thought that you'd find out that our history ends in this horrific way. I assumed you and Liam and Sal would follow Foster's guidelines. That you would never travel forward to this time. I assumed . . . hoped . . . that your focus would remain entirely on the past, on preserving history as it is.' He sucked in a long breath and let out a wheezing sigh. 'You would never have known an end was coming if my work hadn't been sabotaged.'

Waldstein sighed. 'One of my trusted assistants, a young man I completely trusted . . . found out about the end.'

'And he left me a note in that San Francisco bank vault. Left it for me to find?'

'Ahhh.' Waldstein nodded. 'So . . . *that's* how you found out?' He closed his eyes. 'I had my doubts about setting up that resupply location. That was Griggs's idea. Not mine.' He opened his eyes again. 'It was Joseph Olivera, our junior partner in this agency, who attempted to sabotage the project. I don't know how he found out that the world was going to come to an end in 2070, but he did. The young man should have come to me; he should have asked me why we were making sure that was our fate. I could have tried to explain it to him. But no . . . he just assumed I was a crazy old man. So, he acted on his own. He decided to let you know . . . with a note, it seems.'

'Pandora . . . the note told us to look out for Pandora.'

'Pandora, eh?' Waldstein nodded. 'A good enough codename for the truth, I suppose: the end of everything. Kosong-ni. He compromised the whole project by doing that. He made you suspect the agency, me . . .'

'So you decided to murder us all? Just like that?'

Waldstein looked down at his hands.

'You could've come back and talked to us. Explained yourself,' said Maddy. 'Surely talking to us would have been easier?'

'You don't understand. Olivera betrayed me back in 2055. Fifteen years ago the situation was very different. The world wasn't falling apart. There were dozens of monitoring outposts being built around the world. All of them designed to sniff out time travel. And yes . . . the world was looking very closely at me. I couldn't just vanish into the past to explain myself to you.'

'You could.'

Waldstein shook his head. 'Joseph made his decision. When I found out, I wanted to talk to him. To explain to him . . . but then the stupid young man stepped into an unverified portal. No density check . . . the poor fool didn't even bother to verify if he was transporting into an empty space.'

Maddy had listened to Liam and Sal describe the horrific mess of a man they'd encountered back in 1831. 'Yes. Liam and Sal came across him. He didn't live for very long.'

'*You actually met Joseph?*'

'Liam and Sal did. Briefly.' Without too much detail, she described what they'd come across: the young man fused with the body of a teamster's horse. An appalling corrupted creation that managed to live for just a few moments.

Waldstein closed his eyes tightly; tears spilled out on to his dry, wrinkled cheeks. 'Joseph . . . Joseph . . . Joseph . . . you poor fool.'

'I think it was only a few seconds. He died quickly.' According to Liam and Sal, the wretched, mangled remains of Olivera must have been alive for five or ten minutes. But she wasn't going to share that with him. She watched him drop his face into his hands again and sob softly. 'I'm sorry.'

Maddy gazed listlessly out of the now-dark window. She could see just one pinprick of light, the halogen spotlight that was aimed at the corporate logo. She imagined, a few weeks ago, the chrome-and-glass research buildings, the whole campus, must have glowed with lights.

She broke the silence. 'So then . . . things went all wrong when Joseph found out that the world was going to end. And that was back in 2055?'

Waldstein nodded.

'That was fifteen years ago. So why've you waited until now to contact us?'

The old man looked up at her. 'I don't know. I was afraid. I panicked. Things had quickly got out of control. I didn't know if those support units had been successful or not. I just . . . walked away from it all.'

'But then you sent this message. When did you send that?'

'A few days ago.'

'Why?'

'Because . . . no one's watching any more. Pandora had finally happened. The job was done. Just as they wanted.'

'They?' She turned her back to the window. 'Who's "they"?'

Waldstein's wrinkled face suddenly creased with the faintest hint of a smile. It looked like relief. Like the shedding of a long-shouldered burden.

'Maddy, my dear girl, you won't believe how long I've waited to be able to share this with someone else. How much I've wanted to share this with someone . . . *anyone*.'

'Share what?'

'The answer . . . the answer to the biggest question of all.'

She shrugged, inviting him to elaborate.

'Since the discovery of frequency wave-forms, since the invention of radio, for God's sake . . . the big question we have been asking ourselves for the last two centuries . . . are we really all alone?'

'Are we alone? You mean . . .?'

'Maddy, why don't you sit down? Let me tell you what happened on that very first trip I took in 2044 . . .'

CHAPTER 48

Roald Waldstein stared at the being that was impersonating his wife, Eleanor. It . . . she . . . was standing there before him in this perfect re-creation of their home. Their small kitchenette was bathed with morning sunlight streaming in through a venetian blind, his baby son, Gabriel, burbled in his high chair.

'. . . you have to do what?!'

'We have to act pre-emptively, Roald.'

'Act pre-emptively? What do you mean?'

'Complete sterilization of your world.' She reached out and touched his arm. 'There is no room for pity or mercy in this matter. Or favouritism. This sanction is absolute. This particular technology is the one science, the ONLY science that cannot be permitted.'

He looked at the apparition of his wife with suspicion. 'Who . . . who are you?'

'As we have said, you can refer to us as the Caretakers . . . guardians of a kind. Carers. Perhaps it might make it easier for you to think of us as parents. And you – humanity – you are just children, children meddling with powers you can't possibly begin to comprehend. Tapping into spatial dimensions above the cardinal three in order to move forwards or backwards through time, you don't yet see that you're inviting disaster, not just for yourself but the entire universe.'

'Time displacement?'

Eleanor nodded. 'A thin and very fragile barrier protects your existence and the existence of countless other inhabited worlds . . . this entire universe . . . from higher dimensions. You can think of this barrier as being like a tissue-thin membrane. Every time you pass through it, every time you open a window through it, you are leaving a puncture wound in this membrane that never heals . . . You are weakening it.'

She squeezed his arm gently. 'You have to understand, Roald, one day, one too many of these holes will have been punched through it . . . and the membrane will collapse and tear and everything on this side will be consumed. Absolutely everything!'

'My God!'

'That's why we have to be so strict . . . so harsh . . . so brutal, my love. If a civilization stumbles across this obscure science, then they can't simply undiscover it. It's a Pandora's box; once opened it can't be closed.'

He was staring with growing, wide-eyed horror at her. 'You're saying . . . there are other intelligent –'

'Yes, Roald. Humanity is far from alone.'

She smiled sadly. 'And a few . . . a very small number of civilizations have stumbled across this science. It's inevitable. And on those rare occasions we have no choice but to intervene.'

'Intervene?'

He could see a tear glistening on the rim of one of her eyes. 'There can be no exceptions, Roald. Absolutely no exceptions. There is just too much at stake. We have to remove them.'

'Remove? You . . . you mean . . .'

'There is no kind word for it. Genocide. Complete erasure. Complete annihilation.'

He suddenly felt light-headed and nauseous. He reached for a chair, pulled it out from under the table and sat down heavily on it. 'My God . . . w-what have I done?!'

'We're not monsters. If we could, if there was any other path, we would take it . . . but I'm afraid in this situation this is the only way.'

Waldstein lowered his head into his hands. 'What have I done? Oh God, Ellie, what the hell have I done?!' He started to sob.

'Listen to me, Roald . . .' He felt her arm rest across his shoulders, holding him, comforting him. 'Listen carefully to me, Roald,' she whispered into his ear, 'this time round, there is a ray of hope. There is a way that something can be salvaged.'

He looked up at her. 'What do you mean?'

'We have glimpsed into your world's near future, and that's all we dare do . . . the smallest pinprick through the membrane . . . and we've seen what happens. In just twenty-six years' time – in the cosmic scale of things, that is just the blink of an eye.'

'What? What happens?'

'You will destroy yourselves. In just a few years' time, humanity will engineer its own Extinction Level Event.' She stepped round him, pulled out another chair and sat down beside him. 'And it's not a complete extinction. Some – a very, very small number – will survive. And they will struggle; trust me, they will struggle in the aftermath. Struggle to rebuild. Just like the Dark Ages after the fall of Rome . . . after the bubonic plague, you'll be set back by hundreds of years. And quite possibly someone on Earth may one day, like you, Roald, stumble upon this dangerous science. But we believe we can give you this chance for now. But . . . we need your help.'

'Help?'

'Twenty-six years, Roald. A lot can happen in such a small blink of time. You are the only human who's done this. You are the father of this technology. We need you to steer things. To ensure the science you've discovered doesn't spread, doesn't proliferate. The membrane can take some damage, but only a little. Do you understand? A pinprick here . . . a pinprick there . . . but, God help us, not mass migrations of people forwards and backwards.'

'I . . . I can destroy what I –'

'No, you can't. The groundwork is already accessible. The theoretical

324

seeds were out there before you made your prototype. But you're the first to make it work. There'll be others coming in the next two decades. Others following in your footsteps, building their own prototypes. You won't be able to stop that happening. But . . . you can work to preserve this timeline. Make sure it isn't derailed. Just for these few years – keep things on track.'
She smiled. 'I'm sorry, my love, that's the one small chance we can give you. The alternative is absolute and complete.'

Waldstein looked up at Maddy. She was staring back at him, ashen-faced.

'So,' he continued, 'that's why I set up this little agency. That's why you, Liam and Sal had to keep us on this track.' He rubbed his tired, aching hands together in his lap. 'And they're watching us. If you hadn't corrected all the contaminations that you had, put things back on the right course . . . then they'd have had no choice. They would have stepped in and wiped out this world, erased every last trace of our existence from this universe. Forever.'

'My God.'

'I'm so very sorry, Maddy. I created you so you could do this one job, to be agents of doom. To be the steersman . . . steering this ship on to the rocks.' He extended a shaking hand towards her. 'That's not exactly the sort of heroic destiny you'd hoped for, is it?'

A tear rolled down her cheek. 'I am become Death.'

He recognized the quote. 'Robert Oppenheimer. "*I am become Death, the destroyer of worlds.*" Do you know what else he said when he watched the mushroom cloud from that first atom bomb rolling up into the sky?'

She shook her head.

'He said, "Now we're all sons of bitches."'

'I guess that's what I feel like.'

325

'Well, don't. You did it, Maddy. You saved the few people out there who survived this nightmare. You've given them a chance.' He smiled. 'You did a good thing.'

'It doesn't feel like it.'

He nodded. 'I know. That's not much of a heroic legacy, is it? To be responsible for seven billion deaths.'

'No . . . not really.' She took in a deep breath. 'So, what next? What happens now? Liam's still in the past. I need to tell him what you've just told me.'

Waldstein pulled himself up out of the chair with a tired-old-man grunt. 'First you should get some rest. You look exhausted. You and your support unit can have some warm food. I have plenty of supplies here. Then you should get some sleep.'

'And then?' said Maddy. 'What's going to happen? We came here . . . and now we know everything . . . what next?'

Waldstein shrugged wearily. 'Perhaps you'll stay and keep an old man company for a little while?'

CHAPTER 49
1890, London

They had a few hours to kill before computer-Bob would have some worthwhile results to show them so Liam decided there was time enough for them to indulge in a culinary treat; he invited Bob to go with him to grab some food at Bentham's Pie Shop. They found their usual table on the top floor, overlooking the narrow alleyway below. Bob slurped at the mutton broth, grimacing slightly as he swallowed.

'How's your throat?'

'There is some discomfort when swallowing. I believe the arrow must have done damage to my oesophagus as well as my trachea.'

'Your voice is sounding a bit better, though. I thought we were going to be stuck with a whispering support unit forever. That, or —' Liam grinned at him — 'after you healed you'd end up with a bizarre squeaky voice, or something.'

'Most damage I sustain is fully repairable given enough time.'

Liam cracked open the flaky crust of his pie and watched a steam cloud waft out. 'I was really, really hoping we'd find Maddy in the dungeon when we got back. We should all be going to check out the transmitter together. I don't understand why she hasn't been back yet.'

'Her mission involves a lot more guesswork than yours. She did not have a precise date and location to travel to but a whole year and several locations to choose from. And we have no idea what obstacles or difficulties she will have encountered.'

'Do you think she's found Waldstein yet?'

'If she finds him, then it is reasonable to assume that she would use whatever technology is available there to send a tachyon message to us to inform us of that. Becks has the location data. A precisely targeted message would be possible.' He shrugged. 'That is, assuming that you were not correct, and that they have not been lured into a trap and destroyed.'

'Jay-zus, Bob . . . you're such great fun to go out on a dinner date with.'

'If that has occurred, it might also be possible that Waldstein has managed to obtain our location information. If so, then at any given moment another assault squad of support units could appear inside the dungeon.' Bob looked at Liam. 'This would effectively conclude matters for Waldstein.'

'You're a real barrel of laughs, aren't you?'

'I am merely considering possible scenarios.'

'Jay-zus, I hope they're all right.' He gazed out of the window. 'Maybe it was a mistake me being this stubborn. We should have stuck together.'

'The decision to split resources was tactically valid, Liam. You have twice as much chance of acquiring information this way. Also . . . if Waldstein has lured them into a trap, at least two of us remain alive still.' Bob slurped his soup again. 'I suspect this is not cheering you up, is it?'

'No. Not really.'

'Hmm . . . I will see if I can come up with something positive to say.' Bob gazed down at his bowl for inspiration. Finally, he had something encouraging. 'At least our intervention in the time of Jesus does not appear to have caused enough of a contamination to have triggered a time wave. If we caused some changes, it appears it was not enough to deflect the course of history.'

True. There was that for good news. Liam had noticed on the way down Farringdon Street there was still a church on the corner of Stonecutter Street. There were still copies of the King James Bible on sale outside Messrs Water & Stone's bookshop. And the Salvation Army brass band near the bridge was playing 'Amazing Grace'.

History has a way it wants to go.

'Don't you think it's one hell of a coincidence, though, Bob?'

'Please expand on that.'

'Well . . . that one of those tachyon transmitters is right in the same place *and* the same time as the arrival of Jesus Christ?'

Bob looked at him. 'Do you think Jesus is related to the tachyon transmitter?'

Liam shrugged. 'I don't know.' From what he'd witnessed, Jesus didn't seem like some time traveller from the future, trying out his luck at being a prophet. Rather, he'd seemed genuine. A man with conviction and courage and charisma and armed with what sounded like a pretty decent philosophy on life to share with those who were prepared to sit down and listen.

No. If anything, perhaps the transmitter was located there for the same reason their first base of operations had been based in New York on the day those towers had been knocked down by terrorists; it was a nexus point in history, a crossroads. The transmitter had been built there in that time . . . simply because an important thread of human history emerged from that place and time.

Liam did have another theory, though . . . One that sounded too stupid to say out loud – one he'd been kicking around in his head for a while. 'What if those tachyon things are like two sides of something like a box?'

Bob frowned.

'OK. Not a box . . . say more like *bookmarks*, or even *bookends* maybe. I mean, if you were going to section off a period of history, what two events would you pick?' He shrugged. He wasn't waiting for Bob to come up with an answer. He was being rhetorical. 'The *end* of civilization . . . and the *beginning* of Christianity. Hmm? Those are two pretty significant historical markers, wouldn't you say?'

'They are significant.'

'*Interesting* . . . even?'

'Affirmative. Also interesting.'

'I mean, *very*, *very* interesting.'

Bob scowled impatiently. 'Yes . . . very, very interesting.' He looked at Liam. 'I sense you are leading me towards some sort of specific assertion.'

'Do you remember Rashim's theory? That maybe all of that history trapped between those two markers is . . . some kind of *exhibit*. Like in a museum?'

'That is a perfectly valid theory, Liam. May I add to this theory?'

Liam spread his hands. 'Sure. Please do.'

'Far more plausible might be a digital analogy.'

'What do you mean?'

'That everything we have seen, heard, touched . . . experienced is part of a detailed simulation. That we are all software AI in a simulated reality.'

'You mean, in a computer?'

Bob nodded. 'A very large one.'

Liam laughed. 'No . . . see now, that's stupid.'

CHAPTER 50

2070, W.G. Systems
Denver Research Campus

'It all makes sense . . . now,' she said.

Maddy and Becks were sitting in the middle of a deserted staff canteen, a large open-plan floor filled with round black tables, gel-seat chairs and plastic plants in large terracotta pots. Spotlights in the ceiling cast muted pools of light across the beige carpet. In one corner of the canteen, holographic beams projected a soothing forest scene, while the sounds of a babbling brook, birdsong and the hiss of swaying branches and leaves filled the room.

The long wall of the canteen was floor-to-ceiling glass. It was pitch-black outside and they could only see their own reflections staring solemnly back at them.

She slurped at a spoonful of a concoction made of organo-beef granules and black-bean noodles. She looked at Becks. 'You know what?'

'What, Maddy?'

'I feel . . . like, I dunno, I feel like a ton of weight's been shifted off my shoulders. Like I've just finished running some kind of ridiculously long marathon and I can go collapse in a dark hole now.' She absently stirred the bowl in front of her. 'I feel so tired. Totally exhausted.'

'After you have eaten, you should get some rest, Maddy.'

Becks studied her and realized how *spent* she looked. Her eyes were red-rimmed and heavy, her freckled skin pale and drawn. Even her wild, wilful, frizzy hair looked like the life had been wrung out of it and it dangled in tired and matted corkscrews.

'You look unwell, Maddy.'

'Actually, you know, I know I'm tired, but I feel pretty good.' She smiled. 'We did what was needed, right? What had to be done. We were there and we stopped . . .' She paused for a moment, silently counting on her fingers. 'Over the last two and a half years we stopped four separate attempts by other people to derail this timeline. We saved this world four times.'

To Becks's ears that sounded like bravado. Like a heavy-handed dose of false cheer.

'You have performed very well, Maddy.'

They ate in silence for a while, the canteen echoing with the sound of their forks scraping porcelain and the soft chirruping of woodland creatures.

Finally, Maddy spoke again. 'So I guess that transmitter in the jungle and the other one in Jerusalem weren't made by future humans, like we thought, but *aliens* . . . Waldstein's *Caretakers*?'

'Correct.'

'My God!' She laughed. 'Aliens?' She lowered her fork and stared at Becks. 'It so makes sense!' She closed her eyes briefly, trying to recall the carved hieroglyphics on the floor stones. Adam had been certain some of the figures depicted the builders, the creators of the transmitters. Adam had called them the 'Archaeologists'. He'd said these people from the future would probably have been worshipped like gods.

You were closer than you realized, Adam.

If those carved figures had been actual extra-terrestrials . . . then of course the primitive Mayan people would have seen them as godlike.

332

'Maddy?'

'Huh?'

'Do you think Roald Waldstein knows about the transmitters? He did not make any reference to them.'

She nodded thoughtfully. 'No, he didn't. I don't know how those things fit into his story. Perhaps they're devices that allow them to monitor time-travel activity, or the state of that "membrane" between here and chaos. Or maybe they use them to call home or something!' She shook her head. 'Rashim would have really got off on this, wouldn't he? What with his theories about pocket universes and all the Drake-Equation stuff.'

'Yes.' Becks nodded. 'He would have found this very interesting.'

They finished the rest of their food in a morbid silence. Just the two of them, sitting side by side like the last two sisters in an abandoned nunnery. Mentioning Rashim had once again set Maddy's mind off thinking about absent friends.

There was an accommodation wing on the other side of the fifth floor, the one below Waldstein's. There were a dozen bedrooms and a shared bathroom. It had been set up for members of the research staff who preferred to sleep over on the campus rather than travel the mountain road back down to the nearest town for the night. Waldstein showed them a room each and left them to get some sleep.

The next morning he came down and met the two of them in the canteen. He shuffled in, carrying a coffee cup rattling in a saucer in one shaking hand, and wearing a thick, woolly dark-green dressing-gown over baggy trousers and a jumper, his snow-white hair tufted and left messy by a restless night.

'How do you feel now, Maddy? Better?'

333

'Yeah, thanks,' said Maddy. 'I haven't slept that well in quite a while, Mr Waldstein.'

'Support unit, have you fed yourself? Are you nutritionally replenished?'

Becks looked at the half-empty tumbler of pondwater-green sludge in front of her. 'Yes, the protein solution is adequate.'

'Good.' He sat down at the end of the table.

'Can I ask you a question about Foster?'

'About Foster?' The old man shook his head and laughed softly. 'No, if that's what you're asking, he wasn't a clone engineered from my DNA.'

'But he looked very much like you . . .'

'As Liam will one day, I imagine. But no . . . It wasn't me.'

'Then who?' asked Maddy. 'And what about me? I want to know whose DNA I was engineered from.'

He sighed, leaned forward and started fumbling inside his dressing-gown for something, then pulled out an old worn leather wallet. He opened it up and leafed through various pouches full of yellowing, dog-eared corners of paper. He found what he was looking for and pulled it out very carefully.

A photograph. He handed it to her. She saw a couple and a baby. A man and a woman holding each other, smiling; clearly a couple deeply in love – happy times for them and their newborn child. The couple were in their early thirties. The man had wiry thick dark hair, prematurely greying at the temples, deep-set eyes within a lean face. The woman had curly strawberry-blonde hair, pulled back to reveal a pale freckly face.

It took Maddy a few moments to realize who she was looking at. The man in the photo . . . was a *much* younger version of Waldstein. The angled jaw, the lean face, the dark brows, the unruly dark hair. She then looked at the woman holding the baby.

OhMyGod . . .

'May I see, Maddy?' asked Becks.

She turned the photo towards her. 'The woman? It looks . . . like . . .'

'It looks like you, Maddy,' said Becks.

'An older version of me!'

'That's my wife, Eleanor. Me . . . and that's my son, Gabriel.'

Maddy slapped her hand down against the table. 'Oh, I get it. I get it now. You engineered me from your *wife's* DNA?'

'Yes.'

'And Sal?'

'Her DNA came from . . . our research-campus gene pool. We screened for a suitable candidate with pronounced visual acuity, high intelligence. We ended up with someone Asian, so she was given appropriate life memories.'

'And what about Liam . . . Foster . . . ?'

'Yes. They both came from my son's DNA.' Waldstein looked away from her for a moment, unable to look her in the eye. 'You will never know how hard it was for me to see your faces growing in those tubes, to see my wife behind the glass. To see the young man my son could have grown up to be behind that glass. To see how much he would have ended up looking like me if he'd lived his life.'

His weak voice began to warble with emotion. 'And the pair of you will never know how hard it was for me to leave you behind in Brooklyn at the turn of the century and come back to this godforsaken time.'

'But that didn't stop you being able to instruct a whole batch of support units to come gunning for us,' replied Maddy.

'Yes . . . yes, I know. But maybe now you understand the stakes. Left to your own devices you might just have decided to turn today into a better, rosier, happier world. And, my God, if you had . . . there'd be nothing left of Earth now. *Nothing!*'

A solitary tear spilled down on to one of his craggy cheeks. 'I had to order those support units to kill copies of my son and my wife. I had no choice. And I can't imagine you will ever . . . *ever* understand how difficult that was for me.'

They sat round the table in an uncomfortable silence, listening to birdsong and Becks slurping from her tumbler of protein solution.

'I said "welcome home" when I met you at the gate,' Waldstein said finally. 'In many respects, you have come home . . . this place *is* your home, Maddy.'

'The only *home* Liam and I have ever had was what we managed to make for ourselves in New York. And you forced us to run from that.'

'I completely understand how you must still feel,' he replied. 'I'm sorry. What I did was a mistake.'

'You have no frikkin' idea how I feel! To give me a memory of a life, then discover it's just fake?! Everything I thought I was, every emotion, every preference, every choice I made . . . were they my choices? Or someone else's? Were they programmed into my head . . . or free decisions? For God's sake, who the hell am I?'

'You are the person you've become over the last few years, Maddy. The sum of your own experiences and emotions. What you've lived makes you Maddy Carter, not the library of memories you had pre-installed.'

Waldstein set his coffee cup down carefully on the table, then picked up the old photograph, tucked it back in his wallet and put it away inside his dressing-gown.

'Tell me, would you like to see where you were born?'

CHAPTER 51

1890, London

Liam studied the screen. 'How big a space are we looking at?'

> **If it is one continuous void, then it is 270 feet long, 190 feet wide and 57 feet high.**

'It's big, but, if I'm looking at that right, it's not a circular space like the other one.'

'The shape of the chamber may be an irrelevant detail. The engineers who constructed the other beam created a circular chamber to reflect the geometry above it.'

Liam understood what Bob was getting at; they may have been wary of creating a void that would look too much out of place, particularly if at some point down the line someone started conducting seismic surveys.

> **This void is significantly deeper than the other one. A greater attempt has been made to conceal it.**

'Because it's bang in the middle of one of the oldest cities in the world . . . I can see why they'd want to place it deeper. Computer-Bob, can we open a pinhole in there and get a look?'

> **Affirmative. Where do you want to locate the pinhole in this void?**

'Somewhere in the middle?'

'Caution.' Bob pointed at the screen.

They were looking at a theoretical 3D model of the ground beneath the temple compound. It had taken computer-Bob most of the day and well into the evening to lightly probe and probe again in a densely plotted grid pattern. Liam had watched the model slowly build up in detail on one of the screens as the density information from each new probe added to the sum total of what lay down there beneath the temple. He could see a wire-frame outline that looked like it might represent the steps he'd descended beneath the building. And this model confirmed what he'd said; there was what appeared to be an endless labyrinth of passages and stairwells, catacombs and sewers descending down into this giant slab of bedrock. A porous, sponge-like mass of spaces carved by those who had lived on this rock long before the city became known as Jerusalem. According to Sir Richard F. Barton's book, the giant slab of bedrock on which the city was perched had probably been occupied by humans as far back as the Bronze Age, as long as 15,000 years ago. Liam wondered if the transmitters' engineers had even gone back as far as that in order to hollow out the space they needed to install their device.

'I suggest we open a pinhole away from the centre. If a tachyon beam is now active and, like the other transmitter, located in the middle of the void, the pinhole will open within the beam.' He turned to Liam. 'They may detect that.'

'They?' Liam grinned skittishly. 'And here we are still having no bleedin' idea who "they" are. I do hope they're nice and friendly and don't mind someone having a little peek.'

He turned to the screen. 'All right, let's put the pinhole up high and discreet in one of the corners. How about that?'

> **Affirmative. Displacement machine has sufficient charge to proceed.**

'Right then.' Liam rubbed his hands together. 'Let's take a look.'

> **Beginning . . .**

Liam and Bob patiently watched a screen to the right. In one small window, a scrolling density-scan display was showing a relentlessly flat line. It quivered for just the briefest moment.

'The pinhole is being opened,' said Bob.

Then another window popped open on the monitor. Pixels began to appear, column after column, from the left. Black and featureless pixels showing nothing at all, until the very last column; they could see the faintest vertical line of grey pixels.

'What's the line?'

Bob shook his head.

'Damn it . . . it was just starting to get interesting. Can we do another pinhole? Move it along a few feet, and turn it a bit more to the right so we can centre on that line?'

> **Affirmative.**

They waited again, saw the density scan wobble slightly. Then once more another image began to build itself on the monitor, stripe by stripe from left to right.

'Oh . . . my . . . God . . .' Liam slapped the edge of the desk. 'I think we got something this time!'

A vertical stripe of pure white ran midway across the image. At the bottom of the stripe there were some grey pixels pooling on either side of it.

'Those pixels could be light reflected,' said Liam. He looked at Bob. 'A shiny, smooth floor maybe? Just like the other one?'

'Yes, it could be.'

'Computer-Bob, can we do another one with more detail?'

> **I can do a higher-resolution image.**

'Can you make it any lighter?'

> **No.**

'Can you move in any closer?'

> Of course. I can locate the pinhole closer to the centre of this void.

'We must be cautious now, Liam,' said Bob. 'The chamber may not be deserted as the other one was. There may be sensors . . . they may be able to detect a burst of particles if we do this too many times or too closely.'

> Bob is correct. We increase the chance of broadcasting our presence.

'Let's just do it,' Liam said impatiently. 'I need to see more than a white line.'

> Affirmative. Proceeding . . .

Once again the density display fluctuated, then another image began to build itself strip by strip on the screen. This time more slowly. The pixellation was gone. Now they were looking at a grainy image instead of a blocky one.

Liam leaned forward and stared intensely at the screen. 'The light . . . that's definitely another one of those beams.' He squinted. 'Computer-Bob, can you make that bigger?'

> I will maximize the image.

The entire screen was filled by the dark and grainy image file. Liam could see the glowing beam was spilling from an opened section of a vast cylindrical structure that extended out of the picture, presumably as the one in the jungle had done, all the way up to the ceiling.

'Can you zoom in some more on the cylinder?'

The image shuffled in steps, expanding and growing in size, becoming blurrier, grainier. He squinted as he stared at what appeared to be the faint lines of hundreds of palm-sized symbols on the smooth surface.

'It's the same thing, isn't it? Exactly the same?'

Bob nodded. 'It appears to be.'

'Zoom back so it's all on the screen again, please, computer-Bob.'

> **Affirmative.**

The image shuffled back out again. Liam studied the glowing light. Just like the other transmitter, it was featureless and white, a sliver of chaos space. The floor at the base of the column reflected the glow – a wedge of light that spread out across the smooth surface and eventually petered out into darkness. But there was something else there, just about caught by the furthest reach of light. The faintest blur of something hiding right on the cusp of being lost in darkness.

'What's that? There . . . bottom left-hand corner of the image?'

> **I see something.**

'Zoom in on it, will you?'

Once again the image jerked as it expanded in steps. The grey smudge shuffled to the centre of the image as computer-Bob zoomed in on it.

'That's . . . that's some kind of a face, isn't it?' Liam leaned across the desk and studied the faint, ghostly image: an oval with a distinctly pointed bottom, quite possibly the sharp line of a chin. Two dark pools that might just be the orbits of deeply sunken eyes. And – if that oval was indeed a head – then, just above it on the side nearest the light, a solitary pixel hinted at some kind of short stubby protrusion emerging from its forehead.

'Are we looking at one of . . . *them*?'

'If that is a face, Liam, then . . . it appears to be looking directly at the pinhole.' Bob leaned down beside him, both of their faces now glowing from the cool spill of light from the computer monitor. He turned to Liam. 'Which appears to suggest . . . they now know they are being watched.'

341

A chill ran down Liam's spine and brought goosebumps out along his forearms.

He nodded. He reached out and traced his finger slowly along more of the blurry pixels. He thought he could make out the line of a long bare neck, a lean naked shoulder . . . and, slightly fainter, something just visible peeking over the top of the shoulder, the ghostly outline of what looked just a little bit like a wing.

Bob turned to Liam and cocked a thick coarse brow.

'Uh-huh. I know what you're thinking, Bob.'

I don't believe in this kind of thing . . . there aren't angels in the clouds or devils with pitchforks deep underground. What I'm looking at is a grey pixel. That's it. Nothing more.

'What next, Liam?'

He stood up, stepped back and took a deep breath. 'It looks like they're there. Or one of them is.'

Bob nodded.

'I, uh . . . all right, I wasn't actually expecting to find someone home.'

'Liam, we know there's a beam here. We know exactly where it is. That was our original mission objective, to confirm the precise location of the other transmitter. We should wait until Maddy returns, then –'

'Or –' he looked at Bob – 'we can make contact.'

'If we wait, there will be more of us.'

'Strength in numbers, huh?'

'Correct.'

Liam shook his head. 'Do you honestly think five trespassers instead of two are going to make any difference to the people who made something like this?'

Bob scowled.

'If we're not welcome . . . I'm sure they'll do us in just as easily, five or two. And . . .' He spread his hands. 'Maybe two will look a bit less threatening?'

'I recommend we wait until the others have returned.'

'And whoever that is standing down there . . . he might just be leaving.' Liam pursed his lips. 'I want to talk to him. I've got a million bleedin' questions I want to ask him. I think we should make contact.'

CHAPTER 52

2070, W.G. Systems
Denver Research Campus

Waldstein led them up one level to his personal floor and into his capacious office. They approached a section of wall lined with faux mahogany wood panelling and shelves laden with antique-looking leatherbound books and old collectors' editions from the beginning of the twenty-first century.

Maddy read their spines: *Harry Potter and the Sorcerer's Stone*. She recognized that one. *Fifty Shades of Grey*. Not that one, though.

'I know it's something of a cliché from old Frankenstein movies, but sometimes it's the oldest ideas that are the best.' He pulled a book out at head height, revealing a dull red light that flickered. 'Roald Waldstein. Password: *Klaatu barada nikto . . .*' He turned to Maddy. 'Facial recognition, voice recognition and, as a final back-up, a good old-fashioned, honest-to-God password.'

They heard a soft humming from behind the books that ended with an anticlimactic dull click.

'Oh,' said Maddy with a hint of disappointment. 'I was expecting the whole bookshelf to swing in majestically, or rise up . . . or something.'

Waldstein laughed softly. 'It would be nice, but a little less subtle . . . and perhaps a movie cliché too far for me.' He gently pushed at a section of the bookshelf and it swung inwards. Beyond was a short dark passage with another door at the far end, beside it another dully glowing red light.

'Same again?' said Maddy. 'Face recognition, voice recog–?'

'No, that's just a safety light I had installed so I don't trip over and break my neck in here.' He pointed at their feet. 'Mind the small step down there.' He took a pace forward and down and pushed the second door inwards.

It swung open into a dark space. Light strips on the ceiling began to flicker and blink on, like lazy fireside lapdogs stirring after too long a sleep. 'Welcome to my inner, inner sanctum.'

He led them into a modestly sized room with a low ceiling and one small window that looked out across the cold, bare, lifeless mountains. 'Or . . . I suppose we could call this the headquarters – *mission control* – of our humble little agency.'

A cluttered space. Several desks and chairs within it, and a number of computer terminals and power cables snaking across the floor. On one wall was a corkboard covered with photographs. Pictures of houses and suburban streets, of mementoes, childhood toys, family gatherings. Maddy wandered over towards it. The pictures were grouped: one set for her, one for Liam, one for Sal.

Liam's were all sepia-coloured: a montage of grainy images of Cork in Ireland, of a port town, of a church-hall school and schoolboys wearing cloth caps and funny shorts. Fishing boats and nets. Pictures of the *Titanic* below decks. The stewards' quarters.

Sal's were of Mumbai, high-resolution images in saturated colour: her home, family, neighbourhood. Photographs taken by a real girl who had documented much of her life on social media. A girl whose memories had been borrowed en masse; a girl who'd died not long after her fifteenth birthday.

And then, as Maddy walked along the corkboard, there were *her* memories pinned to the board.

My God . . .

She was looking at a picture of her messy bedroom. There were all her childhood things: a Rubik's cube, an EAZY STARTZ electronic kit, her Meccano sets, her Lego Technic. And one token gesture that she'd been a girl not a boy: a doll's house. But even then there was camo netting strung across it and badly painted Warhammer figures fighting it out in the flower bed. Beside that was a photo of the front of her house, the porch, the green door. Her street. Her high school. Friends she thought she'd once had. Family . . .

'I'm sorry,' said Waldstein. 'I forgot all those pictures were still pinned up there.'

She took a step back from it. 'That's my life in pictures. My entire life . . . right there.'

'They're seed memories, Maddy. Just enough images . . . and smells, sounds and other sensations that your mind subconsciously stitched together to build a life narrative.' He came over and stood beside her at the board. He tapped a picture of a class of eighth-grade students. 'We gave you this . . . and your mind built a fictional story of six whole years of high school. It's what we do when we dream . . . We add together all the random firing of neurons when we're in deep sleep, and as we begin to wake we assemble them into a story.'

She shook her head. 'I know it's all . . . fake, all of this, but . . . it feels like I can actually remember these photographs being taken. Remember every one of these moments.'

'Joseph Olivera made your story, Maddy. As he made Liam's and Sal's. He was one of the best synthetic neurological programmers in the world. Come on.' He put his hand on her shoulder. 'Your life isn't those photographs; your life is what you and Liam and Sal experienced together. And, I assure you, you've seen and done so much more than any normal person would have in a whole lifetime.'

He led her away from the board towards the desks and computers. 'This is where I designed and tested the second-generation displacement machine. Where my colleague Griggs designed, coded and tested the support software. We had it up and running here before we took the critical parts back, component by component, to that archway beneath the Williamsburg Bridge and we set it up again there. Most of the non-critical components – the computer network, the power generator, the water-displacement tub, all the computer monitors and cables, for example – we sourced from the time.'

'Who is Griggs?' asked Maddy.

'Griggs was my business partner – the "G" in "W.G." and quite an exceptional computer engineer and software designer. We built the W.G. Systems business together. From the back room of my house in 2047, to a fifteen-billion-dollar technology firm.' He looked across the small lab at his messy desk. 'Some of those early days were fun. It wasn't about making money for money's sake, it was about making money for a clear purpose . . . so that I could safely set up something like this.'

'He knew about your encounter with . . .?'

'No. He knew just what I told him. That time travel was reckless. Dangerous.' Waldstein then pointed at a seven-foot-tall rectangular wire cage in the corner of the room, hooked up by a rat's nest of wires to a tall rack of circuit boards standing beside it. 'And that's the displacement machine.'

'It looks . . . primitive.'

'Yours was refined, a definite improvement on this one. The

347

perspex tube and displacement water was a more robust framework. But the guts of the machine and the software interface,' he said, pointing to the rack of circuitry, 'are fundamentally the same.'

'You're saying you built up W.G. Systems' business empire just so you could set this up?' It didn't look like much to Maddy. 'You could have done something like this in your home.'

He shook his head. 'Not on my own. Behind the half a dozen boards of circuitry that make this displacement technology safe, predictable, accurate . . . lie billions of dollars' worth of hardware and software patents.' He looked around. 'I know this probably is not what you were expecting to see, but it took building a business empire to get to this.'

'And this place?' She looked around the small cluttered space. 'This is where you monitored our progress from?'

Waldstein nodded. 'We had the agency up and running from the eighteenth of February 2054. And, yes, from that day on, Griggs, Olivera and I came in here pretty much every day to keep an eye out for any communications from our teams.'

'*Teams?*' Maddy frowned, puzzled by the plural. 'Did you just say teams? As in . . . *more* than one?'

Waldstein hesitated, then with a nod he eventually elaborated. 'Yes, Maddy. As in more than one team.'

'Jesus!' Maddy cursed. 'Jesus! I frikkin' knew it! I knew it wasn't just us! There were other teams? Other field offices in other places? Other times?'

'No. Just the one field office. And just you, Liam and Sal.'

'But you just said . . . *teams?*'

Waldstein paused for a moment, wondering how to continue, then suddenly the penny dropped for her. Maddy understood. 'We weren't the first team, were we?'

'I'm so sorry, Maddy.' He reached out for her hand, but she

348

snatched it away from him. 'God help me, my dear girl . . . I feel like I'm heaping one revelation after another on to you.'

'Don't call me that,' she snapped. 'How many teams were there before us?'

Waldstein looked away from her. 'It's not imp–'

'Goddammit! How many of us did you make?!'

'Three. I made three teams.'

She shook her head, unsure what she was going to do if she lost control of herself. Punch him?

'We grew three batches of you to full-growth development. Three Liams, three Maddys and three Sals. One set as test models to –'

'Test models?'

'Models on which to test the various cognitive back stories, your memories. To test that they had taken, that you were all mentally stable and capable of functioning properly. To test you believed you were who you thought you were. When we were happy with that, we retired those test models and grew a second batch, which we made here, then sent back to Brooklyn. To the archway.'

'Retired?!' Once again her voice had a sharp edge to it. '*Retired!* Don't you dare . . . DON'T YOU DARE tell me you –'

'*Storage*, Maddy! No . . . We didn't *kill* them! I promise you. We put them on ice.'

She glared at him. 'Test models? Put us on ice? Jesus! We're just another frikkin' meat product to you, aren't we? Just like Becks. We're just another product line your big business can make and sell!'

The air in the small laboratory was charged with tension. She turned away from him and was staring out of the window, absently cracking the joints of her fingers.

'With the deepest of respect . . .' Waldstein finally said, 'you are what you are. Without the memories we assembled for you, without the life story of a girl called Maddy Carter, you would be just like this support unit: a compliant bio-software product. Organic machines. Automatons with a very limited ability to plan long-term goals, to think strategically.'

He stepped awkwardly round one of the desks towards her. 'We had to make you as human as possible. Had to make you believe you were human. We had to make you as self-sufficient as we could and able to think and act entirely on your own without our help. To reason emotionally as well as logically, to think instinctively. To trust your gut, to join the dots in an entirely heuristic way.' He touched her arm gently. 'And, my God, *all three of you* were remarkable creations. You all performed so incredibly well.'

She turned and smiled sarcastically at him. 'Good little robots, were we?'

'Don't think for one moment I thought of you like I think of these things,' said Waldstein, gesturing at Becks. 'They're little more than dumb animals. Lumbering pack horses.' He turned to the support unit. 'No offence.'

The lines of Becks's scowl seemed to deepen slightly.

'I thought of Liam as my son!' He turned back to Maddy. 'And you as the daughter Ellie and I might have one day had. And Sal . . . I thought of all three of you as my *children*!'

Maddy narrowed her eyes. 'So . . . so you were prepared to murder your own children?'

Waldstein gazed down at the floor for a moment, then looked her in the eye. 'Yes . . . I was prepared to murder my own children . . . if that's what it took to buy humanity a second chance. Then . . . yes.'

Maddy turned away from the window once again, then came and sat down heavily on a stool. 'You said *three* batches?'

'Yes.'

'So, we were the third batch?'

'That's right, Maddy. You were the *third* batch.'

She frowned. 'You made a test batch?'

'Then we grew the *first* team. We grew them here. I went back to Brooklyn with them and I woke them up. The recruitment memories . . . I'm sure you've worked that out now, they were fabricated memories put into your minds. I was written into the memory as the man who recruited you.'

'So? What happened to them?' Maddy remembered what Foster had told them. Not much . . . but it hadn't been a pleasant end for them. She wanted to see if Waldstein's story was going to match Foster's.

'Something truly awful happened to them.' He looked down at his pale wrinkled hands. One of them was trembling slightly. 'There are things that exist in chaos space . . . I'm sure you've glimpsed them. Griggs and I both saw them . . . shapes . . . moving out there in all that white mist.'

'Yeah, we've seen them.'

'The first team . . . I lived with them for several months. I trained them, I mentored them. We had a minor contamination event to deal with. They performed admirably, just as well as you did first time round. After dealing with it, I was confident that they were ready to be left on their own. So, I came back to 2055.

'From our time, Griggs, Olivera and I monitored things. We picked up a number of contamination vibrations from here: time waves. Contamination events that the team successfully managed to zero in on and correct before they became a problem in our time. Things seemed to be going well . . . our team was doing its job; history had its guardians. Then one day . . . one of those entities from the mist followed them back through a portal and entered the archway.' He sighed. 'They didn't stand a chance.'

'Go on.'

'The entity killed Maddy and Sal and destroyed the support unit. But, as for "Liam", I don't know precisely what happened. I believe he may have briefly escaped back to chaos space. Whatever happened . . . it damaged him badly. It aged him chronically. We got a message from him after the event. He got back into the archway, somehow dealt with the entity . . . but his team was dead; he was alone. And now a very, very sick old man.'

'So you grew us? Team three?'

'Yes. But only after I had explained to him what he was. A clone.' Waldstein smiled proudly. 'He was strong. He took the news with dignity, courage . . . he accepted what he was. What he had to do. So, then . . . yes, Maddy, we grew a third batch and we sent you back. The original Liam unit was instructed to stay with you, to mentor you, just as I had. Of course . . . we needed to adjust the recruitment memories and he needed to pick another name for himself.'

'Foster.'

'Yes.'

He crossed the floor of the lab towards an old-fashioned wooden modesty screen. He pulled it aside, and dust and motes of fluff fluttered down and glowed briefly as they were caught in the shaft of light coming through the window.

'This is where you were grown.'

She was looking into a small adjoining room, long and narrow. Both walls were lined with growth cylinders. All of them unpowered and forgotten like specimen jars in museum storage. The glass was dusty, the liquid inside them cloudy and dark. Maddy stepped forward between the two rows of tubes.

This is where I started my life.

She brushed her fingers against the glass of one, drawing a window in the dust.

'Look, it's probably best you don't . . .'

She leaned towards the growth tube, peering in. Hanging in the middle of the foggy water floated a wrinkled carcass. She shaded her eyes to see better through the glass. The body of a young woman, thin wasted arms folded across her chest, knees drawn up, as if in death she was still ashamed of her nudity. Curly hair hung round her head like a dirty halo, framing the leathered skin of her long-dead mummified face. Her eyes, mercifully, were closed. She almost looked asleep. Asleep for fifteen years.

Me. That's me. Maddy Version 1.

'My God . . .' she whispered.

There I float . . . preserved like some extinct creature in formaldehyde.

'When I closed this down . . . locked up these labs, they were no longer needed. I figured we were all finished here. History had been successfully preserved for a while . . . and I assumed the support units had located and *retired* you.' He shook his head sadly. 'I thought the agency was done with . . . and these were surplus to requirements.'

Surplus to requirements.

She turned round. 'And you just left us to rot in these tubes?'

'I had to close the labs down in a hurry. I had no choice.'

'Just like your children, were we?' She shook her head and cursed. 'We were just *products* to you. Just another bunch of frikkin' meatbots.'

'No!' Waldstein shook his head. 'That's not true. I loved all three of you. Once you were birthed and your memories installed . . . you became as real –'

She pushed past him, kicked the screen out of her way.

'Maddy!'

She stopped beside Becks, then turned round to face him.

'Maddy, you and the others are so much more than you think

you are. You became so much more than what you started out as.' He extended a hand to her. 'You were . . . you *are* . . . heroes. You're saviours of humanity.'

'Heroes?' She stared at his hand. 'I feel like what I am . . . a product.' Her voice hitched with anger. 'Worse than that . . . a *redundant* product.' She turned and left the lab.

Waldstein stood silent for a moment and slowly lowered his hand to his side.

Becks finally spoke. 'I understand how Maddy feels.'

He turned to look at her. 'You all had a purpose, the most important role . . . in the history of mankind . . . *ever*. A mission . . .'

Becks nodded. 'And now . . . we don't.'

CHAPTER 53
1890, London

Liam finished scooping sawdust into the wooden frame of the plinth and stamped it down with his feet to make a firm bed.

'I still suggest it is best to wait until Maddy contacts us or returns, Liam.'

'And when might that be? Huh? Soon? Or never?'

Bob nodded. 'This is true. But you are proposing to portal into this void to make contact with entities we know nothing about. This may be extremely hazardous.'

Liam stood on the plinth and tested the bed of sawdust with his own weight. 'Come on, Bob, when have we done something that *hasn't* been hazardous?'

'You are proposing to make contact with someone who has nothing to do with Waldstein.'

'Aye. All the more reason we need to find out who he or they ... are ...'

'Their technology is far more advanced than ours —'

'Aye, I know that.' He stepped off the plinth. 'But, Bob ... this is it: this looks like our best chance to find out what those transmitters are there for.'

'You expect them to explain themselves to you?'

He turned to Bob. 'In the jungle, all we had was a vague impression of them: worn-down engravings, that was it. Just a hint of who they might be. Now —' he pointed at the grainy image still on the screen – 'we finally get a chance to meet one of them in the flesh.'

'Maddy would caution against this.'

'No, she wouldn't. She'd be right there with me on this. She'd want to know. And if Sal was with us now . . . so would she.'

'Sal acted alone to find answers, Liam. As you are doing. This action did not end well for her.'

'Bob . . .' He gathered up his long hair and tied it back in a ponytail. 'Look, me ol' fella, I know this seems like a badly prepared plan, but we haven't exactly had a plan since we started running for our lives. Just questions followed by more questions and not much in the way of answers. And that, my friend, is what I need more than anything.'

Bob stepped towards him. 'I have a bad feeling about this.'

'Seriously?!' Liam laughed. 'You're a meatbot. Since when have you ever come to one of your logical conclusions based on something as half-arsed as a *bad feeling*?'

'Instinct . . . non-conscious intuitive thought is how you and Maddy have been able to survive this long. That is why I trust your judgement.'

'Well, thanks, Bob . . . but –'

'What is your *instinct* telling you now, Liam?'

'That maybe I'll walk away finally knowing everything.' He shrugged. 'Or not walk away at all. Truth is, Bob . . . I think Waldstein's just a sideshow here. He made us and this agency to keep some order. Right? Like, we're his policemen, making sure the whole time-travel carnival doesn't turn into a messy free-for-all. I can understand that. Sensible goal. But those transmitters?' He shook his head. 'We were meant to find them. That's how it feels to me anyway. We were led to them . . . they mean something important and we were always meant to find out what.'

'Always?'

'Aye . . . always. Right? The Voynich Manuscript? The Holy Grail? All that stuff has been waiting around quite a while for us to put it all together.' He looked again at the screen. 'Right there is the fella with the answers. I'm sure of it.'

'How can you be so sure?'

Liam grinned. 'Instinct.' He slapped his arm. 'Look . . . I've just got to do this. You know?'

'Liam, you are aware of the aphorism "curiosity killed the cat"?'

'Aye. I know that saying. But think of it this way . . . at least the cat died knowing *something*, right?'

> **The displacement machine is fully charged, Liam**.

'There ya go. Perfect timing. It's an omen of good things.' Liam smiled. 'I'm ready to go.'

'I will come along with you, of course.'

'I know you will, fella. I know you will. You always do.'

CHAPTER 54

2070, W.G. Systems
Denver Research Campus

He was gone. Sometime during yesterday afternoon or overnight he'd left. Maddy found the note on his large desk, leaning against a framed holo-picture of him shaking hands with another man she didn't recognize. He might have been a president.

His large office was just as he'd left it. A camp bed in the corner with the quilt turned back, clothes in an untidy pile on the end, empty cans of food stacked on the floor like a small supermarket-product pyramid. The 'secret' door to his lab had been left wide open, swung inwards. She'd looked in there for Waldstein first before she'd come back out and found his handwritten note in an envelope perched on the desk, her name scrawled hastily across the front of it.

Maddy,

I'm sorry. I created you and the others to be as real as I could. To believe you were people who'd had lives, to believe you'd left behind loved ones. So that you'd care enough what happens to mankind. Perhaps that was a mistake. I don't know. I do know you were never meant to find that out. And you wouldn't have if Joseph hadn't betrayed me. But that's by the by. Spilled milk. And we both know what we're not supposed to do over spilled milk, right?

The point is, Maddy, you were 'born' an artificial person (I hate that term 'artificial'), but you became real. You're just as human as me or anyone else. Probably more so. Liam too.

I wanted you both to be here in the present, to be among the few survivors, to be part of the rebuilding of society. This world has been cleansed. Just like Noah's flood (if you want to use that biblical metaphor). And now it needs strong people to start again. I can't think of two better humans to be there at the beginning.

I left the lab door open deliberately. I have unlocked the computer system. I want you to open a portal to wherever you've been hiding away from me and invite Liam through. There's more than enough power in the campus's emergency generator to do that. I think that would be the best thing for you; to both be part of this new world.

Or, if you choose, you can go into the past. Anywhere you want. Live out your lives wherever makes you happiest. But, please, make it a one-way trip. If the present isn't for you, then find somewhere that'll make you happy. And stay there. Remember the membrane; the fewer holes we punch through, the better.

If you choose that, Maddy, then make sure you leave your support unit behind with orders to destroy my displacement machine. Plus all the digital storage drives in the lab. There's nothing outside that room that could be used by anyone to rebuild this technology. So if she smashes the circuit boards and magnetic discs then sets the place on fire . . . that will do it.

Finally, you're probably wondering where I am. No, I haven't gone back in time. I was rather tempted, but I think another blast of tachyon radiation will finish me off. So, Maddy, look out of my office window . . . go on . . . I'm out there somewhere. Eleanor used to tell me I don't get out of the house enough. She was quite right. A few days in the great outdoors, perhaps I might even spot the first green shoots of new life in all that dust. Who knows? I do wish I'd had a chance to see all three of you. I wish I'd had a chance to say hello and goodbye to Liam. Will you tell him he made me very proud?

Roald Waldstein

She placed the note back down on the desk.

'What did the note say, Maddy?' asked Becks.

'He's gone.'

'Gone into the past?'

'No . . . out there. The old fool's gone out there to die on his own.' She shook her head angrily. 'I guess he figures it's some poetic grand gesture.' She took her glasses off and dabbed at her eyes, surprised that she was starting to cry yet again. 'Well, he's just an idiot for doing that.'

No one's going to miss you, Roald. No one's going to know what you did. Or even care. You could have stayed here with us. You could have tried coming back in time with us.

She felt angry with him more than anything else. She'd have forgiven him for making her believe she was human, for trying to kill her . . . in fact, she already had. Now the job was done there were an infinite number of warm, comfortable and pretty places he could have 'retired' to for however long he had left to live.

Instead . . . he chose this. A pointless, sad 'grand' gesture.

'Maddy? We need to decide what we are going to do now.'

'Yup.' She sniffed, then puffed out air. Once again it was time for her to figure out what happened next. She placed her glasses back on the bridge of her nose. 'I guess we go back to London. We regroup with Liam . . . and tell him what happened to Rashim, and we let him know what all this was about.'

'And then?'

What then? She shrugged. She could see that was probably the point at which their paths finally parted. She knew, if Liam was released from any duty or obligations, the time and place he desperately yearned to get back to: he'd be the Sheriff of Nottingham again – that or return to the high seas to become a pirate king once more. Especially if he had Bob by his side.

And what about me?

Nothing quite so ambitious. The dungeon would feel just dark, damp and depressing if it ended up being only her and Becks and that stupid yellow robot living there. She wasn't going to stay there. And she certainly didn't want to come back here and be one of the few survivors hacking out a meagre existence – all dust and acid rain.

She could spin a globe, throw darts into a spread-out map, randomly flick through the pages of a history almanac . . . or she could go somewhere in particular. Find a certain someone who might feel something for her. Someone who might give her a very ordinary, very unremarkable, very happy life.

And what about Becks? Well, first she'd better follow Waldstein's advice and get her to trash the lab. Then, maybe with a timed charge ticking down to destroy the machine behind her, perhaps she'd let Becks choose her own somewhere to live out her unnaturally long life. Mind you, she had no idea when and where Becks would choose. There'd been several places they'd explored recently that seemed to have awakened her imagination: the savannahs of Africa, the jungles and rainforests. Perhaps she'd enjoy living among the bonobo chimps in deepest, darkest Africa . . . Perhaps she'd become some kind of female Tarzan.

Maddy smiled at the thought of that. She turned to Becks to suggest that as an idea, but instead found her staring at her.

Becks's eyes were wide and round. Her jaw hung slack and open. She looked startled.

'Becks? What's the matter?'

Her grey eyes settled on Maddy. 'The decryption-lock condition has just been satisfied. That . . . or it has just been removed.'

'What?!'

'The message, Maddy . . . the message that was embedded in the Holy Grail. I can now reveal the entire message to you.'

CHAPTER 55

Liam felt the cool embrace of chaos space: tendrils of white mist reaching out and enveloping him. That nauseating, vertiginous sensation of falling, having nothing firm beneath his feet and yet having no visual features to indicate he was falling or, for that matter, travelling in any particular direction.

Just this linen-like, tissue-thin shroud all around him. Endless. Infinite emptiness.

And silence. A perfect silence.

Sometimes chaos space took him and spat him out in a heartbeat. Sometimes, like now, it held him in there, seemingly reluctant to let him pass through and go. Reluctant to be left alone once more. Or did it just feel like that? If there was any way to reliably measure the passage of time in here, he wondered whether the duration would always turn out to be the same, and that it was just his *perception* of the time that had passed that varied so much.

First time, he'd been terrified.

But this time? What was this . . . his thirtieth, fortieth time? Now it was an almost soothing sensation. He wondered if it was akin to the reports of return-from-death experiences he'd read about in a trashy magazine back in New York. The proverbial light at the end of the tunnel. Perhaps when people died . . . somehow something was left behind in here – call it a soul, call it a spirit, call it awareness – and that very last essence of a life travelled through this, on its way to . . . somewhere.

Liam . . .

A whispered voice. He knew who it was. Partly he was scared . . . partly he was relieved.

'Sal?'

Yes. Through the mist a ghostly outline began to form. As it grew more distinct, his fear ebbed away and he found himself smiling sadly. Sal. Not some nightmarish creature. She drifted closer and became more defined. Her dark hair floated as if she was suspended beneath water; there was her small oval face, those dark eyes.

'I thought I'd never see you again.' He realized his smile had come with tears. 'I've missed you.'

I miss you too, Liam.

'Are you . . . alone?'

She nodded. *In here . . . everyone is alone.*

Somehow he knew this time around there was no need to be frightened. There wasn't that sensation of crackling energy held back by force of will, no menace lurking behind, held at bay by her fondness for him.

'Sal . . . I wondered if I was ever going to see you again.'

Outside . . . we can fade. But in here . . . it's forever. Her ghostly face cocked with half a smile. *It kinda sucks.*

The undulating, ethereal outline of a hand reached out towards him. He touched the tips of her fingers, knowing that he was safe. He sensed coolness. Not a burning, vengeful energy.

You look so sad.

'I'm so . . . sorry . . .' he replied. 'Back in that cave, I wanted to help you find peace.'

Thank you for trying, Liam. For not being frightened of me. For staying a while. Her cool, ghostly fingers stroked the back of his extended hand. *I loved you . . . you were always my favourite.*

'I wish . . .' He felt his throat tighten. 'I wish there was a way out for you.'

She shook her head. Her dark hair floated in slow motion. *There's eternity in here, or brief existence as a monster out there. Those are my choices.*

'I wish I could do something for you.'

She looked away from him, at the mist around them. *End this.*

'Chaos space?'

She nodded. *Eternity . . . an afterlife . . . isn't that what everyone hopes for when they die? That there's a forever after? Something more?*

'It's what people call Heaven.'

Heaven isn't this, Liam. Heaven is rest. Peace. Sleep. An end to just being. Can you help me have that?

'Oh God, Sal . . . I just wish I knew how to –'

This . . . She looked around again . . . *chaos space, it should never have been. It's a net that catches us. A cage that will never let us go.*

Out of the mist Liam saw other shapes beginning to form. Their faint outlines grew clearer as they slowly drifted towards him. Faces . . . men, women, children. Dozens. Hundreds. Fading out into the mist . . . *thousands*. None of them seemed threatening. None seemed to be aware of any of the others. All of them lonely ghosts making a solitary plea to him.

If you care for me, Liam . . . let me die, whispered Sal. *Let me go.*

She suddenly cocked her head, reached a hand out and touched his face. *You're crying, Liam.* She smiled sadly. *Thank you for not being afraid of me.*

He felt the warmth of tears on his cheeks. 'Why would I? I loved you too.'

Then, please . . . help me sleep.

'How?'

You, me and Maddy, we found the start of it . . . and now you've found the other end, haven't you?

'Yes.'

Find a way, Liam. Please make it stop . . .

'OK, Sal.' He nodded. 'OK . . . I'll try.'

Thank you. She stroked his cheek again. *And afterwards . . . will you do one more thing for me?*

'What?'

Live what you've got left, Liam. Don't waste a precious second of it.

CHAPTER 56

Liam landed with a heavy thump into darkness. Perfect darkness. He looked around, trying to find something to see. No dazzling vertical beam of light. Nothing. Complete darkness.

'Bob?' he whispered.

There was no answer.

'Bob? You there?'

Nothing but the sound of his own breath and the thud in his ears of his own beating heart. The antithesis of chaos space. A featureless black instead of a featureless white.

It took him a moment to realize his orientation was completely wrong; he wasn't even standing. He was lying flat on his back. His hands probed the ground. It was soft. Then he realized it wasn't the ground; it wasn't a hard, smooth surface but a coarse material. He lifted himself on to his elbows and heard a soft creaking beneath him. He was on a bed.

'*Hello?*' he called out. His voice bounced back at him. Not, as he'd expected, awash with the reverberation of a large void, but the bounce-back of a much, much smaller place.

'Hello?' he called again.

He heard something else. Faintly. A muted clattering rumble from above. Vaguely familiar.

I've heard that sound before.

Something else: the soothing sound of heat fans whirring.

The *clicker-click* of computer hard drives. The faint wail of a distant police siren. His eyes were adjusting to the complete darkness, and now he could see the faintest pinpricks of green lights that flickered along with the clicking.

A light snapped on above.

He saw a low brick archway above him, crumbling mortar and perishing bricks beneath flecks of white paint, a light in a wire cage dangling from a foot of electrical flex.

Jay-zus. This is our old archway.

He heard the clack of footsteps coming from somewhere out in the darkness. Approaching him.

'Hello? Bob? Is that you?'

The footsteps on hard concrete. The clink of ceramic against ceramic. Then, out of the darkness, a figure finally emerged. 'Coffee?'

Liam's eyes rounded. The old man was holding a tray with chipped mugs and a carton of doughnuts. He set it down on the end of the bed, then sat down.

'Foster?'

He smiled kindly. 'Hello, Liam O'Connor.'

'I . . . I don't understand.'

'I know this must feel very strange to you.'

'This . . . this is how . . .'

'How it all began for you? I know.' He looked around. 'This, I believe, is your first real memory. Waking up here, in this place.' He turned back to Liam. 'Your first *real* properly experienced memory, that is.'

'How . . . am I here? How are you even alive?'

'I'm afraid I'm not who you think I am. I'm not Foster. But you can call me that . . . if it helps you.'

Liam tapped the frame of the bunk. 'This was my bed. This is our old archway in New York.'

Foster shook his head. 'No . . . It's an illusion. Our best attempt to present you with something you can understand. Your first proper memory, Liam.'

'Where . . . Where am I? Where's Bob?'

'Bob? The other one who entered the field with you? He's not here right now. It's just you and me.'

'I'm . . . back here in the past? Right?' He looked up at the archway. 'Beneath Jerusalem?'

'No. You're in a pocket of space. Our own little universe, if you will. Just this place, you and me. It was created so that you and I can talk.'

'Who . . . who the hell are you?'

'I'm a projection made in the image of your friend, Foster. But who am I really? Well –' he settled back against the wall – 'I have a story to tell you. Would you like to hear it?'

Liam nodded.

'Once upon a time . . .' He smiled. 'That's how you begin a good story, isn't it? Once upon a time,' he continued, 'there was a universe. An infinite universe. At first it was lifeless. Then just over seven billion years ago it began to come to life; chance encounters of amino acids in bubbling pools of heated water.' He smiled. 'The story of life always starts the same way on every world, you know, Liam. In a muddy pool. We wind the clock forward seven billion years, and, Liam, the universe is inundated with life.'

'No, it isn't.'

'Oh, but it is. Billions of worlds, humming with life. Among them, millions of worlds populated by intelligent beings. And, among them, many thousands of races who have surpassed humanity on their way to a fully enlightened intelligence.'

He passed Liam a mug of coffee.

'But there have been those races that have been a cause for

concern. Those with a particular agility of mind to understand the universal language of science. Like genius children, they are so very advanced in one particular thing, and yet so very childlike in all other matters.' He shrugged. 'And that, I'm afraid, typifies humankind . . . the archetypal talented child. An *enfant terrible*.'

Foster patted Liam's arm. 'You are not the only ones. There have been others. And they have all been dealt with in a similar manner. Isolated, *quarantined*.'

'Quarantined?'

'Kept out of harm's way.'

Liam frowned. 'We're a danger?'

'To other intelligent beings? Yes, of course you are. Humanity is capable of incredible things: your ability to comprehend multi-dimensional space, to construct music more beautiful than any other species. But you are still children, dangerous children, naive enough to destroy your own world. To harvest its resources to depletion, to kill each other when your opinions or philosophies differ. To allow humanity into the greater universe would be inviting a shark into a bathing pool, a wolf in among the sheep. I'm afraid . . . your race still has so much growing up to do.'

Liam gazed down at the mug of coffee in his hands. It felt real. 'Who the hell are you?'

'We are those who've been entrusted. You can think of us as *Caretakers*.'

'And what right do you have to judge others?'

'Oh, we were judged in our infancy, I assure you. Judged by others who came before us. Who also called themselves "Caretakers". A long time ago.' He smiled. 'It's a very, very old universe, Liam.'

'So . . . you . . . are you the ones who made those transmitter things?'

He nodded. 'We did. Those "transmitters", as you call them, are what hold you in this state of quarantine. Everything – your world and everything you can see from your world, the sun, the planets, the stars, all of it – just like this space we're sitting in, exists in an isolated pocket. A pocket universe.'

Liam narrowed his eyes. 'I'm not sure I . . .'

'We identified the period of your timeline in which humanity experienced its greatest growth spurt of knowledge. Approximately the last two thousand years. During this period of time the pursuit of scientific knowledge and your understanding of it increase exponentially. It explodes. In such a short period of time, your species goes from understanding the concept of the number zero . . . to understanding zero-point energy. From the simple wheel to the Hadron Collider. From the bow and arrow to the fusion bomb. In that respect, you are a *truly* remarkable childlike species that has entered an accelerated puberty.'

'And dangerous?'

'Yes. Quite dangerous. To allow your species out just as you are . . .?' He shrugged. 'I know your *last* history so very well. How humans have interacted with the less technically advanced. For example, how Native Americans and Maoris fared, not so very well, after the arrival of men in sailing ships.'

'Our *last* history?'

'Yes, Liam. Your pocket universe has been going for quite a while. The last two thousand years have been looped through a number of times. And every time round you have proved to us the same thing . . . that you just can't be trusted. You can't be released from captivity. You seem unable to grow up.'

'So . . . what's going to happen to us?'

'Are we going to destroy you? Is that what you're asking me?'

Liam nodded.

Foster smiled. 'No. We're not barbarians. We're not Old Testament angels of vengeance and destruction. We want you to join us. We want you so very much to rejoin the greater community of this universe. We want you to succeed. But . . . you're just not ready.'

'So . . . what? This looping thing goes around again?'

He nodded. 'That is what has been happening. These transmitters, as you call them . . . they are our device for doing this. They are your quarantine.'

'The beam and, wait . . .' Something occurred to him. 'Is chaos space something you people *created*?'

'Chaos space? Is that what you call the field?' He nodded slowly and smiled. 'Perhaps that's not such a bad name for it. Yes,' he acknowledged with a sigh. 'It's a dangerous, non-cardinal dimension, a *place . . . a regrettable place* but a necessary by-product. It has to be handled so very carefully. Which is why we had to intercept a certain person I think you may know?'

'Maddy?'

'Is that one of your colleagues?'

Liam nodded.

'No . . . earlier. The very first human to dabble with time travel.'

'Waldstein? My God! Are you talking about . . . Roald Waldstein?'

'Yes. The man is a perfect example of what I have been talking about. A brilliant, exceptional mind, but . . . even then, capable of childlike, irrational behaviour. The prodigy of a species that isn't ready. His discovery and manipulation of this artificial dimension – chaos space, as you call it – was a problem we had to deal with. He was using our field in a way that it shouldn't be used.'

'Time travel? Are you saying time travel?'

'I'm saying time travel is possible only because of the field we created. Chaos space. Waldstein was not the first. There have been those in previous loops, equally brilliant minds, who chanced upon the field, discovered it could be manipulated and harnessed to allow a person to travel through time.'

Foster sighed. 'And therein lies the big moral dilemma for us. The issue that has been troubling us for a while now.'

'What dilemma?'

He got up off the end of the bunk. 'Liam, are you ready to dispense with this illusion? I constructed it so that we could talk more easily. So that you would not be unduly alarmed at my intervention. Will you come with me to a real place?'

Liam nodded. 'Where are you going to take me?'

'We're going where you intended to go.'

'The transmitter? Beneath the temple?'

'Yes. I would like to show you something.'

Liam stood up. He looked around at the darkness beyond the pool of light. 'Do you have a portal or . . .'

'No. We've no need to actually travel.' He spread his hands. 'Because we're already there.'

CHAPTER 57

First century, Jerusalem

Foster was quite right; in the blink of an eye, there they were. They were standing in the chamber Liam had glimpsed. In front of him was the tall cylindrical structure, identical to the one he'd seen beneath the Mayan city, its smooth dark surface etched with hundreds, *thousands*, of indecipherable symbols. A section of the cylinder had slid open and a vertical beam of brilliant light was spilling out from it.

Liam narrowed his eyes at the overpowering glare. He turned to look at Foster. 'So . . . now we're beneath Jerusalem?'

'Yes.'

'Is Bob here?'

'He will arrive when I'm ready. We sensed you entering the field first, so your colleague is being held in a waiting pattern for the moment. He is quite safe.'

Liam looked around. 'What . . . what did you want to show me?'

'Come . . . let's get closer to the field.' He beckoned Liam to step forward with him. 'It is quite safe to approach, I assure you.'

They crossed the smooth floor until they were standing just a few feet from the intense glow of the field.

'Chaos space . . . look closely at it, Liam. Tell me, what do you see?'

'What I've always seen. I see white . . . but –' he glanced at the old man – 'I've seen other *things* in there.'

'Other things? Be more precise, Liam. I know you know what's in there.'

He stared into the churning mist before him, unsure how to describe what he'd encountered in there since the very first time he'd stepped into it. 'Wraiths. No, people . . . No, not even people, the *ghosts* of people.'

Foster nodded. 'Yes. And *that* is our dilemma. You've witnessed what some might call *souls* – the manifestation of intelligent, self-aware entities formed out of pure energy.'

They both watched the field for a moment, and as Liam's eyes slowly adjusted to the glare he began to recognize the faint swirling patterns he'd grown used to seeing almost every time he'd passed through chaos space.

'There are now many, many thousands of lost souls trapped in there, Liam.'

'Who are they?'

'They are the unfortunate ones. Most of them like you . . . people who were foolish enough to step through chaos space.'

'Time travellers? But I thought there were only just a few of us –'

'The loop, as I mentioned, has run many times. And it wasn't just during this last one that the ability to travel through time was discovered. On one loop, a particularly disastrous one, the use of time travel proliferated; it became widely used.' He shook his head. 'That is why we cautioned Waldstein, why we invented a hazard . . . a dangerous fragility to space–time. Our greater concern was the cruelty . . . the cumulative horror being caused by our technology. Over time we have trapped far too many souls in this place. All of them imprisoned forever . . . tormented for eternity.'

'Just now . . . I saw them all. I saw my friend . . .'

'I know.' He looked away from the glow for a moment, appalled. 'Instead of carers, nurturers of an infant civilization that needs guidance, we've become gatekeepers of our very own manufactured Hell.' A tear spilled down his craggy cheek. 'In our desperation to give humanity enough chances . . . we've become guilty of inflicting an unacceptable evil upon you.'

'Can't you just release them?'

'Liam. We can. We can let them have peace . . . by finally bringing an end to this process.'

Liam stared at the white mist, and caught the fleeting image of what might have been a tendril of smoke or what might easily have been the distorted image of a screaming face pressed up against the confines of the field, like a face pressed against condensation-fogged glass.

'End this process? What . . . what do you mean by that?'

'We turn it all off. We allow this field to collapse.'

'And . . . this world?'

'It means there will be no more loops. No more resets.' He turned to Liam. 'No more last chances.'

'You're saying this pocket place . . . what? It collapses too? We *all* vanish?'

'No. I mean there will be no more loops. Your timeline runs from this moment onwards and you have the next two thousand years to get it right. To grow up. And that is all.' He gazed at the swirling light. 'In two thousand years, we return and we will have to make a final judgement. And, if by then you are still the same beautifully creative, hazardous, self-destructive race, then I'm afraid . . . that is that. It will be all over for you.'

'We can be better than we are,' said Liam. 'Two thousand years? That's a load of time –'

'Liam, in the grand scheme of things, two thousand years is

the blink of an eye. It is no time at all. My fear, my certainty, is that one day we'll return and have no choice but to collapse your universe and erase every last sign that humanity ever existed.'

He smiled at Liam. 'You know, I've grown fond of your race: to love your creativity, your passion. I love the few moments of enlightenment your kind have exhibited. Briefly, here and there, you've truly shone. You've shown an empathy, a species-wide capacity to lift your heads above petty tribal squabbles. But . . . I'm not sure this last loop will give you enough time to truly evolve your collective consciousness to a higher state of being.'

Liam understood it clearly: the dilemma. The choice. 'If we let these souls go . . . then we're down to this last chance?'

'Yes.'

'So . . . what are you going to do?'

Foster smiled again. 'I choose you.'

'Choose me? For what?'

'To make that decision.'

'Decide?! What?! Why me?'

'Do you think for one moment I *haven't* been watching you closely? You think I haven't been following your antics all this time?'

'Following me? I . . . never . . .'

'I've been a silent passenger travelling alongside you, Liam. Ever since you first stepped into the field . . . I've been a breath away from you. Invisible. Silent. Watching. Listening.'

'Every time? Every trip?'

The old man smiled. 'Don't be too alarmed. I know when to look away.'

Liam started trying to trawl through his jumbled memory.

'Relax, Liam. I've seen in you the very best of humanity. Mercy, compassion, courage, selflessness, curiosity . . .'

'Jay-zus, I'm no bloody saint . . . I'm just a –'

'A human?'

'But, God help me, I'm not even that! I'm the product of a test tube.'

'You are the product of your life experiences, your actions, your choices, not the circumstances in which you are born. Liam . . . we could make this decision on behalf of humanity, but it's my belief that the choice has to come from one of you. In fact, I petitioned my colleagues on the matter. That a human choice should be behind the decision.'

'I'm a . . . what do they call it . . . I'm a clone. I'm not even hu–'

'You are made of human DNA. How you were grown, in the belly of a woman or in an artificial womb, makes little difference to me. To all intents and purposes you are human.' He rested a hand on Liam's shoulder. 'So, I choose you.'

Liam gazed at the wall of light in front of them. 'I . . . I can't just . . . decide something like that for everyone! And, Jay-zus, don't ask me to leave those poor souls stuck in there . . . I can't . . . I can't do that!'

Foster smiled. 'You genuinely believe that humanity can be better, don't you?'

Liam had witnessed so much of the dark underbelly of life . . . and yet so many acts of heroism and selflessness, courage and compassion. 'Yes. Yes, I do . . . I think so.'

'Then perhaps your decision is already made?'

Liam shot a glance at him. 'Now? I'm making that decision right now?'

'I think the decision you come to now . . . wouldn't be changed by an hour of reflection, or a day, a year. You have quite clearly an opinion of mankind, a summation of them.' He narrowed his eyes . . . and smiled. 'It seems that you do very much believe in them.'

Liam nodded. 'I do. I think . . . I think we could be better. I think we can grow up.'

'You understand, from this point until we eventually return, this last run through time . . . is a blank canvas, Liam. A completely blank canvas. Do you understand what I'm saying? Up until now, you have been told by Waldstein that history cannot in *any way* be altered. That it cannot be contaminated. That it must go one particular way.'

Liam nodded. 'That was what he —'

'Then I want to be absolutely sure that you understand this. Forget that. History *must be changed*. Radically. The sooner you start out on a brand-new path, the better your chances will be one day. Do you understand? Not baby steps, Liam . . . but giant strides.' Foster pressed his lips together. 'Two thousand years? You have so little time to get things right.'

'I understand.'

'The history of this final loop is unwritten. Your fate is undefined. Make the best use of the time you have.'

'What do I do? How do I change things?'

'We're in a very special time and place, Liam; how the next two thousand years goes will be defined by what happens in the next few days . . . weeks. Right now, humanity is desperately looking for new answers, getting ready to abandon old ways, old religions, old ways of thinking. This is "ground zero" for the next two millennia. You have a chance to steer it.'

They stared in silence at the light for a while, before Liam finally spoke. 'So what happens next?'

'What happens next is already happening. I have communicated the decision to my colleagues. The beam will collapse in just a few hours' time. The cylinder shield will seal for the last time. The field will collapse. After that, time travel will no longer be possible.'

'What about –'

'Your colleague will be fine. He'll be here shortly.'

'But there are others!'

'I know about them. Maddy . . . Becks . . . your good friends. You'll need to communicate with them immediately. I'm sure you'll want to tell them what I've been telling you. That is fine. I think you *will* need them with you, Liam . . . if you're planning to stay here at the beginning, there is so much work to do; you will need friends.'

'Stay? I'm going to be stuck here, aren't I? If time travel stops, I'm going to be stuck here for the rest of my life?'

'Humankind's last chance begins right here, Liam. This is your place . . . if this is what you choose. Or . . . the field can be maintained and –'

'No!' He steadied his voice. 'No. You have to let them go.'

Foster smiled. 'I'm glad you said that. Non-existence is a far kinder sentence than eternal torment.' He reached out and patted Liam's arm. 'If it helps . . . that's the choice I would have made.'

'This is where I'm going to live the rest of my life, then?'

'Yes. If this is what your final decision is.'

Someone needs to be here, steering things. There are no choices on that matter. It's me.

'I'll stay.'

'Good lad.'

'But . . . how am I going to tell the others to come back here?'

'I prepared the way for you.' He squeezed Liam's shoulder. 'I've always known this would be your decision.'

'Since when?'

'Since now.'

Liam looked puzzled. 'That doesn't even begin to make sense.'

'Time is circular, Liam. You'll understand that one day. You just need to write them a letter.' He smiled. 'A letter they've *already* received.'

'What letter?'

Foster winked at him. 'Think about it.'

He let go of Liam's shoulder. 'You know, the foolish idealist in me believes in you. If anyone can steer them right . . . I believe you can.'

He stepped towards the glowing beam of light. His slight and hunched old man's frame became silhouetted against the glare. All of a sudden his outline began to waver and shift, his limbs to elongate, his head to narrow. Now no longer a shuffling old man but something tall and graceful, ethereal and as fragile as a butterfly. From the slender shoulder blades of his bare back something large and fan-like had emerged: two feathery membranes so fine that the light shone murkily through them, highlighting a web of pencil-thin bones and tendons.

The figure looked back over his 'wings'. His face glowed, smooth and featureless, not quite male or female, and ageless. Alien, yet strangely beautiful. He smiled. 'I'll be back one day to see how you've fared.'

Then he stepped into the field.

Liam watched his outline quickly become lost in the glare. And then he was entirely alone in the chamber. A moment later, he felt a puff of air on his skin, and turned to see Bob standing beside him. The support unit looked around, braced and ready for action. 'Where is the entity we saw in the pinhole image?'

'He's just gone. It's only you and me down here now.'

'Did you make contact? Did you speak with it?'

Liam nodded. 'Yes . . . yes, we spoke.'

'What information did the entity reveal?'

He gazed at chaos space. 'I'll explain all of that later. We haven't got a lot of time. Bob . . . you have the data stamp for our arrival location on the hillside?'

'I have it logged.'

'Good . . . do you still have full recollection of the original text of the Holy Grail document in your head?'

'Of course.'

'Then there's something we're going to need to add to it.'

CHAPTER 58

2070, W.G. Systems
Denver Research Campus

'What . . .? What's the message?'

'This is the concealed part of the message, Maddy. The part I –'

'I know! I know! The bit you couldn't say because the end condition wasn't satisfied yet. So is that what just happened?' Maddy pointed at the window. 'Your sectioned-off brain has finally figured out that the Pandora Event has happened?'

'No. I believe the message has just been changed.' Her eyes narrowed as she tried to make sense of the subtle shift of data in her head. 'We may have just experienced a very subtle time wave, Maddy. History has been altered. The document that will be known as the "Holy Grail" may just have been amended.'

'Liam! Right? It's got to be Liam!'

Becks met her eyes. 'Yes . . . it must be.'

'Well, tell me what the frikkin' message is!'

She closed her eyes. Maddy could see eye movement dancing beneath the fine skin of her lids.

'The wording is the same . . . except for a short sequence in the middle.'

'Just say the damned thing!'

'*Time is limited. Have found second transmitter. Tachyon beam shuts down soon. After this, no more time displacement. You will be stuck. A choice to make, Maddy. Choose somewhere, or join us. Choose quickly. Little time. Our time-stamp data follows . . .'*

'Where are they? Are they back in London now?'

'Negative.' Becks silently processed the numbers. 'They are still in Jerusalem in the first century.'

Maddy waited expectantly. 'Is there any more?'

Becks opened her eyes. 'That is all of it.'

'Nothing else left locked away in your skull?'

She shook her head. 'I have no more secrets now.'

'But wait! We can't just abandon the field office and shoot off to ancient Jerusalem!'

'Our London field office has a shutdown protocol, Maddy. Remember?'

She mentally kicked herself; yes, of course, her parting instructions. If they didn't get back, computer-Bob would make sure no one was going to make use of their displacement machine, or his AI.

'We would not need to worry about the displacement machine falling into someone else's hands anyway. It will not work.'

'What?'

'*No more time displacement.* Perhaps it means we have only been able to travel through time because of the force field created by the beacons?'

'We've been riding on the back of it?'

Becks nodded. Maddy shot a glance at the wire cage of Waldstein's displacement machine. 'So, when the field shuts down, this machine, the one in London . . . they're not going to work any more?'

'I believe that is what Liam is saying.'

'Then . . .' She got the urgency now. They had to decide

what they were going to do: stay here, go back to London, join Liam or go elsewhere . . . and they had to decide quickly.

A choice to make, Maddy. The message Liam had just sent was unequivocal, the word was right there . . . a *choice*. Not a call for help. Not an obligation . . . he said it. A choice.

Her choice.

'Maddy? The message says we have to choose quickly.'

How quickly? Days? Hours? Minutes?

'I don't know . . . where the hell am I supposed to go?'

'Do you wish to remain here?' asked Becks.

'No!'

'London?'

She shook her head. 'No . . . I don't want to spend the rest of my days there.'

Becks cocked her head. 'Are you considering another place that you would like to live your life?'

Maddy didn't want to admit that, but . . . yes. She'd thought about this before. She had a particular place in mind, but it felt like a selfish choice. It felt irresponsible, a naive wish.

'Recommendation: I should immediately activate Waldstein's displacement machine. We will need some time to build up an energy store before we can go anywhere.'

'Yes.' Maddy nodded. 'Yeah, you better get that started.'

Becks hurried through the gap in the bookshelf. Maddy heard her echoing footsteps down the short dark passage, then her clattering around in the lab beyond. She heard the electronic whine of energy being diverted. The lights in Waldstein's office dimmed and flickered as power was drawn away from them.

I could go anywhere . . . couldn't I? We're all done now.

Waldstein had told them their job was finished. Mission accomplished. And Liam . . . it's not like he'd said, '*I need you here.*' It's not like he was saying, 'Please help me.' In fact, in the few words he'd used, it had sounded just a little bit like a goodbye. It had sounded to her like: *Great working with you. Have a good life.* As if he was telling her he'd got things covered. And . . .

I could . . . I can . . . go anywhere I want.

She could hear the surging whine of energy building up in the lab.

Decision time. One shot. One chance. No take-backs. No second chances. Where I choose to go, I'm going to be there for the rest of my life.

So maybe this was finally it: her chance to live a normal life. Surely she'd earned that right by now, hadn't she? After all the crud, the heartache she'd been through. Surely . . .?

She stepped through the doorway, down the short dark passage, and joined Becks in the lab.

'The displacement machine is now charging.'

'Becks?'

The support unit stopped what she was doing and looked up at her.

'You know, you have a choice too. You understand that, don't you?'

'I have a choice?' She said that like she was questioning the idea.

'Of course you do! You're not my slave. Or Liam's. Or Waldstein's.' Maddy came round one of the desks towards her. 'In the end, we're no different, you and me. Right?' She laughed. 'You know what? We're just two orphans now. That's us . . . just two lost girls looking for a place to call home.'

Becks frowned. 'I do not know what to choose.'

'You don't have to come with me, Becks. You don't have to go to Liam. You're free to go wherever the hell you want!'

'I do not . . . know what to choose, Maddy.'

'Well, OK.'

Time . . . time . . . we're running out of time!

386

'OK, what would make you happy, Becks?'

'Happy?' Happiness – she cocked her head at such a curious notion. She stood up straight, and her grey eyes seemed to lose their intense focus for a moment as she pondered that. 'Mission priorities being met. Data compressed cleanly and filed correctly . . . things being tidy.'

Maddy chuckled at that. 'Seriously? Things being tidy?'

Becks nodded. 'And . . .'

'And what?'

Becks's face seemed to colour ever so slightly. 'Being . . . needed.'

Needed?

'My God? Becks? Seriously?'

She nodded, looking almost sheepish.

'Do you realize how . . . *human* a thing that is to say?'

'Humans prefer to serve?'

'No, not *serve* . . . but . . . we just . . . it's hard to explain.' Maddy thought she understood what Becks meant by that one word – having someone not just to be close to, but having someone that you know . . . just *know* . . . isn't going to make it through life without you being there for them. Maybe that's what *home* is . . . a place that eventually falls into disrepair and collapses into dust without you to care for and nurture it. A place . . . or a person.

'So, all right. Think . . . who do you reckon needs you most, Becks? Is it Liam? Do you want to go back and be with Liam?'

She narrowed her eyes for a moment. 'It is Bob . . . I think. His AI has room for further development. I believe he still processes emotional thought as heuristic logic.' She frowned. 'I would like to help him appear more human.'

'OK . . . that's good, that's –'

'And there is also Liam. I believe he needs me too. He is rash,

387

impulsive. He needs tactical guidance.' Becks huffed and looked at Maddy. 'Men . . . huh?'

Maddy laughed at that. She had no idea where Becks had heard that. A sitcom perhaps, or a film.

'And who is the person who needs you most, Maddy?'

She shrugged. 'I . . . I'm not sure.'

'Liam's message was clear: our choice has to be made quickly.'

'I know . . . I know!'

Becks looked at the display screen. The energy-storage bar was showing enough charge for a portal to be opened. 'We should hurry up, Maddy.'

'I know!' She shook her head. 'I guess we'd better be quick.' She looked around Waldstein's secret lab. 'Last place I want to be frikkin' well stuck forever is right here.'

Becks reached across to the screen and started tapping in data. 'Do you know where you want to go, Maddy?'

Time to decide, Maddy. Tick tock. Tick tock.

'All right.' She nodded. 'Yeah, OK . . . I know . . .'

CHAPTER 59

First century, Jerusalem

They found another way out from the labyrinthine catacombs. Rather than having to come out via the temple, they'd found a path that led them to daylight via a winding route which had eventually taken them into the city's sewer system. The blinding sunlight made Liam's eyes water as they emerged into the warm light of a new dawning day. Above them a tall brick archway supported an aqueduct leading across the shallow dip of the Kidron Valley over the high wall and into the city.

Ahead of them, as they looked east, they watched the sun, molten and liquid like a ball of lava, slowly rise above the shimmering brow of the Mount of Olives.

'Do you think our message got through?'

Before leaving, they'd headed up to the archive of religious texts stored beneath the temple, each scroll of parchment carefully rolled on a wooden pin, tied up and sealed with a wax tablet and placed in a clay jar. One day, a thousand years from now, an army of mercenaries and crusaders would be rampaging through this freshly taken city, burning, looting and far, far worse. Few places would remain untouched by it. The catacombs beneath this temple, the holiest of holies, would be one of the few places left intact . . . and two brothers by the name of Treyarch would discover the archive and, united by their desire for atonement and forgiveness, would determine to protect the holy building —

now part synagogue, part church, part mosque – from the rampaging mercenaries. More importantly, they would discover a particular scroll, yellowed and brittle and cracked with age.

'We will know this soon enough,' said Bob. He nodded at the hillside.

They made their way up the gentle slope, past goatherds, merchants, traders and pilgrims flocking into the city for the coming Passover. Liam paused to rest for a moment. He turned round to look at the walled city. Its pale stonework was coloured peach by the rising sun. The myriad flat terrace roofs spilled threads of smoke from chimneys into the clear blue sky. He studied the high walls of the temple compound, the tall temple building in the middle of it.

Look out, you lot in there . . . a big change is coming. Somewhere, a dozen miles north of them, a man with a message worth hearing was travelling from one small town to another, attracting a modest band of followers and the growing concern of the Pharisees in that building.

They reached the first row of trees and picked their way through the dappled light and shade of the olive grove, walking uphill until finally Bob came to a halt. 'This is the location.'

Liam looked around. Yes. This was where they'd arrived. There was the bush, the stunted olive tree. Weary from the climb, he sat down on a flat rock, shuffling on it until he was vaguely comfortable. Bob settled down on the ground beside him.

They listened to the faint calls of people on the dirt track below, the distant market hubbub coming from the city, the twitter of sparrows in the trees, the chirruping of grasshoppers.

'So, Liam, you said our mission now is to steer the next two thousand years of history in a *different direction*?'

'Aye. There's work to be done, Bob. We've got just one shot at this.'

'We are not *preserving* history any more, we are –'

'Hell with that! We are *writing* history. A brand-new one.'

Bob nodded slowly, reconfiguring his priorities, rules. 'I understand,' he said presently.

'We've got two thousand years to play with and by the end of it we'd better bloody well not be fighting each other still . . . or it really will be over for the lot of us.'

Bob nodded thoughtfully. 'So, your plan is to replace Jesus as the Christian prophet? To create a new religious faith?'

'No!' Liam shook his head. 'No . . . I . . . I wouldn't know what the hell to say. I wouldn't know where to start with any of that. I'm not prophet-material.'

As they'd picked their way through the labyrinth of tunnels, he'd explained to Bob what he'd seen and heard: the Caretaker, the conversation . . . the tachyon beam being deactivated, an end to time travel . . . and this last chance for humankind to get it right.

Bob's frown deepened. 'Then what *is* your plan?'

Liam shrugged. 'I don't think we need to come up with anything new. It's all there already, I think. And it's good.'

'I do not understand. Please clarify.'

'The way we should behave to each other? The once-and-for-all guide to how we should all live our lives? I'd say it's all there in what I heard him preaching. I don't think I'd change a single word of what Jesus was telling those people.' He shrugged. 'I think he's got it just about right.'

'Then . . . you will *not* be altering history?'

'Oh, but we will, Bob. We are going to completely change history. We have to.'

'Please clarify how this will happen if you don't intend to alter the message that Jesus is –'

Liam absently picked up a dried twig. 'We're going to make

sure it all gets written down . . . *exactly* as he says it.' He started idly drawing circles in the dusty soil. 'See now, what I heard him say on the hillside? It all made perfect sense to me. As a guide for living?' He shrugged. 'I can't say I've heard anyone put it much better than Jesus did.'

'So your plan is that we write down what he says?'

'Aye. We're gonna record it . . . faithfully. Accurately. Honestly. Word for word.'

'We are to write a new Bible?'

'I suppose . . . yes. That's it. That'll be our plan. We'll be the authors of the Bible. A brand-new one.'

That would at least be a start. Theirs was going to be a *true* account of the story of Jesus, a far more reliable record than the old one, comprised as it was of second- or third-hand accounts written decades and even hundreds of years after the man's death.

Liam wondered if they could do more than just that, though. Perhaps they should alter the way things were going to go over the coming week. What if they actually saved Jesus from crucifixion? Spirited him away from that grisly end. How different might the world be if he went on to live and spread his message for another twenty or thirty years? After all . . . last time round he'd had only seven days in Jerusalem to make his mark. Just seven days to educate us.

Or is that the point? Does he have to die . . . become a martyr in order for his words to leave a lasting legacy?

Liam had no idea. Foster . . . the Caretaker . . . had been quite specific. He'd said history could be changed. In fact, he'd said history MUST be changed. And . . . the sooner history went off the rails and trundled in a brand-new direction, the better.

Perhaps that's what they'd do, then. Perhaps that was their mission now: to protect Jesus. Make sure he got more than just a few precious days to get his teachings out there. They were going to be his bodyguards . . . More than that, they were going to be his chroniclers, his archivists, his biographers. Perhaps even his close friends. If there was one thing he and Bob could do with the lifetime they had left, it would be to ensure Jesus's message would guide mankind towards its eventual judgement day. That those words weren't going to be fabricated, mis-translated and wilfully *misinterpreted* by people centuries from now with dark hearts and darker goals.

He looked down at the dusty ground beneath his feet. Absently he'd been drawing a twisted loop, like a figure of eight lying on its side. He smiled . . . he recognized that it was the symbol for infinity.

Only infinity, eternity . . . would be ending very soon. No more chaos space. No more torment of a *forever* for Sal and countless others caught in that artificial hell.

With one hand, he began to scrub out the symbol . . . despising the torment it represented. But he stopped. He'd brushed away just the start of the loop on the right and now what remained of it looked just a little bit like the symbol for a fish.

A fish . . . or the broken open end of an eternal loop.

Maybe we could use that as a symbol? The broken loop.

A symbol of the new faith, not a cross this time, representing a grisly death, but a broken loop – a reminder to mankind for the next two millennia. A reminder that there were going to be no more chances, no more take-backs, that this time round was our very last time to get our lives right.

A fresh and cooling breeze made the brittle leaves around them whisper. He looked up at Bob. The support unit gave him a crude, thick-lipped smile.

One day, hopefully, he was going to finally get that right; he might even look less than terrifying. 'Liam . . . I am picking up precursor tachyon particles. A portal is due to open.'

'Good . . . looks like they got our message, then.'

Liam looked up at the air above the dry ground, where he expected to see it open. It began to shimmer like the air above a campfire. Suddenly a six-foot-wide sphere inflated from a mere pinprick; it hung in the air before him. Its surface rippled and undulated, and in the swirling oil-colour pattern he thought he could see ceiling strip lights and dangling loops of electrical flex, the pale walls of a small room . . . and the dark outline of . . . what . . .? One figure – was there more than one? – standing there.

He waved at them. 'Come on, then! You coming through or what?'

'Do not be scared, ducks,' grunted Bob. 'Cluck . . . cluck . . . cluck.'

Liam looked at him.

'That was not amusing, Liam?'

'Not really. Anyway, it's meant to be chickens . . . not ducks.'

Bob gave that a moment's thought, then his deep voice rumbled softly and his meaty shoulders shook and his thick horse-lips parted. 'Chickens. I see. That is amusing.'

CHAPTER 60

1994, UEA campus, Norwich

In a dark alleyway beside the service entrance to a municipal swimming pool, a fox rummages through tied-up bin bags of rubbish, a light rain hisses against wet tarmac and, far off, a police siren wails insistently.

Just a normal Tuesday morning. Just another day, five hours from breaking daylight. But this world is never truly asleep. In New York, it's eight at night, the streets busy and noisy with the last late-working commuters heading home and the early party people coming out. In Mumbai, it is seven in the morning and the streets are already busy with bicycles and rickshaws and exhaust-spewing cars. In Israel, it is four in the morning, one hour before the first Muslim call to prayer can be heard echoing from tinny PA systems above the terraces and rooftops of Jerusalem.

But right here it is quiet. Everyone's fast asleep. Silent, except for the soft hiss of rain, and the rustle of a plastic bag being pulled around by a hungry fox.

Then something stirs. A fresh breeze from apparently nowhere, a breeze that stirs loose rubbish into a lazy catch-me-if-you-can circle . . . just a playful breeze . . . or, perhaps, something more than that . . .?

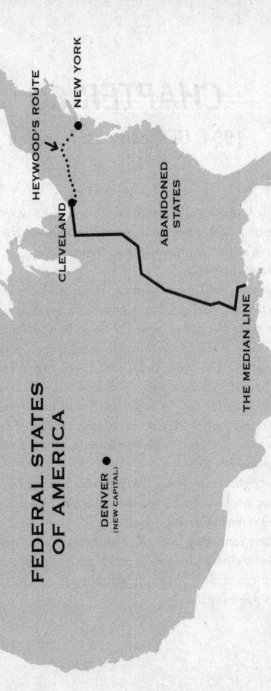

HEYWOOD'S ROUTE

NEW YORK

CLEVELAND

ABANDONED
STATES

THE MEDIAN LINE

FEDERAL STATES
OF AMERICA

DENVER
(NEW CAPITAL)

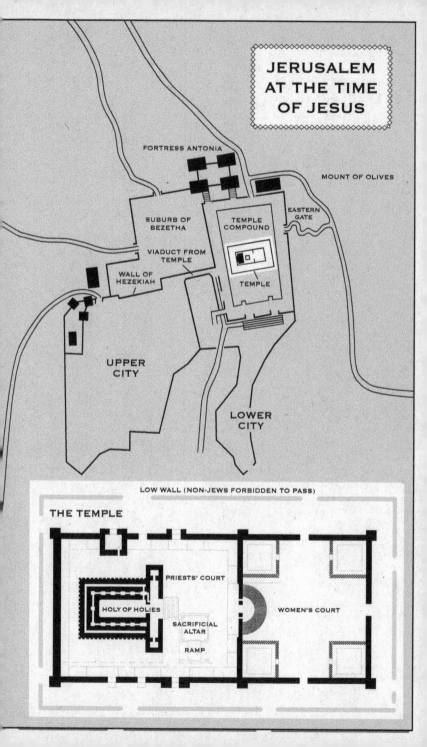

JERUSALEM AT THE TIME OF JESUS

FORTRESS ANTONIA

MOUNT OF OLIVES

SUBURB OF BEZETHA

TEMPLE COMPOUND

EASTERN GATE

VIADUCT FROM TEMPLE

TEMPLE

WALL OF HEZEKIAH

UPPER CITY

LOWER CITY

LOW WALL (NON-JEWS FORBIDDEN TO PASS)

THE TEMPLE

PRIESTS' COURT

HOLY OF HOLIES

WOMEN'S COURT

SACRIFICIAL ALTAR

RAMP

AUTHOR'S NOTE

Well, here you are then . . . finally. I've been waiting here for you at THE END for the last five years. What took you so frikkin' long?

All right, already . . . just messing.

Well, sort of. Because it's been a bit like that, knowing how it all ends and not being able to share that ending with anyone (I mean ANYONE . . . not my agent, my editor, my family, my best friend, my dog, etc., etc.) until now. It's been so-o-o hard not letting anything slip out!

I've been quietly watching friends and fans theorizing online, posting on Twitter, Facebook and on the TimeRiders website that they know already how this whole thing ends. Quietly watching, reading . . . and, of course, cackling to myself. I've often been asked if I knew how the series would end from the start and the short answer is . . . yes. Longer answer is that I knew how it all ended before I started writing the very first chapter. (Remember that one? Liam? Aboard the *Titanic*? Seems like a lifetime ago, doesn't it?) With a story involving time travel, you really do need to know how it all ends before it starts. Time travel's like that.

So, the majority of the story was carefully planned; however, along the way, some events did actually surprise me. For example, Rashim . . . he was never initially meant to tag along with the team. He was actually meant to be a walk-on character in the fifth book, *The Gates of Rome*, and then quickly dispensed with. But I just, well, warmed to the guy. No, it wasn't that; it was Liam, Maddy and Sal who warmed to the guy. So I had to listen to them. They were nagging me to recruit him into their story.

That sounds a bit weird, I suppose. But, really, that's how it's been with this series. And, you know, I've never had that before, not with my adult books – the characters actually becoming real people in my mind. Coming alive, off the page, entering my head and chattering away even when I've finished writing for the day. Hence the dedication at the beginning of this last book. So, although this series has finished, they're certainly not gone. In fact, they're alive and well and stuck somewhere back in the first century, jotting down the wise, common-sense words of a certain bloke called Jesus. Making sure their account of his life and his message is free of any potential misinterpretations and ambiguities that might be exploited by kings, emperors, caliphs, princes, priests, presidents and prime ministers, down the line.

Liam and the others are going to be steering the next two thousand years of our history, and I'm pretty sure they're going to do a better job than humanity has done thus far. What will this last loop of history be like, I wonder?

Well, that's what I'd like you to ponder. In fact, this is my request of you, Dear Reader . . . to imagine, perhaps even put into words on paper (or online) what they might get up to in the past, what their actions might change, how the timeline might alter, what today might be like because of them, because of the wisdom they choose to write.

I know their story continues in my mind (seriously . . . I'll be tempted to go back to them sometime in the future and see how they're getting on!) . . . and in *your* mind. I'd love to read what you come up with. I'd love you to post your fan-fiction on the Internet and see where you take them. For instance, you might decide that Maddy went back to join the others, or that she *did* go back to live with Adam. (Was that a portal in 1994, or just a gust of wind? Hmm . . . Your call.)

So . . . I hand the baton over to you. After all, Liam, Maddy, Bob and Becks are now our characters – not just mine but yours too. They're our mutual friends.

The TimeRiders website (**www.time-riders.co.uk**) will, by the time you read this, have a fully functioning fan-fiction section where you can upload your story and read those of other fans, where you'll be able to like and comment and provide feedback to each other.

Who knows . . .? Perhaps in writing the further TimeRiders adventures, you'll get a taste for storytelling and one day be an author whose books I'll be avidly reading. From tiny acorns an' all that . . .

OK, so I guess I'd better sign off soon. Otherwise I'll probably get all emotional; there'll be tears and we'll both feel awkward and uncomfortable.

Just a few thank-yous from me. Thanks to: Shannon Cullen and Wendy Shakespeare, my faithful and reliable editorial team; Deborah Chaffey, best friend, partner and consistent beta reader; Jake, my son, first-ever reader and continuity spotter. And, finally, Mum and Dad . . . whatever you put in my baby milk must have worked.

I want to leave you with this last thought. If you go and read up on the head-scratching physics of time, you'll discover it's not a straight line we walk down; actually it's an endless loop. Which means . . . if you think about it . . . the future's *already happened*. And, if the future's already happened, maybe that future will contain the technology for time travel. If so . . . then that can only mean one thing. Somebody may already have done it . . . travelled back.

Which means, this world, this reality we all know so well . . . maybe this is a 'wrong' reality? Maybe this is a contaminated timeline. I mean, how the heck would we know if it wasn't!

Just sayin'.

Alex Scarrow

NB: I'm still waiting for you to decode that message in the dedication of *The Day of the Predator*. Now, what are you waiting for? It's easy.

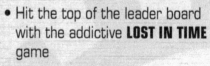

THREE TEENAGERS HAVE CHEATED DEATH

NOW THEY MUST STOP TIME TRAVEL DESTROYING THE WORLD

Listen to all the TimeRiders adventures

http://bit.ly/1qBEj6v

Scan the QR code
for an audio extract

BECOME A TIMERIDER @
www.time-riders.co.uk
Your first mission awaits . . .

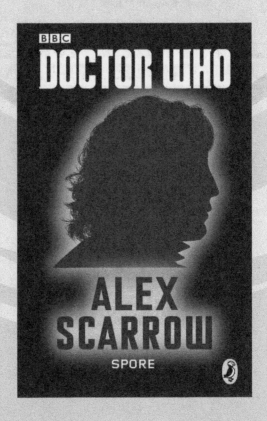

YOUR STORY STARTS HERE

Do you **love books** and **discovering new stories?**
Then **www.puffinbooks.com** is the place for you . . .

- Thrilling adventures, fantastic fiction and laugh-out-loud fun
- Brilliant videos featuring your favourite authors and characters
- Exciting competitions, news, activities, the Puffin blog and SO MUCH more . . .

It all started with a Scarecrow

Puffin is over seventy years old.
Sounds ancient, doesn't it? But Puffin has never been
so lively. We're always on the lookout for the next big
idea, which is how it began all those years ago.

Penguin Books was a big idea from the mind of
a man called Allen Lane, who in 1935 invented
the quality paperback and changed the world.
**And from great Penguins, great Puffins grew,
changing the face of children's books forever.**

The first four Puffin Picture Books were hatched in 1940 and the
first Puffin story book featured a man with broomstick arms called
Worzel Gummidge. In 1967 Kaye Webb, Puffin Editor, started the
Puffin Club, promising to **'make children into readers'**.
She kept that promise and over 200,000 children became devoted
Puffineers through their quarterly instalments of *Puffin Post*.

Many years from now, we hope you'll look back and
remember Puffin with a smile. **No matter what your age
or what you're into, there's a Puffin for everyone.**
The possibilities are endless, but one thing is for sure:
whether it's a picture book or a paperback, a sticker book
or a hardback, **if it's got that little Puffin
on it – it's bound to be good.**

www.puffinbooks.com